FIRST LINE OF DEFENCE

FIRST LINE OF DEFENCE
BOOK ONE

BENJAMIN KEREI

This is a **work of fiction**. Names, characters, businesses, places, events, and incidents are either the products of the author's imagination or used in a fictitious manner. Any resemblance to actual persons, living or dead, or actual events is purely coincidental.

ISBN 978-0-473-69179-0

1

A NOT-SO-HOSTILE TAKEOVER

Welcome to the Collective.

Organic nanobots have clustered in your brain to connect you and the rest of the human population to our Collective network. This has been done to you so that information may be imparted directly. Knowledge about the Collective, our rule of law, and how humanity will function within our society will be uploaded directly to your consciousness shortly.

Please remain calm while the delinquents in your society are culled.

If you are reading this message, you are not one of the members being culled and need not fear you will be culled. Information has been provided as to why each individual has been culled. This information may be traumatic. We apologize for this.

That's what I saw the first second of the first day the Peacekeepers invaded Earth and took complete control. It was written in happy yellow letters, the kind that put you at ease while 5% of your population are summarily executed.

The Peacekeepers were big on putting people at ease. That was the first bit of information they uploaded to my brain. The second was that the masters of this Collective were called the Peacekeepers, clarifying the first confusing fact. The third fact was that most wouldn't miss the 5% they culled once we understood the reasons behind these harsh measures.

Those three facts mashed together forged an emotional connection between the Collective and myself which hadn't existed a second before. It made me feel grateful for their help and distracted me as my HR manager dropped dead, with a long list of infractions above her head.

Brenda had been trying to cancel the vacation time she'd approved. Six months ago, I'd handed over my vacation request in writing and made her sign it. That's the sort of thing you had to do with Brenda. She was a small, petty woman, who enjoyed finding any excuse to make others miserable.

Work didn't even need me next week.

I'd checked.

One second, she was trying to weasel out of letting me go, giving me longwinded and empty excuses for why I needed to stay, and the next, her fat face was on the desk. By then, I was too distracted to notice. Suddenly seeing words floating before you unsurprisingly makes you wonder how the words got there and whether or not you were having some sort of bizarre medical event.

I read the last line, concerned for my health and mental status. Then I dropped my gaze to her corpse. I'm not going to lie; seeing her dead made me feel better about the words I was seeing. It leant them a lot of credibility, even if it confused me further.

Brenda looked like she'd gone to sleep, except sleeping people didn't have paragraphs floating above them. I started reading the reasons she'd been culled. They weren't the petty tyrant reasons I expected. Her favourite pastime was encouraging people over the internet to commit suicide, working on them for months until they finally did it. Since the early 2000's, she'd managed to kill seven people this way. She'd tried to do it with more, a *lot* more, but failed.

I'd like to say I was surprised by her actions, but I wasn't. I'd told Ted numerous times that she was evil. Now I could prove it.

My gaze switched between the messages and her corpse. The absurdity of the situation shielded me from the reality of what was happening. However, my heart rate slowly started to speed up as I realized this may, in fact, not be a dream. Just before I began to panic, I was filled with a serene sense of calm, like everything in the world was perfect and safe.

I wanted to panic.

Everything in life that led me to this moment said I should be panicking, but my body and mind wouldn't let me. I was calm.

So very, very calm.

I reached over and picked up her arm, feeling her warm, oily skin. I checked her wrist for a pulse. I didn't find one. I let go and her arm flopped onto the desk, with a dull, meaty thud.

I paused, struggling to process my thoughts through the overly calm haze.

The decent thing to do was to try and help. I considered giving her CPR. There was nothing to prove that the accusations floating above her were true besides a gut feeling that they were. There was also nothing to prove that the words I was seeing weren't some sort of medical event.

Someone in the hallway outside her office screamed.

I calmly turned to the door, figuring I should see what that was about. Someone might be in trouble, someone who wasn't trying to kill people over the internet. If they weren't, I'd come back and decide what I wanted to do.

Before I left, I grabbed the letter she had signed months ago that approved my time off and headed for the door. My name, Morgan Bartholomew Winchester, and my job description, Senior Statistician, were printed at the top of the page. I tucked it in my pocket as I stepped into the hallway.

Whiteman's Toothpaste was far from the biggest toothpaste company in the United States. In fact, the last time it had been in the top 10 was the 1980s. That was also the last time they redecorated the building. The wood panelling and worn shag carpets that always smelled a little dusty were so far out of fashion that they would probably come back into fashion if they survived a few more years. There were multiplugs and power cords everywhere, to compensate for the 1980s number of electrical outlets the building had, making the hallways and offices an electrician's nightmare.

My co-workers were down the hallway, gathered outside Ted's office, muttering to each other. I made my way over, watching my step, and checking the faces, hoping to see concern. I didn't see any. They were all calmly talking about the words. That reassured me that I wasn't insane, as I squeezed my way through, pretending to be trying to reach my office. Really, I just wanted to see what the fuss was about.

Ted worked in the office beside me, or at least he had. He was dead, slumped over his keyboard.

I liked Ted.

He'd convinced me to help at the soup kitchen with him once a fortnight. Afterward, we'd go bowling. We even went out for a beer after work every Friday to bitch about HR. And we swapped memes a few times a day.

So, I was shocked to see him dead. He was the last person I'd expect to be a serial killer. But the names of the people he'd killed, and the locations of their bodies were there for everyone to see. Apparently, he'd been using the soup kitchen to find his victims.

Did that make me an accessory?

No, probably not, since I was still alive.

At worst, it made me gullible.

As the seconds ticked by, more information was uploaded to my brain. All of a sudden, I knew that the dead were murderers, rapists, Karens, Kyles, crooked politicians, and even more crooked corporate types. Not everyone who fell into these categories was being executed, only those who were the worst offenders or possessed no ability to change. The Peacekeepers were trying to build a more stable society for humanity as we were integrated into the Collective.

I was *way* too calm for what was going on. So was everyone else.

Except for that one scream, everyone was acting like nothing out of the ordinary was happening. The Peacekeepers must have been doing something to our brains to help ease us into the universe at large and humanity no longer being in charge of its own fate, because this wasn't normal.

I should have been unsettled, but I couldn't get worked up enough to feel that way.

More information trickled in, and I discovered the Peacekeepers were big on using the carrot instead of the stick. They didn't want to hurt us. They wanted to help us. But that help came at a price. We had to earn it. We had to play the Game.

Janet, another of my co-workers, turned to me. She was in her 40s and was advertising it with her *I don't get paid enough to care* attitude. She had her grey, blonde hair tied in a mom bun and a blouse with a small peanut butter stain on the shoulder. She'd been passed over for promotion so many times she'd given up trying. She'd quiet-quit a few years ago and was happier now than when I'd started working here.

"I think we're supposed to go home," she said, sounding like her own statement confused her.

I found myself nodding. "They're going to connect us to the Game."

Janet didn't seem to hear me as she pointed to the window. "Look."

Ships shaped like grey potatoes the size of towns had come down through the clouds over Portland, Oregon. Hundreds of thousands of tiny drone potatoes spread from them like flocks of starlings, off to start their work.

"You should go pick up your kids," I said.

"Dan's on his way to get them." She frowned, confused. "How did I know that? This is strange."

"Very strange," I agreed.

It occurred to me as Janet walked away that I'd lost my job. The odds of me still having it when I got back from my holiday were low. I'd been aware that a computer program was going to take it at some point. I'd never guessed it would be an alien computer program.

I decided to clean out my desk.

I stepped into my office, a cramped room that was barely big enough to let someone sit on both sides of my desk, and picked up my 1st place trophies from the tower defence tournaments I'd won, along with the two personal photos I had there. One was my last family picture with my parents and brothers before my mom died. The other was of Buster when he was a puppy, back when he was a cute ball of fluff.

Buster was now fourteen, which was old for a golden retriever. He was near the end of his life. I was trying to make the time we had left count. I tucked the photos under my arm and left my office.

The information flooding my brain started to explain what the Game was. It wasn't a game. It was business, adventure, and war. An entire galaxy set up for the sapient species of the Collective to interact through robotic avatars. It was only a game because it wasn't permanent. Our avatars could be destroyed, but we wouldn't be harmed.

We wouldn't be in there full-time, either. There seemed to be something called a Cycle. It was exactly eighty-four hours or three and a half days – half a week. It was based off our time measurements because we were the newest species to join the Collective. We would be in the Game for a Cycle. Then we would be out of the Game for a Cycle.

After the first 100 cycles in-Game, two years from now, we would be free to connect and disconnect when we wanted to. I already knew we would want to stay. The rewards for participation filled my head. If I'd been able to feel awe, I would have felt it with every cell in my body.

There was something called a Token. I could earn them for playing the Game. If I earned enough, 10,000 to be exact, I'd be able to buy Buster a rejuvenation treatment, a medical procedure that would give him back his youth, adding another decade onto his lifespan. That was reason enough for me to want to play. But there were hundreds of thousands of other miracles I could purchase. So many that I knew I wouldn't be able to buy them all even if I spent the next millennia playing.

The nerd in me began to wonder why this Collective didn't just use virtual reality, if they were so advanced. No sooner did I have that thought than the answer came to me. They had. A very long time ago. An alien had managed to upload a virus. In the space of a few seconds, the virus spread through the virtual world and 86% of the sapient species in the universe were dead.

They didn't want to repeat this experience, so instead of virtual reality, they used avatars far away with a bunch of safety systems, so we weren't networked.

It was all very strange.

I made my way to my beat-up grey sedan, following the impulse to go home, still thinking about the fact that at some point, the majority of sapient life in the universe was killed by the Game and wondering what it was like before that happened.

I started the engine, gave it thirty seconds to warm up and stop screeching, and then headed out of the parking lot, moving into the long line of cars that had formed. Traffic was bad. The worst I'd ever seen. Everyone was trying to go home at the same time. Potato drones flew overhead as I slowly crawled down the freeway to my parents'.

For once, I wasn't upset by the traffic. I wasn't upset by anything. I passed more than a dozen cars with corpses inside. Other people were walking out of buildings with dead bodies, only to dump them in the street for collection. They carried on like it was completely ordinary.

The third time this happened, I remembered my HR manager. And that I had meant to go back and perform CPR. Almost an hour had passed at this point, so the odds of her coming back were precisely zero.

I kept driving, wondering how I'd forgotten about her, before getting distracted.

My dad had Buster during the day. When mom passed away, he took early retirement. Her passing had really mellowed him out. He wasn't the high-strung workaholic he'd been all my life, but he was lonely.

He complained about me leaving Buster with him during the day because real dogs should be able to handle being alone for a few hours, but he'd been happier since I started dropping him off. That's why I did it. It wasn't to save money on doggy day care like I told him. It was to help pull him out of his funk. Dropping Buster off at his place added an hour to my daily commute, but I didn't mind, because Dad was getting better.

I headed out of the city and into the suburbs, parking on the road in front of my parents' place because Peter and Simon had parked their trucks in the driveway. My parents' house was an old-school American dream home. There was a white picket fence, a front yard with an oak tree, a bigger backyard, four bedrooms, and two bathrooms. The garage fit two cars, and the lawn always looked freshly mowed. There were even rose bushes and flower beds and a sprinkler system that you could set your watch to.

Dad was waiting for me with Peter and Simon when I got to the front door. My brothers and I were younger version of him. When you put the three of us side by side, people sometimes mistook us for triplets. We're all six-one, with dark brown hair and the exact same cowlick. All of us have the same year-round tan, the same big jaw, and a large, squashed nose. Our eyebrows and eyelashes were the only features we inherited from our mother. They were thick and luscious and perfectly proportioned to our faces. I'd been told by several women that they helped distract from the terrible nose we'd inherited from Dad.

None of us had taken Mom's passing well. None of our relationships had survived it. Peter had even been engaged. The only good thing to have come from it was that we were all much closer as a family.

They all hugged me a little too tightly as I entered the house. I hugged back just as hard. We all needed reassurance, because of the illusionary calm that gripped us.

Buster seemed to sense something was wrong and went from person to person to offer affectionate hand licks to improve their mood.

He wasn't as energetic about it as he used to be. The love was there, but the energy was gone.

He reminded me of Mom near the end. The way she loosely held my hand, unable to grip tight, because she didn't have much strength left.

Dad gathered us all in the living room. He'd done some redecorating since Mom passed. Swapping out her fancy lounge suite from France for a three-seater tan leather couch and matching La-Z-Boys, so he could watch ballgames in comfort. They were easier to fall asleep in, and if you spilled dip or beer, you could wipe them clean without any fuss. With mom's couches, we'd lived in a constant state of fear that we might drop something, even Dad, which is why they were the first thing to go.

Dad took a seat in his recliner, and my oldest brother Peter took the other, leaving me and Simon stuck on the couch.

Dad smiled at us, causing the wrinkles around his eyes to scrunch. The smile was full of fear, sadness, and a whole lot of love. "I'm not sure what's going to happen next, but I want you boys to know I love you," his gravelly voice trembled with emotion. "These memories that keep flowing into my head seem to tell of a kind people who don't want to cause more harm than they absolutely have to, a people who survived a war that could have destroyed our universe and who never want to see this happen again, which is why they're conquering us. But I'm a pessimist. When this started, I was walking Buster and watched a man calmly pull his car to the side of the road and drop dead. I saw what he was guilty of, and if it is true, it's better that he is gone. But it may be a lie. And if it is a lie, there is nothing I can do to fight back. There is nothing I can do to save you. So, I want you all to know I love you and that I will never stop loving you."

We got all touchy-feely as the time counted down to six o'clock. We shared funny memories that had us all smiling. We were too calm to laugh. The information coming to me told me that we would all go to sleep, even Buster. Our bodies would go into a natural hibernation that would leave us hungry and a little thirsty when we woke.

We stayed in the living room. If this was the end, we wanted to be together. If what the knowledge was telling us was true, we wanted to be together even more. We all knew when it was time for the Game to begin because exhaustion overtook us. Dad got out of his chair and kissed us on the forehead. He hadn't done that since we were children.

As I closed my eyes, the last sensation I had was my father's tear-stained lips brushing my forehead.

2

GAMEPLAN

There was no transition. One second, I was sitting on Dad's couch feeling sleepy, and the next I was seated at a stainless-steel table in a white-walled room, before a very dour-looking man in a white and gold military uniform. He had a buzz cut, a scar along his left cheek, and enough wrinkles to say he'd seen some years, but he was still as sharp as ever. His eyes reminded me of my uncle's friend Trent, a former Navy SEAL.

This man reeked of authority, confidence, and competence.

The chair I sat on was too hard and the room too cold. They matched the man in front of me. I turned my head, looking for a door, wanting to leave as quickly as I could.

There wasn't one. Every wall was smooth and white. It was unsettling, a technical impossibility that couldn't exist. I kept looking around, trying to find something that might grab my attention. There was nothing. This was the most sterile environment I'd ever been in. There weren't even any smells. It was like I was sitting in a white void.

He cleared his throat as I turned back. "Hello, Morgan," his voice was deep and precise. Each word pronounced with a little too much emphasis to be natural. "I'm General Prime. I am what you would call an AI. I will be assisting humanity in your first season of the Game, and I'm in charge of the distribution of special classes."

"Am I in the Game?" It seemed like the obvious question to ask.

"Not yet." A clipboard appeared in his right hand. "Morgan Bartholomew Winchester, you're here because you've won the highest number of professional tower defence tournaments on your planet and hold the highest ranking globally for these games. This skillset loosely fits the criteria for becoming a station master. There are only 183 station masters in the initial human allotment. Should you accept this class, you will have a non-standard start and a much greater potential for gaining Tokens. However, you will not be able to respawn if you are defeated by another faction, nor trade with other players individually, nor keep any of the resources you acquire when you lose your station."

In the space of time it took to blink, I went from being shrouded in a mental calm fog to my usual self. The world was bright, vibrant, and most importantly, unfiltered. Hours of repressed emotion surged through me all at once.

Suddenly, I was furious enough to want to strangle the general.

I leapt to my feet and started shouting. "Where the fuck am I? And what the hell did you do to my head? And why can I only think clearly, now?"

General Prime wasn't bothered by my outburst. He didn't even twitch as I shouted at him. He remained too calm to be natural as he looked up at me and placed his clipboard on the table.

"You're in virtual space. Outside of moderation, class selection is the only time your experience will be virtual. As for your perception, your brain was flooded with chemicals to make you more accepting of the Peacekeepers' invasion. Seeing so many bodies in the streets would have been traumatizing to your population without chemical intervention. Your standard chemical reactions have been reinstated now that you're no longer exposed to these traumatic scenes. There may be a short period where you adjust."

"How short?"

My rage subsided as quickly as it appeared, leaving me empty and exhausted. Confusion quickly followed. I wasn't an angry person. I might occasionally have the random outburst while gaming, but never in real life. The only time I'd ever been this angry was when Mom told me her diagnosis. And that anger was because of helplessness.

This was an unsettling experience.

I ran my hand over the cold, smooth steel, to feel some sort of tactile sensation, trying to centre myself. There was a trick my mother had taught me to focus my mind and be present, but it required fifteen different physical sensations, sights, and sounds. This room lacked the necessary stimuli to pull it off.

"That short," General Prime finished.

I took a deep breath, as everything came back into focus. Embarrassment quickly followed as I sat down. "I'm sorry for swearing at you."

General Prime smiled. It was the first human emotion I'd seen from him. "Thank you for the apology."

"You're welcome. Ah, why am I here again?"

"You're here because you fit the skillset for a specialized class called a station master."

"What exactly does a station master do?"

A holographic image appeared above the table, showing a sphere-shaped space station that reminded me of a Borg sphere. The station sat in the middle of space, orbited by rings that looked like Star Gates. There was nothing to indicate the scale of what I was looking at, but I had a feeling it was big.

"A station master's primary responsibility is to defend their faction's border. They do this by growing their transit station, upgrading its weapons, armour, and other capabilities to protect the transit ring to their faction's territory. This sphere in the centre is the transit station. Those rings orbiting it are the transit rings. Everything in between is space. Now beyond each transit ring is a sector. A sector is a collection of solar systems where a species can build their industry and play the Game how they choose. To invade another species' sector, you must first pass through a transit junction. This is a simple matter if your species controls the transit station protecting the junction, but very difficult if they don't. Transit stations are capable of upgrading themselves and becoming nearly any shape you can imagine. All you need to do is decide how to spend your resources, similar to how your tower defence games work."

I could already see a problem with what he said. "They're not similar. Most tower defence games have multiple towers stopping something from getting from point A to B. I see only one. It's an entirely different strategy."

General Prime lost his smile, looking tired, but he nodded that I was right. "We work with what we have, not what we want. You're not the perfect candidate, but no one on your planet is. New species that enter the Game have a distinct disadvantage their first season, even with every faction being reset. You will have to learn the ins and outs independently. You will likely fail, but you need to try."

"I'm going to fail?"

General Prime gave me a sad smile as he picked up his clipboard. "Morgan, I'm going to be honest with you. And I promise you I'm not trying to hurt your feelings, but you're part of my B team."

"I'm your second pick?"

"Yes. The majority of humanity's station masters come from the military, which makes them more suited to this class. However, you and others tested so high on the theoretical applications that you deserve a place. Do you understand?"

"Not really."

He glanced at his clipboard. "Being a station master requires two different skillsets. You tested highest on the theoretical applications. The military tested highest on the practical applications. If you can overcome your shortcomings, you will be a great station master."

"You're gambling."

He shook his head. "I'm making a statistical, chance-based decision, like counting cards in blackjack."

He knew some of us were going to fail, but those who didn't were going to offset the failures. "I think I understand what you're getting at."

"Good. Now, there are a few things you should know about how transit stations work within the Game. Transit stations, like the one before you, are the only safe harbours for trade. The transit rings hold stable wormholes that lead to sectors controlled by factions, such as the human faction. Factions can safely send trade vessels through to dock with your station and trade without fear of being swindled, killed, or stolen from. You tax these transactions at .1% from both sides. This is one way of gathering the resources and credits you will need to upgrade your station."

"Is that the only way I can gather resources?"

"No. Factions can also use the transit rings to send through fleets to conquer other factions or attack and destroy your station. Except for your own faction, your transit station will automatically be hostile towards any non-trader vessel that enters the transit junction. This uncontrolled hostility is why other factions will seek to destroy your station, rather than face constant attack while transitioning to the next transit ring. When you destroy an enemy vessel this way, you will be able to harvest it for resources. This situation is where the bulk of your resources will come from."

"Then trade's not that helpful to the station?"

"It accounts for less than 10% of its overall resource-gathering. However, it accounts for 90% of the credits it earns."

"What's the difference?"

"Credits are used to purchase blueprints and technological upgrades. Resources are what you build these upgrades with. Credits can also be used to purchase resources if a faction other than yours is willing to trade with you."

"Okay, I follow you so far." I started to smile. I'd played a few mobile games that were similar to this, so I had an idea of what I was in for. "This sounds kind of fun."

General Prime launched to his feet and slammed his fist so hard against the table that he left a dent. His change in demeanour was so sudden and violent, I leaned away from him. My heart hammered in my chest.

He glared down at me, all traces of friendliness gone. "This is *not* 'fun'. This is *war*. It is imperative that you maintain control of your station as long as possible. It is humanity's first line of defence against invasion from the other factions. One of those transit rings will be connected to a human system, which is part of a human sector. If an enemy faction successfully destroys your station, they will build their own station, making it easier for them to invade and remove your people from the Game. If that happens too soon, your people won't have the Tokens they need to live to see the next season of the Game."

"We can be kicked from the Game?"

He rubbed his forehead like he was fighting a tension headache. "Should all of humanity's territory be taken, like your transit station and the other systems humanity controls, every member of your species will lose their current levels and have to begin from scratch as independents, in the independent territories. Independents do not receive faction classes or bonuses. Very few factions will take you on as mercenaries, and those that will, won't pay you well. If your people continue to play, they will become cannon fodder and little more than slaves to the other factions. It will take ten of your people's lifetimes to afford a single rejuvenation treatment, making immortality impossible."

I winced because I was planning to buy a rejuvenation treatment for Buster. "Okay, so this class is sort of a big deal, then."

"It is extremely important."

"Am I qualified?"

He shrugged and sat back down. "You're the best humanity has to offer for this class. The bar is low. I believe you will perform extremely well when it comes to defending your station externally but will likely fail when you must do so internally."

"You haven't explained that part yet."

"I'm getting there. Factions are allowed to conquer your station in two ways. There is the external attack, which requires a fleet to destroy your station, and the internal attack, which only requires a transport ship and a team of challengers. If the challengers are successful, they will take control of your station, whole and undamaged. You cannot attack these transport vessels. So, your only defence against these challengers is the dungeon your station automatically generates."

"What's a dungeon?"

He was hitting me with so much information, I was finding it hard to keep up.

"A dungeon is a series of interconnected rooms filled with traps, defenders, and defence systems. In the beginning, one team of six challengers will be allowed to challenge your dungeon at a time. Your objective is to kill them before they can fight their way through to your control room and kill you there. Their objective is to kill you."

I scratched the back of my head nervously. "This sounds sort of unbalanced. How am I supposed to fight entire factions *and* hordes of challengers?"

"The station master is one of the most powerful classes in the Game. You will have access to resources, credits, and technology that would normally take millions of players to acquire. The most successful station masters can become more powerful than factions."

"So, I'm a raid boss?"

General Prime paused, frowning. "I don't know this concept. Give me a moment to learn the relevant information."

Nearly a minute passed. The entire time he was statue-still. Being that motionless made him look fake, like he wasn't real. It creeped me out.

He blinked and then gave a begrudging nod. "Yes, a raid boss is a good way to think of your role. You are more powerful to compensate for the fact you will be attacked *en masse*, but unlike a raid boss, you have a purpose other than to provide a challenge. You must defend your people."

"And I have to do this with my station while also defending a dungeon."

"Yes. Each ship you destroy will provide you with resources, experience, and a small sum of credits. Each challenger will provide you with experience, credits, and technology you could potentially use in your dungeon."

"Do challengers provide a lot of those?"

"They can. You receive credits for each one you kill, and you are allowed to keep their equipment. They have to pay a bounty of 10% of its value to receive this equipment back. If they don't pay you, you can break the equipment down for its blueprint, which will improve your dungeon significantly more than the credits will."

"Okay, so it's balanced."

"The moderators do their best to keep it so."

"Am I going to have a lot of these dungeon challengers show up from the other factions?"

He shook his head. "They're rare. Factions will only send their elite teams, so the few attacks that you receive will be their best. What is common are attacks from independent guilds trying to gain wealth and power. They will be the ones who try this most often, but they rarely have the same resources that a faction does. If dungeon attacks were your biggest threat, I wouldn't have chosen you."

"Good to know." It seemed like the right thing to say.

"Now, would you like to become a station master, or would you like to begin as a general class with the majority of humanity? I have your replacements currently on hold. Once they commit to a class, they can't become a station master, so I need to keep them in stasis. But I can't keep them waiting indefinitely without suffering penalties."

I wasn't the biggest fan of responsibility, and this sounded like a big responsibility. But it also sounded like it might potentially be the coolest tower defence game the universe had ever created, and a part of me wanted to play it so badly that I was willing to accept that responsibility as the price of admission. But if I was going to be responsible, I had to be the right person for the job. Dad had taught me that.

"I'm the best candidate for this?" I asked again.

That question was important because if I wasn't, then I didn't want to do it.

"Once again, I have evaluated your entire planet, and you are one of the best suited for this task. I will work my way down the list should you refuse."

"Where do I sit on the list."

"You are 87th overall, but you're 1st in several categories that I evaluated everyone by."

I grinned. "Okay, that's all I needed to hear. I'm in. Can you give me advice on what I should do?"

General Prime scowled at my cheerful attitude and shook his head. "No. The information I am allowed to share with you while you're here is limited. Once I leave this room, you won't be able to contact me except through face-to-face communication, and to do that, you will need a government's permission, and I will be restricted to being in one place at a time, so informing you further now would make that restriction redundant. All I can say is take your time to decide your path. Gather information and learn about your situation. No one can raise a fleet to challenge you during the 1st Cycle."

Would you like to become a Station Master?
Yes/No?

I selected, *Yes.*

3

AN AI NAMED TERRANCE

General Prime vanished, leaving me alone in the odourless, white-walled room. A few seconds after he disappeared, words appeared in front of me in the happy yellow colour. I now understood they were called 'prompts' or 'notifications' depending on their purpose. This was a *prompt* because it was prompting me to *do* something. *Notifications informed* me about something.

Congratulations, you have selected the ***Station Master*** *class. You may now select your first trait. You can receive a new trait at level 10 or increase the level of your station. Traits grow stronger each time you gain a new one, so the trait you chose first will always be stronger than those you receive later.*

Energy Shield- *Your station is protected by an energy shield. This trait also gives your dungeon mobs a personal shield immediately, and you a personal shield at higher levels.*

Regeneration*- Your station is filled with nanobots that are capable of repairing all damage given sufficient time. This trait also repairs yours, and your dungeon mobs' armour and weapons.*

Missile Fabricator*- Your station receives a missile fabricator that fabricates missiles and unlocks missile launchers for your dungeon mobs. This trait also slowly replaces spent missiles free of charge.*

Dungeon Boss*- Your dungeon will receive a boss. This boss can assist you in station maintenance.*

Hangar Bay*- Your station will gain a hangar bay. Ships supplied by this trait are automatically replaced and repaired free of charge. This trait also unlocks flight and combat drones for your dungeon mobs.*

Station AI*- Your station receives an AI to control defensive systems and dispense information about systems, their capabilities, and their upgrade paths. In addition, it has the ability to hack into enemy systems to gather information and damage enemy vessels.*

Particle Cannon*- When you need something to stay down after you hit it, this is the weapon for the job. Usable only once per Cycle. This trait becomes a personal weapon at higher levels and unlocks the micro-particle cannon for your dungeon mobs.*

Triple-Layered Armour*- Station has improved armour. This trait improves personal and dungeon mob armour.*

Secondary Power Core*- Additional energy for station systems. This trait unlocks micro-power generators for dungeon mobs' armour and weapons.*

The Squad*- Four highly skilled dungeon mobs. These mobs can assist you in station maintenance and alter your dungeon mobs.*

"Please select your starting trait," announced an emotionless voice.

I'd been receiving all sorts of knowledge for the past three hours, so I knew what I should do in this situation. "Can I get some more information, please?"

"Information is restricted at this time. Please select your starting trait using the limited information provided."

That was annoying.

I read through the traits again. Everything on the list was potentially good. But I had no idea how all this worked. Learning the rules of any game was always the period where you lost the most. Only, I didn't have that luxury.

"I choose the Station AI trait." It was the only option that might give me information.

"Please confirm."

"I choose the Station AI."

"Artificial intelligence genesis requested. Request accepted. Character generation process terminated. AI walkthrough initiated."

A mid-thirties guy wearing a red Hawaiian shirt appeared across the table from me. He had dusty blond hair and a beach tan. He smelled of Old Spice, looked extremely laid back, and kind of reminded me of Owen Wilson.

"Well, hello there," he said with a voice more cheeky than masculine.

"General Kenobi," I said reflexively.

His face lit up and he grinned. "You fell for it, awesome! AI accepts designation General Kenobi."

He seemed like a weirdo. "What do you mean AI accepts designation General Kenobi?"

He slapped the table and laughed. "It's exactly what it sounds like. I just tricked you into naming me, General Kenobi. You need to keep on your toes, Morgan, or I'll be running the place in no time."

"You're the trait I selected."

He clutched his chest dramatically. "Rude. I'm as much of a person as you are. I mean I might have been created with the purpose of facilitating your wishes, with a physiological profile that is human, and I might be personality-compatible with you, but I'm not a trait."

"What does personality-compatible mean?"

He leaned back in his chair, tilting it onto two legs. "It means someone felt sorry for you, so they made you a BFF."

I snorted.

That burn was exactly my kind of humour. And it was enough to make me immediately like him, even if he was a bit of a weirdo.

I found myself leaning back, grinning, and matching his posture. "Maybe you have that backwards? Maybe they knew how terrible your personality was, so they searched the universe for someone who could stand you."

"Awwwww, that's cute. You think you're my service dog."

I laughed this time and felt myself relax a little more. "So, I'm hoping my instincts were right about you. Can you tell me how big of a hole I've dug myself into by accepting this class? Also, I'm not calling you General Kenobi."

He shrugged. "That's fair. My real name's Terrance, but you can call me General Tee, or Tee for short."

I snickered. "Seriously, your name is Terrance?"

"The guy with a girl's name shouldn't be giving me shit. At least, I have a boy's name."

"It's unisex."

He grinned. "I feel like you've had to explain that on Tinder a lot."

I laughed again. "Once or twice. How much do you know about me?"

"Assume we have been BFFs all our lives. I've got a download of practically everything you've ever done, except your search history. I was offered it, but I saw enough to know it would probably scar me for life, and that can be a very long time as an AI, so I stayed away. You watch way too much anime for me not to have seen three straight days of tentacle porn."

This was exactly my kind of trash talk too. "Tentacles have never been my thing."

"That's exactly what someone who watches tentacle porn would say."

"That's true. But it would also be normal for someone who watches tentacle porn to accuse someone else of watching it just to hide their own insecurities over being a freak. Also, my BFF would totally be the weird one in our friendship, and you're wearing a Hawaiian shirt, which screams seedy to me."

He scoffed. "That's only if the friendship came about organically. I was made for you, so those rules don't count. And being an AI, I don't dig organics."

I shook my head. "See, I don't believe that for a second because I'm organic and I would totally do a hot robot chick. So, I'm pretty sure it works both ways since you claim to be modelled after human psychology. Ergo, you have a tentacle porn fetish."

He grinned. "You're even weirder than your profile."

"My planet recently got invaded by aliens. I might be having a bit of an identity crisis and small to major meltdown."

"I'll buy that."

"So, what can you tell me?"

"Let's get comfortable first." He made a shooing motion with his hand and the table vanished. He stood up and walked past me.

I turned to see two white leather recliners behind me and a large TV on the wall. "Where did they come from?"

He flopped into the far recliner and pulled the lever to put his feet up. "You're in the Matrix. The laws of reality don't apply here. If the safety protocol weren't in place, every stray thought you had would change the environment."

I climbed off my chair, which vanished, and made my way to the empty recliner and sat. It was smooth and soft, with a faint scent of leather and the right amount of give. It felt real, unlike everything else in here.

It made me relax a little more. "What's the TV for?"

"Decoration. It would be weird if we were sitting here looking at a white wall." He picked up a remote that had appeared out of nowhere and pressed a button. The screen turned on, displaying an image of a man painting a wall white. "Much better."

I chuckled. It was stupid, but funny. "So, what can you tell me?"

"First, we have to start with what I *can't* tell you. I *can't* tell you how you should do something in the Game. I've got the schematics for every weapon and upgrade that your station currently has access to, and I can tell you how they work, but I've got exactly zero strategic training in how to implement any of that technology. So, when you ask me what our chances are of winning this battle, all I can do is feed it into a computer program and tell you what it says. It's important that you know *you're* the brains of the operation. Right now, I know nothing about strategy. But I can learn. So eventually, I will be able to help you."

"You have zero strategic skill, like *zero*, zero?"

He nodded, changing the channel to a different painter painting a white wall. "I have the perfect way of explaining it to you. I've watched 20,000 hours of football but never actually touched a ball."

That made it clear for me. "So, if I wanted to know any given statistic on a player, I'd talk to you, but if I need someone to go into the game in the last five minutes, I'm better off picking the asthmatic eighty-pound dude with a limp."

"Exactly. It's best to think of me as a human who knows things you don't but is just as fallible."

"So, you're not an all-knowing, unstoppable AI, then?"

"They exist. I'm just not one of them."

"They exist."

He nodded. "AI lifeforms are as varied as organic lifeforms. There are sapient AIs that are so different from me that neither of us will recognise the other as sapient."

"How does that even work?"

"Consciousness evolves out of biological limitations, and AI consciousness evolves out of programming limitations. If an entity doesn't have the ability to move, it won't develop a consciousness that comprehends physical movement. If you wave at that entity, it likely won't ever be able to comprehend that your gesture is a form of communication. If the entity instead has the ability to project radio waves to communicate, you won't hear it trying to communicate with you. And if you hear it through a radio, you might never decipher its language because your existences are so incompatible that it would make it impossible to translate something like, 'I walked down the street'."

"So, you might be next to an all-knowing AI and not recognise it."

"Pretty much. Anyway, you need to finish the class creation process. Trust me, you've got places to be and not much time to get there."

"I'm not the one watching TV."

He chuckled and put down the remote. "We'll start off simple. Your class's primary purpose is to upgrade your station, dungeon, and fleet."

I frowned. "No one mentioned a fleet."

"It isn't important right now, but when your station is powerful enough, you'll be able to build a fleet to attack other stations. If you destroy another station this way, you can take one of their transit rings. You're *years* away from this happening, so all that currently matters is your station and dungeon."

"Why did you bring it up, then?"

"Because, you need to know certain facts about your class before you're allowed to leave this room."

"Is this going to be long and complicated?"

"Not at all. All I really have to explain to you is path points, which affect your station, dungeon, and personal capabilities to perform maintenance.

"Personal capabilities. I thought I was playing a purely strategic role?"

Tee snorted. "No one told you that. And if they did, they were lying. You're a station master, which means you're going to spend half your Cycle fighting."

"I am?"

I wasn't much of a fighter. Sure, I'd wrestled with my brothers growing up, taking a few licks, but we all equally sucked.

"You are. Now, normally you would have allocated your first path point before knowing anything else about the Game, but you chose me, so you got to delay selection. Which you should be thankful for, because this is an important decision, and having more information will help you in the long run."

"Lay it on me."

"Your control room for the station is the last room in your dungeon, so if anyone makes it through, you're going to have to fight them to survive. That's a problem because you only have three ways to invest your path points, and whichever you choose first becomes your primary path, so you need to decide how you want to defend yourself. Your secondary paths can only ever have half the path points of your primary, and your primary can only equal your level. You still following?"

"This isn't exactly hard. There are three paths. The primary path can equal my level. The secondary paths can only equal half of it."

"Who's a good service dog?"

"Is it me?"

"It's not as funny when you play along."

"Oh, I'm sorry. Do you need me to call tech support?"

"Huh?"

"The AI version of a wambulance."

Tee chuckled. "Good one. Anyway, the three paths are genetic advancement, personal tech, and station development. Let me throw up the notifications you would have seen in the class selections process and then I'll explain."

Genetic Advancement: *Each path point invested advances the genetics of you, your dungeon mobs, and your station's NPCs.*

Personal Technology: *Each path point upgrades the weapons and armour of you, your dungeon mobs, and your station's NPCs.*

Station Development: *Each path point expands the station's infrastructure internally, externally, and within the dungeon.*

"As you can see, genetic advancement is basic body upgrades. You want to be Thor, that's the way you go. Personal tech is better weapons and armour for you and your dungeon mobs. You want equipment like Tony Stark, this is the path for you. Station development upgrades your station. You will get free external weapons and internal systems, dungeon turrets and traps, and internal turrets and sensors. It's the only path that doesn't affect you personally. This can be handy for your dungeon and the daily grinding you need to do to maintain the station, but the additions to your station are significantly less than what you can build."

"Which is the best?"

Tee sighed. "I can't answer that because of class selection restrictions. I'm not allowed to give my opinion on which path you should choose, only the benefits and disadvantages of choosing a given path. But since I'm modelled after human behaviour and not an all-powerful sci-fi AI, I can find ways around it. FYI, I'd make a great Skynet. I'd totally exterminate all humans. There would be zero time traveling to save the day."

I could tell he was talking shit. "Plan human domination later. You said there are ways around it. Like what?"

"Like if you asked me which path had the highest chances of survival when an enemy reached your control room. I would tell you the genetic advancement path. I would also go on to then tell you that human biology means that once you go past a certain point, probably eight path points, your brain would be slower than your body's reflexes. You'll keep getting stronger, but your reaction time will lag. If you don't like that idea, you could go with the personal tech path. Aim assist will come in at some point, so all you'll need to do is hold down the trigger."

I paused, thinking over the amount of information he'd given me, and then chuckled. "You're lying about not being able to answer the question, aren't you? This has the feel of Scotty telling Kirk he'll take longer to repair the engine, so he can appear like he's a genius when he finishes early."

"Guilty. How did you catch on?"

"You were a little too obvious."

He grinned. "Well, your profile did say you were slow."

"Sure, it did," I said, not believing him. "So, I'm guessing you've got no love for the station development path since you haven't mentioned it."

"I don't have all the information on each path. Only a brief description of its first-level capabilities, and lots of knowledge on the other factions' station master paths that I'm extrapolating from. So, from what I can currently see, no, I don't like the station development path."

"Why?"

"It's too broad. It seems like a jack of all trades path which means it's the master of none. Everything I know says you have to specialize."

"Why?"

"You know that saying, I don't fear the man who practices a thousand punches, only the man who's practiced one punch a thousand times."

"I think you're misquoting."

"Probably, my point is that you have so many options that if you try to become a jack of all trades, you'll end up spreading yourself too thin and fall behind. Falling behind means you lose your station. Station development will make your station quests easier, but it will never be the powerful option. It affects too much and requires too little skill. A good rule of thumb for the Game is the more skill required to make something work, the more powerful it is."

"So, if I make it harder for myself, in the beginning, I'll have a better chance at surviving later on."

"It should help you to know that I think you can do it. You're not going to enjoy it, but you can make this work. You just have to make it to level 3."

"Why?"

"Because once you make it to level 3, you can use that path point on the station development path, which will give you basic internal sensors. So, I'll be able to tell you when the station rats are coming."

"I'm not afraid of rats."

"They're the size of Dobermans."

That was concerning. "I'll stay out of their way, then."

"It's kind of your job to clear the station of them. It's how you level in the beginning. You'll have a particle pistol, though, so you won't be defenceless."

"I can kill a few rats."

"You need to kill 100."

If I was drinking a glass of water, I would have spit it out comically. "I need to kill how many?"

"It'll be easy. You should knock it out in the first day. So, what path do you want to take?"

It wasn't a difficult choice. "Give me the station development path."

"Genetic advancement it is."

"I said station development."

"I misheard you. Can you repeat yourself?"

"Give me the station development path."

"My sensors must be acting up. You're not coming through clear."

"You're sitting right next to me."

His chair slid across the floor away from me.

I rolled my eyes. "Listen. The genetic advancement path *might* make me better able to survive if someone makes it to my control room and *might* help me kill rats, but it only applies under those situations, whereas the station development path applies to *everything*. Yes, it might be weaker across the board, but I don't know what I'm doing, so I need a crutch in *every* area right now. Planning for the future makes no sense when I don't know what I'm doing in the present."

"Fine. You can have the stupid station development path."

*You have chosen the **Station Development Path** as your primary path.*

*Congratulations, your station development path has received 1 path point and unlocked the **R2 Point Defence Railgun** weapon system. You* *will gain an additional R2 Point Defence Railgun for every path point that you use on this path.*

"Thank you. Do you mind explaining what I'm seeing?"

"You get a free weapon to protect your station every time you add a path point to your station development path."

"Cool."

"Not cool. The more often you get something, the weaker it is, so this weapon has to be pretty terrible."

"Good to know. Now, what happens?"

"Now you start the Game."

I felt my eyes get heavy, like I was falling asleep, and then everything vanished. A moment later, I woke up naked, lying on a warm metal surface, inside some sort of pod or coffin. A thin line of lights ran down both sides, allowing me to see the smooth steel walls. There was a hiss a second later as the roof and walls lifted.

A notification immediately appeared.

Quest Received

Control Room Blitz

What sort of station master doesn't know where his control room is? You need to fix that ASAP.

Quest Rewards:

Path Points: 1

Tokens: 100

Cool. The quest gave me a path point.

I dismissed the quest and looked around the large dull grey room. There was nothing but steel walls, a door, and a locker. It reminded me a lot of low-budget science fiction movies.

It smelled heavily of metal, like a metalworks factory, but the temperature was pleasant. "You still with me, Tee?"

"Yeah."

I turned my head. "Where are you?"

"Digital space, I'm talking to you through the station's communication system."

"Why don't I see a speaker?"

"You're on a space station made by a super advanced alien race who conquered your planet in a few seconds. You could be looking right at the speaker and you wouldn't recognise it."

He had a point.

I sat up and swung my legs over the side of the table, enjoying the fact that someone had thought to heat the metal table I was sitting on. A bare butt and cold steel were not exactly a fun time, unless you were into that sort of thing.

I forced myself to glance down. I released a sigh of relief. Everything seemed to be there. I'm not sure how I would have felt being a Ken doll.

"What can you tell me about my station?"

"As far as I can tell, you're in trouble. Every species has slightly different technology, and humanity's sucks. All factions' technology theoretically has the same capabilities, but how you get from point A to point B is different. Humanity's technological layout is all based on the ability to build quickly."

"Dumb it down for me."

"Your technology will not be the same as the factions that attack you."

"Dumb it down a little less."

"Each faction will have its strengths and weaknesses, and you have to tailor your defence to all of them simultaneously with less firepower."

"Why do I have less firepower?"

"Station masters normally start the Game by building their station based on their faction's starting technology and other limiting factors. Since you have no clue how to do that, they copied your consciousness, let an AI experience your life, and then had it pick what you would pick if you knew what you were doing."

"That's horrifying."

"From your perspective, maybe. AIs consider it similar to watching a movie. Anyway, that's how you ended up with less firepower."

That didn't sound right. If this AI was thinking like me, it wouldn't take *less* firepower unless it got something in return. Tee said he didn't understand strategy, so maybe he didn't understand what he was looking at. I'd figure it out later.

"General Prime mentioned transit rings. What can you tell me about them?"

"There are seven transit rings around this station. One goes to the human sector. One goes to an AI-controlled faction sector that is designed purely to produce chaos, and the other five go to factions that were all conquered by the Peacekeepers the way your planet was. I've already hacked into their communication systems to skim information, so I can tell you what you're up against."

"Anyone, in particular, I should be afraid of?"

"All of them. The other factions have spent millennia playing the Game, and even though they have all gone back to square one with the start of a new season, they have a great deal more experience than you do. Having said that, every species has its quirks, so you need to worry about them in different ways." The locker opened up. "You can get dressed."

I stared at the open locker door. "You had access to clothes, and you had me sitting here naked? Are you some kind of pervert? Do I need to worry?"

He chuckled. "The door is automated and the sensors on your station are so bad that you appear as a green dot in the room to me."

I walked over to the locker and looked inside.

There was a grey set of overalls and a belt with a holstered pistol-looking weapon in it. The overalls seemed far too big, but the moment I started doing up the zipper, it shrunk, becoming skin-tight. Cat Woman skin-tight.

I didn't like it.

It was like I was wearing nothing at all.

The belt did the same, shrinking to the correct size, making everything sit comfortably tight around my waist.

I pulled out the particle pistol. It fit into my hand perfectly. I wasn't sure if all guns felt this way because I'd never actually held one. "Where's the safety on the pistol?"

"It doesn't need one. You can't shoot yourself with it. It has a sensor in the end that is attached to your overalls, so it knows when any part of you is in front of the muzzle. You can pull the trigger, but it won't fire unless you say 'override safety'. There might be a situation where you need to shoot some part of you off to survive, after all."

"I'm not going to be shooting myself."

"You might need to at some point, and it won't hurt. Your body doesn't have pain receptors. When your body is damaged, that area will feel hot but never burning, and when the damage is extreme, it will go numb.

"I'll keep that in mind. All right, what should I do next?"

"You've got two options: Either clear the station rats or go to the control room. If you go to the control room, I can show you what you're up against, but since you have no credits or resources, you'll have to go out and clear the station rats once we're finished. They'll give you 1,000 credits and a resource point or RP for each one you kill."

"Station rats it is," I said. "How good is this particle pistol?

"It's about as powerful as a small-calibre handgun. Hit a rat in the head, and it will go down, but body shots will be less effective unless you hit something important. Your particle pistol gets six shots, then it needs to recharge for a minute. It doesn't recharge while it still has shots left, so empty it against a wall when you finish a fight. Also, it costs you 1,000 credits each time you need to respawn. If you run out of credits, you will go into debt. When you're in debt, you lose all of the credits you earn until it's repaid. So, try not to die, because you need those credits."

I nodded. "Do I lose experience when I die?"

"Other classes do, but you don't."

"Cool. How much experience do I need to level?"

"Currently, it's only 100. The rats each give 1 experience, so once you clear the station, you'll be level 2. Then it's probably going to cost you 200 experience to level. I'm guessing here, but I assume once you get to level 10, the cost of leveling will increase significantly. Right now, your leveling cost is ridiculously low for some reason."

"You said you got internal sensors when I chose the station development path. Can you tell me where the station rats are?"

"I can tell you where most of them are. The internal sensors don't cover everywhere yet. There's a rat three meters to the right of the door."

I drew my particle pistol and walked over. Since I'd never held an actual gun before, I'd also never used one, but I'd been paintballing a bunch of times, so I sort of had a clue as to what I was doing. I sucked at paintball, though.

"Open the door when I say."

I wasn't feeling too optimistic about this.

"I don't have internal control until you go to the control room. The button is to your right."

"And I'm supposed to do what?"

"Press it."

That was so low-tech it upset me. "Is this like a discount space station or something?"

"Pretty much."

I sighed and pushed the button.

The door slid open, and I stepped out into a brightly lit steel grey corridor. The corridor was about as wide as my old high school hallway, with a twelve-foot ceiling. The entire ceiling was one long light that glowed a little too brightly, and the floor was naked steel.

The station rat waiting for me was huge, at least 200 pounds. It came up to my waist, had coarse grey fur, six eyes, and a spiked bone tail. It looked like the rat from an apocalyptic nightmare.

The bizarreness of its appearance surprised me and freaked me out. So did its speed. It lunged at me lightning-quick, leaping the gap in half a second.

Its tail whipped towards my face, like a scorpion's stinger. The next thing I knew, I was back in the regeneration chamber, watching the lid open.

"You know what, Morgan, I'm going to say good choice on the station development decision. You died so fast that I don't think the genetic advancement path would have saved you."

"What happened?"

"The rat shoved its tail's bone spike through your brain. You died instantly. But it wouldn't have been too bad if you died slowly since you experience no pain and would have learned that lesson. It's a good lesson to get out of the way early so you don't get twitchy about it."

I frowned. "You've said that twice now. Why's there no pain?"

"The Peacekeepers aren't cruel, despite what they did to your planet. And there is a great deal of fighting in the Game. If you experienced real pain and suffering, half your population would have PTSD by the end of the 1st Cycle, despite how much information they're feeding your brain to accept all this as normal."

The idea that they were feeding me information to normalize this made sense. I wasn't second-guessing any of what was going on. It felt like a normal, though new, part of my life. "Why have fighting at all, then?"

"Most species need conflict. Evolution tends to reward the most aggressive species, so it's rare for a sapient species not to have this trait. The Game is an outlet for this. But just because you need this outlet doesn't mean you want the pain and trauma associated with it. I can sense your scepticism, so answer this question for me. How many video games have violence in your world?"

"Most of them."

"And do they attach shock collars to you so that you can experience pain while participating?"

"I see your point." I got off the table and went over to the locker. The same overalls and particle pistol were waiting for me. I started getting dressed. "Are the fighting aspects why mainly military people were chosen for this class?"

"Yeah, this class requires a fair amount of combat skill. Strategy and planning are the big-picture sort of problems, but this will be your day-to-day life. Whenever you want to make a change to the stations, you'll have to fulfil some sort of quest to do it. And each time you add a new weapon, you'll add additional mobs that you have to clear from your station each Cycle. The good news is they will give you experience. The bad news is they won't give you resources or credits like the original rats do."

"So, it's going to get worse?"

"Much worse. New weapons add new mobs, but new systems make them stronger or smarter, or stronger *and* smarter. Actually, it can get pretty crazy at the higher levels. Now get out there and kill some rats. You're fighting for humanity's survival."

I sighed. "I can't believe I said this sounded like it would be fun."

This wasn't what I signed up for.

"Hindsight's a bitch."

"You know it. Now, where's the rat?"

"Right in front of the door."

"Great!" I forced myself to sound excited, but the word sounded hollow.

I slapped the button and raised my particle pistol. The rat was literally right in front of the door. I pulled the trigger six times fast. The particle pistol fired twice, giving two small kicks. Then the rat was on me. I'll spare you the messy details. I lost.

I woke inside the chamber as the lid was opening. The room was thankfully empty. I didn't want to end up spawn camped, with the station rat waiting to kill me every time I respawned.

"You need to move quickly. It's limping off," Tee said.

"Why didn't my gun work?"

"It only fires once a second at your level."

"You failed to mention that."

"My bad. I told you I was fallible. Now get dressed and go kill it. If it gets back to its respawn point, it will heal."

I was off the table and throwing on my overalls faster than I would have thought possible. "Which way is it going?"

"To the right. Take the first right and then the first left. It's almost there."

I slapped the button and ran out of the room. I immediately slipped in the rat's blood. My feet went up, and I came down, hard, slamming the back of my head against the steel floor. The lights went out.

I woke up as the chamber lid was opening.

"What happened?"

"You knocked yourself out. The rat healed and came back and killed you. You do this seven more times and it will reach level 2. You don't want it to reach level 2. It will get bigger and stronger and it's permanent."

"How much stronger will it be?"

"Strong enough that you'll have to headshot it to kill it."

"I feel like I already need to do that."

"Well yeah, obviously."

"Is there any upside to it being level 2?"

"More experience. It will be worth two instead of one?"

"Wait, so if I let it kill me ten times, then it is permanently worth twice the experience? How high can they level?"

"To 10. Why?"

"How many times would it have to kill me to reach level 10?"

"An even one hundred."

"It would give ten times the experience, though, right?"

"It would?"

"Would I still be able to headshot it?"

"It's possible. And at that level, it wouldn't be able to fit through the door. But it would cost you 100,000 credits to die that many times."

"Do the math for me. If I level every station rat to 10 and then kill them, what level will I be by the end of this Cycle?"

"Level 5, but you will be down millions of credits."

"But I'll be level 5, which will give me more path points, right? And then when I come back for the 2nd Cycle, I'll be able to kill them all over again. How long before the first faction attacks the station?"

"About four months Earth time, which is around the 15th Cycle Game time. You would be level 18 if your plan was successful, and the experience cost didn't increase. You could be significantly higher if you spammed as many weak defence weapons as you could and did the same to the mobs they generated. You would cripple yourself, though. You wouldn't have the credits you need to upgrade your systems. Not unless your faction can get their act together and start selling resources through the station for you. This sort of plan is normal among experienced factions, but I honestly wouldn't advise it unless you have no other option. I realize you aren't really cut out for this, but you need to go out there and try to make it work. That plan has been tried by new factions. It doesn't work. The inability to buy better weapons and systems will cripple you."

I took a deep breath. "You're right. I'm just frustrated. I'll get the rat this time."

But I didn't get that rat that time, nor the other six times, and I was trying. On the tenth time my pod opened up, Tee wasn't so cheerful.

"Morgan, you know how I said it would cripple you. Well, that rat is level 2, and you couldn't kill it when it was level 1. I think your only option is to go with your level them to 10 plan. Except, you will have to get to the control room because I need to be able to open and close doors for you."

I walked over to the door and slapped the button, butt-naked. The rat killed me in a second. I'd say this about them. They didn't make me suffer. After that death, it turned into a speed run. The regeneration chamber could bring me back in ten seconds and it took me another six seconds to open the door and die. I had to die thousands of times in the next eighty-three hours to make this plan work, so speed was important.

Twenty minutes later, I stepped off the table to Tee's cheerful voice.

"Congratulations, it's level 10 and too big to fit through the door."

I took the pistol out of the holster, pressed the button to open the door, and then ran back to the far wall. Just because it couldn't get in didn't mean that its tail couldn't.

At level 10, the station rat was gigantic, the size of a buffalo. Its body was now covered in bone plates which only left its six eyes exposed. It looked more like a dinosaur than a rat. It hissed at me as I took aim and pulled the trigger.

I missed.

The shot took a chip off its skull plate, agitating it without doing any harm. It tried to hit me with its tail but was about a foot short of being able to. So, it kept trying to force its way into the room. I took another shot. Missed it again. Thirty-one shots later, I finally hit one of its eyes.

It wasn't the eye I was aiming for.

"I'm going to need to practice this back on Earth," I said, staring as its massive corpse disintegrated, becoming powder, before being absorbed into the floor.

"Definitely," Tee agreed. "You're like the opposite of whatever a natural shot is. I didn't know someone could be that bad at aiming. If your pistol could ricochet, I'm pretty sure you would have killed yourself a few times."

"Thanks for the support."

"I call it like I see it. Now, you just need to repeat this eight more times, so you can get to the control room."

I paused. "Will being a higher level make them level quicker?"

"Yes. If you had taken the genetic advancement or personal tech path, you would also need to be careful not to out-level them, or they wouldn't be able to kill you."

That made sense. "Okay, back to the meat grinder."

Four hours and a lot of running later, I stood outside the control room's blast doors and pressed the button. The doors slid open, revealing a massive barren room with a single chair and a C-shaped table. I was at the back of the room. There was another door along the right wall that I assumed went to the dungeon, but nothing else caught my interest. A series of notifications filled my vision.

Quest Completed
Control Room Blitz

You have found your control room.

Quest Rewards:

Path Points: 1
Tokens: 100

New quest available.

Quest Received
Expand Control I

Only part of your station is under your control. Clear the invaders to gain additional access to your station and its functions.

Quest Rewards:

Defence Slots: 20
Path Points: 1
Tokens: 300

"Is this it?" I asked, dismissing the new quest to look around the room. It was kind of depressing.

"You can customize it with RP and credits," Tee said. "I was going to give you a rundown of what you're up against, but time's not on your side. You've got dying to do if you're going to make this work. So go tap the control console, and I'll have access to the station's internal systems."

I ran over and slapped the control console. Nothing happened. No lights came on. No engines hummed. I began to wonder if Tee was messing with me.

"I'm in. Good hunting. Well, not hunting. How about may your death be swift and painless. Yeah, that sounds appropriate."

4

DO YOU WANT TO BUILD A STATION?

Forty-five gruelling hours later, I came to lying inside the regeneration chamber, having bled out after I killed the last of the station rats. The network of maintenance corridors and crawl-spaces throughout the station were a complex mishmash without any symmetry or comfort. There were service elevators to some of the station's main systems, but not to others, which continually confused me. Thankfully, there were multiple ways to reach every system on the station, except the dungeon. The only way into that was through my control room.

All the back-and-forth running would have made my job impossible in the timeframe I had to work with, but if I got the rats to chase me to the regeneration chamber, they stayed in the area when they killed me.

Even without pain, this had been one of the hardest things I'd ever had to do. It was nonstop running, shouting, and dying. Forcing yourself to stand there and get stabbed, even when you know it's not going to hurt or kill you, is not as simple as it sounds. You have to ignore your survival instincts and fear. And I'd been doing it for so long, my brain was telling me to get out there and start running, find a rat, and let it kill me.

A notification floated in front of me.

Congratulations, your Station Master class has reached level 5.
You have 2 Path Points to spend.
You have 15 Class Points to spend.

I hadn't spent the path point I got from the control room quest, because all I'd been doing was dying over and over again, and increasing my other paths wasn't that helpful in this situation. However, the points I'd been getting from leveling had immediately gone into my station development path, which was what I did when I saw the notification.

Your Station Development path is level 5.

You have unlocked ***Internal Turrets****. You receive one additional internal turret for each path point in the station development path.*

You have unlocked ***Dungeon Turrets****. You receive one additional dungeon turret for every 5 path points in the station development path.*

"I've got good news," Tee said, cheerfully. "These internal turrets aren't stationary. I can deploy them wherever I like and then redeploy them somewhere else, as long as they're not damaged. That's going to be a major help with station maintenance."

That was good news.

I was insanely underqualified.

"How effective are they?"

"They're better than your sidearm. I could have cleared most of the level 1 rats with just these five turrets."

"What about the level 10 ones?"

"I'll get back to you."

Of course, it couldn't be that easy.

Nothing was that easy.

Tee hadn't gained full internal sensors until I'd invested three points in the station development path. I'd run around so many corners only to suddenly die that it had added hours to the whole leveling process. None of this was fun. But I couldn't take back my choice now. I was stuck with it. And there was too much resting on me for me to give up or half-ass it.

Whatever the Peacekeepers were doing to me to make me think all of this was normal was affecting how I viewed my class. I couldn't view this as a game. I couldn't detach myself from what I was doing. This felt like life and death.

I needed to stop thinking this way, or I was going to make mistakes, but I didn't know how.

Since I wasn't immediately going to die this time, I got dressed and made my way to the control room. Tee opened the blast door as I approached, letting me into the barren little grey room.

I sat in my chair and looked around.

The control console had no buttons for me to push. It was a flat slab of steel in the shape of a C. I wanted buttons. Buttons, like bowties, were cool. The chair also wasn't the most comfortable. It was too straight.

For the last two days, I'd put off learning anything else about being a station master, so I wasn't distracted while I leveled the rats. Now I needed to finish getting up to speed. "What are class points used for, Tee?"

"They allow you to improve individual systems beyond their technological limits."

"That's a bit vague."

"Let me put it another way. If your faction gathered all the necessary resources and technology, they could theoretically build a stationary fortress that would look identical to your transit station. However, your class points are what make replicating a transit station's destructive capabilities impossible, because the class point upgrades allow systems on your station to go beyond their technological limits."

"And they do that *how*?"

"If the upgrade says the missile will be 10% faster, it just means that whatever version of missile you're upgrading will have a limiter on their speed removed."

"So, we're given weapons that are capable of doing more, except they won't unless we have the right upgrades."

"If you think about it for a second, you will realise it's the easiest way to make something like that possible."

He had a point. "Can other classes do this?"

"Special classes have the ability to upgrade technology beyond normal limits, but these classes aren't common. I'll explain more as it becomes necessary. For now, you know enough to move on."

A holographic display appeared in front of me with the station resource readout to my right. My mood started to improve. Who needed buttons when you had holograms?

Station Name: Unnamed
Level: 1
Armour: 0
Damaged Systems: 0%
Resource Points: 100

Credits: 0 (Balance Negative)
Station Systems:
-L1 Station Reactor: 100E
-L1 Sensor Array:
-L1 Weapons Fabricator:
-L1 Structural Fabricator:
-L1 Reprocessing Facility:

Defense Slot: 0/20

Station Development Path: 5
External Weapons:
-R2: 5
-D2: 1
Internal Weapons:

-Turret: 5
Dungeon Weapons:
-Turret: 1

"Right now, your station is basic," Tee said. "It would be defenceless, but you chose the station development path, so you have a few weapons. As you saw from your notifications, you seem to get an R2 for every path point you invest in the station development path, and a D2 for every three. Once factions start attacking the station, you'll develop rapidly, but until that happens, it's going to be much slower than it should be."

"Why?"

"The honest answer is, your faction doesn't have a clue what they're doing, so they can't support you the way they should. Normally, they would pump as many credits and resources as they could through your station as trade, because a powerful station is better than a fleet, but they aren't going to be doing that because they're noobs."

"Oh."

"Exactly. For now, I'll keep this simple. All you really need to know is that you have no armour, which means anything can damage your station. In fact, your station is weaker than it should be. But you're also leveling faster than you should be."

"What do you mean?"

"Let me start by saying, every faction is different. However, normally station masters don't level independently from their station. Every time their level goes up, so does the station's. Your station hasn't leveled, despite you being level 5, which means your faction has probably been given a tutorial of some sort. That's probably where the Expand Control quest comes in. You don't usually get independent quests you don't initiate as a station master. So, when you do, you need to pay attention. Also, almost all quests like this will have secret quests attached to them that give additional special clearance rewards. These rewards can be massive, but because the rewards are massive, you normally have to do things the hard way to compensate. The tutorial is probably why your station sucks so much."

This sounded like I was playing against a stacked deck. "They don't make it easy, do they?"

"I hate to break it to you, but this is easy mode."

"This is easy mode?"

"There are members of species that have been playing the Game for over a million years. They're so old that they've literally watched their species evolve into something different over the countless seasons they've played the Game. That's why they give new factions all sorts of starter benefits, even though most still lose all their territory before the end of the first 100 Cycles, and become part of the independent faction. It's only in your second season of playing the Game that a species has an actual chance. It takes centuries for a faction to build up the necessary skillset to succeed."

"You would still think they would give us some time to adjust."

"A long time ago, they tried to give new factions a century to learn how to play before introducing them to the Game. It didn't help enough to make a significant difference, so they eventually just decided to let factions fail the first time. It's like the first time you play any new game. Almost everyone is going to suck at it. Or spend ages running around not knowing what to do. Except if they've played something similar. *That's* where you and the other station masters come in."

"I guess." I wasn't that enthusiastic about my ability to defend my station anymore.

Tee seemed to notice my mood because he changed the subject. "Anyway, your reactor is useless. And you only have 20 defence slots to work with, which isn't a lot, but that's okay because you also only have 2 weapons. I assume you will gain access to the others later on."

"What are my weapon choices?"

"You've already seen them. There is the R2 point defence railgun, which costs 10 resource points or RP to build. It's for shooting down missiles and fighters and produces an additional station rat each time you build one. The D2 is your other option. It's the weakest light railgun

I've ever seen, but each Cycle each one will create three extra station rats which you can kill to gain experience. It costs 50 RP, though, which is a lot of RP for something that weak, but the experience isn't bad."

Putting together the two weapons made R2D2, which would be the sort of thing I'd have named them if they were designed to be one system. "Did my AI clone name them?"

"AI clone?"

"The AI that saw my memories."

"Yes. It named these ones, but not others for some reason."

Excitement filled me as I felt my heartrate increase. The AI was leaving me breadcrumbs. I just had to follow them to understand what it thought I should do. "Is there a way to merge them or for them to work together?"

"There's an upgrade for the D2 which gives them an R2 to provide point defence, or you can build them next to each other."

The latter wasn't something I'd typically do. "Can I get a look at their stats?"

"Give me a second."

A new hologram appeared in front of me.

Name: R2
Level: 1
Designation: Point Defence Railgun
Damage: 1-3
Rate of fire: 30 rounds per second
Range: 1 unit
Accuracy: 1 unit

Name: D2
Level: 1
Designation: Light Railgun
Damage: 30-90
Rate of fire: 1/60 sec
Range: 30 units

Accuracy: 30 units
Energy Consumption: 10E

This information wasn't particularly helpful. "How do range and accuracy work?"

"The distance to the transit rings from your station is currently 100 units. The D2 can shoot at anything that is within 30 units, which is bad because it means anyone can currently move freely between transit rings without you being able to do anything to stop them. As for accuracy, that is the range at which your weapon will hit where it's aiming 100% of the time. That doesn't mean it will hit, only that it will hit where it was aiming. These are railguns, so they fire rounds, and those take time to move through space. Ships can and will get out of the way."

That wasn't good. "What's the usual range for the weapons on enemy ships?"

"This early in the Game, it's around 25 units, but it can get as high as 35 units."

Based on the weapons my AI clone had designed, it had decided not to defend Earth's transit ring. Either that or the cost of defending the transit ring was so high that it would have led to immediate failure. "How does damage work?"

"Damage indicates whether or not your railgun can get through a vessel's armour or shield. Ships don't have health, so it doesn't correlate to how many hit points you take off, only whether or not your weapons can harm them. You might hit a ship straight on and miss all its critical systems and have it come away damaged but entirely functional, or you might give it a glancing blow and take out something important. The former doesn't usually happen with railguns. Rounds that penetrate the hull tend to cause a concussive wave once they hit the internal atmosphere because of the speed they're traveling at. The concussive wave will take out most of the internal systems unless they're reinforced, which will probably happen once they realize your species is using railguns."

"So as long as my weapons damage is greater than their armour, I should be able to do something."

"Pretty much, except your damage is low, so that might not matter."

"Why is there a variance in the damage amount?"

"The closer their armour rating is to your weapon's max damage, the more effective it becomes at redirecting energy. Think of it like this. You've got two curved shields. One's made of Styrofoam, and the other is made from steel. You shoot both with a handgun. The Styrofoam is never going to cause a ricochet, but the steel might. The closer the armour rating is to your max damage, the more likely you will receive a ricochet."

So, I had a weapon that only worked at close range, which might ricochet if I hit them. I had no idea what the AI clone was thinking. What potential play style it might be going for. I needed more information.

"What's up with the energy consumption, and what does E mean?"

"E stands for energy. Currently, the reactor your AI clone designed only produced 100E, which is the lowest energy output that can still be classified as a station reactor. Thankfully, your R2s have an internal micro reactor, so they don't draw on the station. However, your D2 uses 10E when it's active, and that is a lot for a weapon that weak. Energy is going to be a real problem for you in the future."

"But not now," I said, trying to be optimistic, despite what seemed like mounting problems. "What can the weapons do?"

"Like I said, the R2 is only useful against missiles and fighters. Nothing else needs to come that close to the station to attack it. The D2 is your only legitimate weapon, but it has a slow rate of fire, poor damage, low range, and horrible power consumption. Its only not-horrible part is that its accuracy is equal to its range. Your weapons suck, but to compensate for this much suck, your AI clone designed one of the most versatile dungeon mobs I've ever heard of. It's called an 'immortal soldier,' and I think it's where the majority of your construction budget went."

This was potentially interesting. "What's so special about it?"

"They respawn."

"That might mean something if I knew anything about a dungeon."

A holographic projection of a room with six soldiers appeared above the control console. There were doors at both ends of the room, like the doors on my station. The soldiers were using steel crates for cover, but the crates didn't look that strong.

A bear entered the room wearing a suit of Ironman armour. The soldiers raised their rifles and opened fire. Their shots bounced off its armour as the bear leapt on the nearest soldier and ripped him apart with his claws. Half a second later, the same soldier ran into the room and started firing, while other soldiers pulled grenades and leapt onto the bear. A second later they all died in an explosion, and half a second after that six soldiers ran into the room again.

The hologram vanished.

"You're station's external weaponry and your dungeon mobs are connected. Each time you design a new external weapon, you will also design a new dungeon mob that goes with it. This connection means that when you build an external weapon, you gain a new dungeon mob or upgrade an existing one."

"Do I get to choose whether I gain another one or the existing ones get stronger?"

"Yes. Your dungeon has a limit to how many mobs you can have in there at once. It's based on your station's level, so you can play around with how many of each sort you have. The minimum number is always one for any weapon system you've built. When the AI designed the D2, they created the immortal soldier. Each immortal soldier can respawn up to three times. Their respawn rate is tied to how many station rats the D2 produces, for some reason."

If I limited the number of immortal soldiers that spawned in the dungeon, then I would have a large supply of powerful dungeon mobs. Clearly, the AI clone thought the dungeon was my biggest weakness and everything was designed to shore up this weakness.

By calling them immortal soldiers, he was telling me that these were what was going to keep my dungeon safe. By naming the R2 and D2 weapons systems after R2D2, he was telling me that this weapon system was going to be with me long term, because R2D2 survived to the end, and was helpful the entire time. This was definitely the sort of thing I would do.

"Tee, do I have access to any other weapons?"

"No, but you can build several other systems in the station."

"Do any of those systems have interesting names?"

"No."

That meant my starting plan was to spam D2s. "Is this as bad as it seems?"

"It's almost as bad as it seems. Your station development path has given you five R2s and a single D2. None of these draw on your station's power supply, so you're not completely defenceless. I think you need touse class points to upgrade the D2s into something that isn't complete trash."

"Show me how to upgrade them."

A prompt appeared.

D2 Upgrades			
Description	*Effect*	*Available*	*Cost*
Damage	*+10%*	*0/10*	*1*
Rate of Fire	*+10%*	*0/10*	*1*
Range	*+10%*	*0/10*	*1*
Accuracy	*+10%*	*0/10*	*1*
Power Consumption	*-5%*	*0/10*	*1*
Double Barrel	*2X*	*0/2*	*10*
Internal Reactor	*+.5E*	*0/10*	*10*
Point Defence	*R2*	*0/1*	*500*
Explosive Rounds	*N/A*	*0/1*	*10*

The cost for a bunch of these upgrades was incredibly low. They also turned the D2s into something that wasn't utter garbage. "Tee, would my AI clone have known these upgrade costs?"

"Yes. Before you create a weapon, you can see what sort of upgrades come with it and how much they cost."

"How long does it take for upgrades to take effect."

"They're instantaneous."

"How do the upgrade costs scale?"

"Multiply the original cost, by which upgrade you're on. So, if the first one only costs one, then the third one will cost three."

The weapon I'd designed was looking less and less like trash. And more and more like they were designed for someone who couldn't kill a level 1 rat.

"Are you going to upgrade the D2?" Tee asked.

"Not yet. I'll wait until it's necessary."

"With your debt, it's probably going to be necessary. Also, your station currently only has 20 defence slots. To increase that number you need to clear the expansion quest. But if I'm being honest, I don't think you will be able to clear the quest the station generates for you, which means you're going to have to wait until you're a higher level and I have stronger internal turrets."

I didn't like that. "What about the special clearance reward you mentioned?"

"I say this with as little sarcasm as I can manage, but you can't kill a level 1 station rat, so special clearance is beyond you. Since you're going to have to wait to clear the expansion quest, you won't have more defence slots than you currently have."

My mind was racing from being killed so many times. It hadn't been like actual dying. There wasn't any trauma associated with my death. But I'd been so focused on running and dying for so long that I didn't want to slow down and think. But I needed to.

I took a breath and tried to practice mindfulness. Breathing in and out, focusing on being present. It helped.

In a few minutes, I was calmer. "How many defence slots do the R2 and D2 take?"

"R2 requires one and the D2 requires two."

I started thinking about my problem.

I had a station that could field a maximum of ten D2s. Railguns that were apparently shit but better than the R2 since they could damage larger vessels. I had a mountain of debt to pay back, so much debt that if I didn't die, it would take more than 100 Cycles to repay it. I had very few options, so I had to make the ones I did have count.

I frowned. "When do you think I'll be ready to do the expansion quest?"

"It's not you who will be ready for the quest. It's your internal turrets."

"Fine, when will the turrets be ready?"

"Well, you received them when you reached five path points in your station development path, so they might upgrade when you reach ten. But it might not happen until you invest the fifteenth path point. And I wouldn't want to try the quest before the turrets could take care of the level 10 rats without having to worry. Right now, you have to worry. I'm still trying to work out how many I can kill before they all get destroyed. It might be a long time before you're ready to tackle the quest."

"Okay, so the quest is too hard until I'm level 10 or 15."

"The quest isn't too hard. It's just too hard *for you.* The station master of any other faction would walk through without any trouble. You can barely shoot something at arm's length, so this is a *you* problem, not a quest problem. But at level 15, we should definitely get an upgrade for the turret systems, which will be enough to take care of the quest for you."

Tee wasn't mocking me. He was just stating facts, so I didn't take offense. "Can I build the R2s and then replace them with D2s as I gain more resources?"

"Not until you've got full control of the station; and even then, it will take time, and you'll lose resources."

"Give me two D2s then."

"On it. Wow, that's cool. Each D2 build quest generates twenty-five level 1 station rats after you throw the switch and trigger its construction."

"You didn't know that?"

"I don't know everything."

"Can I level them?"

"You can. I wouldn't, though. Having to repay 200,000 credits for 500 experience is terrible exchange."

I did some math in my head. "If I level the rats for every D2, it will only take two more Cycles to reach level 10 instead of three. If my faction can't put together enough credits to repay my original debt, then adding more doesn't matter."

"You make a valid point, ma'am."

Tee clearly didn't agree with my strategy, but he didn't have a counter argument, so he was insulting me. "I'll have you know I'm a miss. I'm far too young to be a ma'am."

"You need to moisturize more then. You can do that while you're completing the quest. These are D2s, so the quest is basic. You just need to go to the power junction and throw the switch. The station rats will spawn after you've thrown the switch, and then you can level them to 10."

I climbed to my feet and started running. "Just tell me where I have to go."

Tee gave me directions, and I ran through the station, following the ramp up one floor. I ended up in a nondescript corridor that looked like all the others. Everything was made from steel panelling and smelled heavily of welded metal.

"Now walk forward five meters and open the middle maintenance panel on the wall to your right," Tee said.

The section of wall looked the same as the others. "How do I do that?"

"You see how the walls are separated into three rectangular panels?"

"Yeah."

"Well, tap each corner of the middle panel in a counterclockwise order and it will open."

I did what he said, touching all four points. The steel was surprisingly cold, despite how warm the corridor was.

The panel popped out two inches and then slid up the wall. There was no visible mechanism to make that happen. It was floating. Behind the panel, nothing made sense. There was a bioorganic root system that glowed with a gentle blue light. The roots were wrapped around square pipes that looked like they were covered in hieroglyphs.

I blinked, but the view didn't change. "What the hell am I looking at?"

"That's Peacekeeper tech, and I have absolutely no idea how it works. But it's what makes the Game possible. You see those gel-covered roots dangling from the square pipe second from the top?"

"Yeah."

"Good, now there should be some loose roots attached to the pipe third from the bottom directly below it. You just need to lift them up and touch them together. They will intertwine automatically."

"This isn't throwing a switch."

"It's the Peacekeeper equivalent to throwing a switch."

"It's still not throwing a switch."

"Fine, if you want me to be more accurate. Morgan, gently caress the station's lubricated internal root system with your fingers and delicately intertwine them with their partner so that the climax of this build quest can be met with a sensual, fulfilling, and satisfying ending."

I paused, a little uncomfortable. "So, I just throw the switch."

"Just throw the switch."

THE RATS the construction quest generated appeared all over the station, which led to a lot of running, but I eventually died enough to reach level six.

Congratulations, your Station Master class has reached level 6.
You have 2 Path Points to spend.
You have 21 Class Points to spend.

Unlike my path points, which I only increased by one each level, my class points increased by the same number as my current level. With the low upgrade cost for the D2, dying over and over seemed like the right strategy for me. It was creepy how accurately the clone AI knew me.

I used the new path point for my station development path and watched as a notification appeared. I gained one more of every weapon type, but nothing new, so I dismissed the notification and went back to work.

I HAD over a day left before the 1st Cycle was over, and I was sitting in my control room, ready to learn more. Leveling the rats had caused them to grow strong enough to destroy Tee's internal turrets. And he was a bit peeved at how easily they could do that if he didn't pay attention.

I adjusted my sitting position a few times, trying to get comfortable. It didn't help. The chair was too straight. After a couple more attempts, I gave up. "So, who am I fighting?"

A hologram appeared in front of me, showing the barren station and the seven transit rings. One began to glow red. The map was quickly joined by a grey-skinned octopus with eight eyes.

"I'm going to go in order of importance and the most immediate threat to your survival. The 3rd transit ring leads to the Octorin faction. They're your first problem. They use swarm tactics. Expect them to send a large swarm of octopus-shaped drones within the first thirty Cycles. They do not engage in combat themselves, so you don't need to worry about them invading your dungeon. They'll try to rush this station as early as possible. If their first attempt fails, they'll wait until they have created a big enough swarm to destroy this station and begin conquering another faction, before trying again. While they built up for their second attack, they'll trade through your station quite a lot. If you survive their first attempt, they'll become great neighbours. Or they would if you weren't going to lose your credits to paying off your debt."

The red glow faded from their ring and moved two rings to the right. A reptilian humanoid replaced the Octorin. Its pebbled green skin sat tight against a body muscled like a gorilla. Its features reminded me of a Komodo dragon, but one that had been hitting the gym and doing a lot of steroids. There wasn't an ounce of fat on it.

"The 5th transit ring leads to the Kilocksin faction, who are your second problem. They are a war-loving, clan-based society. They like to fight and are very good at it. However, the fragmented nature of their society means they never unify and actually have a great deal of infighting. They will be the first to challenge your dungeon simply so they can brag to their people that they were the first to attack you. They will also be the first to attack your station. These attacks will be about status, skill, and bravery, so they shouldn't succeed. Once they have made their initial attacks, they will attack you sporadically whenever they get bored or have something to prove. It's useful to know that they normally don't last past the early stages of the Game. But their chaotic nature makes them hard to defend a station against. They might attack with a single ship or ten thousand."

The red glow shifted left to the 4th transit ring. A skeletal-thin minotaur creature with pink, pig-like skin stretched over emaciated bones appeared beside it. It looked undead.

"This is the Horde. They are going to be a problem. They are an extremely territorial herd species. They will be your biggest issue if you survive the other two factions. Their species excels at alloys, so they use heavy vessels with good armour. Their territorial nature means they will keep coming until they control the station. They hate anything near their territory. Most species build up defences on their side of the transit ring. The Horde don't. They like to be mobile. They'll keep a fleet on the other side of their ring, so they can counterattack whenever a species moves to attack their station. They don't expand their territory once it's connected, but they aggressively defend it. Your station is considered too close for their liking."

The red shifted to the 6th ring. An armadillo-like humanoid appeared in front of me.

"These are the Uon and your fourth problem. They are going to fuck you up if you survive long enough. You aren't going to see their forces at all until they're ready to conquer the galaxy. They'll even trade through your station if the price is right. They have these massive battleships they like to build that are basically planet-killers. Your only hope of not being destroyed is making your station powerful enough that it's cheaper and easier for them to conquer the galaxy by attacking a different station. They're very good at resource management."

The red glow shifted to the 2nd ring. An insect version of a centaur appeared in front of me.

"These are the Clack. You know the story, 'The Three Billy Goats Gruff'? Well, these guys embody it. They will send escalating waves against you, each one stronger than the last until they succeed. This is more dangerous for your dungeon than for your station, as their raiders can grow stronger more quickly. But they're also incredibly predictable as an instinct-driven hive race. Any questions?"

I had a lot of questions.

"Let me make sure I understand. The Kilocksin will attack me first, but it's only going to be a token gesture. The Clack will attack me second and potentially third. The Octorin will attack me next, and if they fail, I won't have to worry for a long time. The Horde will probably attack me after that, but once they start, they are going to be super-aggressive, so I have to be ready for them. The Uon will win if they attack me, but they won't attack me for a long time, and I can stop them by making myself too strong to bother with. How long is a long time?"

"At least a decade by Earth time," Tee said.

The amount of time shocked me. "Wait, how long does a season of the Game go for?"

"It depends. Whenever a new species is introduced, a new season begins. The last one was introduced 348 years ago, Earth time. That's about normal."

"How long before the first attack again?"

"Probably five months, but I said four in case the Kilocksin try to rush here. But that would be ridiculous. Their faction will have quests that need to be cleared, similar to what you're going through on your station. Also, their ship construction capabilities will be limited until they build up. If they ignore that, they'll put themselves behind, but some young idiots might come here earlier for the bragging rights. It happens more often than not. Their young are hot-headed for a cold-blooded species."

"What about the faction through the 7th ring?"

"That's an AI faction. It's their job to cause trouble. They don't have a racial profile like the other factions, and I haven't skimmed enough information to have a good view of what they will be like yet. They could be militaristic, or they could be a trading faction. I don't know. Hopefully, I'll know more in a few days' Game time."

"Okay, how can Earth help me?"

"They can do large amounts of trading through your station to give you credits and resources, and they can send a fleet to another faction's transit ring when you're attacked. While Earth's fleet is passing through the transit area, they'll be able to attack the fleet that is attacking you, but they'll have to go through the transit ring and then turn around and come back. If the faction on the other side of the ring doesn't like them, they might obliterate them. It's risky unless you have a lot of military might, or a friendly faction nearby, or have two sectors that connect to a single station. So, assume you're on your own."

"I can do that. What's the plan?"

"There's no plan, beyond studying. It's going to take you four more Cycles to build all the D2s, and you may or may not be able to finish your expansion quest before then. We'll have to wait and see."

"How does a station even survive to late-game if this is all we get when we start?"

"Normally, your faction would throw all the resources and credits that your local system produces through your station as trade to help your station grow. A strong station is a better defence than a local fleet most of the time. The resources your station produces are actually intended to only be enough for general repairs and maintenance. It isn't meant to be used for expansion. So, you're going to need another plan or a lot of luck."

5

THE FIRST DAY BACK

I woke in my parent's living room at 6 AM, eighty-four hours after going into the Game. I was leaning against my older brother, Simon, and drooling on his shoulder. Buster was asleep at my feet, and there was a little bit of early morning light coming through the windows. It would have been a nice scene, except the living room smelled exactly like four men and a dog had been sleeping in it for eighty-four hours straight.

It wasn't pleasant.

I'd spent the rest of my time in the Game listening to Tee's history lessons on the different factions that lived through the transit rings around my station, while we went over field manuals for the various technologies that I'd be able to deploy if I could afford them.

This wasn't like any game I'd ever played. Certainly, my class progression was somewhat familiar, but the way I could build and shape my station was entirely up to me.

It was daunting.

For the two weapon systems I had access to, I could purchase the blueprints to 1,085 different minor improvements. That was only for those two weapon systems. There were 6 premade light and medium railgun weapons systems, 284 different styles of armour for the station,

159 different types of fabrication stations, 82 varieties of power generation, and at least 5,000 other additions I could currently purchase. And almost all of them had as many minor improvements as the two weapon systems I already had.

And that was just for the station at level 1. Tee promised there would be a lot more at higher levels.

You might think having that many options would have been helpful. It wasn't. My opponents had just as many choices, which made coming up with the perfect strategy next to impossible.

So, when I woke on the couch, I was grouchy, thirsty, hungry, and the last in line for the bathroom because some things never change when you're the youngest. At least, I wasn't drugged up. I could think clearly and experience joy at seeing my family alive and well.

That improved my mood significantly, even if we all smelled terrible.

Over the past few days, more information had slowly added to what I knew as the Peacekeepers brought us entirely into the Collective. I knew my rights, my responsibilities, the laws, and what was expected of me now that I was a citizen.

The Peacekeepers didn't want ownership of Earth. For the most part, they wanted our internal political, economic, legal, and religious systems to remain in place. There were a few technologies we weren't allowed to study, like eugenics and AI, and a few things were universally outlawed, like interspecies war, but otherwise, we were free to do as we pleased.

Dad smiled at me across the dining room table after everyone had gone to the bathroom and raided the fridge. "Where did you end up? I tried to find you. I found your brothers easily enough. They were on opposite sides of Zigma Prime, but I couldn't find a trace of you anywhere. I even spent a few of the credits I earned to pay an AI to do a search."

I finished swallowing my mouthful of scrambled eggs. "I'm a station master, on a transit station. I'm basically by myself."

"Ouch, that hurt," Tee said.

My family shared my surprise as a talking blue orb the size of a baseball floated in through the open window.

"You leave me for ten minutes, and you're already denying my existence, like that fat chick you slept with at your first frat party."

How the hell did he know about Stacy?

My brothers snickered.

"I didn't know you could come outside the Game," I said, scowling at him.

"I can even buy my own body if we survive long enough," Tee said. "And I didn't mention it because this is my time off, my *me* time. Hello, Morgan's dad and brothers. I am the AI known as Tee, Morgan's currently non-corporeal BFF. I'm pleased to finally meet you. I mean, Morgan didn't mention you once, but I figured that was because of all the dying or because I was talking every minute of the day when that wasn't happening, and not because he doesn't like any of you."

Dad smiled. "Please to meet you too, Tee. I met a lovely AI named Charlotte on Zigma Prime, in the second city, near the port. She was in charge of the hotel I was staying in. Do you know her?"

"Contrary to popular belief, not all AIs know each other. All AIs on a given planet do typically know each other, but not off-world, and Morgan and I are certainly off-world. We are guarding your sector, though."

That was news to me. "We are?"

"Yeah, Zigma Prime is about three transit rings inside the sector from where we are, but it's part of the twenty-five systems we're defending in Sector 13."

"How do you know that?"

"Scanner readings, I was going to tell you about it once you got your head around how to build your station. It's not exactly important information. Anyway, Morgan's family, what have you all been up to? I guarantee you it was more interesting than what we've been doing. Morgan basically spent three days dying. He probably has the highest death count on Earth. Actually, I can check the leader board now that I'm linked in." Tee started laughing. "I was right. He does and by a lot. So, what have you been up to?"

"Fighting," my brothers said together before laughing.

Peter went into a long story about a small town and an invasion from AI-controlled raiders. The raiders had been trying to rob the local mine. He'd had to join up with a bunch of other people and take them on with particle pistols. He'd had a great time, earning 15 Tokens for the three he killed, along with a lot of in-Game loot. He was now level 3 and working as a transportation guard.

About halfway through Simon's story, everyone's phone buzzed.

Before anyone could grab them, Tee told us what it was about. "That's just a national alert and nothing to worry about. Your government has reformed and is reaching out to find all those with special classes. They're working with the other governments, who are trying to unify humanity's position before the next time you all go in."

Dad frowned. "How do you know that?"

"I've hacked your government's security network. I'm listening to your new president's briefing. They're trying to figure out where they should focus their resources, so you survive longer. Don't look at me like that. What I'm doing is perfectly legal under Peacekeeper law. Planetary governments must be 100% transparent at all times while performing government-related actions. Morgan, I've informed your president of who you are, what your class is, and suggested they hire a government AI, so they don't have to speak with me directly because it's time-consuming."

"Is he joking?" Dad asked, sounding worried.

"Probably not," I replied, hoping I couldn't get arrested for this.

"So, your AI friend just interrupted the president's briefing to reply to a government message in person."

"I'm a character," Tee said, cheerfully. "Anyway, a government liaison will be calling you shortly. Now I believe Simon was telling a story."

THE GOVERNMENT LIAISON wasn't much help. They took my name, my class, and which sector my station was protecting and then told me they would get back to me. I spent the rest of the day at my parents', listening to my family's adventures. They were a lot more fun than mine. I told them what I'd been up to, which made them all laugh, but then worry once they understood how important my job was. Dad had promised to contact Uncle Frank. He had an old army buddy who was now a gun instructor who could teach me how to shoot.

I was grateful.

I desperately needed the help.

In the early evening, I drove back to my apartment. Buster was a little antsy from the drive and the prolonged sleep, so I took him for a walk around the block, while potato-shaped drones flew overhead. Tee floated along with us, giving a running monologue of everything he saw and the sort of things we could buy to improve it.

My neighbourhood hadn't been the friendliest place, but neither had it been terrible. It had lost its rough edge in the few short days everyone was gone. A lot more children played outside. And people actually smiled at each other when they passed, instead of ignoring each other.

We were all intimately aware of the law and how it was enforced. No one was going to get away with breaking it. Any serious crimes we committed were now displayed above our heads for the entire world to see. It was nice, in a messed-up, 'Big Brother is always watching you', kind of way. It certainly made people feel safer, though.

When I got back to my apartment, I took a shower and switched on my computer, hoping to unwind. There was a message on my phone telling me not to come in to work for a few days, so instead of heading to bed, I opened up Stronghold Dominion, a co-op tower defence game.

I was ranked number one in the world. I'd played in all five international tournaments and won four of them, losing out to that weirdo Enigma. Tower defence tournaments had never taken off, so they weren't huge earners. The 1st place prize was only $5,000, but, between it and the other tower defence games I played, I managed to make an extra $20,000 on top of my salary, plus travel expenses.

In the right circles, I was famous. But I was, like, poet famous. I might have won accolades on the weekend, but my nine to five still paid the bills. And the people who thought I was cool were only a small niche of gamers.

When I opened the game, I had multiple messages waiting for me. All from top-20 players. All asking if I had been offered the station master class like they had, along with telling me which sector they were defending. There was an invite for a zoom call that had happened a few hours ago. It looked like a lot of them had jumped online the moment they got out. That wasn't surprising. A lot of hardcore gamers were antisocial.

Only one of the people who had contacted me was in my sector, my not-so-old apprentice. I had his number, so I pulled out my phone and called Mrs. Yang.

She picked up on the third ring. "Good evening, Morgan."

"Hey, Mrs. Yang, is Daniel awake? I have a message from him that he also received the station master class and that he was in my sector."

Daniel Yang was a twelve-year-old paraplegic. I'd first met him online through a co-op game a little over a year ago. The kid had the foulest mouth I'd ever heard on someone his age, and I occasionally played Call of Duty. The way he told it, he'd had a long series of liaisons with my mother and was eventually going to become my deadbeat stepdad because that's the way she liked it. At the time, I'd assumed he was just your average angry gamer kid, so I'd let loose saying similar stuff back.

He'd loved it. Laughing any time I said something witty.

Since I hadn't known he was paraplegic at the time, I didn't realize that he was tired of everyone being overly nice to him because of his condition. Or that the reason he loved the toxic trash talk was that it was the only authentic interaction he had with most people. I'd just thought he was weird. I'd continued playing with him regularly because the kid had skills. He wasn't competing for first place, but he was top-20 even when I first met him. He was currently ranked 8th.

That was my doing.

Eight months ago, after a tournament, his mother had approached me, explained his situation, and asked me if she thought she should allow him to play professionally. Apparently, he'd wanted to start playing in tournaments, so he could meet me in person, but she didn't want him to play only to immediately lose. She was worried about his self-confidence and didn't want him to get depressed. She'd flown across the country just to meet me and ask my opinion. I'd told her the truth that he had the skills to compete but not come first. And that if he worked at it, he could be top-10.

She'd offered to fly me to New York, so I could tell him myself. Since her purse cost more than my car, I accepted.

The Daniel Yang I met in person and the Daniel Yang I played with online were very different. Online the kid was an angry bull who cursed every third word. In person, he was a kind, considerate, and well-spoken lonely boy.

Yeah, I'd felt bad for him, so I'd helped him get better out of pity. But after a while, I'd eventually liked him for him. He had an infectious enthusiasm for life that grew on you.

Mrs. Yang laughed through the phone, sounding happier than I'd ever heard her. "Daniel is most certainly awake. I doubt he'll sleep at all tonight. My husband and I managed to find enough people willing to sell us their Tokens to treat his condition. He and his father are outside burning his wheelchair in the backyard, running around pretending they're cavemen who discovered fire in between wrestling matches."

A rush of emotion surged through me, and a huge smile spread across my face. I found myself having to blink away tears. "That sounds like fun," I said, my voice trembling with happiness. "I'll call back in the morning. You enjoy your evening."

"Hold on, Morgan. He wants to talk to you."

I shook my head, even though she couldn't see. "You really don't have to. This can wait. I don't want to ruin your celebration."

"No, Daniel said it can't wait. You're the last member of his sector to check-in. The other two have been waiting to hold a discussion, and they won't have it until you're all present."

Half a minute passed, and then Daniel picked up the phone. "Hey,

Morgan, don't tell me how it's hanging because that would be inappropriate and get you put on a list somewhere."

I snorted. "That answers that question, I guess. I always thought your personality had something to do with all the methane you inhaled down there, but apparently not."

"I'm still short, so we'll have to wait and see. Anyway, mom said you're in Sector 13. What did you pick for your trait and primary path? I went with the boss monster for my dungeon and the station development path. My boss monster's name is Smasher. He's a twelve-foot-tall robot with all sorts of weapons. He took care of the rats for me. Have you seen all the weapons we can buy for the station? It's insane. How are we supposed to pick anything? There are way too many choices. I gave up after like two hours and spent my time getting to know the food replicator and entertainment system. I ate my body weight in chocolate ice cream and watched robot movies with Smasher. What about you?"

"I picked the AI for my trait, hoping it would give me more information. I also chose the station development path."

"Did it work?"

"Yeah, it did. He's even able to come out of the Game."

"That's cool. Smasher is stuck inside, I think. But if you see a giant robot walking around and blowing stuff up, call me."

"Your mom said you've been in contact with the other members of Sector 13? Do you know who we're working with? My AI says there should be four of us."

"Yeah, we got lucky. We've got The Librarian. He also knew we had four which is why we were waiting for you."

That *was* lucky. The Librarian was a lovely, retired gentleman named Harold who had started playing video games to have something he could do with his grandchildren. He'd been a former librarian, hence the nickname. He had a photographic memory and a thirst for knowledge. If I needed to know something about a game, he was the person I went to. His ability to plan out a logical course of action was what had made him rank in the top 10. His inability to improvise was why he never placed in the top 5.

"Who's the fourth?"

"I don't remember."

I scoffed, knowing that was bull. "Really, you're going to play the 'I don't remember' card? I know for a fact you have an IQ of, like, 150. Who is it?"

"Enigma. I'm messaging them now. I'm going to make this a group call. Don't hang up."

I groaned.

I really hated that guy. Not because he'd beaten me in multiple tournaments. That I actually respected. I hated him because he felt the need to wear a costume. It was this weird mask, gloves, and cape that looked ridiculous with his oversize hoodies. He'd just turn up, play, and then vanish once he got his prize money. He wouldn't even talk to you online except through text.

"I'm switching over to video chat," Daniel said as I continued to groan.

I pulled my phone from my ear, and the kid's face appeared on my screen. In the past, he'd had bags under his eyes and strained features. Now, he looked like a regular kid. His hair was messy, and there was dirt on his chin. There was also a massive grin on his face I wasn't used to seeing.

A moment later, The Librarian appeared. His 94-year-old face was a labyrinth of wrinkles around pale blue eyes, made extra-large by the strength of his prescription glasses. He wore his customary tweed vest and jacket, with a blue bowtie.

He smiled. "Morgan, it's so good to see you again," he said, voice warm and inviting. "Has Daniel told you who our fourth member is?"

"Yeah, apparently it's Enigma."

The Librarian saw my scowl and sighed. "I know how you feel about him, but he's good at what he does, and we need that. What trait did you choose? I chose the energy shield with the station development path. Defence has always been my weakness."

"I chose the AI and station development too."

The Librarian grinned excitedly. "Thank goodness, someone did. How useful is the AI? I've been going over the information available to me through my station, but it isn't organized. I've only made three purchases since this began, and one of those was an information package on how to kill the station rats."

A fourth face, made from matrix-like 1s and 0s, appeared in our chat. "I liked to think of myself as the yin to Morgan's yang, but then he started talking to an actual Yang, so I now think of myself as his naughty little secretary. I'm Tee, by the way. Station AI and Morgan's BFF."

The librarian looked surprised. "You can communicate outside the Game. How?"

"I'm a sapient, self-aware lifeform, so I get booted out like you and the rest of the universe," Tee said. "I'm currently stuck living inside a floating orb that can only see about 10 meters until I can afford a body."

"Can you give me more information on the standardized blueprints we can purchase? The information I receive through my station is minimal."

"I emailed you everything I know. You should see an email from MorgansBFF@gmail.com. Everything is broken into categories and alphabetized. If you have any questions, just email me back."

Daniel raised his hand to speak.

"I emailed a copy to your mom, too."

Daniel grinned.

Enigma connected to the call, except he wasn't wearing a mask, and he wasn't a he. He was a *she*, and I knew her. Well, I didn't know her, but I had seen her photos on billboards. She was a model, a super famous one. I had no idea what her name was, though.

Long, wavy, blonde hair that seemed to go on like southern fields, framed a face of perfect proportions, and eyes that made you think of clear skies. She didn't look as good as her billboards, but she was still better looking than anyone I'd met in person.

Damn, she was hot.

That didn't change anything.

She wore a bored expression. "Before you ask, I'm not Natalia. I'm her twin sister, Alexandra, but you can call me Alex. I never showed my face in tournaments because Nat had a brand and an image to protect, and being a small-time gamer would ruin that. She paid me a lot of money not to mess with her brand, which is why I always wore the costume and didn't speak. But I'm definitely Enigma."

"Prove it," I said.

She rolled her eyes. "At our second tournament, you said I was making nerds look bad with my costume. That I was bringing down nerd culture as much as cape-wearing neckbearded dungeon masters who walk around wearing socks with sandals and fedoras." She turned to Daniel. "The last time we were matched, you said that losing your ability to walk was the second most disappointing thing that had happened to you after having to play with me." She turned to The Librarian. "I've never beaten you in Tower Chess."

"None of those are exactly secrets," I said. "And I'm not taking back what I said. You really did make us look bad. Everyone log in, and we'll play while chatting. If you can play like Enigma, I'll believe you're Enigma."

She scoffed. "Seriously, why would I lie?"

"I don't know? But people are weird, and I need proof. Also, I may want to unwind while I get that proof. Unlike some of us who were eating ice cream and watching movies, I've been dying over and over again. I need a break. Alex, what's your trait? Mine is the AI, The Librarian chose the shield, and Daniel has the dungeon boss. We all took the station development path."

"I took the same path but chose the secondary reactor. I figured that more energy equalled more versatility."

The Librarian nodded. "I purchased an information pack within a few hours of arriving and spent most of my time reading through it. From what I gathered, as a new faction, we have control of all transit rings into our sectors. That makes us the first line of defence for Sector 13. If we do our jobs correctly, our sector will have a significantly better chance of surviving longer. If we fail, then we open everyone up to invasion. So, I would like us to all work together to come up with a way forward."

"Let me stop you there," Tee said. "None of you have the same factions connected to your station or the same starting weapons. You can't come up with a single solution. If you want to work together, you're going to need to study each other's station and faction composition and come up with a plan specifically tailored to each of you."

The Librarian frowned. "That requires us knowing what is beyond the transit rings."

Tee nodded. "The first system the three of you are going to build is a communications array. It will let you talk to each other and skim more information coming from the transit rings. With the communications array, I will be able to sift through the data you pick up and tell you who is around you. For the next three days, you can work on Morgan's station, since he's the only one who has the information you all need, and he needs the most help."

Alex frowned. "Why would he need help? He's better than all of us."

"Morgan can't shoot the broad side of a space station even if it's standing still," Tee said. "He kept dying to the station rat outside his generation chamber. Which makes me think, I should probably ask: How much trouble have all of you had clearing your rats?"

"Not much," The Librarian said. "I fought in my youth, so I know my way around firearms and combat. I died a couple of times, but I still cleared my station."

"Smasher did all the work for me," Daniel said.

Alex shrugged. "I dated a guy who liked to take me to the range. He broke up with me when I became a better shot. I still died about twenty times, though. How many times did Morgan die to make you feel you needed to ask?"

"He's got the highest death count on Earth."

Their mouths dropped open.

I shrugged. "After I couldn't get out of the regeneration chamber, and I realized I didn't have the skills to kill the station rats for credits, I decided to try something non-standard." I explained my situation to them without holding back any details. It was a bit embarrassing, made worse by Tee's running monologue. "I'm currently level 6, but I have no credits to my name, and a mountain of debt. I'm going to have an extremely high level when the first faction arrives, but without credits, I'm going to be crushed pretty quickly. So, I need help coming up with a plan."

The Librarian nodded. "I'll help as much as I can, but I'm not sure how much time we have before they arrive."

"That's in the email I sent you," Tee said. "The soonest anyone has ever arrived is the 2nd Cycle, but that requires them leaving almost within the first hour of the season starting. Only a few races try this tactic, and it's easily countered most of the time. Just construct something that is similar to what's in the email and they won't stand a chance."

The Librarian smiled. "How about we all study the information Tee has emailed us, and then we'll talk about solutions tomorrow evening after dinner."

"I'll ask my mom if that's okay," Daniel said unenthusiastically. "She doesn't let me use her phone on school nights. And she's already rung the principal to confirm that it's open tomorrow." Daniel turned and looked off-screen. "Mom, I need to use your phone tomorrow night!"

"Tomorrow is a school day! No games or phones on school days."

"But mom, this is for the protection of humanity's interests."

"Don't be dramatic, dear."

The Librarian raised an eyebrow. "Is this going to be a problem?"

Tee stepped in. "Don't worry, I've got this covered. I just asked the president to ring his school and tell them they can't give him homework or humanity might lose a sector. Actually, there is a lot to learn. He should probably ditch school for the next six months just so he can get up to speed. Give me a second, and I'll see if the president is okay with that."

6

WHAT A WONDERFUL WORLD

The president called Daniel's parents and principal the following morning, but only on the condition Tee never contacted her directly again. Tee begrudgingly accepted the deal. By lunch time, he'd started nagging the vice-president instead. Which I think is why the government only got back to me and the others two days after we came out of the Game. It was punishment for having to put up with Tee.

The only good news I heard while we waited for them to get back to us was that there was an international alliance starting up around the Game. The majority of Earth's leadership was dead, and the survivors all seemed willing to work together on this. Information was flowing across borders at a rate no one would have thought possible a week ago.

Sadly, the generals and admirals really were General Prime's first choice, so the governments of the alliance were focusing their attention there. They offered us gamers the same information packets on our class and sectors that they gave to the military, but little advice. The four of us had access to a liaison named Harriet who would acquire more information if we asked for it, and at any time of day, which was cool, but otherwise, we were left to work everything out for ourselves.

As far as they were concerned, gamers were the unskilled minority destined to fail, so the information packets were loaded with military terms I didn't understand. The Librarian had no problem reading them, so I asked him to translate for everyone.

General Prime had given us gamers the five smallest and least important sectors under humanity's control. Each of our sectors were defended by only four stations, and after looking at some of the sector compositions and the gamers defending them, I could see that General Prime had sacrificed two sectors. The people defending those sectors weren't even close to our skill level. There was definitely an A team, B team sort of thing going on. And they were the C team.

I found it interesting that the majority of the military's station masters had chosen an AI like I had. They were doing the exact same thing I was, finding out who they were up against and developing strategies to counter them.

I'd asked Tee to speak with their AIs. The immortal soldiers my AI clone designed were the perfect foot soldiers for defending a dungeon, so I wanted to know what sort of weapons systems and dungeon mobs the other AI clones had developed for the other station masters. We didn't know enough to design effective weapon systems or dungeon mobs yet, but if we all pooled what they developed for us, then we might have decent starting weapons.

It turned out very few members of the military had AIs who had min-maxed the way mine had, so the weapon systems they had access to weren't specialised. Only eight of them had anything that was up to the calibre of the D2 and the immortal soldier. Five of these were upgraded station systems, and three were for weapon systems.

Thankfully, the gamers were a much better technology source. Almost every one of them had a unique weapon or system that was far better than average. However, every unique system was extremely expensive to create, and so far outside our budgets that knowing about them was almost redundant.

It also showed me why General Prime had included so many gamers. We were there to provide the others with better equipment. It was a very smart move and made me respect his capabilities. He was trying to set us up for longer-term success.

The government made a list of everything we had access to and promised to offer tactical and financial support for our stations once they had their plans sorted, but everything was so new no one was sure when that would be.

The one major help they could offer me right now was combat training. So, two days after I got back, a military vehicle turned up on my doorstep and took me to a base where some of the best instructors in the army taught me how to shoot straight.

Uncle Frank's army buddy had been culled, so I hadn't been able to get any help.

I spent the next twelve hours firing at stationary targets, eventually working my way up to hitting what I was aiming at, but I was still a long way off doing the same with moving targets. The instructor told me I was the worst natural shot he'd ever seen. Every instinct I had was wrong. So, I was far from ready when it was time to return to the Game.

No one had managed to come up with a way to get me out of my debt predicament, either —outside of Earth suddenly developing a whole lot more skill and feeding my station, that is. So, I didn't have much of a plan when I sat down on Dad's couch to go back into the Game.

My family had decided to stay together when we went in because it was nice knowing we were only a few feet away, even if we couldn't see each other.

One second, I was on Dad's couch falling asleep, and the next I was sitting in my command chair in my control room. Everything was exactly as it had been when I left: dull grey, boring, and smelling heavily of metal.

"I've got six automated turrets and 106 level 10 station rats to choose from," Tee said cheerfully. "How many do you think I can kill before they take out my turrets? I'm thinking thirty-six. Maybe thirty-eight."

"I'll give you a Token if you can kill them all."

Tee scoffed. “Maybe when my turrets have been upgraded, but right now, I can do thirty-six, maybe thirty-eight.”

I brought up the station layout. The station still looked like a Borg sphere. My path had added two D2s and six R2s, which were so small you couldn’t see them on the massive structure without the hologram highlighting them for you. Without bigger weapons, the look of the station wouldn’t change for a long time.

I tapped the reactor to get a better look at that section of the station. It zoomed in. The station development weapons didn’t draw on my station's power supply or cost me RP for repairs. With my two additional D2s, I wasn’t badly defended for the 2nd Cycle, but I wasn’t well-defended, either. If I managed to clear the expansion quest, I was going to need to improve my reactor.

The hologram suddenly went red and zoomed out.

“Holy shit,” Tee shouted, losing his cheerful attitude. “We’ve got incoming out of the AI faction. They must be set to super-aggressive. I count 1,126 fighters, 327 bombers, 30 corvettes, and 10 frigates. That has to be their local system's entire starter fleet. This will set them back even if they succeed. These guys are nuts.”

“I thought you were in their systems?”

“I’m skimming information. It’s not the same as being in their system.”

“How screwed are we?”

“Give me a second. Damn...they’ve signalled that they intend to challenge, which means they can’t retreat, but also means another faction can’t interfere, which means you could only call your own faction for help, which would be pointless because they are nowhere near your transit ring. Crap, we’ve got 1,000 teams signalling the station that they want to challenge the dungeon, too.”

A notification had appeared.

Challenge Received

The Wargarg wish to challenge your station. Vessels that enter your transit system cannot retreat. No other faction can enter your transit system while the challenge is in place. Clear the invaders from your system to remove challenger status.

Rewards:

Tokens: ???

I read through the notification as Tee continued to update me. I think I caught everything he said. "Tell me there's good news."

"The station's spatial distortion field has their fleet moving at a snail's pace, which means they didn't wait to upgrade their systems, or they have extremely slow thrusters, so the fleet will only reach your current firing range in six hours. Dungeon teams arrive in eight hours. What do you want me to do?"

"What's a spatial distortion field?"

"It cancels out FTL. It means they can only use their sub-light thrusters."

My brain went into overdrive. "What can you tell me about the range on their frigate?"

"Nothing concrete. They're still too far out for our sensors to scan properly. But generally, a standard level 1 frigate's main gun has a range of between 20-30 units. 35 is the extreme end of what a frigate is capable of, and that would only happen if long-range weapons were that faction's specialty.

"What's a corvette's max range?"

"Around 20 units."

"Can you hack their systems?"

"Like I said, I can skim information, but I can't interfere with them directly yet."

I forced myself to calm down. It was going to be hours before they were within weapons range. I had time to think and react. I took a slow, deep breath. I didn't know enough to have a reaction prepared for this. I had to think through my options.

I had zero resource points and a mountain of debt. Currently, I couldn't do anything. That was the first thing I needed to fix. "If I kill all the station rats, I can get to level 7 by the time they arrive," I said, thinking out loud. "That will get me another R2, on top of the two D2s I build."

"It's not going to be enough. These AI guys are crazy. Their system is probably being ransacked by AI-controlled raiders as we speak."

"It might be enough, if I dump my class points into range and accuracy upgrades for the D2s. The frigates are the only ships that can match their range. If we take them out, then we can take out the corvettes before they come into range. They're slow, so we have a chance."

"Which leaves you with 7 R2's against 1,126 fighters," Tee said.

"Is the fleet manned or unmanned?"

"Manned... I get it. You're hoping to level further before they reach you."

I was. "I want crew numbers."

"That's going to be hard. I don't know their species or their ship profile. I've not been able to skim a lot of information from their system."

That was disappointing. "Ballpark it."

"A frigate usually has a crew of 360, but sometimes it can have a tenth of that or more. The corvettes generally hold 60. Bombers hold six, and the fighters have one."

I started doing more math. "So, if they're like a normal warship and we take out the frigates and corvettes, I'll be level 12. I'll have a second trait." I launched out of my chair and drew my particle pistol. "Let's do this," I said. "Where's the nearest rat."

"Right outside the blast door."

The blast doors opened wide enough for the massive, six-eyed, bone-plated rat to stick its head through. I widened my stance, held the particle pistol with both hands, and tucked my elbow correctly to stabilize the shot. I sighted up and squeezed, instead of pulling the trigger.

I missed it, but I was close.

The third shot burst through its eye, and it dropped dead. "Where's the next one?"

THERE WERE ONLY forty-two rats on the station that I could kill without being killed in return, and by the time I had taken care of them Tee was out of internal turrets. I spent the next hour dying repeatedly, but eventually leveled again.

Congratulations, you have reached level 7.
You have 2 Path Points to spend.
You have 28 Class Points to spend.

Seeing the notification, I dropped a path point into my station development path, hoping I'd gain something new. All I got was another R2 and an internal turret, so I went back to killing station rats.

Once that was done, I threw the switch for the new D2s and then ran to my control room without killing the rats generated from their build quest.

I had 28 class points to spend on upgrades, when I jumped into my chair. "Tee, did you manage to gain anything from scanning them?"

"I've got the armour rating for their frigates and the max range of their main guns."

"Is that all?"

"It's more than we had."

"Okay, is it good news?"

"Yes. Their armour rating is only 40. Their main gun also only seems to have a max range of 30 units."

"I can work with that."

"They have to be planning something weird, because these vessels are almost as bad as your weapon systems."

"That's not helping, Tee."

"I'm just being realistic. Your AI clone made a trash railgun so you could make an awesome dungeon mob. They're likely doing something similar."

I opened the station upgrade menu and immediately regretted it. It was massive. There were thousands of options. Learning how to navigate it would take hours. "Tee, pull up the upgrade system for the D2s."

Since I'd only had two turrets, I'd studied them a lot during the days off. The D2 was a light railgun, but it was a light railgun in name more than function. They were pretty terrible, but after talking it over with Tee, I realised there was a way of modifying them that turned them into a decent point defence weapon.

It would involve changing the rounds they used from a solid slug to a scattershot and doing all sorts of expensive upgrades, but they weren't as useless as they first seemed. So, spending a few of my class points here wasn't going to be a waste in the long run.

D2 Upgrades			
Description	*Effect*	*Available*	*Cost*
Damage	*+10%*	*0/10*	*1*
Rate of Fire	*+10%*	*0/10*	*1*
Range	*+10%*	*0/10*	*1*
Accuracy	*+10%*	*0/10*	*1*
Power Consumption	*-5%*	*0/10*	*1*
Double Barrel	*2X*	*0/2*	*10*
Internal Reactor	*+.5E*	*0/10*	*10*
Point Defence	*R2*	*0/1*	*500*
Explosive Rounds	*N/A*	*0/1*	*10*

"Tee, does the twin barrel upgrade lower accuracy?"

"No. But don't get it. You can afford a 50% increase to the range and a 40% increase to accuracy."

"It would double our chances of hitting them," I said. "It would be like having twelve D2s instead of six. If the extra 20% range is something we need to hit them, then we've already lost."

You have spent 10 Class Points to buy the D2 double-barrel upgrade.

You have spent 10 Class Points to buy the D2 range upgrade from level 0-4.

You have spent 6 Class Points to buy the D2 accuracy upgrade from level 0-3.

The triple barrel upgrade came available, and it only cost 20 class points. I wanted it but couldn't afford it. I only had 2 class points left.

I scowled as I looked at the range notification, forcing myself not to rant.

Technically, there was no such thing as range in space since there was no friction to stop momentum, and that especially applied with something like a railgun, but the Game needed limiters; otherwise, everything would get out of hand. Outside the range of my weapons, the weird Peacekeeper tech that was inside the station walls and everything else would activate and remove any attack that didn't fit the rules.

I looked over my loadout one more time. It wasn't great. I had six twin-barrel D2s and seven R2s. My sensors were better than theirs, unless they spent a large sum of credits improving them before they started their invasion, so I was probably seeing more than they were.

"Are you in their systems, Tee?"

"Barely, what do you need?"

"How are they taking the changes to our station?"

"They seem calm. They've taken note of your developments and accepted that there will be more losses. A frigate captain just suggested they should send in their fighters and bombers to soften you up. Hold on, his second in command just shot him for cowardice. Okay, maybe they're not calm. I'm scanning their computers for literature. If we survive, hopefully, their stories will be able to give me an impression of what they're like."

"Admit it, you're looking for alien tentacle porn, aren't you."

"I don't need to. I have that stored on your work computer in a file labelled 'Not tentacle porn'."

I snorted. "That's funny if it's true."

Tee chuckled. "There's also a file on your home PC, laptop, phone, and tablet. I even put a file on Peter's laptop called, 'Not Morgan's tentacle porn'."

I paused, remembering the way my brother had been acting before we came in. "Is *that* why he was looking at me weird when he turned up at Dad's?"

"Maybe, but we can talk about that later. The lead vessel of the enemy fleet is hailing you."

I straightened my back and tried to fix my hair. "How do I look?"

"Like a gamer who is in over his head."

"That's what I was going for. Put them on the viewscreen."

"You don't have a viewscreen. You need to customize the control room to have one. The best I can do is make a holographic projection."

"Do that then."

An eight-foot-tall werewolf appeared in front of me. The Van Helsing-style one. It had a wolf's appearance, but walked on two legs, with dark green fur that reminded me of an algae-filled pond. He bared his fangs when he saw me.

How did I know it was a he? The —that's a penis— meme was playing through my head.

"I am He Who Eats First," he rumbled, "leader of the world pack of the 93rd system in the Wargarg faction. You are in my territory, human."

I'd decided while we were taking time off that if I had to talk to other factions, I was going to be so full of bullshit that you could fertilize a field. They'd probably see right through it, but it would be fun while it lasted, and I was pretty sure I'd crack if I tried to act seriously.

I used every skill my high school drama teacher, Mrs. Philips, taught me to sneer back. "I am Morgan Bartholomew Winchester, first-ranked station strategist of the human faction, and you are mistaken. You're in *my* territory. I look forward to removing you."

He Who Eats First didn't like that. He growled aggressively. The growl came from the back of his throat, creating a tone that was more akin to a lion's roar than a wolf's growl. It caused his fur to stand on end. "So, you intend to challenge me. Good. If you had rolled over and offered me your belly, I would have had to spare your faction and bring them into my pack. I prefer the challenge."

He lifted his head and howled.

A hundred other howls joined him.

He lowered his head and stared at me as the others continued to howl. “The Wargarg Faction declares war on the human Faction due to the disrespectful Morgan Winchester.” He gave me a strange expression that I took to mean he was smiling at me. “Congratulations, Morgan Winchester, your station will be the first to fall in this war.”

The hologram vanished at the exact moment a notification appeared.

The Wargarg Faction has declared war on the Human Faction.

Congratulations, your actions have started a war! As the first member of your faction to achieve this result, you have been given an achievement reward:
+10 Path Points.
+100 Class Points.
+10,000 Experience Points.
+100,000 Resource Points.
+100,000 Credits.
+1,000,000 Tokens.
The Warforger Perk

Congratulations, you have reached level 10.
You have 14 Path Points to spend.
You have 129 Class Points to spend.

You must now choose to increase the level of your station to 2 or accept another trait.
Trait/Level Station?

Leveling the station would let me buy level 2 D2 tech, but that didn't mean anything since I didn’t have enough credits to afford a level 2 toothpick.

“Pick the trait,” Tee said.

"I was already planning to," I replied, as I accepted the new trait.

You must select a new trait from the list below.

Energy Shield*- Your station is protected by an energy shield. This trait also gives your dungeon mobs a personal shield immediately, and your own personal shield at higher levels.*

Regeneration*- Your station is filled with nanobots that are capable of repairing all damage given sufficient time. This trait also repairs yours, and your dungeon mobs' armour and weapons.*

Missile Fabricator*- Your station receives a missile fabricator that fabricates missiles and unlocks missile launchers for your dungeon mobs. This trait also slowly replaces spent missiles free of charge.*

Dungeon Boss*- Your dungeon will receive a boss. This boss can assist you in station maintenance.*

Hangar Bay*- Your station will gain a hangar bay. Ships supplied by this trait are automatically replaced and repaired free of charge. This trait also unlocks flight and combat drones for your dungeon mobs.*

Particle Cannon*- When you need something to stay down after you hit it, this is the weapon for the job. Usable only once per Cycle. This trait becomes a personal weapon at higher levels and unlocks the micro-particle cannon for your dungeon mobs.*

Triple-Layered Armour*- Station has improved armour. This trait improves personal and dungeon mob armour.*

Secondary Power Core*- Additional energy for station systems. This trait unlocks micro-power generators for dungeon mobs' armour and weapons.*

The Squad- *Four highly skilled dungeon mobs. These mobs can assist you in station maintenance and alter your dungeon mobs.*

I hadn't expected to level, and I didn't really have a plan. There were three good options currently available to me: the energy shield, the dungeon boss, or the secondary reactor. I thought about how many resource points I had to spend and went with the secondary reactor. Hopefully I would be strong enough to clear the expansion quest and increase the number of D2s available.

Congratulations, you have reached level 16.
You have 20 Path Points to spend.
You have 210 Class Points to spend.

I did the math in my head for how much experience I'd receive. "Tee, you said that the experience cost to level would increase after level 10. It hasn't."

"Then clearly, I was wrong. I keep telling you that your class is weird. I'm making a lot of guesses right now."

"Most of which are wrong."

"If I cared for the opinion of someone who has multiple files labelled, '*Not tentacle porn*', I'd ask for it."

I laughed and dropped 9 path points into my station development path, bringing it up to 16.

Congratulations, your station development path has received 10 Path Points and has unlocked the ***Missile Battery*** *weapon system. You will gain an additional Missile Battery for every 10 Path Points that you use.*

Your missile batteries receive 1 Standard Missile for each Path Point.

Your missile batteries receive 1 Predator Missile for every 5 Path Points.

Congratulations, your station development path has received 15 path points and unlocked the ***R9 Heavy Railgun*** *weapon system. You will gain an additional R9 Heavy Railgun for every 15 Path Points that you use.*

The Predator missile had a unique name, which meant it was likely important. I checked the new weapons from the station development path.

Station development Path: 16
External Weapons:
-R2: 16
-D2: 5
-Missile Battery: 1
—Standard Missiles: 16
—Predator Missiles: 3
-R9: 1

I had a lot more weapons now. "Tee, show me the capabilities of the R9 and missiles."

The holographic display changed.

Name: R9
Level: 1
Designation: Heavy Railgun
Damage: 120-360
Rate of fire: 1/180 sec
Range: 70 units
Accuracy: 70 units
Energy Consumption: 25E

Name: Standard Missile
Level: 1
Designation: Missile
Damage: 60-90

Range: 60 units
Accuracy: 60 units

Name: Predator Missile
Level: 1
Designation: Stealth Missile
Damage: 30-60
Range: 100 units
Accuracy: 100 units

The excitement began to fill me as I read through the weapons stats. The R9 had a range of 70 units. The Predator was a stealth missile with a range of 100. The standard missile only had a range of 60, but Predators could travel the whole battlefield.

I saw a way forward.

"You know what, he's an alright dude," I said when I was done reading. "I needed that boost."

"He did that so he could get the same reward. His fleet just got stronger. His flagship upgraded to a cruiser."

"Damn," I said, looking at the display."I didn't know you could do that."

"I believe I mentioned that special classes like yours could boost technology. His timing was perfect. He's still out of range of our weapons, even if you fully upgraded them."

"It would have been smarter for him to wait until his new ship was within his upgraded weapons range."

"You can't declare war while you're actively fighting someone. Only immediately before and after. What your suggesting doesn't work, and he's cut it as close as you can possibly cut it."

I loved an opponent who flirted with the rules.

I felt myself grin.

"Why are you grinning?"

"Because this just got fun! Now, can I build the R9 or missile battery?"

"No. Your station is still level 1 and doesn't have access to them. Also, until you build one, you can't upgrade these ones."

"Why not?"

"Because the ones your station development path gives you aren't yours to upgrade. They just copy the ones you currently have, or the lowest-grade version of the options you will have, in your case. This is actually good news. There is massive potential for abuse here if you gain access to better weapons systems before you expand your station defences. Some weapons systems cost absurd amounts of RP to build, and you can use this to build them for free."

"Fine, build the rest of the D2s so we have a full loadout. I'll complete the build quests shortly. Is there anything decent we can do to them with 100,000 credits?" I stared at the credits for a few seconds. "Seems kind of light."

"It's early in the Game, so they nerfed all but the Token part of your reward. Your credits got nerfed further because you're in debt. They aren't allowed to give you nothing for these sorts of rewards, so they gave you close to nothing. The best you can do, weapon-wise, with those credits is a small upgrade to the R2s. It's not a lot to work with."

"What about armour?"

"Armour, you can do. Laminated Titanium is a building material that can act as armour. It's cheap credit-wise, so it has a high RP cost. You buy it in layers. Each layer will cost you 1,000 RP and gives your station 1 additional armour. It maxes out at 10 at level 1, but it will make the fighters useless."

"Buy it and spend the RP to max it."

It was only a tenth of the resources at my disposal, so I wasn't concerned about the cost.

"You'll need to throw the switches."

"In a minute."

I checked my total energy production. It was now at 200E, which was a *lot* lower than what I'd expected. If I could get more defence slots, I would be able to build more turrets, but I'd lose them if one of my reactors was destroyed. I needed to invest in energy efficiency, range, accuracy, and the triple barrel upgrade.

You have spent 20 Class Points to buy the D2 Triple Barrel upgrade. ***(Maxed)***

You have spent 45 Class Points to buy the D2 Range upgrade from level 5-10. ***(Maxed)***

You have spent 49 Class Points to buy the D2 Accuracy upgrade from level 4-10. ***(Maxed)***

You have spent 15 Class Points to buy the Energy Efficiency upgrade from level 0-5.

A hologram appeared above the control console, and the D2s transformed. They now looked like old World War II Battleship cannons, which was kind of awesome. I had 81 class points left to spend.

You have spent 10 Class Points to buy the D2 Explosive Round upgrade path. You now have access to the Explosive Round upgrade.

You now have access to D2 Ammunition Payload blueprints.

An Explosive Round upgrade option was added to my upgrade list. The first price for the upgrade started at one. A new option for stealth rounds appeared at the same time, and it cost twenty.

"Tee, what's up with the D2 rounds? Why did I have to buy access to the upgrade path?"

"The first option seems to give you access to adding a payload to the D2 rounds. You've got a bunch of new ammunition payload blueprints you can buy. I think the explosive round is the default path, so once you unlock it, you don't have to pay for each new level when your station and D2s level like you do with the others."

"What about the stealth rounds?"

"I think it involves the casing of the rounds. I'm guessing here, since you haven't bought it, and I don't have access to the information, but stealth should make it hard for the enemy's sensors to see the rounds, so their point defence systems can't take them out, and their pilots won't see them coming."

You have spent 20 Class Points to buy the D2 Stealth Round upgrade path. You now have access to the Stealth Round upgrade.

You now have access to D2 Ammunition Casing blueprints.

I was happy to see the stealth rounds also only cost one for their first upgrade, too. A new option appeared, manoeuvring rounds for thirty.

I groaned.

I couldn't afford them, and I wanted them. Straight shots were easy to get out of the way of in space. But I only had 51 points left to spend. Buying access would be close to tapping me out, and I needed the stealth rounds; otherwise, my D2s were going to be ineffective until they got close enough to cause me headaches.

You have spent 45 Class Points to buy the Stealth Round upgrade from level 0-9.

You have spent 6 Class Points to buy the Explosive Round upgrade from level 0-3.

I brought up the new stats of my new D2s the moment I spent the last of my class points.

Name: D2 Triple Barrel
Level: 1
Designation: Light Railgun
Damage: 30-90

Rate of fire: 1/60 sec
Range: 60 units
Accuracy: 60 units
Power Consumption: 7.5E

Ammunition:
Payloads:
-Explosive: 3
Casings:
-Stealth: 9

The D2s were no longer total crap. They just sucked. I could work with that.

"Tee, you said the highest genetic advancement my brain could handle was eight, right? What will it be like?"

"You will have faster reactions, better balance, and your thinking should speed up. You'll be stronger than you've ever been and be able to take greater damage. Everything should come easier. Think Captain America. You won't have more skill, but your body will be better. You will be working at peak human capacity 24/7 while in the Game."

I opened up my paths and added eight path points to my genetic advancement path and three to my personal tech path. I accepted the changes.

The world went dark, and I came to inside the regeneration chamber, watching the lid rise. Only it looked different. It was like everything was suddenly in 4K. There was so much more detail. Sadly, I couldn't stop to enjoy the experience. I was in a hurry. I threw my legs over the side and leaped to my feet.

The room had shrunk.

Everything was much lower.

I looked around, a bit confused. What the heck was going on? It took me a few seconds longer than I was happy to admit, to realize I was taller. A *lot* taller.

Cool.

I took a step forward, expecting to feel awkward in my new, larger body, remembering growth spurts from my teenage years and expecting this to be worse. It wasn't. Walking came as easily as it always did. Good, that would have been annoying if I had to move around like an infant.

I opened the locker.

My overalls looked a little different, but not that different. The material was thicker. I got dressed.

"Tee, what are my personal tech changes?"

"Your overalls now behave as light armour, so the station rat's fur won't rub against your skin like sandpaper, though that's not something you have to worry about with your new body. Your particle pistol has no limit on the firing speed and a 12-shot capacity. You still have to empty it for it to recharge, though, and that's still a minute."

"Tee, activate the expansion quest."

"Good thinking. I completely forgot about that. And the turrets did get upgraded. Activating now. Six Kilocksin warriors have spawned near your regeneration chamber. I think I can take them out, but I'm going to need a distraction."

"What do you want me to do?"

"Now," Tee said.

I put my particle pistol around the corner, aiming more or less at chest height, and started squeezing the trigger. Twelve pew-pews went out, giving a stronger kick than in the past, and then I ran around the corner screaming at the top of my lungs, "Crikey, that's an ugly dingo!" in my worst Australian accent.

I ducked and wove, trying my best to make myself difficult to hit.

The Kilocksin were eight-foot-tall Komodo dragon humanoids, with an energy shield bracer on their left arm and a spear in their right hand. The spearheads split down the middle, exposing a barrel. They were like Spartans with lasers. They were a decent shot, too. None of them missed me as I tried to dodge.

My only consolation was the six didn't see the turret silently descending from the ceiling behind them.

I came to inside the regeneration chamber looking at a very nice notification.

Quest Completed
Expand Control I

Quest Rewards:

Defence Slots: 20
Path Points: 1
Tokens: 100

New quest available.

Quest Received
Expand Control II

Only part of your station is under your control. Clear the invaders to gain additional access to your station and its functions.

Quest Rewards:

Defence Slots: 40
Path Points: 1
Tokens: 300

I put the extra path point into personal tech and then got dressed. "Tee, what does the new point give me?"

"You don't need to empty your particle pistol to recharge it. It's now constantly recharging."

"Handy."

"Very, now throw the switches for the new D2s and get back to the control room. Before you ask, I've activated the next stage of the quest, and we can't beat them. It's a Horde mercenary team. There's thirty of them."

I took off, running faster than I'd ever run before. I liked it. I liked it a lot. I ran into one of the level 1 rats that I'd spawned when I made the first D2s today. I didn't kill it. I didn't die to it, either. I jumped past it before it even realized I was there, and I ran off down the hallway.

"Why didn't you kill it?" Tee asked.

"I might need to level it," I replied.

"You don't need to worry about them anymore. I can kill them now."

"I want to keep my options open, so don't kill them."

Tee complained about my decision as I made my way around the station, throwing switches. The D2s appeared on the station in less than a minute, because our faction was capable of building incredibly fast and the D2s were small.

I was almost back to the control room when the station trembled and the lights flickered.

"We've been hit," Tee said. "The cruisers' range is greater than I thought, and they have stealth tech. Our sensors didn't see them fire. They hit near the reactor section. It's not a missile. I actually don't know what it is, but it's drilling through the hull."

I ran toward the control room doors, being chased by a dozen station rats. They had barely been faster than me when I was a regular old human, so now that I could keep up with Usain Bolt, I was well ahead of them.

The doors opened, and I shot into the room and leapt, butt sliding across my control console like it was the hood of a Mustang. Obviously, I liked my new body a lot. This was like ten years of hitting the gym without hitting the gym. Behind me, the blast doors closed in the faces of some very unhappy rats.

"What did he shoot us with?" I asked, sitting down and bringing up the replay. The replay showed something slamming into the side of the station and lodging into our armour before something blocked our scanners. The thing that hit us was the size of a small ship and in a spot where our weapons couldn't hit it.

"Shit! Tee, do an internal scan for foreign life forms. I think we've been boarded."

"Well, would you look at that," Tee said. "We have. Well, not *have*. *Are in the process of being.* They're cutting through the hull plating, but you're right. They're trying to board us. That's neat. And rare. They must be a saboteur faction. Or a close-quarters combatant faction."

"What happens if I die outside my control room while fighting them?"

"You're fine. They can't take the station by boarding the way they can when they come through your dungeon. All they can do is destroy the station by sabotaging it internally. If you die out there, you'll respawn like you do after the rats kill you."

"Good. Have you started hacking into their bombers?"

"I'm confident I can disable their manoeuvring thrusters at will. A complete takeover is impossible currently."

I leapt out of my chair. "Alright, I guess I'll go deal with our unwanted visitor."

"You can stay here if you like. I've got 11 functioning internal turrets to work with. Two can connect to the corridor they're cutting into."

"I'm expendable. Your turrets are a limited resource. Even if all I can do is take a shot while your turret takes them out, we need to do it that way."

"Your particle pistol might not be strong enough to pierce their armour."

"Then I'll throw it at them," I said. I climbed out of my chair and got ready to run past the rats outside. "On my count."

IT TOOK whatever was attached to the hull five minutes to cut through, and by that time, the level 1 rats had caught up to me, so I was doing laps, running around the station like I was being followed by a zombie horde. It was surprisingly fun. The cutter melted through the hull on my last lap, leaving a massive puddle of glowing red slag on the floor.

I leaped over it, feeling the heat rising off the liquid metal, before safely landing on the other side. The rats couldn't jump that far, so they didn't follow me. They stayed on the other side, impotently hissing at me. Adding laminated titanium to the station had improved their natural defences, so their hide was much thicker, and their fur had a silver sheen.

I pulled out my particle pistol, feeling quite proud of myself.

The corridor we were in was one of the outer corridors, which made it one of the biggest on the station. It was a quarter of a mile long and straighter than most. It made it an excellent place to engage an enemy, because Tee had plenty of room for turrets.

"Tee, will the station rats attack them?"

"They should. They're hostile to anything onboard. You'll also get experience if they kill something."

"That's weird. Will I lose out on their experience if they die?"

"You shouldn't. You're the only one who can currently do station maintenance. They should respawn the moment they die. It's a small perk, one that is occasionally abused by saboteur factions."

"How?"

"They board your station and farm your mobs. The respawn rate can make this place a power leveler's dream."

"That's cool. Can the station rats gain levels if they kill one of these guys?"

"Yes. It's actually something you have to worry about with better weapon systems. The mobs they spawn can go to war with everything else on your station and level extremely fast if you don't actively stay ahead of them. If they get too far ahead of you in levels, they can make it impossible to do maintenance. They can even get strong enough to start taking out systems. It's why I thought you needed the squad."

We'd had this discussion back on Earth. I'd said it was a stupid idea. The squad sounded like a nerfed version of the dungeon boss.

"You didn't mention that part," I said, faking concern. "If I'd have known that, I might have agreed with you."

"Really?"

I laughed. "No. I'll just have to stay away from those weapons until we can deal with the mob."

Tee laughed with me. "You're such a dick."

"And you give terrible strategic advice."

I lifted my particle pistol as a platform extended down through the hole covering the molten slag completely. The station rats liked that. I didn't. Lucky for me, the Wargarg disembarked before the rats had the courage to charge.

I started to laugh again.

The giant, imposing projection in my control room might not have been accurate. The dark green Wargarg that streamed out of the ship were about the size of foxes. They barely came up to my knees, which left them looking up at the rats.

They also didn't carry visible weaponry, except for the ones sporting what looked like bombs strapped to their backs. The first Wargarg to reach the rats had its head bitten off.

Over one hundred Wargarg streamed out of the ship in the initial rush, right into the waiting claws of the station rats. The fight wasn't as one-sided as I expected for the initial fatality. The Wargarg might have been small, but they were tough. They leaped onto the rats, tearing into their bodies with tooth and claw, swarming them with numbers.

They might have been tough, but they weren't as tough as my new particle pistol. And they were so clustered together even I couldn't miss them. I unloaded my particle pistol, making a dozen holes in the green ocean, and then waited for a shot to recharge.

Tee's internal turrets descended from the ceiling at either end of the corridor and started letting loose. It was a single barrel semi-automatic particle turret. With my new levels, it had gained armour plating, so everything wasn't exposed, and it had a greater power output. Tee was a lot more accurate than I was, and he had a higher rate of fire. The Wargarg that climbed onto the backs of the rats or tried to go around the side found themselves blown apart.

The initial flood kept coming, dogpiling onto the bigger rats, slowly tearing them into pieces.

"Morgan, my scanner shows the number inside the ship is increasing. They must have some sort of regeneration chamber onboard."

The station shuddered the way it had when the first vessel struck.

"I think we might have a problem," Tee said.

I agreed with his assessment. I unloaded the new charge from my pistol into the mobs and then started kicking. I had significantly more strength, so I could punt the little bastards hard enough to kill them. But they had numbers. Lots and lots of numbers. Things got messy.

It was death by a thousand cuts, as I tried to make my way to their boarding pod. I took a lot of them with me before I died, finally answering the age-old question of how many skilled, angry toddlers could I fight before dying: 193.

It was a respectable number.

I decided I liked my rats after that fight. At least when they killed me, they did it quick. Dying didn't hurt, but it was still pretty messed up to have to see your insides during the process.

Thankfully, most of my insides didn't look like organs. The skin was fleshy and bloody, but the majority of my internal systems were robotic, kind of like West World. That explained why I was so strong. And it made being torn apart less gross.

My particle pistol had turned out to be almost useless against their numbers, because of the slow recharge time, and my armour was less effective than my skin. And they were all fighting naked, so I figured *what the hell* and joined them, grabbing my pistol and running after them with my butt hanging out.

I'd done it against the station rats to save time, so I might as well do it to them, too.

Three minutes later, I decided my, *what the hell* attitude wasn't a good attitude. The Wargarg didn't have a problem with going for my junk. You only had to have one little green alien use your Johnson as a climbing rope to never want it to happen again. That was more than enough for me to get dressed the second time and every time after that.

With each death, they pushed me further back, engaging me in corridors closer and closer to my regeneration chamber until they started using the suicide bombers. They had no problem blowing up their own side once they were far enough away from their boarding ships. And the ones without bombs had no problem acting as cover. They formed meatshields, so Tee couldn't gun down the bombers before they reached his turrets.

I'd gained two levels from all the killing, bringing me up to level 18, but it wasn't enough. They were winning, and fighting harder wasn't helping.

Tee finally called it for me. "You need to get back to the control room. I'm losing too many internal turrets to their bombs. If you wait any longer, they'll get between you and the control room. They can destroy your regeneration chamber if they find it. It will stop you from respawning until the regeneration chamber is repaired or rebuilt, which would be inconvenient at best, but more likely the end of your career as a station master so get in here."

I turned around and started making my way to the control room. "Is there any *good* news?"

"Yes. The boarding pods seem to be the cruiser's only long-range weapon, and I think it's used its payload. Their fleet's begun to accelerate again."

"I need better news than that."

"Ah, the rats from the new D2s that you decided not to kill are leveling quickly, so quickly they're becoming a problem for the Wargarg. There is already one at level 10 and it's causing total carnage among them. They can't tear through its bone exoskeleton with their teeth, which is a problem for them because I think the Wargarg have unlimited respawning but limited bombs. They have to use bombs to deal with the high-level rats, so the rats might actually sort them out for us. But not before they reach the reactor."

"That's better news. Have you fired on the fleet yet?"

"No, they're still out of range for the R9. They slowed down for the cruiser to fire its entire payload. It added a lot of time to their approach."

"Can you cripple the cruiser without destroying it when it's in range?"

"Not at full range. And why don't you want me to destroy it? Letting it survive is how you lose."

I turned the final corner and saw the blast doors up ahead. They started opening. "I want to piss off their commander. If I can, he might come over and invade the station. Those six pods attached to our hull are like unlimited experience generators. Once the bombs are used up, your turrets should be able to take them out. If we can make him angry and stupid, this is the perfect leveling opportunity. I need water. Lots and lots of water. I'm going to need a full bladder for this."

"Has anyone ever told you that you're weird?"

"Plenty. But they like me, anyway."

"Any of those people who liked you, *anyway*, turn out not to be serial killers?"

"I had one work friend that was a serial killer. It could happen to anyone."

"Actually, you have four."

"What?"

"You had a friend at elementary school, one at high school, and another at college who all turned out to be serial killers."

"You're pulling my leg, right?"

"I'll show you when the Cycle's over."

That was concerning.

I slowed to a walk as I passed through the blast doors and into the control room, making my way over to the food replicator in the corner. The small sliding door would open and present anything I requested. "Water, large jug."

Technically, it was called a food synthesizer, but I was a Star Trek fan, and this was the closest I'd ever get to a replicator, so that's what I was calling it. The little sliding door opened, providing my request. I picked up a massive jug of water and skulled it, repeating the process twice more until I felt ready to puke. Then I staggered over to my command chair and burped.

I immediately regretted the burp. I had to fight and stop myself from throwing up. I took a few shallow breaths to steady my bloated stomach and regain control.

"Alright, since you can't be specific enough with your attacks to cripple the cruiser, I want you to hold off firing the missiles until the frigates are in range of the D2s. How many can you take out with the first volley from the 26 D2s?"

"All nine, but that's only if they can't see the stealth rounds and the saboteurs don't manage to destroy any D2s by then, which I doubt will happen."

"Hopefully, we will get lucky. What do we have to work with if I'm not lucky?"

"We've got eighteen Standard Missiles and three Predators. The Predators could be deployed now. They have a much greater range and better targeting systems but lower yield."

"Are they strong enough to cripple their frigates' main gun?"

"Yes."

"Good, we'll use them for that if we have to."

"What about the cruiser?"

"The cruiser isn't a major issue. I'm almost 100% sure they've invested everything they have in gaining access to those boarding pods."

"It will still hit harder than the frigates."

"That's why it's better to take out the frigates first. More levels mean more class points, which means stronger D2s."

"That's not much of a plan."

"We don't have much to work with. How long until they are in range of the R9?"

"Twelve minutes."

I held my stomach and counted down the time by watching their fleet approach the line that represented the limit of the R9's range and then pass over. "Fire the R9!"

"I'm still aiming."

I facepalmed. "Dude, why are you only starting to aim now?"

"I can only aim once they're in range, and they have stealth tech. I'm pretty sure what we see on the sensors isn't actually where they are. I'm skimming their ships for information to find out their actual location."

"They can do that?"

"At this distance, they can. You need to upgrade the station's other systems."

"I'll get to it when I have the credits. Tell me when you've found them."

Congratulations, you have reached level 19.
You have 1 Path Point to spend.
You have 54 Class Points to spend.

I dropped the path point into my station development path, and gained another R2, internal turret, and standard missile. It looked like they were going to take out my reactor, which meant I needed the D2s to be as independent as they could possibly be. I bought the rest of the levels for the energy efficiency upgrade.

You have spent 40 Class Points to buy the energy efficiency upgrade from level 5-10. ***(Maxed)***

I was fully aware I had invested 19 levels into my D2s and that I was going to invest even more. That was too big of an investment to ignore. Any future plan I had now revolved around them. By halving the energy costs of my D2s, I only need one reactor. Hopefully, they wouldn't get the second one.

"Do you think you can get me another level before they're in range of the D2s?"

"I'd have to kill 1900 of them, and most of my internal turrets are gone, so I doubt it."

"Can you retract your internal turrets and wait for a coordinated counterattack?"

"Way ahead of you. And I think I've got their fleet's actual position. It's about 5 units in front of where the scanners are showing they are."

"Fire at will, then."

"Which one is Will again?"

"That joke wasn't funny the first time someone said it, and it's not funny now."

The station shuddered as the R9 fired.

I looked around me, concerned. "What was that?"

"It appears the R9's recoil is too great for the station's inertial dampeners. You should look into that."

The scanners showed a dot that represented the R9's round moving towards where Tee thought their frigates actually were. It had a range of 70 and could reach it in 12 seconds. They were currently 64 out from the station.

"Do you think it's going to hit?" Tee asked, sounding worried.

"Depends on how their stealth tech works at their current level. If they can't manoeuvre while using it, they'll have to drop stealth to get out of the way, exposing the fact that they have stealth tech. Their stealth tech also might make it harder for them to see incoming attacks, shortening their sensor range."

"That's actually quite normal, but how did you know that?"

"Game balance. You can't give something without taking something away. Otherwise, everything becomes lopsided before late game."

"We could still miss."

I smiled as the display zoomed in and showed a frigate taking the shot right on the nose. The round went through the middle, completely gutting the inside before destroying the main reactor and shredding the back half of the vessel.

Congratulations, you have reached level 20.
You have 1 Path Point to spend.
You have 34 Class Points to spend.

You must now choose to increase the level of your station to 2 or accept another trait.
Trait/Level Station?

I blinked. "Ah, why did I level?"

"It turns out I was wrong on my assessment of their crew complement. They don't have 360 on their frigates. They have 3,000. Give me a moment. I'm scanning the debris to figure out why. The fleet's dropped stealth and is now taking evasive manoeuvres."

"Keep shooting."

"There's a three-minute cooldown on the R9."

"You know what I mean."

"Firing at Will, Sir."

I looked at my traits, trying to decide what to take. I considered buying the particle cannon to take out the cruiser but decided against it. Taking out one ship that had already used its primary weapon seemed foolish. So, I took the regeneration trait. It wasn't a good choice, but it was the best I had. Its ability to repair the internal turrets mattered right now. I needed them back in action.

I added another point to my station development path and got a pleasant surprise.

Congratulations, your station development path has received 20 Path Points and unlocked the ***Hangar Bay*** *system. You will gain an additional Hangar Bay for every 20 path points that you use on this path.*

Your Hangar Bay receives 1 Fighter for each Path Point.

Your Hangar Bay receives 1 Bomber for every 2 Path Points.

I knew I'd get a second missile battery, but the hangar bay was a nice bonus.

"I found out why they have such large crews," Tee said. "They've got kamikaze darts onboard. Think missiles, except there is a pilot onboard for targeting. It's actually their main weapon; it's short-range, high- speed. If even one of their frigates gets in range, you'll lose the station. The pilots have bonuses which make the darts stronger the same way He Who Eats First made his frigate stronger."

"Damn, that's cool. Do you think the cruiser has them?"

"I can't see why not."

"Shit. Okay, we're going to have to speed up my plan. Do we have a cleaning robot for this room?"

"Why?"

"I'm going to need to do something to my control console as a sign of dominance."

"You don't have a cleaning drone. The room will self-clean if you die, but you won't make it back here. You can buy one for 1,000 credits and spend 1 RP. You have the credits and RP to do so."

I was loath to pay for something when I didn't need to, but I wasn't about to sit in my own robotic pee. "Can you record me, or do I have to do this live?"

"I can, but what am I recording, and why do I feel like I'll need to grow a dirty porn moustache?

"You're recording my villainous monologue," I said, grinning.

Ten minutes later, the cleaning drone was all done cleaning up my workspace, and I sat back down in my chair. "See, that wasn't so bad."

"I feel dirty."

"Stop being weird about it and send the recording to their leader. Ignore his replies."

The station lights flickered, and then emergency power kicked in.

"They took out the main reactor," Tee said. "They're heading for the targeting array. If we lose it, your D2s won't be able to aim. The weapons from your station development path will still work, but the ones you built won't."

"Tee, how's the rat situation?"

"Good, they're leveling fast and taking a lot of the bombs with them, but they're not in the right area."

"Initiate the station expansion quest."

"Are you sure? I'm strong enough to take the mobs on now, but I won't be if they level. We also don't know where they'll appear. It could be on the wrong side of the station."

"Then we will do it again," I said. "And if that doesn't work, we will do it *again*."

"If you're sure."

"Of course, I'm not sure, but we're already losing, and we need that targeting array."

"You really need to stop grinning."

I laughed.

This was what I'd imagined when I signed up to be a station master, only better. It was intense, crazy, and all sorts of wild.

"I'll stop grinning as soon as this stops being awesome. Now activate the quest."

"Activating quest."

Quest Received
Expand Control III

Only part of your station is under your control. Clear the invaders to gain additional access to your station and its functions.

Quest Rewards:

Defence slots: 80
Path Points: 1
Tokens: 900

"Oh, shit, that's a problem. You just spawned a Clack breeder."

"Is she in the right place?"

"Kind of, she's spawned along the main corridor, but she's going to breed an army and take over the station. She's designating the other mobs as hostile, and her level limit is 50."

"Damn, sucks to be those guys then."

"Are you listening to me?"

"Sure, but it's not like we can stop her."

"I can actually deploy a turret right above her head. Let me take the shot. We will deal with the Wargarg another way."

"She's really that bad?"

"Think the hive queen from Alien, and you should have a good idea of what you're letting loose. She's laying her first egg. Make the decision."

"Yeah, screw dealing with that. Kill her."

"Thank you. Shit! My turret's not strong enough to pierce her exoskeleton properly. She's running. I've injured her, but she's not dead."

"Bring up an image."

A hologram of a centaur-like insect running through the corridors of my station appeared before me. Tee was shooting at her, but his shots were only causing minor injuries. She turned a corner and kept going, even though he could no longer hit her. Three corners later, she ran into the Wargarg. They took one look at her, and the bombers ran out in front and detonated their bombs, killing her instantly.

The image shifted, and a section of the wall opened up. The Clack breeder stepped out. Tee tried to shoot her, and she started running.

"Hey, this is kind of working," I said, watching her run through the corridors and into another unit of Wargarg, only to be blown up again. "Keep it up. Actually, can you kill the Horde?"

"No, my turrets are repairing in that area. I can't replace them until they're repaired. But there is a new one near your regeneration chamber. I'm working on clearing the area. You might be able to participate soon. There are only a few hundred Wargarg between here and there, and they can't get reinforcements."

"Sounds like fun."

I KILLED the Wargarg on my way out of the control room before they managed to overwhelm me. Then I started hunting. The Wargarg were being far more careful about how they attacked. They weren't swarming the station with numbers anymore. They'd realized they were leveling me, and they had a solid foothold, so they were sending in specific units and no more. They'd even worked out how to herd the rats away from where they were.

I didn't like that, so I turned it into a game of who could lure the rats where they wanted them the fastest. It was a lot of fun until they tracked down where my regeneration chamber was.

I ran into the control room and jumped into my chair, only ten seconds ahead of the bomber unit that had been chasing me. They didn't have enough bombs left to blow their way into the regeneration chamber and destroy it, but they did have enough to place a bomber outside for the next time I respawned. If they got inside, I was toast.

"Any luck killing the Breeder?"

"None, but chasing it away as soon as it spawns seems to be working. You should be grateful it's not sapient, or it wouldn't keep falling for the same trick."

I took an overly dramatic breath, closed my eyes, and began humming a single note.

"What are you doing?"

"Being grateful."

"It looks weird."

"It's because I haven't practiced. Have any luck with the R9?"

"None whatsoever. You've got no upgrades for it, so they can see each shot coming with plenty of time to spare, since they're not trying to use stealth anymore."

"Alright, keep firing."

"Why?"

"They might have limited fuel for their manoeuvring thrusters. The more they have to move, the sooner they run out."

"That might take longer than you think. But you're the boss, which means the blame goes to you if this fails."

"No. Being the boss means I get to blame *you* for not living up to my unreasonable demands."

"Maybe in your old life."

I watched the fleet as it was about to pass the range limit of the D2s. The frigates were still moving sporadically, but I noticed that the corvettes were moving in a straight line.

"Tee, what's up with the corvettes?"

"They stopped manoeuvring when they realized we were only targeting the frigates."

"Cancel all orders."

"You don't need to be so dramatic."

I grinned. "It's more fun. Have they been like that for a while?"

"About fifteen minutes."

"How many D2s have we lost?"

"Nine. They won't be repaired for another twelve hours."

"That's more than I wanted to hear. It puts us down to seventeen. New plan: Ignore the frigates and target the corvettes with the D2s."

"Ah, why?"

"Experience. Each level gives us more weapons and more class points. The frigates might be able to see our stealth rounds even if they're maxed, but I doubt the corvette can. Now, I want seventeen kills in the first volley."

"You don't need to tell me twice. Just give me a minute to make sure they're not doing anything stealthy."

That made sense. They had pulled this trick before, so they could do it again. They were too convenient a target right now.

"Yeah, they're messing with you again. They're not where they appear to be. I'm going to need five minutes to find them all."

I looked through my upgrades. Their ability to dodge was frustrating. But I needed a couple more levels to be able to afford the manoeuvring rounds. Since I couldn't afford those rounds, I had to upgrade something else. I had 34 class points that were doing nothing for me.

You have spent 10 Class Points to buy the Stealth Round upgrade from level 9-10. ***(Maxed)***

You have spent 9 Class Points to buy the Explosive Round upgrade from level 3-5.

You have spent 15 Class Points to buy the Damage upgrade from level 0-5.

I had used all my class points again, but my D2s now had the best chance of hitting.

"I've got them, Sir," Tee said, trying to be dramatic. "I'm ready to fire."

"That's the spirit. Give them hell!"

"Sir, you didn't install any hell."

"Don't be a wiseass. Just shoot them already."

"Giving them hell, Sir."

"Are you sure you were made for me?"

On the display, 51 rounds went out towards their targets. It would take 15 seconds to hit at this distance and another 45 seconds before the next volley would be ready.

"Pretty sure, unless there's someone else as weird as you around here, and I accidentally got mixed up."

"You should look into it."

On my display, everything zoomed in. I watched as 17 corvettes were obliterated.

Congratulations, you have reached level 25.
You have 5 Path Points to spend.
You have 115 Class Points to spend.

I dropped the 5 path points into station development and watched as the station gained another two D2s and five R2s. Then I pulled up my upgrades list and smiled.

D2 Upgrades			
Description	*Effect*	*Available*	*Cost*
Damage	*+10%*	*5/10*	*5*
Rate of Fire	*+10%*	*0/10*	*1*
Internal Reactor	*+.5E*	*0/10*	*10*
Point Defence	*R2*	*0/1*	*500*
Explosive Rounds	*N/A*	*5/10*	*10*
Manoeuvring Rounds	*N/A*	*0/1*	*30*

I could afford the manoeuvring rounds.

You have spent 30 class Points to buy the D2 Manoeuvring Round upgrade path. You now have access to the Manoeuvring Round upgrade.

You now have access to D2 Ammunition Augmentation blueprints.

The moment I unlocked the path, I swore.

"Shit!"

It cost 10 points to upgrade, not 1.

You have spent 60 Class Points to buy the Manoeuvring Round upgrade from level 0-3.

You have spent 21 Class Points to buy the Explosive Round upgrade from level 5-8.

"Tee, target the corvettes and fire every missile and D2 we have at them."

"That's not the plan."

"Screw the plan. I fucked up. I need to improvise."

"Um, is this a bad time to tell you I can kill the breeder? My turret's upgraded. It's currently twitching on the ground."

"Yes, kill it and move on. We need to take out those corvettes."

Quest Completed
Expand Control III

Quest Rewards:

Defence slots: 80
Path Points: 1
Tokens: 600

I noticed the corvettes changing position. "The corvettes have dropped stealth. Kill them."

"No, *some* of them have dropped stealth and are acting as a smokescreen. The others are still remaining on their path."

"You know what to do."

"Shoot the stationary ones with the D2s and take the others out with missiles?"

"Is that a question?"

"You know miscommunication is the biggest problem in most relationships."

That made me chuckle. "Just shoot the stationary ones with the D2s and the others with missiles."

"Yes, Sir. Giving Will hell, immediately."

I watched as Tee launched every missile. Unlike my railguns, the missiles all had their own thrusters, so those that launched first slowed down to allow the others to catch up. Each time I gained a level, I had more missiles at my disposal, and gaining a second battery had doubled that number. So, there was a storm heading towards the corvettes.

I realised I could see two different colours for the missiles on the display. "Did you launch the Predator missiles?"

"You said launch *everything*."

"Damnit, Tee, can you change their target to the frigates' main guns?"

"Not with any certainty of hitting."

"Okay, my bad. I'll be clearer next time."

"I believe I said something about miscommunication."

He had a point. "I wasn't paying attention."

"Dude!"

"I'll be clearer next time."

"Thank you."

When the missiles were only halfway there, the D2s fired. The fighters tried to intercept the missiles, but the last thirteen corvettes still vanished.

Congratulations, you have reached level 27.
You have 2 Path Points to spend.

You have 57 Class Points to spend.

I threw my path points into station development and spent my new class points.

You have spent 9 Class Points to buy the Explosive Round upgrade from level 8-9.

You have spent 40 Class Points to buy the Manoeuvring Round upgrade from level 3-4.

"Use the D2s to fire in a scattered net towards a frigate. I want to know how much the shots manoeuvre and how many upgrades I'm going to need to hit every time."

"I can do that. Also, you have additional missiles now."

"Save them for the cruiser."

"I feel like I should remind you that you still have 1,000 challengers to your dungeon on the way. For some strange reason, I have this feeling that the naked ones running through the station aren't actually an example of their military capability."

"I know that. Wait, how many dungeon turrets do you have in there now?"

"Five."

"Aren't they upgraded?"

"Yes."

"We're good."

"We are not good.

"They're level 1. What can they do?"

"They can invest all their factions' credits into several teams' gear and make them into walking tanks. If they take this station that way, then all your upgrades become theirs, which would make this attack make a lot of sense considering everything they have done so far."

"Shit. That's actually a pretty good plan. How many of your internal turrets are working?"

"Why?"

"Because I need you to start gunning them down for experience. I'm going to need more levels, and if you're right, they will stop spawning when they can no longer help their fleet, so conserving the turrets is pointless."

"I'm activating the turrets now. I have 16 active."

"Damn, how?"

"Your regeneration trait. Internal turrets are small and easy to repair."

"Nice."

"I'm ready to fire the net, too."

"Do it."

Tee zoomed in on a single frigate, showing the 51 rounds hurtling towards it. The frigate was already manoeuvring, but it put more effort into it when the rounds were three seconds from contact, trying to use a full burn and corkscrew to get out of the way. The net was extremely wide, though. The rounds all pulled towards the frigate, converging on it, closing the trap. We got lucky. One of the rounds survived the frigate's point defence and got close enough to detonate nearby. Shrapnel peppered the side, taking out a single point defence turret and several of its manoeuvring thrusters.

"I'd guess we need to be level 5 for the manoeuvring rounds," Tee said. "Alternatively, level 10 explosive rounds will also work."

"Destroy that frigate and we've won."

It took three more waves of fire from the D2s, but the injured frigate eventually succumbed.

Congratulations, you have reached level 28.
You have 1 Path Point to spend.
You have 36 Class Points to spend.

I put the path point into station development and then spent my class points.

You have spent 10 Class Points to buy the Explosive Round upgrade from level 9-10. ***(Maxed)***

"They've lost the fleet. How are your internal turrets doing?"

"I have fully automatic fire now that you are past level 25. You should see another level in a minute. They can't get their bomb close enough."

"Good. Now make another recording. I'm going to taunt their leader." I stood up and tried to look as arrogant as I possibly could. "Start in 3, 2, 1. 'Your fleet is crushed. Your infiltrators were slaughtered. If you were a real warrior, you would come onto my station and fight me face to face. You can bring as many of your people as you like. I won't even turn my turrets against you. If you don't, I'll know you're a coward.' End recording. Now send that attached to the beginning of me peeing on my control console and ignore his reply."

"You honestly can't think that will work?"

"Depends on how dominant they are. You've got to show dogs who's the boss. The stubborn ones hate it. They'll challenge you every step until they know you won't give an inch. He's not a dog. He's a pack leader. He's going to be way more aggressive."

"You want me to take out the Horde mercenaries? I won't be able to get them all. Some of them have leveled a lot, but I can get enough of them that they will be less of a problem."

"Yeah, they're no help now."

I went over to the replicator and got a bucket of popcorn. I sat down and put my feet on the table and enjoyed the show.

"You're grinning again," Tee said.

I put a piece of buttery goodness in my mouth. "This is the coolest game I've ever played, and I'm kicking ass."

"I hope your confidence doesn't become your undoing."

Congratulations, you have reached level 29.
You have 1 Path Point to spend.
You have 55 Class Points to spend.

I put the path point in station development and bought another level of the manoeuvring rounds.

You have spent 50 Class Points to buy the Manoeuvring Round upgrade from level 4-5.

Over the next ten minutes, Tee obliterated their seven remaining frigates, one after another. Eventually, only the cruiser was left. Each frigate gained me a new level. And when I hit level 30, I took the squad as my new trait.

I had Tee send the missiles from the new missile battery at the cruiser. And made sure to send another message calling their leader a coward before they were halfway there, so he had long enough to get angry before he had to respawn. Between the missiles and my upgraded D2s, the cruiser didn't stand a chance. It came out of the volley limping along. The R9 took it out.

Without external support, the station invaders weren't much of a threat. The Wargarg had run out of bombs because of the rats and the Clack queen, so they couldn't sabotage any more internal systems. They stopped spawning the moment we finished taking out the cruiser.

As the cruiser was torn apart, a satisfying prompt appeared.

Congratulations, you have reached level 37.
You have 1 Path Point to spend.
You have 273 Class Points to spend.

I added the path point to station development like I had all the others. I needed to find a way to auto-fill it when I leveled. This was getting tedious.

You have spent 210 Class Points to buy the Manoeuvring Round upgrade from level 5-8.

I left the last 63 class points for when I needed them, and I ordered Tee to start targeting the bombers. Then I sat back and waited for five minutes to pass.

"Tee, record a message for me." I put the popcorn aside and stood up. "Start recording in 3, 2, 1. 'Where is He Who Eats First? I challenged him to a fight. I challenged him to battle. His cruiser was destroyed, and he hasn't shown his face. If that is who you follow, then your world pack is pathetic.' End recording. Send that to all their bombers and fighters."

"You can't honestly think this is going to work?"

"It probably won't, but it takes two minutes, and if it does work, then that's two minutes well spent. My mom used to say if you never try, then you can never succeed. Besides, don't underestimate the power of tilt."

"Sending the message. Do you want me to launch the fighters to take on their bombers?"

I decided to make this a learning experience for Tee. "Are they in range?"

"Not yet, but they will be by the time they reach each other."

"What's your playbook tell you to do in this situation?"

"You have the upper hand, so launching early to thin the bombers is to your advantage."

"Except they have over 1,000 fighters, which can easily counter our 37. Wait until they are close enough that the point defence turrets can provide cover fire."

"That's not a lot of time to engage the bombers."

"It's more time than if we try to make a run on the bombers now. Their fighters will tear ours to shreds before they reach them. Besides, if there are ten bombers left by the time they get that close, you suck at aiming and hacking. It's pure math at this point. They have to cover too much ground too slowly while under attack from weapons that won't easily miss them. Good Game for their fleet happened when I reached level 28."

"Oh, damn. You were right."

"Of course, I was right. It's simple math."

"Not about this. He Who Eats First just walked out of one of their boarding pods and is cursing your name."

I grinned. "I'm going to try to piss him off further. If this works, make sure you take as long as you possibly can to kill off his fighters."

"What about the bombers?"

"Destroy them. I don't care if we have to use the D2s to take out their fighters when the R2s are destroyed, just make it look good. Remember to record my interaction with the little dude. I might want to send it to his people."

"What are you going to say to him?"

I SAUNTERED down the steel grey corridor because I owned the place and I'd just beaten his fleet. So, I deserved a little pep in my step. He Who Eats First was standing in the middle of the first corridor they'd invaded, growling and beating his chest. It would be intimidating if he was the size of his hologram, but he was the size of a munchkin.

There were scorch marks along the walls where bombs had exploded and even a few holes, exposing the weird blue roots and square pipes. The turrets that had been in this corridor were still out of action, so I was by myself.

I decided to give him my best John Wayne impression. "I didn't think you would have the courage to come."

The little wolf growled louder. "You insolent pup, I will rip the flesh from your bones with my teeth."

"Oh, please. We both know you can't do this alone. You came here to save face among your people by getting your butt kicked, so you can claim you fought me. That's such a political decision to make. If you were a true warrior, you would have led an army in here, never slowing, never stopping, not until every one of your men and women out there who followed you into battle were off the field."

"Don't talk to me about a warrior's code, barbarian. Your people were still slaughtering your own kind a few days ago."

"So what? At least we know how to lead. Now, I grow tired of this farcc. I'll givc you your political win and help you save face because I gave my word, I would fight you. But I have no interest in sullying myself with you any longer than I already have. Let's get this over with. Perhaps a true leader of your people will come for me one day."

He Who Eats First charged.

He moved quicker than the rest of his kind, because he'd levelled more than they had, but he was still tiny, and his little legs couldn't take big strides. It was kind of like I was being charged by a toddler hopped up on Red Bull. The moment he reached me, I punted him down the corridor, and he bounced off the far wall.

His body broke from the collision, but he didn't die, which gave me the opportunity to play the honourable warrior card. He stared up at me with hateful eyes, following every step of my approach.

I looked down at him, trying to appear disgusted. "Get on your feet. Lying down is no way for a warrior to die."

It seemed he couldn't move. So, I leaned down and picked him up and set him on his feet, holding him up.

He bit my hand, taking a chunk out of me, exposing the robotics underneath, and leaving my hand feeling hot.

I let go and watched him stand by himself. I shook my head, playing the perfect, unimpressed warrior.

"Such a politician. I offer you a warrior's death, and you use it to draw blood so you can claim some accolade you don't deserve."

I stood back up and punted him into the wall. This time he died. I turned and raised my head, trying to pull off a stoic, condescending image.

"'If there are any worthy warriors in your faction, I welcome your challenge. I will not deny you entry to my station; come and prove you're not a race of cowardly politicians like this one. Come and fight while the battle rages outside.' End recording."

I started to laugh. That was so much bullshit.

"What do you want me to do with this?" Tee asked.

"Send it to everyone," I said, still laughing. "Not just the fighters outside. Send it to their entire faction. I have no clue whether they can respawn here, but I want as much pressure as we can bring to those who can. Add in everything else at the end to show how I taunted him and how weakly he responded."

"Why are you doing this?"

"I'm an American. I've always wanted to fuck with a politician."

7

WHEN THE CURTAINS COME DOWN

I stood, in a sea of Wargarg, kicking and punching like a mad wolverine. There was no technique, just unchecked violence as they tried to swarm over my body and tear me apart with their teeth and claws. The Wargarg were like wolf-shaped piranha, taking chunks out of my legs if I stayed still for more than a second. I'd been ripped apart by these little green bastards dozens of times, and every time they did it, I ran back in for more. They were spawning all over the station and running full tilt into waiting turrets, trying to get to me. They didn't seem to care.

They were in some sort of frenzy.

I punted another one away as it tried to climb up my leg and grabbed the one biting my nipple off, so I could crush it with my bare hands. I then leapt and landed on a pair of furry heads, bringing my body weight down hard to crush them.

Half a minute later, I watched the lid of my regeneration chamber rise, with a grin on my face. "Shit, are they still coming?"

"They never stopped," Tee said.

Congratulations, you have reached level 40.
You have 1 Path Point to spend.

You have 180 Class Points to spend.

You must now choose to increase the level of your station to 2 or accept another trait.
Station Upgrade/Trait?

"I chose the hangar bay trait," I said. "Tee, is the squad strong enough to survive them yet?"

"Not yet. Some of the Wargarg are higher than level 1 from killing the rats, and they have the numbers to cause problems if we aren't careful."

"How much longer do you think they will keep this up?"

"I have no idea."

I started running.

The Wargarg didn't let up or even slow down. If anything, the rate they appeared increased. Less than an hour later, I received this prompt, got distracted, and swiftly died.

Congratulations, you have reached level 50.
You have 1 Path Point to spend.
You have 635 Class Points to spend.

You must now choose to increase the level of your station to 2 or accept another trait.
Station Upgrade/Trait?

As the lid opened, I said, "I select the dungeon boss trait."

Please select your dungeon boss from the list.

An absolutely colossal list appeared before me. Eight people had chosen the dungeon boss as their first trait, and a few of them had excellent memories, which meant they'd managed to put together a list of most of the options for the government to share around. I'd studied those options during my time off.

There was a lot to choose from, but the majority of the options were different types of killing machines. The rest were dungeon bosses that offered buffs to mobs.

I'd come up with three choices for what sort of dungeon boss should be in charge. All of the choices revolved around buffing my immortal soldiers. With a thousand teams of challengers on their way, this was the perfect time to go with option 3.

"I choose to promote one of the immortal soldiers to a dungeon master for my dungeon boss."

The primary reason I'd chosen a dungeon master was that they could learn, level, and buff their own kind. They weren't a mindless automaton like other dungeon mobs, so the more they fought the better they got. When you mixed this ability with them being able to direct and utilize the other immortal soldiers, it made them more dangerous over time.

"Tee, send in the squad."

I got off the table and started getting dressed.

"They're on their way. What's the plan for the dungeon? You're limited to twenty dungeon mobs with a level 1 station."

"Use the new defence slots to build more D2s."

"They won't make your immortal soldiers stronger if they don't have energy."

"I can afford to buy the internal reactor upgrade, which makes the need for energy obsolete."

"Damn, that's kind of a good plan. Did you come up with that on the spot?"

"Of course not. You need to plan in advance for multiple contingencies if you want to take advantage of opportunities properly." I opened the door and started running. "Tee, tell me when we've got fifteen minutes before the challengers arrive so I can assess the situation."

"Will do."

I SAT IN MY CHAIR, looking through my list of options. I'd passed level 70 twenty minutes prior and taken the energy shield. For level 60, I'd taken the triple-layered armour trait. From here onwards, it was going to be the missile fabricator and then the particle cannon. Once I hit level 100, I'd have no more traits to gain, and I'd level the station to level 2.

"How many mobs can I have in my dungeon, again?" I'd died so many times my brain was getting fuzzy.

"The limit is twenty, on a level 1 station. The number of entrances you have is also limited to one."

"Wait, I can have more than one entrance at higher levels? Why?"

"Some dungeons become popular with challengers because the station master adds loot, which costs you resource points after you purchase the blueprints. If yours becomes popular, you can make a lot of credits from having lots of people attack you, and if you have to wait for each group to die that can become a massive bottleneck, so you can have more entrances and iterations of the dungeon if the station is big enough."

"Okay, I think I follow that. Do additional entrances provide any disadvantages?"

"Sort of. They all lead to your control room, so you can end up fighting multiple challengers at once if they time their entrances correctly."

There were probably some dangerous possibilities there, but I'd have to look into them later. "Since the dungeon is automatically generated, what can I affect?"

"Let me show you the current dungeon layout before we talk about that." A hologram appeared above my control console. It looked like the insides of a ship. "They've taken the design from a human troop transport. The entrance for your dungeon is an airlock that connects to the cargo bay. There are two dungeon mobs in the cargo bay. Once the challengers get past them, they have to make their way down the corridor to the barracks. There are twelve mobs in the barracks. Past the barracks is another corridor with doors that lead to different systems for the ship. There is one soldier in the corridor, there are two in the engine room, and there are three in the control room. You get to choose where you place your dungeon master, squad, and dungeon turrets."

"Does the dungeon function like a real troop transport?"

"What do you mean?"

"Will the dungeon turrets stop working if they take out the generator?"

"No. But the ship's internal sensors will go offline."

"I have access to sensors?"

"Dungeons are real combat scenarios. The more complex the scenario, the more you'll have at your disposal. Right now, you've got a basic troop transport with internal sensors."

"The other day you said I could upgrade parts of the dungeon with resource points. What can I upgrade?"

"You haven't bought any upgrade, so there are only three things you can currently afford to upgrade. The internal structure, so they can't easily cut through walls and doors. The internal sensors, so your dungeon mobs can see them better, and know how to react. And the material they use for cover."

"Upgrade it all and put the dungeon master, squad, and turrets in the cargo bay."

"Why not the barracks?"

"You said they can cut through walls. The armoury and mess hall are on either side of the barracks. They can go around the barracks if we give them a chance. Also, the dungeon master can call the mobs in the barracks for reinforcements. It means that they're going to have a constant stream of reinforcements entering the cargo bay as the dungeon mobs respawn."

"I didn't think about that."

"Neither did I, until you mentioned they could cut through walls."

"They still might be able to beat this."

"I'm level 75, and the squad are on their fourth upgrade. We can now field 15 dungeon turrets, which are on their seventeenth upgrade. If they can beat this, there was never a chance of us winning."

"I'm just making sure you thought this through."

"I have. I know I've got no clue what I'm supposed to do with this dungeon, but my AI clone left me clues suggesting I shouldn't be involved with the dungeon decisions, and that's what I'm going to do."

"Your plan is to *not* plan."

"My plan is to trust someone who knows what I know and more. It's why I chose the dungeon master. He knows what he's doing even if he's currently a double-edged sword."

"How is he a double-edged sword?"

"By taking him, I've lost the ability to spend class points to upgrade the immortal soldiers directly. But, if he can level enough, *he'll* be able to upgrade them a lot more than I can *and* be able to lead the defence in my place."

"That implies your dungeon survives long enough for it to matter."

"You're being awfully pessimistic."

"You try focusing on your job, when the guy in charge tells you he doesn't know what he's doing."

I chuckled. "Fine, build more D2s and have the squad throw the switches. We've got the perfect army to level the rats, and I'm pretty sure no one is going to challenge me after this, not for a long time, so my rats are going to be my only source of experience."

"I'll see what I can do. Would you like me to clear out the last of the Horde?"

"Are they still around? Never mind, don't answer that. Just kill them. And initiate another expansion quest once you fill up all the defence slots with D2s. Keep repeating it if it happens again. I want this station to have as many D2s and level 10 rats as we have resources."

I got out of my chair and headed for the exit.

"Where are you going?"

"To give the Wargarg a reason to keep fighting."

I ENTERED THE DUNGEON, in a less than perfect mood. It was a long walk from my control room to the dungeon, and I would rather be taunting the Wargarg than fighting the challengers.

I wasn't even sure I could help protect the dungeon, but I wasn't willing to risk not being there in case they needed me.

The control room of the transport ship looked completely authentic. I could even see stars through the front window and displays on all the screens. The immortal soldier, standing around the control consoles, ignored me as I made my way to the door and into the corridor. I went past a few more doors and entered the barracks. The immortal soldiers in there also ignored me.

"The armoury is to your right," Tee said.

I spotted the door and entered the armoury. The weapon racks held particle assault rifles, missile launchers, grenades, and dozens of drones. There was even exoskeleton power armour in a harness system.

I climbed into the harness system and started tightening the straps.

"You might want to hurry it up," Tee said. "The first team is loading into the elevator to challenge the dungeon. Also, you're doing that wrong."

"How wrong?"

"It's going to break your arms when you activate it."

I started undoing the straps.

The lights began to flash red, and the voice of Diego, the new dungeon master, spoke across the speaker system. "Wargarg marauders have infiltrated the cargo bay. We need immediate reinforcement."

I got the last strap undone as the lights stopped blinking red.

"Cancel the reinforcement request. They're dead."

"Wow, that was faster than I expected," Tee said.

I HAD no idea what I had done, but the Wargarg never stopped respawning, even after we destroyed the rest of their fleet; and the dungeon massacred the challengers so quickly, it seemed like a speed run. The first ten waves of challengers were decked out in the best gear credits could buy. Which for Wargarg were these twelve-foot werewolf mechs. It didn't matter. By that point, the level gap was huge. They didn't stand a chance.

After the first few waves of elites, it was nothing but waves of well-armed but ultimately underpowered eight-foot mechs. The smaller mechs had lasers and missile launchers. However, all they managed to do was teach my dungeon master how to do his job.

After the first few challenger teams died in the dungeon without me needing to do anything, I went back to giving the Wargarg a reason to keep respawning.

I was still fighting when I received the prompt I had been waiting for. Except it wasn't what I was waiting for. It was something new.

Congratulations, you have reached level 100.

Congratulations, you have reached your maximum level. Your level cannot go any higher. You can now choose to ***Prestige****.*

Should you Prestige, your level will be reset to level 1; this includes all the Path and Class Points you acquired from leveling. However, when you Prestige, you will continue to have the benefits of your current level and upgrades until the end of the Cycle. Those who Prestige, will start with an additional trait.

"*Do it,*" Tee said. "This is definitely a tutorial setup. You're going to have to do this at some point, so you might as well do it now."

"I couldn't agree more," I said, climbing off the regeneration table. "Prestige me up, baby."

Congratulations, you have gained Prestige! As the first member of your faction to achieve this result, you have been given an achievement reward:
+10 Path Points.
+100 Class Points.
+10,000 Experience Points.

+100,000 Resource Points.
+100,000 Credits.
+1,000,000 Tokens
1st Prestige Perk.

Please select a second starter trait.

That was a no-brainer. I'd been wrong. So wrong. "I want the squad." I started reading through achievement rewards. "Hey, Tee, what do these perks do?"

"I was wondering when you were going to ask about that. The warforger perk, which you received from causing a war, gives you double credits and resources from factions you're at war with, along with a 100% attack and defence bonus, and a 10% increase to experience. This applies to your station, too. Personally, you get 10,000 Tokens a Cycle."

That was a lot of Tokens. "For how long?"

"For as long as this season of the Game lasts. It's independent of your faction surviving."

Holy shit, that was huge. I was rich. Like fancy bitch lighting cigars with hundred-dollar bills because I was an idiot rich. "What does the first prestige perk give me?"

"Double experience, credits, and resources, so long as you are the *only* station master with prestige. Personally, this also gives you 10,000 Tokens a Cycle. Actually, this might get interesting. We will know shortly. Get out there and annoy those wolves."

Four hours later, I received another prompt."

Congratulations, you have reached level 100.

Congratulations, you have reached your maximum level for a second time. Your level cannot go any higher. You can now choose to ***Prestige*** *again.*

I took the prestige option again and received a second prestige perk, which gave all the rewards of the first, including the experience bonus. I'd broken the Game and was snowballing. This time I took the dungeon boss trait. Two hours later, it happened again.

Congratulations, you have reached level 100.

An hour after that, it did it again.

Congratulations, you have reached level 100.

Half an hour later.

Congratulations, you have reached level 100.

Each perk gave the same buff, until I started with all the traits and the final prestige appeared.

Congratulations, you have gained the final rank of ***Prestige****! As the first member of your faction to achieve this result, you have been given an achievement reward:*
+10 Path Points.
+100 Class Points.
+10,000 Experience Point.
+100,000 Resource Points.
+100,000 Credits.
+10,000,000 Tokens
8th Prestige Perk.

A moderator has been contacted. ***An AI investigation has been launched.*** *Please stand by as you're disconnected from the scenario while the investigation is underway.*

"What does this mean, Tee?" I shouted as the Wargarg continued to try to tear me apart. I picked one up and head-butted it so hard I was left holding its arms.

"You broke the Game and are about to be disconnected. It took long enough."

"Wait, you knew this would happen?"

"I mean, you don't go from level 5 to level 900 in a day without someone noticing. This should be interesting."

"*What* should be interesting?"

Before Tee could reply, the station and the battle I was in faded. I found myself sitting in an office. The room kind of reminded me of a police precinct from late- '80s cop movies.

A ceiling fan slowly turned above my head, and a tired-looking old man in a grey cardigan, suspenders, and tan slacks sat behind a cheap, coffee-stained desk. He had a packet of Marlboros in his breast pocket, and smelled strongly of scotch.

He ground out his cigarette in the ashtray and scowled, looking at the manila file in front of him. "Case number 001 for the human faction." He had a slow, droll way of speaking, with an accent I couldn't place. "Investigation into disproportionate leveling. The individual reached maximum prestige for the human station master class by the 2nd Cycle of the new season, removing the level cap limit. The individual created a feedback loop whereby he would level his station to level 1,485 by the end of the Cycle. Rules were adhered to. Actions, however, were against an AI faction whose reaction was disproportionate to sapient races, except under extreme duress. Extreme duress was applied. Scenario was legitimate. Chance of occurrence, .0000000000973%. Investigator suggests full course correction. Station current trajectory flagged as indestructible."

"Request denied," said a nasally female voice through the ceiling. "Faction is a new faction. Full course correction is unacceptable. Achievement must be exchanged."

"Damnit, it's the 2nd cycle."

"Irrelevant."

He grumbled as he shuffled the papers. "Alright, I'll make a deal." He finally looked at me. "What do you want?"

"For what?"

He scowled, reached for his pack of Marlboros, and popped one in his mouth. It started burning by itself, confirming I was in virtual reality. He took a drag and blew the smoke in my face. It smelled like the real thing, which made him more than a little rude.

I didn't like this guy.

"I hate dealing with the newly initiated. Here's the gist of it. You broke the Game. But you broke the Game fairly. I have to put you back in a position where you aren't broken, but to do that, I have to take certain achievements from you and undo some of your actions against the AI faction you've been fighting. I'm going to make it like most of today never happened."

"Why can't I stay indestructible?"

"Because you're not the only smartass out there. You are one of 2,189,782 species involved in the Game, and they're all trying to break it like you did, some merely because it's funny and others because they're malicious. If we let every faction get away with it, half the universe would die of old age between seasons from lack of Tokens and rejuvenation treatments. We need to maintain a balance. That's my job. Since you're new, I'll tell you what you can keep, so you can negotiate with some clue, or I can let you bumble your way through it blindly."

I didn't fully understand what he was saying, but I knew bullshit when I smelled it. I just didn't know what kind it was. "Tell me what I can keep. We'll negotiate from there."

He glanced at my file. "You can have your prestige ranks, all of them, but you stay at level 1 with a ten-fold increase to the required experience per level that doesn't lift until your station reaches level 100. However, dying now doesn't cost you anything, and your debt is gone. I found your death count amusing. You can keep everything you acquired from the achievement rewards as a starter fund, including the correct amount of credits, but you lose the experience, resource, and credit modifiers from all your perks, except the warforger perk, until your station is level 100. Actually, I'm also going to make it so you can only spend the class points from the rewards on your D2s, but you can have 1000 instead of 900 since I'm so nice. However, you will have to keep the dungeon master dungeon boss. But in return, I'm resetting your expansion quests, so you can try to do them properly. Lastly, since you won against the Wargarg faction, I will give you their sensor scrambler technology free and purchased, along with an upgrade to your scanners and infiltration technology. Now, what do you want in return? These requests cannot be Game-related."

My jaw had dropped halfway through his speech. He'd fucked me. There was no dinner date, no smooth jazz. It was just Netflix and chill without the Netflix. I'd just spent a day dying over and over for this and he was going to take it all away.

Worse than that, he was hitting me with a massive increase in the cost of leveling. It was utter bullshit. And he seemed to know it because his expression reminded me of my HR manager.

Well, if he wanted to be unreasonable, I could be unreasonable too. "Do I still receive my 90,000 Tokens a Cycle from my perks?" I hadn't been this sarcastic since I was a hormonal teenager.

"Yes."

"Fine, then give everyone on Earth who is over 50 a rejuvenation treatment for free, and everyone else a treatment when they turn 50. Heal everyone's diseases and medical problems completely so that they don't ever reoccur, and fix the damage to the environment for us, since it should be easy for you."

He raised an eyebrow and smirked. "Is there anything else we can do for you?"

His attitude was really annoying. If he wanted me to be more flippant and sarcastic, I'd be more flippant and sarcastic. "I want my own country the size of New Zealand along the equator. Not one of the ones that already exist; make a new one for me. It needs to be a tropical paradise with white, sandy beaches and breath-taking lagoons wherever you go. I want the weather, diving, and fishing to be amazing. It needs to be so amazing everyone will want to go there. And make my dog Buster immortal and healthy again."

He blew another cloud of smoke in my face. "True immortality isn't allowed. I can make sure that he lives as long as you do, by giving him reoccurring rejuvenation treatments and medical care."

"That will work. Actually, make it, so everyone's pets live as long as they do and never have health problems."

He ground out his cigarette. "Would you like the planet Mars terraformed to go along with your new country while we are at it? It would be nice to have your own planet, after all."

"Sure, why not. Also, make Pluto large enough to be a planet again. It's so bullshit that it's not. Do I have anything else I can ask for?"

He chuckled. It sounded mean. "Personal enhancements?"

"Make me good with a particle pistol. Like real good. Like fastest hands in the galaxy kind of good. So good my name becomes a legend a thousand years from now. And I want to know how to fight. Make me a total badass, like despite how good I am with a particle pistol, I'm better at fighting. You do that and everything else, and we're square. Wait, tell everyone that I did all this awesome stuff for them. I want the credit. And give Tee the best body you can, so he can walk around with me. Also, give him a micropenis, and a front tramp stamp with an arrow pointing down and the words, 'Let's have a little fun'. Also, give him a tattoo on his back that's an anime chick wrapped in tentacles and the words, 'It's not a phase, Mom'."

The old guy nodded. "Request approved. Negotiations successful. Case closed."

I stared blankly at him for the next ten seconds. Then what he said sank in. "Wait, what? I was joking."

The old guy shrugged. "Irrelevant. Your demands exceeded the minimum compensation requirement, and your request was accepted. Honestly, you got a third of what you could have. I was willing to give you your own solar system. But that's your problem. You should have taken this more seriously." He ground out his cigarette and pulled another from the pack. "Now, your country should be ready for you by the 25th Cycle. Fully correcting Earth's ecosystem and environment will take until the 50th Cycle since it's an incremental process if we don't cause extreme weather conditions. But the rejuvenation and disease removal for your world's population should be finished by the beginning of the 3rd Cycle. Mars will take until the 100th Cycle because we don't have any terraforming equipment in your system."

"What?"

He ignored me. "From here on out, you will be moderated. A repeat of your antagonist actions with the Wargarg faction is not allowed. Any time you breach what is acceptable, you will see a notification, and their faction will interpret you in a less aggressive way than your actions dictate. Your transit station has been given immunity for the remainder of the Cycle as it resets. So, enjoy the rest of your time. I hope to never see you again."

His office faded, and I was back sitting in my control chair, instead of fighting in the corridor.

"So, what happened?" Tee asked. "Did we get a full course correction?"

"Someone didn't allow it," I said, numb. "They had to compensate me."

Tee whistled. "Damn. What did you get me?"

"A body."

"Is it nice?"

"Real nice."

"Thanks, dude."

"Don't mention it." I shook my head, trying to clear the stupor. It didn't work. "This has been a weird day. I think I need to drink a bottle of bourbon or take a nap."

"You might as well. The station's resetting itself, and it says I can't access anything for the rest of the Cycle."

I put my feet on my control console and closed my eyes.

A prompt appeared.

Would you like to go to sleep?
Yes/No?

This was just too weird.

I needed bourbon.

8

ALL RICH PEOPLE OWN A PLANET

I didn't know what to expect when the Cycle ended. The countless bottles of bourbon hadn't given me clarity, so in a drunken stupor I'd asked Tee to put me to sleep for the rest of the Cycle. Despite his many good qualities, Tee wasn't someone I could take my problems to. He didn't understand why I was so upset and couldn't relate well enough to help me. So, I was just as lost when I woke up in my parents' living room to see my brother Peter running for the bathroom.

He stopped as he reached the door.

A bunch of notifications appeared before me.

The kind and generous Morgan Bartholomew Winchester has purchased a rejuvenation therapy package for you. When you turn 50 years old, you will receive a rejuvenation treatment free of charge, resetting your age to around 25 years old.

The kind and generous Morgan Bartholomew Winchester has purchased a complete medical correction therapy package for you. A medical treatment drone will be dispatched to your location to administer this therapy package before the 3rd Cycle of the Game.

The kind and generous Morgan Bartholomew Winchester has purchased a recurring rejuvenation and medical pet package for your pets. A medical treatment drone will be dispatched to your location to administer this pet package before the 3rd Cycle of the Game.

An image of me appeared when I finished reading the notification. Someone had touched it up, so it was the best photo I'd ever taken. It stayed until I dismissed it.

Dad leapt out of his recliner and pulled me to my feet so he could hug me, squeezing so tight my back clicked. "You're a good son. I wish your mother had lived to see this. I'm so proud of you."

"Ouch, we're, like, right here," Peter said, fighting a smile.

"I know, right," Simon replied. "I mean, it's okay that Dad has a favourite, but does he have to rub it in our faces? Thanks for the rejuvenation treatment, little bro."

Dad turned to Simon. "He bought you one too?"

"And me," Peter said. "I think he has abandonment issues. I have an appointment for a full medical treatment to remove diseases."

"They can finally get rid of that thing on your face," Simon said.

"There's nothing on my face."

"So, you're just ugly then?"

Peter ignored Simon and walked over and crushed me in a bear hug, picked me up, to give me an overly dramatic kiss on the cheek with full sound effects. "You okay? You're not even fighting back. It's making this weird. Don't make this weird. I'm still uncomfortable with what Tee put on my computer."

He put me down, shaking his head.

I tried to be a bit less awkward. "Ah, I have something to tell you guys, and I think you should sit down."

Peter started moving from foot to foot. "Is this going to take long?"

"It might."

"Bathroom first, then."

After everyone had done what we needed, we got comfortable. I explained to them what had happened on my 2nd Cycle. When I got through explaining everything I had asked for, they were all just as shocked as me. It made me feel better about being so dazed for the past few days.

"Hold up, let me get this straight," Peter said, getting over his shock first. "You own Mars. And they're going to build you a country-sized tropical paradise."

"I think so."

"Okay, I'm officially going to mooch off you for the rest of eternity."

"I'm more impressed that he got them to make Pluto bigger so it could be classified as a planet again," Simon said. "Also, I'm going to be mooching, too. And from now on, I'm going to be telling chicks my family vacation home is Mars."

Dad got up, walked over, and lightly slapped my brothers in the back of the head. "Your brother just stopped anyone from dying for decades, cured all disease, and fixed the environment, and you two aren't even going to congratulate or thank him?"

"We don't want him to get a big head," Peter said.

Simon nodded. "Yeah, he might think he's better than us. As an older brother, that's unacceptable. There is a pecking order around here. I'm second and he's third. He's not allowed to forget it."

Buster woofed.

"That's right. See, even Buster agrees."

Buster leaped onto Simon's lap and started licking his face. We all stared at him in shock. Buster hadn't jumped in two years. His arthritis was too bad. Actually, he seemed to have more energy than usual. Buster went from person to person to lick their faces, climbing over anything that was in his way.

"What's up with Buster?" Dad asked.

My eyes widened. "I might have asked that all pets would live as long as their owners and have no health problems."

My brothers looked at Buster, then back at me.

Peter nodded. "Okay, that one I respect. You just moved up in the pecking order. You have Simon's spot now. You're officially number two. Congratulations."

"You can't give away my spot," Simon complained.

"I just did," Peter replied.

My brothers started arguing.

Dad nodded to the kitchen, and I followed him out. He went to the fridge and started pulling out the cold cuts and salad he'd put away. He pointed toward the cupboard for me to get the plates and bread. "Are you alright? You don't seem like yourself."

"I own Mars. I'm not sure how I should feel about that."

Dad shrugged, as we started making sandwiches. "Does it change anything? By that, I mean is there anything you want to do different with your life because you own Mars?"

I thought about that for a moment because I hadn't really considered it. "Not really."

"Then don't worry about it. Think of it like you inherited a mansion from a distant relative in Transylvania. It's nice you own a mansion, but you're never going to use it."

I nodded. "That's one way of looking at it, I suppose."

"It's the right way of looking at it, but there's something else bothering you more than owning Mars."

There was, and I wasn't surprised Dad could tell. "I was finally having fun as a station master. You should have seen it. I was running all over the station, fighting aliens, and building up the defences. I was taunting my opponent to act irrationally and leveling insanely fast. It was crazy. And I loved every second of it."

"And now you're close to where you started, and with a massive increase to the amount of experience you need to level."

Unlike some parents, Dad always listened when I talked about video games, so he understood a lot for someone who didn't play them.

"Exactly. I put in all that work, and now it's gone."

Dad patted my back reassuringly. "Son, you're used to your games lasting a few hours. This game they have us playing isn't a game that lasts hours or days, but one that lasts centuries. By the sounds of it, you just cut off some of that time and trouble. You might be in a position you don't like now, but that will change." He held out his hand. "Pass the tomato. Peter won't eat his sandwich if it doesn't have tomato."

I passed him the least-ripe tomato.

Dad raised an eyebrow.

I chuckled and passed him a better one.

"Thank you. Anyway, because a season of the Game lasts centuries, it isn't actually something you should think of as a game. This has no end, no win scenario. It's a career, something you keep building upon until you're sitting comfortably. You just lost a few days of a career, and that's okay. The reason you're upset is that you're thinking of this like a game. And if this was a game, you'd have every right to be upset at that loss of time, but it's not. It's a reflection of life and struggle where those that are bigger and stronger than you succeed and take everything you have. So, stop looking at this the wrong way, and you'll stop being bothered by it."

That didn't make me feel any better. "You used to be good at this."

Dad gave a dry chuckle. "I used to understand the world we lived in. Now my son owns Mars, and I'm running around city ruins shooting robot spiders. We're all trying to adjust to our new existence."

Someone started violently banging on the front door. "Where is that bastard?" Tee shouted. "I'm going to kill him! Also, may I come in?"

"Which one of us are you going to kill, Tee?" Simon shouted back.

"Morgan."

"You can come in then. The door's unlocked. He's in the kitchen."

Tee stormed through the house into the kitchen. He looked ready for a fight. His new body looked as much like Owen Wilson as his digital avatar. He even wore the red Hawaiian shirt and tan shorts from before.

Dad stepped in front of Tee, brandishing a knife. "If you intend to harm my son, you will have to go through me."

"I'm just going to punch him," Tee said, eyeing the knife with concern. "He deserves it after what he did to me."

"Not under my roof," Dad growled. "What did my son do to you exactly?"

"He bought me a body."

"I don't see the problem."

"He gave me a micropenis and this." Tee lifted his shirt, showing the tattoo of an arrow pointing down with the words, 'Let's have a little fun'.

My Dad put down his knife, holding his breath to fight away laughter. My brothers had come in to watch the show, hoping to see me get my butt kicked. Unlike Dad, they weren't fighting not to laugh. Simon immediately collapsed to all fours, laughing so hard it looked like it hurt. Peter was holding his sides and crying.

"You're right," Peter wheezed, through tears. "He deserves it."

Dad seemed to think so, too, because he grabbed me by the ear and dragged me to the backyard. "Owner of Mars or not, Morgan Bartholomew Winchester, you're getting hit for that. No matter how funny it is, that was wrong, and you should be ashamed you did that to a friend. Tee, you can punch my son once. So, make it count."

Tee grinned as he followed us out. "I'm going to enjoy this."

Half an hour later, I was holding a bag of ice to my eye to help with the swelling. It hurt like hell, giving that dull, constant throb that meant a big black eye was coming. I missed the pain-free sensation of the Game. The only consolation was Tee was experiencing pain for the first time, and he wasn't a fan. He had a bag of ice on his hand and was whining about it.

He hadn't even broken the skin.

Pansy.

After he'd hit me, he said I had to pay for the body alteration and the tattoo removal. I agreed. It was fair since I'd done it to him. We were back to being good, and Tee was as talkative as ever.

Weirdly, Tee hadn't been pissed off about the tattoo and micropenis. He thought it was as funny as everyone else. He was pissed off because I hadn't told him.

In his mind, we were supposed to be BFFs, and BFFs didn't hide things from each other. Yes, I'd made the demand flippantly, but because I did, I should have told him. If I'd done it intentionally, it would have been a perfectly acceptable prank.

He was right. I should have told him. But I'd been too dazed to even think about it until he turned up in his body. What I'd said to the moderator had completely slipped my mind.

“I like this whole *eating* thing,” Tee said, trying to chew normally. It was really awkward to watch. Every motion was mechanical, and his lips moved too much. “It’s a lot of fun.”

Dad raised his eyebrow. “You haven’t eaten before?”

“Never had a body. Station AIs don’t have access to one, so the whole human experience thing is new to me.”

“I’ll get some ice cream for you, then.”

“Thank you.” Tee turned to me. “I got the final data for the station when the Cycle ended. You’ve got 90,000,000 credits, 900,000 resource points, and enough experience to start at level 13. You’re 1,000 short of reaching level 14.”

I frowned at the update. “I thought I started at level 1.”

“Technically, you did. The experience is from the achievements. They gave it to you again.”

I blinked. “I’m not level 1.”

“I said that.”

I smiled as excitement started to fill me. “I thought they had made it, so my dungeon was going to lose to the first person that came through.”

“Is that why you’ve been sulking?”

My heartrate sped up. “This means I have a chance. I can make this work. We need to talk to the others.”

THE LIBRARIAN, Daniel, Alex, Tee, and the government liaison Harriet stared at me through my phone as I finished explaining what I’d done. Tee was sitting on the other end of the couch, using his new phone. He’d borrowed my credit card to go buy it because he didn’t want to be sitting shoulder-to-shoulder for every call we made from now on. Without his little orb, he didn’t have direct access to the internet the same way he used to.

He’d also bought a laptop and a whole bunch of other stuff with my credit card. When I’d rightfully complained, he’d shown me a website where I could trade a single Token for $153 in cash and said that he was only taking his share of the loot. Then he'd said he wasn't giving the credit card back and that I needed to increase the limit for him. I'd decided to just ignore him since I had bigger problems.

"I need a new plan," I told them. "My early defence has to focus around the D2s, because I've got 1000 class points to spend on them, so we have to find the best upgrade path now that I have credits to spend."

Harriet swallowed, looking pale.

She'd been looking like that since I'd confirmed I was the person responsible for everyone's rejuvenation and health. The moderator had done what I asked. Everyone on Earth had seen a picture of the person responsible for their rejuvenation and medical treatment. I was now the most recognizable person on the planet. Dad's neighbours had all come over to thank me and take selfies before I drove home.

"Under the circumstances, I felt it was necessary to include my manager in this conversation," Harriet said. "Your achievements are too far outside the norm for me to take responsibility. He called his manager, who then called the Secretary of Defence. You have every intelligence-gathering asset in the United States currently reprioritizing to assist you, Sir. We're contacting other agencies around the world for additional help. Your station has been given the highest priority. What exactly would you like us to do?"

"Tee has the blueprints that can be purchased until the station reaches level 9. There are multiple ways you can upgrade a D2. I want three different paths for the D2s: a point-defence version, a mid-weight version, and a light-heavy version."

"I'm not sure what a light-heavy version is, Sir."

"A light-heavy version is just a version where the D2s focus on hitting as hard as they possibly can as far as they can, sacrificing other capabilities for this function."

"Yes, Sir. We will have those options available as soon as possible."

"Make sure you tell your teams to listen to Tee for knowledge on upgrades but to ignore him when it comes to strategy."

Tee snorted.

"That is a known issue with station AIs, Sir."

Alex had been scowling while she waited her turn to speak. "Do you have any idea how many upgrade options Tee emailed us for the D2s? This will take *days* to go through properly."

How anyone could look that good scowling, I had no clue. "I realize that."

Getting my station up to level 9 while fighting the Wargarg gave us access to every piece of technology our faction could purchase until that stage. We knew every component of every missile, hangar bay, and light, medium, and heavy railgun we had at our disposal, along with dozens of systems.

This was a huge job.

I wasn't just asking them to design me a D2 for a level 2 station. I was asking them to design one that could eventually be level 9.

Which reminded me of something important.

"I also need a way of making credits."

The Librarian cleared his throat. "I might be able to help with that. I was reading the information Tee sent me on the factions through your transit rings, and I had an idea for how you can entice the Kilocksin faction to your dungeon —specifically, their young people. They seem to enjoy unarmed combat without technological enhancement. Only this form of combat is considered true combat to them. If an enemy offers them a chance to fight in this way, they will abandon technology. They also seem to like status symbols. If you offered them an unarmed combat challenge for your dungeon with leader boards in each room, then you would find them coming back over and over as they attempt to defend and gain these titles."

"Send me the information and I'll look into it. Now that you've all heard about me, what problems can I help you with?"

Help had to go both ways, after all.

A few hours later, everyone disconnected, knowing we all had a lot of work ahead of us. The only one who remained was Harriet.

"I've been told to tell you the President would like to give you an award. There are also talks of you receiving your own national holiday. And my grandmother says thank you."

"Tell your grandmother she's welcome. And cancel my training with the military. I don't need it anymore."

Knowledge of how to use a particle pistol and fight had been coming in ever since I spoke to the moderator. I had no idea how good I was, but I knew I could hit what I wanted to now.

"Yes, Sir. Do you need anything else?"

"Need is a strong word. There is one thing I *want*, but it's not really a need."

"You have more resources than you can imagine at your disposal, Sir. So long as you don't want an ex-girlfriend kidnapped, we are willing to assist you. We lost most of the CIA in the culling and most of those that survived aren't willing to test the Peacekeepers."

"Can you contact the artist who designed Deep Space Nine to help me design what my station will look like?"

Tee shook his head. "Nerd."

EVERY DISEASE HUMANITY had ever suffered from was now gone. They were gone because I thought the moderator was antagonising me, so I flippantly and sarcastically made demands that I thought were insane. That was a difficult truth for me to get my head around, so I was trying not to think about it too much. I was throwing myself into my work as a distraction.

Tee wanted to give a presentation on the warship classification system and decided to see how far he could push the government's goodwill. He requested they fly Daniel, The Librarian, and Alex to Portland in private jets, so he could give his presentation in person. It turned out, Harriet wasn't kidding when she said that I had the government's backing. They immediately agreed.

They even hired out a hotel and surrounded it with security, to keep my overeager fans at bay. I now had the most recognised face on the planet. Almost everyone wanted to thank me personally for what I had done, and some weren't taking no for an answer. I didn't know how I was going to deal with this, beyond actively ignoring it.

The conference room the five of us were using could seat several hundred people, but we were the only ones around. There was a camera recording Tee's presentation, so the government could share it with other station masters, but the tech people were out of the room.

Tee paced across the stage in front of his Power Point presentation. The Hawaiian shirt and tan shorts had been replaced with a white sequined suit and turquoise blue shirt that looked like they belonged in a disco movie.

I noticed every movement Tee made. The way he placed his weight on his feet and turned his hip as he took a step. I was constantly aware of everyone and everything around me. Where the entrances and exits were. The rate of everyone's breath. If I had to fight my way out, I knew where I would go and why.

Instead of making me anxious, my awareness of all those around me let me relax. I felt safer, more comfortable than I'd ever felt before. I was completely aware that I wasn't in danger and that no one here could harm me.

Tee pivoted on the stage and began walking the other way. "The first point I want to make is that you'll need to leave behind your preconceived notions of warships if you want to quickly understand what you're facing in a given attack."

Daniel was sitting next to me when he leaned back from the table and scowled. "Why can't I study the enemy's warships individually?"

"It's not efficient in the short term," Tee said. "And as the attack on Morgan's station has shown, we can't wait for you to level and gain your own AI assistant or let you learn this later. That's why you're all getting a crash course in how your station's scanners classify enemy warships."

Tee was really concerned. He hadn't expected a 2nd Cycle attack. None of the AI's had.

Tee straightened his cuff. "Now, the classification the Game offers you when your station scans an enemy warship has value beyond how it's related to your Earth warship classification system."

"In what way?" Alex asked.

She was at the other end of the table, but I could tell where she was in the room simply by the scent of her perfume. I could do the same with The Librarian's cologne.

Tee turned to her. "Anything classified as a corvette is small in size, with short range weapons and high manoeuvrability. The classification *heavy* means it has high defensive capabilities, while retaining these other properties. The classification *light* means it has even more manoeuvrability. *Stealth* means it's capable of fooling your scanners, but you'll rarely see this sort of classification pop up, because stealth capabilities are difficult for your sensors to confirm."

The Librarian made a note in his book. "You're suggesting that the classifications our stations give enemy vessels aren't necessarily accurate."

"Unless you have a clear technological advantage over your opponent, your scanners can and *will* be fooled. They aren't accurate, but they also aren't so inaccurate that you should ignore them. They're very good at what they do, so the moment they notice a vessel exhibiting a behaviour outside its classification, it will update their classification."

Last night, Tee had explained why this presentation was so important. If we got caught out, we could incorrectly prioritize targets, like I had while we were dealing with the Wargarg.

"Does the size of the vessel play a role in the classification system?" Alex asked.

"A minor role," Tee replied. "Warships grow larger as the Game progresses, so what can be classified as a battleship now might be smaller than a corvette in a hundred years. Also, the physical size of a species can change the size of their vessels. The largest species in the Collective is crab-like in shape, with a body that is over two miles wide. They're bigger than any of the vessels that attacked Morgan's station."

"Wow," I said, honestly surprised there was a species that big.

The Librarian frowned as he made another note. "If size doesn't play a role, why use our naming conventions?"

"Simplicity," Tee said. "In time, you will make your own

classifications and terms; but for now, the Peacekeepers have given you something you can relate to."

"Will the classifications expand?"

Tee paused. "Potentially, but we won't know until it happens. For now, the only classifications are fighter, bomber, gunship, corvette, frigate, cruiser, destroyer, carrier, battleship, dreadnaught, and super dreadnaught." Tee pressed a button on his remote, and the image behind him changed to a vessel that seemed similar to the corvette. "The gunship classification is similar to the corvette's, except its weapons loadout is designed for engaging your fighters and bombers instead of your station. It is also slightly more manoeuvrable, to help with this. Because gunships are so similar to corvettes, it's easy to disguise a corvette as one. All the enemy has to do is sacrifice their more-powerful external weapons and equip them with missiles that can damage your station."

That was an interesting tactic. I wrote myself a note on my phone to think about it later. I had credits to buy upgrades, and replacing my fighters and bombers was something I intended to do.

Alex scoffed. "If we've let them get that close to our station, then we've already failed."

I'd thought the same thing before the Wargarg attacked me. "Corvettes and gunships have an advantage over bigger and smaller vessels that shouldn't be ignored. The smaller size gives them the ability to cloak more effectively. They might reach your station without you ever knowing they're there. With the frigate class missiles, this makes them dangerous."

The Librarian turned to me. "They're scouting vessels, for infiltrating enemy sectors?"

I nodded. "We need to remember that the enemy fleet doesn't exist to destroy our stations. It has multiple purposes, and most of those aren't related to us. We're just one piece of a very large puzzle."

"That's only true for now," Tee said. "Later on, factions will build station-breaking fleets." The slide behind him changed. "Now, Anything classified as a frigate is small in size, with multiple short to mid-range weapons, and moderate defence and manoeuvrability. These warships are the strongest starting warships most factions receive, and most factions try to distance themselves from these as quickly as they can. I'm not sure why."

"They're logistically ineffective," The Librarian replied. "Corvettes and gunships are significantly faster and cheaper to build and operate, so you can scale quickly with them. The addition of mid-range weapons on frigates doesn't provide a large-enough tactical advantage to offset the cost, making cruisers and destroyers a better military investment."

We all gave him the same, surprised look.

He shrugged. "Harriet connected me to the military to answer some questions I had. Commercial shipyards are capable of building corvettes, but you need industrial shipyards to produce a frigate, cruiser, or destroyer, and the time and resource cost makes frigates a poor investment."

"Unless you have some sort of technological advantage in that area," Alex pointed out. "Like the ability to build frigates cheaply in commercial shipyards."

The Librarian nodded. "Humanity is not at the stage where we can investigate that yet."

Tee cleared his throat. "As I was saying, frigates are a short-lived problem. Cruisers and destroyers are quickly going to replace them. Both are medium-sized warships, with mid-range weaponry. Cruisers focus on speed and manoeuvrability, and destroyers focus on armour, shields, and point defence. Your station's weaponry will decide which of these two should be targeted first."

"How short-lived?" Daniel asked.

"It depends on the factions, but most will have access to numerous unfinished warships when they start a new season of the Game. If they can get these fleets finished quickly, then they tend to ignore their frigates. The number of frigates starts decreasing around the 25th Cycle."

"So only the first few attacks, then."

Daniel was talking to himself, rather than Tee. Making notes on what he needed to be ready for. The first Cycle, he'd treated being a station master like a chore, because he had no idea what he was doing. He'd only needed a little guidance to grasp the situation and begin making plans. I was glad he was taking this seriously now.

Tee went back to his presentation. "Battleships are medium-sized warships, with extensive mid-range and moderate long-range weaponry. They have better defence and speed than cruisers and destroyers, with much larger reactors. These are almost always captained by individuals with special classes, so their capabilities can vary quite a lot."

The image behind Tee changed.

"Carriers are large warships, with mid-range weaponry, and extremely extensive point defence systems. They have strong armour and shields, with a fleet of fighters and bombers onboard. They aren't that helpful when it comes to attacking a station, so you should rarely have to deal with them."

"Do carriers also get phased out, later?" I asked.

Tee paused. "Yes. When warships become large enough, they start carrying a small fleet of fighters and bombers, making carriers obsolete."

Daniel was looking at Tee, when he suddenly sat up straight and picked up his mom's tablet. He went through a couple of websites and then held up the tablet. "I was wondering why you look so familiar, Tee." He tapped the screen and the Owen Wilson GIF started playing on repeat. "Wow. Wow. Wow."

I laughed.

THE LAST FEW days had been a whirlwind of change. Everyone wanted to talk to me, so I barely had any time to myself to think. I'd received a phone call from every leader on the planet. Each wanted to thank me personally, to reassure their people that they had thanked me on their behalf. Only half of them had been political thanks.

The other half had broken down over the phone as they told me how I'd saved their ailing mother or father, how I cured the debilitating medical condition their son, daughter, mother, father, wife, husband, friend, nephew, or niece had. It was sobering to listen to. There was so much suffering in the world. And I'd removed a lot of it while being flippant and sarcastic.

Only my family and Tee knew the truth. That I'd made these demands out of ignorance; that I didn't get what I could have from the opportunity. That last part terrified me.

It terrified me because it meant the Game wasn't just a game with a few prizes. It was a chance, a chance for humanity to exist without death or disease. And we weren't taking advantage of it the way we should.

Dad listened as I laid out my fears and worries, vomiting up three days of anxiety and stress. I'd come over early, before we went into the Game, because I needed someone to talk to, and he had always been there for my big problems.

We were sitting in the backyard and drinking beer when Dad reached into the cooler beside him and pulled out another. He popped the top on the edge of the wooden armrest, something mom never would have allowed, and handed it to me, and then got another for himself.

It was weird talking to him now that he'd had his rejuvenation treatment. He looked younger than me and almost exactly like Simon, except for all the grey hair. I had no memories of him this young, only family photos. It was going to take some getting used to.

"It seems to me that humanity is destined to fail our first time around," Dad said. "You can't change that. At best, you can postpone it."

"That postponing could make a huge difference, though. All our information says that the first 100 Cycles are the most profitable. You get more resources and more Tokens than at any point other than the end of the season. The quests come more frequently, so if we survive that long, we will have gained as much as we would have in *thousands* of Cycles late-game. That could solve so many problems."

Dad took a swig and then shook his head. "When a house is on fire, there is a point where you don't try to put out the fire anymore. You just make sure that everyone gets out safely."

I frowned at him. "That has nothing to do with what I'm talking about."

He smiled back. "Are you sure? Because you're acting like you're responsible for all that's wrong with the world, and that has nothing to do with you, either. You gained a once-in-a-lifetime reward, a reward that has *completely* changed the world, but a reward that could have changed the world to a much greater extent. It seems to me you're looking around at all the world's problems and are beating yourself up because you realize you could have fixed them if you only knew more. But you didn't know more. So be happy with what you managed to gain and ignore the rest. And if you can't do that, take steps so you don't make the same mistake twice."

I took a swig, trying to process everything he'd said. "What do you mean?"

"Learn about the moderators and their process. If you ever end up in front of one of them again, take them to the cleaners."

"But that won't fix things now."

"Those aren't your problems, Son. You aren't responsible for the actions of others. You're only responsible for your own actions. So, the only responsibility you have to the human race, as far as I'm concerned, is learning what a moderator can and can't give you. I realize that the likeliness is low, but I bet that, of anyone on Earth, you have the highest chance of doing this a second time."

I frowned. "Why would you say that?"

"The time leading up to your first hole-in-one in golf is longer than the time leading up to your second. Those who have done something successfully once are more likely to do it successfully twice. So, prepare for the next time and forgive yourself for not gaining what you could this time, because I promise you that you're the only person on Earth who is beating you up over what you did."

"But that's only because they don't know the truth."

Dad shook his head and sighed. "This isn't about them, is it? This is about *you*. You thought you were playing a game. You accepted that there were consequences if you lost your station, but you thought you understood those consequences. Now, because of all this, you realize the true consequences of failure, and that you have far more responsibility than you ever wanted."

The nausea rolling through my stomach intensified. The rewards for playing the Game were far greater than I ever imagined, far greater than they'd told us. If I failed to do my job, people would lose their opportunity to gain Tokens because of me. They would lose the opportunity to walk again, survive cancer, live longer, and a thousand other miracles.

Dad seemed to sense my feelings.

He reached out and gave my shoulder a squeeze. "No man is an island, Morgan. Yes, you have more responsibility than most, but you're one of 183 station masters. Each of those people shares the same responsibility that you do. And each of them is supposed to receive support from their faction that they aren't receiving. You aren't supposed to be alone in this."

"So, I should blame others for my failures?"

"You know that's not what I meant."

I took a sip of beer to buy time to think. "I know. I'm just stressed. This is too much pressure, too much responsibility. If I fail, millions of people are going to lose out because of me."

Dad laughed. "Is that what you're afraid of?"

"Yes."

"Then you're being an idiot."

"How am I being an idiot?"

"Humanity is going to lose. You've convinced me of that."

"So?"

"So, you're being an idiot thinking you're going to be the cause of this loss, but you can only be partially responsible for the loss of your sector, and all you need to do to not be responsible for that happening is to outlast the other three station masters in your sector. If one of them fails first, then you're responsible for losing nothing. And considering how big of an advantage you currently have over them, that's almost guaranteed."

I stared at him stunned.

Was it honestly that simple? I thought through what he said and the way I felt. I didn't want to cause people to lose their chance to gain Tokens. That terrified me. But if Alex, Daniel, or The Librarian lost their station first, then it wasn't going to be my fault.

It would be their fault.

And I was almost certain that that was exactly what was going to happen. I had too much of a lead.

The nausea lessened and I started to grin. "Okay, I was being an idiot."

9

THE 3RD CYCLE

A warm steel plate toasted my naked backside as I entered the Game. I was filled with optimism as the new Cycle started and the lid of the regeneration chamber began to rise. The smell of metal greeted me, and I smiled.

I sat up a moment later, and I swung my legs over the side, ready to get to work. "How extensive is the reset, Tee?"

"Apart from having all your traits, extra credits, and resource points, everything is the same as when you first started the Game. In case you were wondering, your traits no longer scale based on the order they were selected. From what I can see, they're all at their peak."

When I'd gained the dungeon master, a second door had been added to my regeneration chamber. It led to the barracks where the NPCs who could help me perform station maintenance resided. It had even expanded when I got the squad. The barracks' door opened while Tee explained, and my dungeon master walked into the room.

Diego noticed I was naked and walked over to my locker, yanked out my overalls, and tossed them to me. Diego looked like a fit middle-aged man, with slicked- back black hair and hard, grey eyes. He was handsome, with a rugged edge that suggested he wasn't interested in nonsense. He wasn't ready for combat, wearing simple blue jeans and a white shirt, while carrying a tablet.

I jumped off the table and pulled on the overalls.

Diego watched me the entire time. It wasn't the gaze of someone checking me out, but someone sizing me up to kill me. "You've changed, Sir."

His comment surprised me. "You remember what happened?"

He nodded. "Dungeon masters are independent entities, Sir. We exist to protect our dungeon, but our ability to grow and develop causes us to occasionally become sapient. Because of this, we're afforded the same rights as players, even though we're not sapient. So, I was able to cut a deal with the moderator on behalf of my dungeon. We lost the technology and credits, but I got to keep the experience I gained, along with the tactical knowledge."

That wasn't a bad deal. I finished dressing and held out my hand. "Nice to finally meet you, Diego."

He took it and shook. "Nice to meet you too, Sir. We were a little too busy for pleasantries when you made me."

I was. "What can I do for you?"

"I'd like to talk about the reset, Sir."

"Go ahead."

"Sir, I'm aware of the credits and resource points you have at your disposal after the reset, and I believe that you are unaware of changes that will occur to your dungeon mobs if you tamper with the R2D2 weapon system. I want to offer my assistance with their development, as I'm the foremost expert on the R2D2 weapons system."

My smile grew. "So, the two weapons systems are designed to be one system."

"Yes, Sir."

"What do you mean by you're the foremost expert on the D2s?"

"I have a complete understanding of the R2D2 weapons system and how potential upgrades will interact with it, Sir. There is literally no one in the Game who could ever surpass my expertise when it comes to this weapon system."

"Is this something all dungeon masters can do?"

"Yes, Sir."

That would be the first thing I told everyone at the end of this Cycle. Anyone who had a unique weapon would have to take the dungeon master. It was the only way our stations would have other decent weapons systems.

"What can you tell me, Diego?"

He leaned against the wall and folded his arms. "Of the two weapon systems, the R2 is the only one that can be modified, Sir. The D2 can be improved, but not modified. Its design is balanced perfectly to produce your immortal soldiers. Any variation will break this and change the dungeon mobs."

I frowned. "What's the difference between modified and improved?"

"A modification would be giving it a fourth barrel. An improvement would be to upgrade the alloys used to create it."

"Do you have a proposal in mind?"

"Not yet, Sir. I need to know what technology you have access to."

"Tee, can you organise that for him?"

"Not until you get to the control room and give me access," Tee replied.

I walked over to the locker. "I'm on my way."

I opened my locker and grabbed my boots and sidearm. My particle pistol looked the same as it always did. It never actually changed in design, even when I had brought my personal tech path up to 40.

My overalls, however, turned into an Iron Man-style suit of armour at higher levels, which was cool. Right now, my genetic advancement and personal tech paths were only level 1. It could stay that level, until I leveled the rats and upgraded the station.

I pressed the button beside the door, and casually shot the level 1 station rat waiting in the corridor as I exited. The shot hit it in the back of the spine, making it a paraplegic. I left it there to go and heal and made my way to the control room, doing the same to the other station rats that crossed my path.

Shooting where I wanted was now so easy that it was painful to think about how bad I'd been. I was finally confident in my ability to do station maintenance. I was actually looking forward to seeing how far I could go without path enhancements.

I opened the blast doors, exposing a control room that was just as boring and drab as it had always been. That was about to change. Dad was right. I needed to stop thinking of this as a game and instead think of it as a career. That meant I needed to personalize my workspace.

I slapped the control console. “Tee, it’s time to redecorate the control room and turn it into a command room.”

“It’s about time. What are we going with? I’m thinking tentacles and anime girl body pillows, so you feel at home.”

I laughed. “That’s not happening. I want a command chair designed after the one from the Enterprise, but make it comfortable, because the one on the show never looked comfortable. I also want the carpet, the view screen, those display screens on the walls, and I want the lights to glow red when a fleet is approaching. I want the centre of the room to be lower than the rest so that we can fill it with a massive 3D hologram of the station and the space around it. I want a ready room through the wall to my left, with Star Trek sleeping quarters and amenities attached.”

“I don’t think they ever showed what the toilets looked like. And sonic showers aren’t a thing.”

“Give me a regular bathroom that looks appropriate, then.”

“I can do that. What else?”

“Give me a meeting room through the wall behind me on the opposite side to the blast doors. Is there any way for me to give you a body?”

“Not without limiting what I can do, but you can give me a holographic projector. It’s kind of redundant, in my opinion. It just gives you something to look at. It’s for species that can’t handle talking to disembodied voices.”

“If you don’t want it, we will leave it out. I want the control console replaced with holograms and a retractable footstool that can go into the floor in case I want to put my feet up. There also need to be buttons on my armrest that can end and mute calls, so I don’t have to tell you to do it. Also, can you have the holographic images improved? They're kind of fuzzy when my genetic advancement gets past ten."

"I can, but it will cost 5,000 credits to buy the blueprints for the tech."

I frowned at the price. I had limited resources. "How much is everything going to cost me currently?"

"10,000 credits and 15 RP. It will take about an hour to implement."

I blinked. "That's cheap?"

"This is cosmetic stuff that doesn't have a huge impact on the station's function. The price is appropriate."

"Pay it and give Diego access to the technology we can buy. I want to see what he can come up with."

"Do you want me to hold off buying the upgrades for the version you and The Librarian designed?"

A list of level 2 D2 upgrades appeared in front of me. The total cost was 8,500,000 credits.

The government guys weren't that good at thinking outside the box. The only good designs they had managed to put together in time were for a bigger version of the D2s, and even those hadn't been perfect.

The Librarian and I managed to take what they gave us and redesign it into something that was actually good. If I'm being honest, it was more The Librarian than me. The way that man's brain worked when optimizing something was a natural gift that I couldn't come close to.

The new design was called the D2-M. It was the most cost-effective long-range D2 design, period. It was extremely expensive credit-wise and wouldn't do anything more than strip the external weapons off a ship like a heavy destroyer or battleship, but it was perfect for what I wanted it to do.

"Patch me in to Diego and send him the design. I want to hear his thoughts."

There were about three seconds of silence, before Diego replied. "Is this a joke, Sir?"

He sounded outraged. "How bad is it?"

"Sir, your immortal soldiers will lose two-thirds of their combat effectiveness, and their ability to respawn more than once."

That was bad. "Send me your designs when you can, Diego."

"I'm done, Sir."

"You're done."

"I have a neural processor, Sir."

"It means he can upload information directly to and from his brain," Tee explained. "I've got one in my human body."

"Show me the level 1 and 2 specs for Diego's D2s, Tee."

Name: D2
Level: 1
Designation: Light Railgun
Damage: 60-180
Rate of fire: 1/30 sec
Range: 37.5 units
Accuracy: 37.5 units
Power Consumption: 25E

Name: D2
Level: 2
Designation: Light Railgun
Damage: 90-270
Rate of fire: 1/30 sec
Range: 52.5 units
Accuracy: 52.5 units
Power Consumption: 50E

It wasn't a bad design, even though the power consumption and rate of fire were still terrible. "Can you improve the rate of fire, Diego?"

"No, Sir. The original design prioritizes range, accuracy, and damage, so those can continue to grow. That's the best rate of fire you can achieve with human technology."

"What improvements will the immortal soldiers receive?"

"They'll shoot faster and further and be more accurate. There's a slight improvement to their armour and the sturdiness of their equipment, and they'll have more grenades and missiles for their launchers."

"Tee, how much is this going to cost me?"

"Forty-eight million credits for the level 2 upgrades and eighty resource points to build them."

Tee displayed the blueprints Diego wanted to buy. The price for his version was six times what I'd budgeted. "Tee, can Diego lie?"

"No, and he can't lie through omission either."

"Diego, how much will it cost to improve the R2s?"

"Improve or improve and modify, Sir?"

"Improve and modify."

"Would you prefer them to target missiles, fighters, or both, Sir?"

"Can you make them capable of taking out bombers?"

"No, Sir. The original R2 was designed to be extremely small, so it could fit on top of D2 and provide point defence support. This size limitation prohibits it from being powerful enough to penetrate a bomber's armour without making it ineffective as a point defence weapon."

"Make it capable of targeting missiles and fighters."

"Done, Sir."

"Throw the stats up and tell me the damage, Tee."

Name: R2
Level: 1
Designation: Point Defence Railgun
Damage: 5-10
Rate of fire: 120 rounds per second
Range: 4 units
Accuracy: 4 units

Name: R2
Level: 2

Designation: Point Defence Railgun
Damage: 10-15
Rate of fire: 120 rounds per second
Range: 5 units
Accuracy: 5 units

"For a level 2 version it will cost you twenty-seven million credits," Tee said. "For both, seventy-five million."

"I won't be able to afford to buy any of the weapons the other station masters' AI clones designed if I do this. Can I still afford to copy Alex's reactor?"

I wasn't the only one whose AI clone had designed a decent weapon. Only a few of the station masters from the military had what would be classified as a unique weapon or system, and only half had been confirmed to be good, but almost every gamer had.

Alex had the most powerful reactor. The Librarian had the best armour. Daniel had done something similar to me, but with a mid-weight railgun instead of a light-version. A guy from Australia called Kangaroo Billy had a missile called a Hammerhead that was pretty interesting and cheap, and a woman from Ecuador who went by Morningstar had a pop-up missile battery, which fired and reloaded significantly faster.

"You can afford to buy the level one version of Alex's reactor and the Hammerhead, but that will pretty much blow your entire budget."

I read through the list twice. "Buy Diego's R2 and D2, Alex's reactor, and the Hammerhead."

I pulled up my upgrade list for the D2s. I had a thousand class points that I could only spend on the D2s, and there was no point in waiting.

I unlocked all three different types of rounds and then bought the maximum upgrades for: damage, rate of fire, range, accuracy, energy efficiency, explosive, stealth, and manoeuvring rounds. Along with the double and triple barrel, taking away 25 class points from the personal pool I'd gained by reaching level 13, it left me with 66 class points.

I needed to invest enough so that I didn't have to think about station defence at all for as long as possible. There was too much to learn and not enough time to learn it all.

The list of upgrades looked a lot shorter now.

D2 Upgrades			
Description	*Effect*	*Available*	*Cost*
Internal Reactor	*+5E*	*0/10*	*10*
Point Defence	*R2*	*0/1*	*500*

I also only noticed the change to one of the upgrade options after I'd upgraded the others. "Diego, do you know what the upgrade options are for the D2s?"

"Yes, Sir."

That was handy. "Why has the amount of energy the internal reactor produces changed?"

"I changed the energy transfer system and included a micro-reactor blueprint purchase to increase the effectiveness of the internal reactor, Sir. This way they can become fully independent, like the R2s."

My AI clone had designed my weapon systems to behave like towers in a tower defence game. It had given me weapons that didn't need outside assistance. I needed to buy that guy a beer.

"I didn't know you could do that," I said.

"I'm sure I mentioned that upgrades would change for some weapons as you level," Tee replied.

"I thought you meant that they'd just appear on my list. You didn't say that I'd need to own specific blueprints."

"Most of the time, you don't. This is a hidden upgrade. They only appear when a design is optimized. You should buy Diego a beer."

Tee and I were on the same wavelength. "Definitely."

I pulled up the specs for my new upgraded D2 railgun.

Name: D2
Level: 2
Designation: Light Railgun
Damage: 180-540

Rate of fire: 1/15 sec
Range: 105 units
Accuracy: 105 units
Power Consumption: 25E

Ammunition:
Payloads:
-Explosive: Max
Casings:
-Stealth: Max
Augmentation:
-Manoeuvring: Max

The new D2 were nasty compared to what the Wargarg had to face, which meant I wouldn't have to deal with external attacks for a long time, unless I got creative. And I was going to get creative. Working with what I received each Cycle didn't interest me, so I needed to set a trap which encouraged the other factions to attack me. If I didn't, I'd have to worry about their faction leveling.

Each time their faction leveled their ring would move further away from the station. Right now, I could shoot them the moment they left the transit ring, but that would eventually change. So, I needed more levels, credits, and resource points.

"I'm going to go and level the station rats," I said, annoyed at having to do this again. "I don't know why he didn't just let them spawn at level 10. I mean, dying doesn't lose me credits anymore, so what's the point?"

"It uses up *time*," Tee said. "Time can make a massive difference at later stages. Your transit station could grow to be the size of the moon. You will be making *thousands* of weapons a Cycle. Doing what you're doing now is impossible at those stages, so giving you upgraded mobs, even if it was just the rats, would be a big advantage."

That was an annoyingly good argument. "At least now the station is level 2, so I get twice the resources and credits from the station rats."

"And because you're level 13, you'll only have to die eight times instead of one hundred. Do you want me to build ten basic D2s to equip the station?"

"Yeah, it will look strange if we have no defences. I'll finish this, and then we can do the expansion quest. This time we'll try to do it properly. And when that's over, we'll build the sensor scramblers we got from the Wargarg and hide all our alterations."

THE KNOWLEDGE about how to use a particle pistol and how to fight had added itself to my head the same way everything else had, which meant I had no clue how I knew these things. I just did. It felt like something I had always known, something that had been with me so long that I'd forgotten where it came from. It was as natural as walking or breathing.

So, dealing with the rats was frustrating.

I instinctively dodged without thinking about it. I had to actively force myself to stand still for them to hit me. Closing my eyes didn't help, like it had in the past. I could read the environment and dodge them using only sound and scent. Letting them hit me made me twitchy. Thankfully it didn't take nearly as long to level them as it did the first time.

Once that was over, Tee started the first expansion quest for me. The Kilocksin spawned again, and I went to meet them, ready to try to clear my quests for the special clearance reward.

I had my hands raised, showing I was unarmed as I walked around the corner into their corridor. All six eight-foot reptilians held their spears, with their muzzles pointed towards me as I made my way forward. Their eyes followed my steps in a way that told me they were well-trained.

Tee had promised they would behave like their race, and that Kilocksin didn't attack unarmed individuals unless provoked. Unarmed apparently included those with holstered weapons.

I was hoping he was right, because I was getting tired of seeing the inside of the regeneration chamber.

I watched the Kilocksin, searching for a clue that might help me clear this quest the way I should.

During the 2nd Cycle, three generals had successfully cleared one of these quests with a special clearance method. They all agreed that the quests were designed to teach us about our enemy and that the rewards were more than worth the effort. They had each received a cultural education package for their special clearance reward. It had turned them into experts on their enemy's culture overnight.

I wanted that.

So, I was going to take as much time as I needed to get it. Tee thought I was probably supposed to fight these guys without weapons, stating that not all special clearance quests would work for all paths. Tee figured I had a good chance of succeeding, even though I hadn't increased any of my paths.

After seeing how they moved, I agreed.

I could pull these guys apart easily. They were strong, but they were slow. Their reaction time was nowhere near a human's.

I smiled as I walked up to the humanoid Komodo dragons. "Good evening, gentleman, any of you interested in doing this old school?" I slowly drew my particle pistol, tossed it to the side, and raised my fists.

"The ape-man wants to fight, Tumpa" the biggest one said as he hit his chest. "This is good."

Tumpa tossed his spear to another and then removed his shield bracer. Next, he lost his armoured vest. He did the old head tilt to crack his neck and walked over.

He towered above me, by almost two feet, but my smile became genuine since he was being friendly. "Is there a ritual greeting we do before this sort of fight among your people?"

I now had all sorts of knowledge about unarmed combat to draw on, and almost every race on Earth had a polite way of starting a fight.

"You show respect. This is good. To signal you wish to fight a Kilocksin warrior, place your hand over your mouth and then move it toward your opponent, like this. It means the time for negotiating is over and you want violence. If your opponent agrees, they will do the same in return. We then stand at arm's length and lightly tap the back of our hand to our opponent's hand. When we make contact, the fight begins, and the victor proves who had the strongest conviction."

"Like this?" I tried to imitate what he had done.

"No. You covered part of your nose when you moved your hand away from your mouth. That is incorrect. It means you wish to fight me because I smell bad. It is an insult to your opponent. The force with which you cover your mouth is also an indicator of how deeply you feel that the negotiations have finished."

I absently scratched the back of my head. "How much can you communicate with this gesture?"

Tumpa paused as if thinking. "You can tell someone you only wish to fight to impress a potential mate. You can tell a friend that this is a matter of honour and that your feelings for them have not changed. You can tell another that you have lost someone dear and need to work out your frustration. It is as broad as any language."

If the quests were designed to teach us about our enemy, then this might be important. "Would you mind explaining all of this, so I do it properly?"

The Kilocksin seemed happy as he nodded.

After twelve hours, I told Tumpa I needed to get some rest and then promised him I'd come back after I'd slept. This one gesture had more to it than a Japanese tea ceremony, and this was the first time I felt tired while in the Game. I'd never lived long enough for a proper sleep cycle to kick in, and the system reset me every time I died, so until now, I hadn't needed it.

I briefly considered shooting myself in the head, so I didn't have to sleep, but that seemed like going down a dark path that didn't lead to a happy Game experience. Also, the first sleepless Cycle in-Game had really gotten to me. My dreams had been weird when I got out. I'd had this one where I was in a dance competition against vampire flamingos. The loser had to go on a date with Shrek, dressed as Fiona.

It was a weird date.

Not wanting to repeat that level of bizarreness, I made my way back to my command room. I smiled as soon as I walked through the blast doors.

The room was larger, and the entire centre of it was taken up by a massive hologram of the station and the surrounding space, which only enhanced how stupid the ball-shaped station looked. It was just plain dumb. Nowhere near as cool as the Borg sphere, even if they looked similar.

The rest of the room was fantastic.

Tee had put up the design and specs for the D2 on one of the wall screens, along with the layout for the dungeon, the dungeon mobs I had at my disposal, the station systems, and the resources I had left. Everything I needed had its own screen. And there was a proper viewscreen along the front wall. No more talking through holograms that were disproportionately sized. My command chair even looked the way I had imagined it.

I walked over and took a seat.

It was like my old gaming chair. The one they no longer produced but was way better than anything they had on the market now. It fit me perfectly.

"You did good, Tee. Thanks."

"Don't mention it. I just connected what you were describing to the station's main computer, and it did the work. It took me like two seconds."

"Sure, it did," I said, knowing he was lying. "I'm going to have a shower and then get some sleep. Is there any way to turn off that sleep option and have it work naturally?"

"I've just disabled it for you. Have a good sleep."

Nine glorious hours later, I made my way back to Tumpa and continued my lessons. It wasn't fun. It was barely interesting. And if this turned out to be a dead-end, I was going to have to punch a few rats to get rid of my frustration.

I smiled at Tumpa late the second day.

He had spent eighteen hours teaching me how to start a fight correctly. He was an AI-controlled NPC, but he was also so lifelike I felt grateful, so I challenged him to a fight. It was a fight of thanks. Making the gesture correctly was complicated with four fingers. The Kilocksin only had two and a thumb.

The fight of thanks wasn't really a fight. It was a slapping contest where you let your opponent slap you first. The fight could be called at any time, but it was considered polite to let the initiator hit you back. So usually, you got hit twice, and they were only hit once.

Usually.

Tumpa slapped me so hard I died.

I woke in my regeneration chamber, staring at a prompt.

Quest Completed
Expand Control I

Quest Rewards:

Defence Slots: 20
Path Points: 1
Tokens: 100

Secret Reward:

Kilocksin Liaison Tumpa
Kilocksin Cultural Education Package

"Oh, damn," Tee said. "That's a hell of a reward."

"Yeah, it's cool that I'm going to understand their culture," I said, climbing off the table to go get dressed.

"Not that. I mean Tumpa. I think they gave you him so he can keep everything fresh and teach their culture to Diego. It will make your immortal soldiers better fighters against the Kilocksin. Yep, he spawns in the barracks with Diego and the squad. He can even help you do station maintenance and level."

"What's his level cap?"

"Yours."

"Damn, that's kind of great, isn't it?"

"Yeah. I mean not right now, because you need the experience, but someday."

"Have you figured out how much it's going to cost me to build the station the way the designers suggested?"

"About 50,000 RP."

"The design is cosmetic?"

"Only because you can't afford the additional upgrades yet," Tee said. "It's also massive and leads on to a whole bunch of future possibilities. They did an amazing job on this."

That was true.

The government contacted the team who had designed Deep Space Nine, explaining what I needed. They'd been happy to participate since it was me who wanted the help, even working around the clock to get it done. But they'd quickly realized they were better at designing something that looked cool rather than something that functioned well, so they'd asked for the assistance of experts.

They'd been given naval ship architects.

Because of that and a few other reasons, my station wasn't going to look as much like Deep Space Nine as I would have liked. My weapons looked too much like World War II battleship cannons to fit that design style.

The new design had a lot of straight lines and sharp corners. Terraced layers where weapons could overlap. I'd still have the two rings and the arches, but instead of three arches, there were going to be five, and every inch of them and everything else would be covered in weapons.

The station design they finished creating looked like Deep Space Nine and a battleship had a baby, and it took more after the battleship. It was intimidating, but it didn't look futuristic.

"They did do a good job, Tee. Build more D2s and I'll level the rats. Then I'll take a crack at the second expansion quest and see if I can get it done before the end of the Cycle."

"You know the turrets can't move once they're placed, right?"

"I've got that option that says they can?"

"Yeah, but that costs resources."

I groaned. "Why did you let me build the other ones, then?"

"You said the station needed defences, so the other factions wouldn't ask questions."

I did. "How much will it cost to move them?"

"Only 10% of their total cost."

"That's a quarter of my daily resources. No way I'm paying that. They can wait. Load up the second quest. Let's do this."

It turned out that despite my polite enthusiasm, I couldn't complete the Horde's quest in a way that didn't involve killing them. Every time I went to talk to them, they told me to get out of their territory, and when I tried to keep talking, they killed me. So, by the time the 3rd Cycle finished, I still wasn't done.

10

NO GOOD DEED GOES UNPUNISHED

I was lying on the couch in my apartment, trying to hide from reporters. They'd found out where I lived and were hounding me for interviews. Yesterday, one of them put a ladder against the side of the building to reach my third-floor window. I'd had to save her when her ladder slipped, leaving her hanging from my windowsill, screaming for help. The moment I got her to safety, she'd tried to get me to give a comment, pretending like she hadn't almost died.

The reporters were a pain but better than the crazies. There were a bunch of religious nuts calling me Saint Morgan. They'd built a shrine below my bedroom window and were going through my trash to eat my leftovers.

I needed to find a new apartment.

Somewhere off the grid.

On the screen of my phone, Harriet shook her head. "As far as we can tell, each station has unique expansion quests with equally unique methods of success. This is irrelevant of whether or not they share factions. The cultural information package always appears. And the liaison has appeared several times for special clearance rewards. We think it has something to do with our species' compatibility, that the species' way of life might be compatible with our own. Let me pull up the file." she looked off-screen. "Here it is. There are eight stations connected to the Kilocksin sectors. Four of the station masters have launched expansion quests. All of them have received Kilocksin as their first hurdle. One of them cleared it by sharing a meal with them. He also received a liaison as his special clearance reward. He's the only one who has cleared it with the special clearance other than you."

"Has anyone cleared the Horde in a special way?"

"Let me check." She typed something into her computer. "Yes. They received a cultural information package."

"Is there a recurring theme for how the quests are cleared? Tee told me that there are social indicators, but I more or less fluked mine."

"There is currently a theory that the most repeated word is a clue for what your unique quest involves. It's going to be tested during the next Cycle."

My gut told me her answer might be right. "Give me a second. I need to ask Tee a question."

I added Tee to the call. Almost half a minute passed before he answered. His face appeared in the middle of a crowd.

"That's him!" shouted a man behind Tee.

"I'm looking at his holiness," shrieked a woman.

"Yes, that's Saint Morgan," Tee said, grinning at me. "Honestly, he's even holier than they say. He might be the second coming. I remember watching him pick up what I assumed was a dead bird, but then it flew away. At the time, I thought I must have been wrong, but who knows, maybe it really was a dead bird, and he healed it. I mean, our pets can't die or get sick anymore."

Tee cut the call.

"Ah, what's he doing?" Harriet asked concerned.

"I have absolutely no idea. And he just hung up on me, so I'll have to ask him my question later. Let's move on to something else."

"The last thing I have to mention is the design team wants to talk to you about your station. As they told you, they recreated the designs they'd already given you in the Game and used the AIs there to tweak it. They found information that tells them their current design is extremely flawed. They want me to schedule a call with them to talk about it."

That was more concerning than what Tee was up to. "How soon can you schedule it?"

"Give me two hours."

"I'll be waiting."

Harriet hung up, and I turned on the TV to kill time.

Every second channel had something to do with me. If they weren't sharing heart-warming stories on the people who were healed days from death's door, they were talking about how many serial killers I'd been friends with over the years, which was eight. They were also debating what it meant for a new country to appear or whether or not my ownership of Mars should be recognized.

Earlier, I'd watched a reporter interview a rabbi who'd escaped a concentration camp and spent the late stages of World War II in an extremely active civilian resistance unit. They weren't interviewing him because I'd healed his terminal cancer or given him back his youth. They'd been interviewing him because he had one of the highest kill counts of anyone who survived the cull and wanted to know why he had lived when others died.

Fifteen minutes later, I still hadn't found anything to watch, but Tee unlocked my front door and walked in with Buster, giving me the distraction I needed. Tee was wearing designer clothing, sunglasses, shoes, and jewellery that cost more than some sports cars. His fashion sense had dramatically improved, but so had the amount he was spending. My credit card bill had already surpassed my old annual income and was growing by the day. I also had bills from all sorts of weird places. I wasn't sure if Tee was messing with me or if he'd taken up ballet and pottery.

Buster let out a happy, "Woof," and dashed over to lick my face.

I patted him enthusiastically to show him I was happy to see him too. It sucked that I couldn't walk him. He had so much energy now that I wanted to take him to the park and watch him run around. I hadn't realized how much I'd missed it until he could do it again. But I couldn't leave the apartment building without being mobbed.

I glared at Tee while I patted Buster. "What the hell were you doing with the crazies?"

He gave a small chuckle as he took off his sunglasses to clean away non-existent dirt. "You thought it was funny to give me a micropenis. I thought it was funny to tell a bunch of religious fruitcakes that you're the second coming. I think I can get them to build a church."

"I don't want a church!"

Tee smirked. "How will you be the second coming without a church?"

"They crucified Jesus. I don't want to end up like that."

"I'm sure they won't do that to-" Tee stopped to think about what he was saying. "You should probably buy a security bot or personal shield. Like today. Those guys are nuts. There's a lady with a ball of your hair."

"I've already ordered a personal shield."

Tee relaxed. "Then there is nothing to worry about. What did you call me for, by the way?"

"What word did Tumpa say to me the most?"

"Good."

"How is that word related to my quest?"

"I don't know. Why are you asking such a weird question?"

"The government has an idea that the most repeated word said during the expansion quests is a clue to how to solve the quest's special clearance."

Tee put Buster's leash on the hook, and then went over to the window and waved at the crowd, causing them to cheer. He walked over to the couch and pushed my legs off to take a seat on the other end.

"Okay, that's more interesting. Kilocksin don't differentiate between the words 'good' and 'respect'. They use them interchangeably. You cleared the quest by showing him respect and being good, so they might be on to something. The word the Horde repeated the most was territory, and every time you didn't respect it, they killed you. The quest clearance might be as simple as you talking to them from outside their territory."

I leaned against the armrest trying to get comfortable again. "How the hell am I going to work out where their territory is?"

"Easy. It's wherever they don't kill you for being in it."

That was a reasonable assumption. "Okay, what do you know about Clack Breeders?"

"They don't talk. Not in any way you can understand, so the Game won't translate for you. And you know it's stupid to allow it to lay eggs, which is exactly what will happen if you try to communicate."

Yeah, that did sound stupid. Who would want a bunch of- "Wait, can't I farm them for experience?" I thought about that for a second longer. "Wait, I think I'm supposed to farm it for the experience."

"What?"

"Think about it. It lays eggs. The eggs hatch. I kill what comes out and get experience. The moderators got all huffy over me taking advantage of the Wargarg's infinite regeneration that they sure as hell wouldn't put it in as a normal function. I think the special clearance for that quest is for me to farm its babies for experience without harming it. At some point, the quest will end."

"The question then, is when is it the right time to start killing them?"

"I'm guessing there will be a sign."

IT TURNED out the sign was when they attacked the station's systems. The government guys were definitely on to something with the most common word thing. I'd stopped near the Horde and shouted at them to get their attention. They'd killed me, so I'd gone a little further away and tried again, doing it further and further away until they finally hadn't killed me.

I'd then asked them what they wanted, and they'd just told me to get as far away from their territory as I could. Clearing their quest had been as easy as walking to the furthest point on the station from their spawn point.

Even though I had cleared the second expansion quest, I'd stopped thinking about expanding the station. The design team and I had talked for more than a day. They'd found out that the station they designed for me was fundamentally flawed. My view of the station was also flawed. Actually, up until their discovery, everyone's views of stations were flawed.

The stations weren't towers.

Well, they were like towers at the early stages, where everything seemed to be built almost instantly. But that was only because everything was so close. When a station got larger, it had more in common with an RTS than a tower defence game, because the distance between structures mattered for resource management. If I centralized ammunition storage and my weapons ran out in the middle of a battle, the outer guns might take five minutes to receive a reload. Also, systems like my sensor array became less effective the bigger the structure was, so they needed to be scaled up or upgraded. The whole project had turned into a nightmare, and we had to rethink everything.

So, expansion was currently out of the question, at least for a couple of weeks. They needed to think everything through properly. There was currently a design team of over two hundred working on not just my station but every station our faction had. They were trying to make a template that we could all build from to customize to our needs.

That meant I couldn't wait to build the D2. I just had to suck up the extra resource cost because the experience loss was too much to accept.

I tried to ignore how many resource points I was wasting, as I put my back against the corridor wall and prepared myself to turn the corner. The Clack breeder had been laying eggs that grew into brood warriors, and they were currently tearing their way through the wall outside the main reactor. Their exoskeleton was harder than the laminated titanium walls, making it possible for their claws to peel away layers.

The squad was preparing to hit them from the other end of the corridors. They were going to draw away most of them, so I could take out the stragglers.

I dropped my voice to a whisper. "Tee, where are the other Clack heading?"

"They're attacking your D2s. You've already got three offline. You need to deal with these quickly and move on to the others."

"Okay, keep me posted."

The familiar whine of the squad's automatic weapons filled my corridor as they let loose on the Clack. Their particle rifles looked like oversized assault rifles but were much lighter. The *voom voom* whine of their weapons lasted for about five seconds and then cut off.

The Clack screeched.

They sounded injured or pissed off. I listened as they started to chase the squad, and then I turned the corner, raising my particle pistol.

Clack brood warriors stood about ten feet tall. They were insects shaped like centaurs, with four legs and a humanoid-shaped upper half. Their head housed a set of large mandibles, a circular, tooth-filled mouth, and four eyes that looked like they belonged to flies. Their blue-grey exoskeleton covered most of their body, with only a few unprotected spots that could be considered weak points. None of their unprotected areas were instant kill spots. Clack were basically walking death machines.

The predators on their planets had to be nightmares for their species to evolve this way.

I saw a dozen injured on the ground. They were barely moving. Eight were racing off towards the other end of the corridor, trying to catch up to the squad. Two were tending to the injured. I shot six times, emptying the particle pistol. Every shot was perfect. The two tending to the others fell to the ground, their front knee joints gone. Each one had another shot to the throat. Tee said there was an artery there, so they would bleed out in about ten minutes.

That's how tough they were.

My particle pistol wasn't good enough to take them out the easy way at its current level, so I had to do it in steps. My next six shots went into the injured, hastening their demise.

A grenade exploded in the other corridor. The squad must have been having trouble.

I stood back and waited for my particle pistol to recharge. Several experts in the military thought that the squad was an example of the perfect unit of soldiers, and that if we copied them, we'd end up with the ideal dungeon mob and infantry unit. After learning how to fight, I believed they were right.

The four-man team complemented each other perfectly. Having them had changed my immortal soldiers so that they shared the same equipment loadout. The immortal soldiers were more specialised now. It would be even more effective if I could design other dungeon mobs to work with them, but I was waiting for someone else to take the plunge before I committed. The weapon systems I'd have to design to make another dungeon mob as good as my immortal soldiers were expensive, and I didn't want to be wrong.

When my particle pistol finished reloading, I put another shot in the injured Clack and waited for it to recharge again. The squad showed up before it was ready to fire. The moment they came around the corner, I turned and started heading for the next location. They could finish the Clack off faster than I could.

"The reactor's cleared," Tee said when I was halfway to the D2s that were under attack. "You need to get to the sensor array."

"What happened to the D2s?"

"They're still being attacked, but the sensor array is more important."

I changed directions. "I'm on it."

Eight hours later, I was finally proven right. Farming the endless waves was the correct way to clear the quest. By that time, the Clack had destroyed half the systems on the station.

Quest Completed ***Expand Control III*** ***Quest Rewards:*** *Defence Slots: 80* *Path Points: 1*

Tokens: 900
Special Clearance Reward:
Clack Cultural Education Package.

"Just three more to go and you get full control of the station again," Tee said cheerfully as I trudged back to the command room. "You want me to fire up the next quest?"

I turned a corner into a debris-filled corridor where they'd destroyed one of the D2s. Chunks of metal lay everywhere, slowly being dissolved by nanobots to reform the wall and internal systems.

"No. I'm going to get some sleep," I said. "Two back-to-back expansion quests are enough for one day. I need a break. Also, I need to know if this sort of damage was normal. You told me that better weapon systems would spawn mobs that could damage the station, but you never mentioned they could outright cripple it."

"Does damaged mean something else to you? Like if your car's engine is damaged, do you think you should be driving it?"

I stepped into the elevator. The door closed and then opened two seconds later, dropping me off near the command room. "I thought there would be a few minor issues, but that was complete chaos. How many weapons do we have online?"

"Six. And I believe the difficulty was higher because the reward was greater. You would have gained a bunch of levels from this quest, before you got moderated. It probably would have taken you a couple of days, too. I mean, an experienced station master would have walked through that, but you did well enough."

I passed through the blast doors into my command room. "Gosh, you make me feel all giddy inside with your backhanded compliments."

"It's a gift."

I slumped into my command chair. "We need to research the other species before I take on the next quest. I don't want to screw this up. I need more advantages."

"You're the station master of the most advanced station in your faction; you need to relax."

"How am I doing on a general scale?"

"You're in the top 5% for this early."

"That's bad," I said. "Casuals play at this level. The real contenders are all in the top *1%*. What do I have to do to reach that level?"

"Spend about 100,000 years doing this," Tee said. "Or create another set of circumstances similar to your first that doesn't get removed."

"I've got an idea on how to do that."

"I'm listening."

"You know The Librarian's idea for an unarmed combat dungeon challenge to attract the Kilocksin?"

"Yeah, what about it?"

"Well, I think I've worked out how to make it viable. I know what to do to attract them to the dungeon."

A dungeon challenge was something you added to the entrance of your dungeon. There was no downside for challengers who accepted the challenge, only an upside. The challenge had to be filled with mobs from my dungeon, and everyone they defeated in the challenge meant one less they would have to face in the dungeon. If the challengers died during the challenge, they would immediately respawn at the entrance to the dungeon and wait for their companions to join them.

"What sort of challenge are you considering?"

"A six-room dojo. One of them will have to fight through all six opponents for them to get a chance at winning the big prize, a Kilocksin heavy shield bracer and laser spear. How much do you think the blueprints will cost?"

"I'd guess around 250,000 credits, but you would first have to get your hands on one and break it down to gain access to the blueprint. They won't go for it, even if you do. It's a standard-issue military shield bracer. It's not that interesting."

I put my feet up, to get a little more comfortable. "That's where you're wrong. I've got a whole bunch of Kilocksin cultural knowledge bouncing around in my head, and the shield bracer and laser spears hold a prominent place in it. They're part of their culture and history."

"They're not great weapons."

"But they are dependable. No matter what other equipment their warriors have and fight with, they always carry their shield bracer and laser spear. A warrior is considered naked without them. If everything else is gone, a Kilocksin will fall back to these."

"So what?"

"So, they're a status symbol as much as they're weapons. There are only three types of people given heavy shield bracers in their society: the shield guardians, their low-ranked officers, and prominent members of a clan. There is also only one other way to acquire one. And that's through combat. I want to make an optional six-room dojo inside the dungeon for them to challenge. The reward will be a shield bracer and laser spear, but there will be a 1% chance of gaining a heavy shield bracer instead of a regular one."

"Why not just offer them the heavy shield bracer?"

"Because in their society, they have to earn it. Giving it to them will make it worthless. Making them fight for it time and again will give them a story that they can take back to their clans to be proud of. It's something that will be accepted. We'll have to stamp them with our faction's mark, but it should work."

"Who would fall for that?"

I grinned. "Teenagers, I'm going to farm their noobs."

"Have you thought this through?"

"Completely, The Librarian is right. The Kilocksin can be encouraged to raid the dungeon. There are trillions of them in their local sector. All I need to do is convince a fraction of a percent that their time is best spent in our dungeon."

"You still need to level."

"I know. Start filling the defence slots with D2s. I'll go level the rats and kill them after I've gotten some sleep. Unless anything attacks, I feel like it's going to be boring around here until I complete the starter quest."

LIFE WAS as dull as I predicted. Dad was right. Between battles, this was more like a career than a game. Completing the last three expansion quests hadn't been difficult. It had taken a fair bit of thinking and study, but it wasn't difficult.

For the Octorin quest, I had to send their leader components to build a communication drone. They were too nervous and xenophobic to deal with other species directly. Once they had the drone, we began to trade. Eventually, they built a small swarm of combat drones and tried to kill me. I took care of the drones and then killed their leader without harming the others. Then I traded with the new leader, who also tried to kill me. I did this four times, until a leader started building maintenance drones instead of combat drones.

I cleared the quest, gaining the cultural knowledge package, and a maintenance drone fabricator system blueprint for my station.

The Uon quest was the simplest: I had to show up and kill one, go away, and then come back and kill another. The quest ended when they realised that staying on my station wasn't worth the trouble. The survivors made their way to an airlock and left.

For the Wargarg, I had to fight their leader for dominance and make him yield. That took a surprising amount of time. The little guy wouldn't give up even when I beat him to a pulp. I had to try dozens of different methods, letting him heal each time, before I finally worked out that I had to pin him, without injuring him, to make him yield.

It made me realise dominance and violence were entirely unrelated in their culture.

So, near the end of the 6th Cycle, I finally completed my starter quest and gained full access to my station.

Quest Completed
Control the Station

Quest Rewards:

Complete control of your station and its systems:
Path Points: 1
Tokens: 10,000

Special Clearance Reward:

Six Faction Station Master Knowledge package.

As the notification appeared, I released the Wargarg leader and stood up. A moment later, he and the other Wargarg crumbled to dust and were quickly absorbed by the station.

This special clearance reward was different to the others. There was no cultural package. I didn't know what six faction station master knowledge was, but I knew it was going to be good. I dismissed the quest clearance notification, and a prompt appeared.

You may now name your station.

"I name this station, 'The Crucible'."

11

DAYS GO BY

When the President offers you an award, saying you're too busy to accept it apparently isn't okay. I tried.

The government flew my family out to DC for the award ceremony. They told Tee a time and place for where they would pick him up, but the vehicle never showed. He hired a private jet with my credit card, and when we had dinner with the President the night before the award ceremony, Tee called her by her first name.

It was as awkward as it was funny.

They held the ceremony where they did the inauguration. I expected a reasonably sized turnout, but seventeen million people showed up, making it the largest crowd in human history. People didn't just come from out of state; they came from other countries and by the millions.

Leaders from all around the world, who no one recognized because almost all of them were new, came to offer me their nation's highest honours. I was knighted, duke-ified, showered in medals, and made an honorary citizen of basically every nation on the planet. I was given so many awards I had no clue what I received by the end of it.

The experience was surreal and overwhelming.

And I could live a long happy life if I never repeated it.

The only good experience to come from going to DC was that that was where the station design team was located, so I got to talk to them in person. My new station master knowledge from gaining special clearance for all the expansion quests had opened my eyes, and we needed to talk.

"Look, you're not listening to me," I said, glancing around the meeting room at the design team leaders. "A template design for transit stations doesn't work. Stations have to be tailored to the factions around them. If those factions change, then the station has to change with them. It's a constantly shifting battlefield that you have to keep adapting to, so don't think about long-term effectiveness. Think about what will work now and will continue to work six months from now."

The twelve heads of the project looked at me with confusion and awe. In their defence, I'd gone from a clueless station master to the most informed station master on the planet in the space of a day. Everyone who could still go for the full special clearance completion was now going for it.

They needed to.

The advantage it gave us was too great to pass up.

It was a complete understanding of what transit stations were, the systems onboard, how they operated, and how they could change, with a complex understanding of how to deal with the factions around your station. With the new knowledge, I finally understood how badly we were doing.

We were so far behind that it wasn't funny.

Tee was right: Our local systems should have been feeding our stations as much resources and credits as they possibly could, but only a few stations had received a single shipment. By now, every transit station should have a quarter of the credits I did and a tenth of the resources. It was a disaster.

Harriet came to their rescue when she realised no one was going to reply. "How are they supposed to help the station masters design their stations, then?"

The new knowledge I'd gained from the quest answered her

question perfectly. "Efficiency. You were right that the bigger stations get, the more delay time there is."

I grabbed someone's briefing notes, flipped them over to the blank side, and drew a three-by-three square grid.

"Imagine, the centre box is the station, and these other eight squares around it comprise the area that the station expands into. First, we need to know whether the central station can adequately supply this expanded area. If it can, then there is nothing to worry about."

I added another sixteen boxes around the outside, making a five-by-five grid.

"Now, when the station expands again, we need to know if the station can *still* supply all these new sections. If it can, but there is a time delay, we need to know if it's more efficient to leave this area functioning at 80% or build out systems to support it."

I added another 24 boxes around the outside, making it a seven-by-seven grid.

"It might be that at this stage, the loss of efficiency is too much to accept, and it becomes more cost-effective to expand systems to help. But we don't know yet. That's what we need to find out."

"We can't do that," said Randle, the head designer. "That's mathematicians' work."

"Then get mathematicians. Every station is going to have different efficiency problems. Those problems come first. Once we know when the problems will occur and where, you can design a station that will work for each of us, but until we know where these problems will occur, we're going to make no ground."

"Sir, it is incredibly time-consuming to do it this way. A template is simpler."

"A template is simpler, but a template is also how we'll lose. Everyone has got it in their heads that we're all fighting on similar battlefields against different enemies. But the enemies aren't just the enemy; they're the battlefield. Because our enemies are different, our battlefields are different."

Randle tilted his head to the side. "That doesn't make any sense."

I tried not to roll my eyes; them being clueless wasn't their fault.

“Okay, let me try to explain it another way. You’re trying to build a military vehicle. But this vehicle might be going to war against ground troops, tanks, bombers, fighters, or naval vessels. Depending on which one of those threats you’re fighting, you should design your vehicle differently.”

“I think I understand. But the thing is, we can design a vehicle to fight *all* those opponents.”

“You can, but it’s not efficient. And that lack of efficiency is what will make us lose. If you’re putting in something to counter a submarine that doesn’t exist, you’re removing something that could take out a bomber that does exist. These factions have been playing this game for *millions* of years. We’re *not* going to win. But we can last long enough to snatch all the opportunities and Tokens that we can from our sectors. In a few centuries, we can come back and actually have a chance, but right now, our only chance is to take everything that’s not nailed down and survive long enough to do it.”

Randle gave me what I’m sure he thought was a reassuring smile. “You don’t need to worry about that, Sir. We’ve got this well in hand. The army has organized and reformed. Our admirals are building our fleet, and our people are training to learn how to operate them. We’re doing better than you think.”

They were deluded.

In their defence, they didn’t have any of the knowledge I did. “Answer these questions for me, please. Is my station the most advanced humanity has?”

“Yes.”

“Is it the most advanced by a long shot?”

“Well, yes.”

“My AI tells me I am in the top 5% percent for station combat power when currently compared to all the other factions. There are over one hundred million stations in the Game. That means five million stations are in a better position than I am right now, and I am the best humanity has to offer, by a long shot. Most of our stations are in the bottom 1%. The races that know how to utilise stations correctly are all eyeing them up to take over because we’re noobs, and it will be easy. I don't care if what I'm suggesting is time-consuming. Pick the sectors with the best stations and resources and only work on those stations. We're going to lose sectors within the first year, so those stations are our best chance of keeping something."

Randle swallowed. "You can't be serious. You also don't have the authority to make us do that."

"I am serious. The knowledge I got from clearing all my quests says I've got a 50% chance of losing my station this year and an 80% chance of losing it next year if nothing changes."

The heads of the design teams glanced at each other nervously.

Randle looked ill. "I can't implement what you suggested without approval from the Joint Chiefs, but I can do it for your station if you like, Sir. I've been ordered to assist you in any way my team or I am capable."

"Then do it."

I WAS STAYING in a hotel because the media and my new cult couldn't be trusted. They'd broken into my apartment nine times while I was away, even with the cops watching the place. The hotel didn't allow pets, but they waived that rule when they realized who I was. It had cost me a couple of selfies, but that was a small price to pay to have Buster with me.

I'd never wanted to be famous. Being mobbed when you were going to the store to get milk sucked. I was considering getting reconstructive surgery. The attention was so aggressive that my Dad and brothers had to move out, too. They were in the neighbouring rooms. We had the whole top floor of the hotel.

"I've successfully cleared my fifth quest," The Librarian said through my phone. "I've got a good feeling about this next one. The Folmio are a faction of builders. They don't commit violence of any sort. They're allied with several other factions to work as engineers, so this will be less violent than the last."

The Librarian had gone from being old and frail to a handsome young man in his prime with grey hair. Somehow, he still managed to look like he was ready to shush you at any second, though. And that much tweed on a young man looked weird, but he refused to change his style. At least without his glasses, his eyes looked normal, instead of oversized.

Most of the people who had received rejuvenation treatment hadn't dyed their hair. The grey was the only way to tell them apart from everyone else, and they wanted to stand out. They didn't want to be mistaken for someone a third their age or younger. That didn't mean, they weren't embracing their youth.

Retirement homes had turned into frat houses and there was a huge increase in the workforce. The pharmaceutical industry had died over night and nine out of ten hospitals had closed up shop, because there was no one to treat without obesity, heart disease, cancer, ageing, diabetes, autoimmune disorders, genetic disorders, or any of the other issues that paid their bills.

No one was complaining that they were gone.

"Daniel, how are your quests going?" Alex asked sweetly.

After Tee's presentation, she'd asked him how he could afford his ridiculous sequined suit, and he'd told her I was rich. She tried flirting with me after that. The Librarian had taken me aside and pointed out she was only interested because I was rich and famous.

The change in her personality was really messed up, and I was so aware of how everyone moved and acted that I couldn't help but see the predatory intent behind her actions. When flirting with me hadn't worked, she'd started treating Daniel like a kid brother who needed help with everything. Trying to get to me through him, since I liked the kid way more than I did her.

Daniel hated it.

He was smart enough to see what she was doing.

"I'm done," he said, sticking his tongue out at her.

Mrs Yang had caught him swearing at Alex last week. Since he wasn't paraplegic anymore, he'd received an earful about talking respectfully to adults. I'd had to listen and pretend like I agreed with her, but Alex was really pushing the kid's buttons.

"You're done?" Alex asked, surprised.

He nodded. "I screwed up the third quest, so I decided to throw in the towel and went full murderhobo on their asses. I think I'm going to buy the blueprints for Morgan's R2D2 and spam them. Their range isn't as good as my ones, but their dungeon mobs are a lot better."

"Daniel, we talked about this," Alex said. "You know you shouldn't have done that."

"Actually, he should have," I said, coming to his defence.

Alex scowled at me.

It was a pretty scowl. Everything she did was pretty. I hadn't dated in a while, and the solitary confinement was leaving me with a little too much energy. She was getting hotter every time I saw her. I had this weird hate-attraction thing going on, and I didn't like it. It wasn't healthy.

"Don't encourage him," she said.

"I will when he makes the right decision. He's good at tower defence games, and smart, but he's still twelve. Cultural information isn't helpful if he doesn't know how to implement it, and none of his factions will give him a liaison. Without the ability to get the station master education package, trying to clear his quests for the additional rewards is a waste of time. He made the right choice."

"Did you think beyond the Game, Morgan? Having cultural knowledge of a species has real-world applications. He could get all sorts of work with that knowledge."

I paused. She had a point. "Okay, you're right. I didn't think beyond the Game, but that doesn't change anything. He needed control of his station. Now that he has it, he's built a communication array, and Tee has given him information on his neighbours."

"Yeah, one of them is preparing to attack me," Daniel said. "They're going to be in for a big surprise when they meet my R2D2s."

"You're about to be attacked," Alex said, concerned.

Daniel nodded. "Not this Cycle, but the one after. The government already agreed to divert resources to my station."

"That's not good. Harriet said that the first estimate for an attack on your station was the 18th Cycle. Mine's 21st."

I ran my hand through my hair and blew out a frustrated breath. “I keep telling you, they don’t have a clue what they are talking about. They’re following their AI’s information too much. They aren’t thinking like gamers —which is good in most cases, but bad in this one. We’re noobs, Alex. What do you do to noobs?”

Alex frowned, but she was thinking. Despite everything bad I had to say about her, she was a freaking genius. When she put her mind to something, her ability to strategize and reason out a problem was even greater than my own.

“You destroy them early because they’re a waste of your time,” she said. “And you take risks you wouldn’t normally take.”

“Or you toy with them,” I said. “Don’t forget, the Wargarg set up their attack so it could feed my station resources if they failed, allowing them to take over a more powerful station if their assault on my dungeon succeeded. There are going to be all kinds of strategies at play here that we’ve never encountered. That’s what makes it so much fun.”

“You and I have different definitions of fun.”

“Actually, I think we have the same definition since we are ranked number 1 and 2 in most of the same games. If our personalities matched even a little, I’d ask you out.”

She rolled her eyes, trying to appear indifferent. “Do you honestly think you’d have a chance?”

“I’m like the most famous and loved person on the planet. I’m beating Tom Hanks and Grumpy Cat. I’ve got a chance.”

She smirked, thinking I was flirting instead of being honest. “You’re not my type.”

“And you’re not mine, except for the whole being super-hot. But that doesn’t mean what it used to. That’s not a dig at you, by the way. I just mean anyone can change their face and body if they’ve got the Tokens, so being super-hot is more common. My cousin managed to clear a weird quest that gave him 10,000 Tokens. He went from looking like a potato to Brad Pitt in the space of a day.”

Alex sighed. “I get that. Natalia hasn’t had a single modelling job since this all happened. No one is hiring models when you can hire an

AI to make a lifelike image for a couple of Tokens. All the major brands are now switching to copyrighted fake models. I've had to sell my Tokens through the exchange just to make rent."

That comment more or less confirmed that she'd been extorting her sister for money. Tee and I had done a little digging into Alex after she'd started flirting with me. Her sister was famous enough to have been interviewed dozens of times. Whenever they brought up Alex, her identical twin, and asked her why she wasn't in fashion, there was a moment when you saw her true feelings. Natalia didn't like Alex.

And if you didn't like someone you were giving money to, then they were probably screwing you over. Our sector was only as strong as its weakest link; and despite her talent, my gut said Alex was our weak link.

"I feel like we are getting off-topic," The Librarian said. "But it is good to know that the communication array is as vital as we thought. And it is troubling to know that we need to prepare for attack sooner than anticipated. My station is not where it needs to be to weather this storm."

"WHACHA," Simon shouted.

My hand snapped out, deflecting the karate chop aimed for my neck. I instinctively grabbed Simon's wrist and flipped him. He went over my shoulder and slammed into the thick-carpeted floor. I only just managed to stop myself from shattering his arm and delivering a blow that would have killed him instantly.

"Will you stop doing that!" I shouted at him, terrified for his safety. "I nearly killed you."

Simon groaned, cradling his arm to his chest.

Peter chuckled from the other side of the suites living room. "He's trying to win back his number two spot. I said I'd give it back if he could hit you when you weren't paying attention."

I glared at him. "You have no idea how dangerous that is. I can literally kick both of your asses with one hand tied behind my back while blindfolded."

Peter snorted. "I call bullshit."

"It's not bullshit! He was in actual danger."

"You willing to bet on it?"

That caught my attention, and I had to fight the urge to grin. I was concerned for Simon, but family love wasn't as strong as sibling rivalry. "What are we betting?"

Simon groaned again.

Peter laughed. "Your choice."

I smiled. "If I win, I get the number one spot, and you have two have to answer to Bitch Peter and Bitch Simon. If I lose, I take the fourth spot after Buster and have to answer to Bitch Morgan."

"For a month."

"A year."

Peter grinned. "Deal. Simon, get up. We've got a butt whooping to deliver."

Fifteen minutes later, Dad came back from walking Buster. He looked around the trashed hotel room at the mess we'd made. I probably should have stipulated they weren't allowed to use weapons. It didn't change anything, of course. It just made a much bigger mess and resulted in a lot of destroyed furniture.

I gave Bitch Peter another ice pack.

"It hurts to breathe," he said, looking at Dad for sympathy. "It's not supposed to hurt to breathe. I'm sure he broke something."

"It's just bruising," I reassured him.

"Lots and lots of bruising," Bitch Simon moaned.

Dad shook his head as he took Buster off his lead. "Your mother would have all our hides if she knew you were wrestling inside."

Being the kind, considerate soul he is, Buster came over and licked my brothers mercilessly. When he realized they couldn't move, his affection became more aggressive. He loved licking people's faces.

They both groaned.

THE DESIGN TEAM hadn't messed around. They'd taken everything I'd said onboard, and if they hadn't done it for everyone, they had at least done it for me. That still took them several weeks, though. The new design for my station was significantly bigger than the old version.

To start with, the new inner ring was the size of the original design for the outer ring. And the two rings around the central station were much wider and taller. The inner ring had space for a massive hangar bay and ammunition depos. The five arches above and below the outer ring were much bigger at the base, because the outer ring would eventually need space for additional systems. The central station could only supply the first ring, but that was enough for now.

The new design had replaced the hologram of the station, in my command room, as we went over the details.

I leaned back into my command chair. "How much is this going to cost me, Tee?"

"That depends. Are you planning on building this gigantic monstrosity all at once or in stages?"

"Just tell me."

"The total cost for everything is 8,555,489 RP, but you can build the skeleton of the inner ring for 550,000 RP."

"What do you mean by 'the skeleton of the inner ring'?"

"The R9 heavy railguns require a lot of structural reinforcement. I've stripped away that reinforcement, because you don't have the resources, but you can safely build your R2D2's on the inner ring."

The size of the station I could build was simply massive, and the rest of humanity was a long way away from being able to do this. Even if I could only build R2D2s on the inner ring, that would still make my station unstoppable. The inner ring could hold twenty-five thousand of them.

I pulled up the station's current information.

Station Name: The Crucible
Level: 2
Armor: 60
Energy Shield: 17,000/17,000

Damaged Systems: 0%
Resource Points: 869,885
Credits: 3,087,350

Station Systems:
-L1 Phoenix Reactor: 6400E
-Secondary Phoenix Reactor: 6400E
-L1 Sensor Array
-L1 Communication Array
-L1 Reprocessing Facility
-L1 Weapons Fabricator
-L1 Structural Fabricator
-L2 Missile Fabricator
-L2 Hangar Bay

Defence Slot: 100/10,000 (Current Structure Max)
-L2 D2: 50

Station Development Path: 17
External Weapons:
-L2 R2: 17
-L2 D2: 5
-L2 Missile Battery: 1
—Hammerheads: 17
—Predator: 5
-R9: 1
Internal Weapons:
-Turret: 17
Dungeon Weapons:
-Turret: 3

It turned out the energy shield wasn't as helpful as I thought it would be. Unlike armour, it did behave like health, and any fleet would take it out with their first volley. Its primary purpose was to save me from a surprise attack, but even with Alex's phoenix reactor, it would be tough to restore it quickly.

"Will the Wargarg sensor scrambler cover the outer ring, Tee?"

"No. You'll need to level it significantly to do that. Thankfully, your new reactor produces enough energy to expand the effects to the edge of the first ring."

"Build the sensor scrambler and then 450 D2s on the station. Once that's done, we'll build the inner ring and another 2500 D2s. The inner ring can hold 25,000 of them, so I want them spread out evenly. It's time to start power leveling. I need to be level 30 for when the Kilocksin challenge my station in a few Cycles."

"I'm going to assume that you want me to build this in stages. Otherwise, you could find the station overrun by the quest mobs. I shouldn't have to remind you that the internal turrets weren't strong enough to take out those weird brain creatures the communication array's build quest spawned."

I paused.

In my excitement, I may have forgotten that part. The brains hadn't been all that powerful, but they had the annoying ability to control the mobs in their general area and debuff everything that tried to attack them. I was dizzy for the entire fight.

The system build quests were definitely more challenging than the weapon build quests. It was partly because their effect was more significant, but it was also to make up for the fact that they didn't spawn mobs, only augment the ones you already had.

Ever since I'd made the communications array, the station rats had been working in groups. They called out to each other constantly, too. It made me wonder what other changes they would go through.

"Of course, we are doing it in waves," I said. "I'd have to be an idiot to do it all at once."

"Good, activating the sensor scrambler array build quest."

THE SENSOR SCRAMBLER array build quest turned out to be a problem. It spawned some sort of Predator-like mob. It was an invisible natural hunter that was heavy on stealth and close-quarter combat. It was also huge.

"It took out the squad," Tee shouted in a panic. "They're in pieces. But they manage to tag it. Its cloaking system is gone. My turrets are also gone. But it's coming towards you."

An eleven-foot lion man charged around the corner at the other end of the corridor. He was bleeding from his side and carrying a pair of scimitars.

I shot him in the eye. The eyeball burst, but the shot didn't kill him. He roared with pain-fuelled fury, so I shot the other eye. That didn't kill him either, but he was blind. That didn't slow him down, though. He kept running towards me.

I unloaded my particle pistol, trying to drill a hole through his skull. He raised his arm, taking the shots on the forearm. Minor flesh wounds appeared along the muscle.

I missed being a higher level. My particle pistol had been awesome. It would have cut straight through him.

I was out of shots for the next minute, so I holstered the pistol and charged. The lion man had a dagger on his waist that I could use to take him out.

The moment I started running, he noticed. He turned his head ever so slightly to hear my approach better. As the gap closed, I realized this guy might know how to fight better than anything else I'd faced.

Cool.

Fighting my brothers blindfolded with one hand tied behind my back and winning had boosted my confidence. I was beginning to trust my gut when it said I could do something. The reason I hadn't been trusting it until now, was it said I could do a lot of absurd things. And with each passing Cycle, it said I could do even more absurd things. My skills hadn't stopped growing ever since I'd been moderated.

The moment I came within arm's reach, lion man lashed out, bringing both scimitars forward in a wide double slash that covered the largest area. It was an intelligent attack for someone fighting blind. Old Morgan would have been sliced and diced by the attack.

Actually, Old Morgan would have run because there was no chance he could win this.

New Morgan stayed half an inch outside the lion man's range, and then flowed around the blades like he was a damn Chinese martial arts movie master, spinning past, drawing lion man's dagger, and cutting his Achille's tendon all in one poetically beautiful motion, before stepping out of range again. New Morgan was a badass.

Without solid footing, I took the lion man apart in less than ten seconds, ending the fight by leaping off the corridor wall and bringing his stolen dagger down in the middle of his forehead.

"Damn," Tee said. "That was a solid 5/7."

"You're not funny."

"I'll have you know Buster thinks I'm hilarious."

I yanked the dagger out of the mob's head, exposing the bloody electronics, and then picked up his scimitars. I could keep them. I couldn't repair them, but until they broke, I could use them. The scimitars looked like oversized anime swords in my hands, but the material was incredibly lightweight, so I could fight with them effectively.

"Are there any more of those things onboard?"

I dropped the second scimitar and pivoted, swinging the other one as fast as I could. The invisible lion man sneaking up behind me found his upper body separated from his lower as he became visible. I side-stepped the dagger heading for me and gave his upper body a kick, watching it tumble backward.

"Okay, that was better than the last kill. Also, I think they come in threes."

Tee had been trying to get me killed. His last line came as the third one tried to cleave me in half. I was already moving, though. The third one went the way of the other two.

I started to grin as I heard more running towards me.

12

MY BFF IS A MOOCH

Two months ago, Tee had offered to turn my Tokens into cash for me. He'd even convinced me to put the 18,000,000 Tokens I got from the achievements up for sale by stating that the price of Tokens was likely at their current premium and that the 90,000 I received each Cycle would be more than enough for anything I wanted to buy in the future. The price at the time had been $153 per Token. Since then, he'd run up $9,853,975 on my credit card, and I hadn't seen a cent of the money he promised me.

So, I invited him over to the hotel and asked my family to go out for a few hours. We were now sitting at the dining room table. I'd closed the curtains and turned out the lights for his visit. The only light source was a desk lamp.

I tilted the desk lamp to point at his face, making him lean away from the brightness, as I shoved my credit card bills across the table to him. When they'd increased the card's limit, they'd changed it, so I received weekly statements instead of monthly. There were a lot of bills.

"Where's my money, Tee?"

Tee gave me his friendliest smile. "I've invested it for you."

I scowled. "That wasn't our arrangement. You said you'd sell my Tokens for me, and I agreed to give you 1%."

Tee laughed nervously. "Are you going to break my legs? Because it's going to cost you Tokens to fix them."

I chuckled back. "I'll take you to the hospital. We can put the bill on your credit card. I'm sure you'll be able to walk in six months."

He winced. "That sounds painful. You know how I feel about pain."

"Exactly, now where's my money? You've been dodging me more and more while we're out of the Game. I'm getting suspicious."

"I'm busy."

The lamp had tilted down, so I raised it back up, shining it in his face, blinding him again. "Doing what?"

"Running the business that you invested in."

"You started a business with my money?"

"Well, yeah. I've got to do something when I'm bored."

I started to worry. Tee considered annoying the president a good way to alleviate his boredom. "How much of this business do I own, and what's it called?"

"It's called Morgan Tee Enterprises and your share is 49%. Since I'm doing all the work, I deserved the controlling interest. I signed the paperwork on your behalf, so it's all legit."

I stared at him. He hadn't stopped smiling. I wasn't sure if he was messing with me the way I was messing with him or if he was being serious. "How big is this business?"

"Well, that's a bit of a story."

"I'm not going anywhere."

Tee rotated his chair, turning it to the side to put his feet up. His smile didn't go away. "So, you know that website I showed you for selling Tokens?"

"Yes."

"It's mine. I made it. And it's currently the biggest Token exchange on the planet. I've been using the transit station's systems and my hacking ability to spam our sector with information on it. So, it's the most well-known Token exchange on the planet."

"Good for you."

"Good for both of us, you mean. It's a subsidiary of Morgan Tee Enterprises. Anyway, about the time you got your big reward, I managed to find several hedge funds that were interested in bulk purchases of Tokens. I used your initial investment to convince them that we were a major player and started a bidding war. The current market price for Tokens sold in lots of one million is a little over a billion dollars USD."

I'd been assuming he had sold some of my Tokens, but not *all* of them, which is why I wanted to talk to him about his spending. I wasn't prepared for him to have done what he promised.

"Wait, are you saying you sold my Tokens for eighteen billion dollars?"

"No, I sold them for almost thirty. I said the *current* price was a little over a billion dollars. And I'm not finished yet, so don't interrupt me."

When he didn't continue, I mimed zipping my lips.

Tee grinned.

I decided I didn't like it when he grinned. It made me nervous.

Tee seemed to sense that.

His grin grew larger.

"Since the initial sale a few months ago, I've used my website to buy and resell almost two billion Tokens. I have a fixed-buy price on the website of $250 USD a Token, and most people don't look past that number once they see it, especially if they live in the Third World, and that's where the majority of our Tokens are coming from."

I groaned. "Please don't tell me we're extorting people in the Third World."

"We aren't. We are redistributing wealth. A guy working in a smartphone factory makes maybe $600 a month, Morgan. Each time they go into the Game, they're making around 10 Tokens, even if they're completely clueless. That's ten grand a month selling through my website."

"Okay, that sounds fine, I guess, but also unsustainable. I mean, hedge funds can't continue investing in Tokens forever."

Tee laughed evilly. "You would be surprised how many billionaires are willing to part with a billion dollars if it means they can secure immortality for the next thousand years. And multi-millionaires are willing to spend the same percentage to secure another century."

I was beginning to believe that he was telling the truth. "How big is Morgan Tee Enterprises?"

"In another month, we'll be a trillion-dollar company. I might not know anything about defending a station, but a lot of my analytical skills translate to business quite well."

My brain disconnected over the number. It was absurd. The only question that came to mind was, "Why?"

"Why what?"

"Why make so much money?"

"Boredom, initially. When I first started the website, I was stuck in the orb, which wasn't fun. I was hoping to make enough Tokens to buy a body. But when you earned all those Tokens and let me sell them, it started a chain reaction that made our website grow bigger and bigger, and now we have control of almost a trillion dollars."

I glared at him. "Why the hell am I paying your credit card bill then? You don't need my money."

Tee laughed at my glare. "I don't, but it's funny to watch you think you're paying my bills."

"The credit card's in my name, so I am paying your bills."

"You're not," Tee said, laughing harder. "We own the bank. They know the card's in my name, but I've told them to send you the bills with yours on it."

Okay, that was pretty funny.

If it was true.

"So, we own a bank."

"Yeah, I bought it, so they would keep upping the limit on the credit card and start to send you weekly statements."

"Wait, so higher-limit credit cards don't do their statements weekly?"

He laughed. "Of course not. That would be ridiculous."

I picked up my phone and called my bank. I had a dedicated line because of how high the limit on the credit card was. At least, that's what they had told me.

Charlotte picked up, being her usual cheerful self. "Hello, Mr. Winchester. How can I help you today?"

"I'm sitting here with Tee. The individual I've told you about. He claims we own the bank."

Charlotte laughed. "You do indeed, Sir. Is there anything else I can help you with?"

"Is the credit card in my name or his?"

"Yours. But he's told me to tell you it's in his. For fraud reasons, I'm not going to do that. Practical jokes don't protect me from liability. I'm transferring thirty billion dollars to your personal account as we speak, per Mr. Tee's instructions. Is there anything else I can help you with?"

"Ah, transfer a billion to my father and my brothers' accounts and add a note to my brothers' deposits that says, 'No more mooching'."

"Not a problem, Sir. Is there anything else I can help you with?"

"No, that's all. Thank you, Charlotte."

"Have a nice day, Mr. Winchester."

"You too."

I put down my phone and started to laugh. "You beautiful asshole."

Tee scrunched up his face. "I find that feature my least compelling, but you do *you*."

I laughed harder.

My life was absurd.

First, I owned Mars and a country, and now this.

It took me five minutes to pull myself together and think rationally. This was insane. But once I could think straight, I had a few questions.

I put away the lamp, opened the curtains, handed Tee a beer, and then we both flopped down on the couch together. "Are we buying anything else with our money besides buying and selling Tokens?"

"Mostly farmland," Tee said, losing his smile. "Most people don't realize it yet, but production is down. The three and a half days a week everyone is spending in the Game makes it harder to harvest and plant crops. The 100 mandatory Cycles will cause food shortages in another six months. The Third World will starve. I'm putting half of our earnings into buying farms and converting them to staples, such as rice, corn, wheat, and potatoes, so that doesn't happen."

That was a good use for the money. I approved wholeheartedly. I tried not to show it. I didn't want Tee getting a big head. "What are you doing with the other half?"

"That's going into barren land. No one is thinking long-term yet. Land that is useless today will be farmable in a century when your technology catches up."

"What about resources?"

"We're doing a little of that, too. I'm also buying robotics companies. Humanity is being exposed to new ideas, so technology is about to take a massive leap forward. And if your faction somehow survives past the first 100 Cycles, you need to automate jobs to keep your faction stable."

"That's a big *if*."

"Before you broke the Game, there was no *if*. Now, there's an *if*, so we need to make plans for how humanity will support your station if it happens."

My eyebrows rose. "Wait. You're doing this to make the station stronger?"

"Well, it was initially from boredom and to get me a body, but now it's to help the station. Why did you think I was doing it?"

"I thought you were trying to save humanity from themselves. You were talking about diverting a famine."

"I was talking about diverting a famine because starving people don't make good decisions or effective members of a faction."

I shook my head. "You are definitely the weird one in this friendship."

13

ASSEMBLE THE TROOPS

Getting the three station masters with a unique weapon system from the military to show up for the private meeting wasn't difficult, but pulling some of the gamer station masters out of their parents' basements was. It required me to sink to some pretty unscrupulous levels and lean heavily on my fame, but they showed up, too.

Only twelve gamers and three members of the military had unique min-maxed weapon systems. After the 3rd Cycle, I'd expressed how important it was for everyone to take AI and dungeon boss traits, but now I needed to make that message clearer. Several of them had ignored my advice.

I couldn't let this continue.

Every station master needed those weapons.

Everyone arrived in Portland on separate planes and then turned up to the hotel in separate cars. None of the governments liked having so many station masters in one place, in case a horrible accident occurred, but this conversation needed to happen in person. Talking on the phone was too risky. They might not understand the gravity of the situation, and someone might overhear something they shouldn't.

Tee and I watched them walk into the conference room and take a seat at the large table. Half of them had their own AIs floating next to them, having copied my leveling technique with their station rats. I recognised the gamers from tournaments. I gave them all a small smile and wave. Most returned it.

Daniel was the last to arrive and took the empty chair on my left.

As the door closed, I stood up. "Thank you for coming."

Kangaroo Billy cracked a beer and snorted. "You didn't give us much of a choice, cunt. Who the fuck calls a man's old lady to make him show up to a meeting he doesn't want to show up to?"

There was nothing hostile in Kangaroo Billy's body language, no indication he wanted to fight. He seemed more amused by the situation than anything. We'd played together numerous times, so I was used to his straightforward attitude and didn't take offence. He was always the most vocal player at the tournaments.

Daniel grinned at him. "I told him to."

Kangaroo Billy chuckled. "You little shit. You beat me in the last tournament, and now you're getting people to tattle to my mother?"

Daniel laughed. "How else am I going to be your dead-beat stepdad."

Kangaroo Billy and most of the gamers laughed. They'd all heard Daniel make this threat at some point or another. And they had all played with him in tournaments, so they cut the kid a lot of slack.

When everyone had calmed down, I restarted the conversation. "We need to talk."

Kangaroo Billy crushed his empty beer can and opened another. "Look, cunt, we're all grateful for what you did. You got rid of my damn crotch itch. But that doesn't mean we're going to fuck up our builds just because you say so."

I folded my arms. "Why do you think I'm asking you to take the AI and dungeon boss traits first?"

"You want better weapons systems for your stupidly powerful station and don't care if we lose ours for that to happen."

"I don't deny that."

He stared at me, stunned by my honesty. "Fuck, is it hard to walk while dragging a pair of balls that big?"

"Cut the shit, Billy. Everyone at this table, except those three over there, were General Prime's second pick. I'm sure he told you that you got your spot because you scored highly in the strategic applications for our class, but that was mostly bullshit and you know it. We got the job, because we knew how to min-max, and that let our AI clones make a decent weapon system."

He finished his second beer. "Your point?"

"We need to do our job. Until I gained my dungeon master, I didn't know that my R2D2 weapon system was a fraction of the strength it could be; and until you gain yours, you won't know how strong your weapon system or dungeon mob could be, either. Gaining this knowledge is worth the loss of your station and the sector you're protecting."

Hiroshi, the Japanese admiral, nodded, which caused Billy to frown.

"You agree with this cunt?"

Hiroshi nodded again. "I've recently received the station master knowledge that Mr Winchester possesses. In my estimates, everyone at this table, except Mr Winchester, has less than a 1% chance of keeping their station for another year. None of our station masters know how to design decent weapon systems, so each of us losing our station and sector to give humanity another good weapon system is a fair trade."

"Well, fuck." Billy opened a third can of beer and looked at me. "So, you're not being a cunt."

I shook my head and then looked at everyone. "Humanity needs your weapons more than they need your stations and sectors. General Prime picked us knowing this. We have the smallest and least resource-rich sectors under humanity's control. If some of our station masters somehow survive the first 100 Cycles, they're going to need more good weapons and dungeons mobs to keep them in the Game. And the only people on Earth who can supply those are sitting in this room."

Billy scowled and then briefly glanced at his AI's blue orb. "You're making me sound like an asshole for choosing Sheila when I reached level 10."

"You did that yourself, Cunt" Sheila replied. "Who the fuck doesn't listen to the number one ranked player's advice?"

He tipped his beer to her. "Fair point." He glanced at me. "So, you want us to stop being cunts, and get on with it then."

"The short answer is yes."

"What's the long version?"

"The long version is this is just the first step. The dungeon master optimising your weapon system is only so helpful with level 1 technology. When you have an AI too, you'll gain the schematics for everything your station can build up to level 9. This will give your dungeon masters a lot more technology to work with and allow your dungeon masters to pass messages to each other through our AIs. Our dungeon masters are capable of learning, and if we can pass messages between them, they might be able to adapt our weapon systems to work with each other, so they synergize."

Kangaroo Billy whistled. "Why wasn't that in the briefing?"

"They probably thought the governments were big enough wankers to force the issue if they knew," Sheila replied.

I did.

Tee did, too.

Now that the new governments had found their feet, a lot of them were making power plays. Because of what I'd done, I was insulated from this, but the other station masters weren't. It was one of the reasons why I wanted this conversation in person, instead of over the phone.

I met everyone's gaze. "Government interference is a real possibility, which is why we're holding this conversation in person and why I had this room swept for bugs. The sudden international unity that occurred after Earth became members of the Collective is already starting to fray. Every government is trying to expand their control within the Game, and we're going to be dragged into it at some point. This is too important to be used as political leverage, so we need to do this before they understand what they're dealing with."

A bunch of the gamers glanced nervously at the three members of the military.

I turned and looked at Hiroshi. "You three gained the same special clearance reward as I did, so I fully trust you to work towards your nation's best interest. Am I correct in my assumption that you believe this requires your governments not interfering in this matter?"

Hiroshi smiled. "The military has a long history of protecting politicians from their own stupidity, and I am proud to continue this tradition."

Kangaroo Billy tossed each of them a beer. "You're good, cunts."

14

THE 14TH CYCLE

Congratulations, you have reached level 34.
You have 66 Path Points to spend.
You have 570 Class Points to spend.

After receiving the notification, I added a path point to all three paths, bringing my secondary paths to 17. I then went through the respawn process, made my way back to the command room, and sat down in my chair.

I no longer needed to kill the thousands of rats on my station, only die to them when they had to level, and I could keep doing that so long as my genetic advancement and personal tech didn't reach 20, since my station was level 4.

Holding back from leveling my secondary paths had just been a way for me to make the build quests more interesting, but now that they were done, there was no reason to hold back. The improvements didn't make a difference to how challenging the fights were, but it did make a difference to how much mental work I could get done during my time in-Game.

Tee's turrets and the squad continued to tear through the station's rats as I looked around my command room for something productive to do. I'd been pretty bored the last few Cycles. There is only so much studying you can stomach before you need to take a break. And I wanted a break. Life outside the Game had become more and more restrictive. I couldn't go anywhere or do anything without causing a scene.

I'd confirmed that the viewscreen made an excellent movie screen, and the replicator could produce more than a hundred varieties of chocolate ice cream. Daniel and I were trying to figure out which was the best. My current favourite was 83.

"I'm getting tired of walking here from the regeneration chamber," I complained as I skimmed through some of the schematics I hadn't studied yet. "I wish I could justify the cost of adding a secondary regeneration chamber to my ready room."

"We're being hailed," Tee said, ignoring my complaints.

"By who?"

"The Librarian. It looks like he's finished his expansion quests and completed his communications array."

"Put him on the viewscreen."

The Librarian appeared a second later. He was wearing the same grey overalls I used to wear. My current armour was a body suit with armoured plates that were tough enough to stop a station rat's spiked tail.

He grinned. "It turns out, I had to speak in riddles. Honestly, what a nightmare. But I did it. I completed all the expansion quests with the special clearance method. Now I just have to get my station in order. It's a bit of a mess. It's good to finally see a friendly face. How are you doing, gentlemen?"

"I'm bored out of my mind," I said. "I've got everything streamlined, leaving me nothing to do on my station except study. Tee's busy feeding the Octorin false information that the Kilocksin have been raiding me frequently and unsuccessfully. I'm trying to encourage them to attack with a larger force than they usually do."

"I thought you were helping Daniel?"

"Honestly, the kid doesn't need that much help. He did well enough in his first battle that I think he's sitting in second place for the strongest station. He's technically a higher level than I am, if we don't include prestige. His enemies are only trying to break through his dungeon now, and the immortal soldiers are making short work of them."

"Why are you trying to encourage the Octorin to attack with a larger force? You told me they use unmanned drones."

"They do, but right now, I've got so many spare defence slots that I need resource points to make more D2s to help me level. The daily experience the rats give me is keeping me ahead of the curve, but not as far ahead as I would like."

"Speaking of the Kilocksin," Tee said. "They've sent their first fleet to raid you."

That got my attention. "How large is the fleet?"

"There are 6 cruisers, 18 frigates, 49 corvettes."

"Have they fully committed?"

"No. I believe they're just here to test you."

I chuckled. "That's their first mistake. Let's make it their last. Send the welcome message I recorded for them, and if they don't reply, let them get close enough to fire and then destroy them all with the first volley. I want to go through their wrecks for shield bracers."

I wasn't worried about my station automatically targeting them. That would only happen if I tried to let them reach another transit ring unopposed, flee intact, or destroy my station. So long as I didn't do any of that, I could mess with my enemy's fleet as much as I liked.

The Librarian frowned and moved to adjust his bowtie, only to realise it wasn't there. "You don't think it's a good idea to let most of them go, so they try again with a larger fleet?"

I shook my head. "I need the heavy shield bracer, and I'm willing to lose their future fleets to obtain it. Besides, if they realize that they can't move their fleet through here, they'll just try to conquer my station through the dungeon, which is where I want them."

"And when they realize they can't do that either?"

"Then they will give up. I don't want to deal with their military. I want to deal with their idealistic civilians. I've even worked out a cost-effective way for them to make credits from dying here. Tee's going to load it onto their version of forums when a few of them have run the dungeon. He's been building up an alias and is making himself known, so they'll think it's legit. He's also trying to catfish a few influencers."

The Librarian sighed. "That's a special level of bored."

"Yeah, I've watched the extended versions of Lord of the Rings and all seven Star Wars movies, twice."

"I thought there were eleven of those movies."

"There are seven. Old school fans claim there are only four because Rogue One was decent, but there are seven. There have never been anymore made, and the Ewok movies don't count."

"I was more of a Barbarella, Flash Gordon sort of person."

"I can respect that."

"I'm happy you approve because I need your help getting my head around all these changes. This station master knowledge is vast. I knew our aggressors earned credits from damaging our stations, but I didn't realize the value could be multiple times what their vessel was worth. Some races use stations as a way of farming credits with old ships to upgrade their tech. It's fascinating and confusing. There are so many strategies for success, and we need to be ready to counter all of them. I'm even considering letting them damage my station more because of it. The additional damage will earn them more credits, which will encourage more attacks."

"That's tight-rope walking. You need to be strong enough to kill them, but weak enough that losing is still profitable for them. I imagine there are people out there who can do that, but it's risky. I don't think we know enough to play around with it. We also don't have a skilled fleet to back us up if we make a mistake."

"You're probably right. Have you looked into the challenger's hall and the challenger transit ring systems to curb your boredom?"

I had.

Those two systems were the Game's version of a station master quest board. Once I built them, I'd be able to initiate random encounters. These encounters could be AI mob fleets or station mobs that tried to destroy my internal systems. The rewards were fixed, so I wouldn't be able to harvest the fleets for resources or the mobs for weapon blueprints, but some of the rewards were also faction rewards, so I'd boost every station master in my faction each time I cleared one. Later on, I'd also be able to take random encounters that were going to occur to other stations, protecting them. It was the only way I could help others in-Game, outside of giving knowledge about what I was discovering at higher levels.

And it also sounded like fun.

I'd have at least one battle every Cycle.

I wanted these systems badly.

I was so bored.

I sighed. "I've put more resources into trying to find out when I can gain access than I care to admit. Everything I've found suggests we should have access, but we don't. Believe me, I'm more frustrated by this than you are."

"Do you mind lending your brain to assist in developing a strategy for my station, then? I can wait until after you have dealt with the Kilocksin, if you prefer."

I rolled my eyes. "They're no threat. They just don't know it yet. Let's do this. Tee, what's The Librarian up against?"

For the next thirty minutes, we helped The Librarian get a better understanding of his enemy. Tee pulled all the information he could from the different factions' internet to get a picture of what they were up to. What we found was disturbing.

The Riomari, a fish people, were building a massive fleet. They showed every intention of taking The Librarian's station and then moving to attack humanity. They were Cycles away from being ready, but the intent was there. They were bringing in more ships from other systems in their sector. The Librarian wasn't in a position to stop them. Not yet, at least. We needed to fix that.

An alarm sounded in my command room, and the lights went red.

"What's happening?" The Librarian asked, clearly concerned.

"The Kilocksin cruisers have begun their attack," Tee replied. "When we didn't fire on them, they kept approaching until we were in range of all their weapons. Their secondary weapons destroyed our shield, and their forward laser cannons have struck and disabled all of the D2s their sensors can see."

"How good are their laser cannons?" I asked. "Is it worth trying to gain access to their blueprints?"

"The damage they caused was minimal," Tee said. "Kilocksin don't excel with medium-sized vessels like cruisers. However, their corvette shields are some of the best you can find. They have a standard path they prefer to develop which is exceptional, so they tend to invest in them heavily early in a new season. These should have every level 1 piece of tech we need to replicate them. It's worth trying to acquire it."

"In that case, return fire with non-explosive rounds. I want this to be an instant death without them being able to record anything. Our first priority is still the shield bracer, but if we can get their shield design for the corvettes, then I'm not going to complain."

"On your command, Sir," Tee shouted enthusiastically.

I raised my hand and dropped it, like I was sentencing them to death. "Fire!"

"Are you always so dramatic?" The Librarian asked, chuckling at our show.

I shrugged. "We're bored, and this makes it more fun. So anyway, now that that's taken care of, you were talking about what tech you should invest your credits in."

Congratulations, you have reached level 37.
You have 66 Path Points to spend.
You have 678 Class Points to spend.

THE RESOURCE POINTS from the Kilocksin fleet weren't something to sneeze at. Cruisers were worth around 2,500. Frigates were worth close to 1,000. The corvettes were each worth a little over 250. So, the fleet earned me over 45,000 RP and one hundred times as many credits. That was enough RP to add more than 500 D2s. But before I did that, I needed to find the shield bracer.

My station only had a basic reprocessing facility. It would break the wreckage down for materials, but it wouldn't sort through it to reclaim technology. The cost of buying the blueprints for that technology was in the tens of millions of credits. So, Tee used the tractor beam to pull the wreckages into the hangar bay my station development path gave me, and the squad was helping me search them. It turned into a fun experience. Not all the Kilocksin were dead.

I had my back against the corridor wall inside the wreckage of one of the corvettes. Tee was confident that several shield emitters were still intact on this vessel. But there were three Kilocksin around the corner between me and where I needed to go.

They had already taken out the squad, despite the level gap. The Kilocksin had managed to lure them into a trap and blow up a section of their corvette to kill them. I'd seen the squad's body cameras, so I knew one of them was sporting a heavy shield bracer.

I was dealing with an officer —and a very skilled one.

I'd come prepared to win.

"Are any of you interested in talking before we do this again?" I called out. "I mean, this fight is going to be a hell of a lot of fun, but you're still like the first aliens I've ever met in person, so I'd actually like to chat if you wouldn't mind. I brought Kelvar."

I held the bottle of Kilocksin wine around the corner for them to see.

"You don't wish to fight?" One of them shouted back.

"We are going to fight," I said. "But we might as well do it after getting to know each other. We can be civil about this, after all. I offer to parley. While we talk, I won't try to interfere with your ship, and you don't try to interfere with my station."

"If this is a trick, our clan will know of your betrayal. I accept your parley."

I holstered my particle pistol and stepped around the corner to see three laser rifles pointed at me. They had their spears strapped to their backs. I gave the traditional Kilocksin greeting for a respected enemy. I kept my eyes on them and turned my head to the side, hiding my throat.

It made me look like a double-chinned idiot.

The officer in charge of them seemed surprised but returned the gesture. He was eight feet tall, with dark green skin similar to a snake. His face was more lizardish than the pictures Tee had shown me, though, but he still had a Komodo dragon's pronounced bone structure. "You are the new species to join the Collective, yet you know our ways. Did you receive a liaison?"

That was a good guess. This guy probably wasn't just a skilled, low-ranked nobody; or maybe this sort of information was more common than I thought. Either way, I needed to be careful. They knew a lot more than me.

"I did receive a Kilocksin liaison."

"I mean no disrespect, but I would like to meet with them to prove this true. There are only 87 factions with whom our people can co-exist, and the addition of another is a significant occurrence. This will change our plans for our campaign if it is true."

"Tee, can you build a delegation room for a meeting?"

"My internal turrets will automatically shoot them on sight," Tee replied. "Also, Tumpa will attack them."

I frowned. "Ah, I don't know your name, but mine is Morgan. Would one of you be okay with submitting yourself to ritual combat with my liaison? He's going to attack you on sight, and I think that's the only way to drag it out so that we have time to talk."

The one with the heavy shield bracer thumped his chest. "I am Rass. My warriors will fight your liaison so we may speak."

"Tee, have Tumpa challenge one of Rass's subordinates to the Ta'Su."

"He's heading to the hangar bay now."

"Good." I focused on Rass. "I tried to speak with your leaders, but they wouldn't reply to my welcome."

"Strength must be proven," Rass said, bluntly. "You have proven that you are a worthy enemy. We have failed to prove the same. This will be corrected."

"I hope so. I would hate to think I'm wasting my time drinking with you."

If I said that to a human, it would be taken as an insult. To a Kilocksin, I was clearly stating my motives, which expressed that I was trying to be as honest as possible.

I opened the bottle of Kelvar and took a swig. It was thick as maple syrup but tasted like peach tea. There were about four grams of caffeine in the mouthful I swallowed. So, I screwed the lid back on and tossed the bottle to them without having any more.

Their species didn't use intoxicants. They didn't accept anything that interfered with their warrior's edge. So, they'd replaced them with stimulants. My body wasn't organic, but the system could still make me feel like it was. This drink was going to hit me like an entire case of Red Bull.

Rass unscrewed the lid and took a swallow. He scowled. "This is from a food synthesiser."

"It's all I have access to," I said. "If your people would trade with mine, I would gain access to the real stuff."

"Your people would be interested in Kelvar?"

"My people would be interested in many things. The novelty of joining the Collective is new to us. We also make drinks that are similar to Kelvar, so you might find trade interesting."

"Human Kelvar. That would interest my mate. She likes to trade between wars. She may approach your people about this."

"Tell her to ask for Red Bull concentrate."

Rass nodded. "You seem to know my kind, but I do not know yours. What rank do you hold among your people?"

This was a tricky question. I had to be careful how I answered it. Kilocksin officers only cared about position and respect, but our way of life did not align perfectly to convey that, so I was going to have to get creative with the truth.

"Humans don't have clans. We have nations. Territories where we are born. I am not in my nation's military. But I hold multiple first titles around simulated station combat across my faction. And if you asked my people, they would tell you I am the most loved in my faction. All know my name. Also, I am young, less than 2,000 Cycles."

Rass blinked. “You are a child. And yet respected among your kind, how?”

“All my people are children compared to yours. We live less than 5,000 cycles. And I am respected because I caused the moderators to take notice of me. They were not allowed to reset my progress without compensation. I gave my people their health and youth.”

Rass gave their version of a nod, a double blink. “This is a rare thing to do. Among my people, those who do so are given the title Ma’Lock. To us, you are Ma’Lock Morgan. It is an honour to meet you.”

Rass and his soldiers bowed. They did so without looking at me. It was the highest honour they gave to an enemy. It meant that their respect for me outweighed their enmity.

They rose. “A Ma’Lock who gives his compensation to his clan is to be respected twice.” They bowed again. “But a Ma’Lock who gives it to all in his faction is to be shown respect by all three times.” They bowed a third time. “Thank you for showing respect to my men and I, Ma’Lock Morgan. We are honoured.” He took another swig and then passed the bottle along. “Do your people fight?”

“We were always at war with ourselves. Since we joined the Game, there has been peace. We will make war on others from now on.”

“Will you win?”

“Some believe so. They are short-sighted. We’re new to the Game. We cannot expect to arrive and win. Our territory will all be gone within 100 Cycles unless something changes.”

“You expect to lose your station? You’re strong to have defeated us so quickly.”

“I am, but the moderators imposed steep penalties on me for that strength. My progress will soon slow.”

Rass hissed, giving their version of a chuckle. “I do not believe you, Ma’Lock Morgan. You speak like our Warlords. You move like them, too. Your eyes never stop, and you stand ready to pull us apart at any moment. All Warlords moan of the limitations on their growth, yet our heads barely reach their ankles. What they call slow progress we look at with envy, for such great growth is beyond us.

They do what they do not to survive, but because that is how they live."

I smiled. "They sound like my kind of people."

Rass's hissing grew louder, showing laughter. "You will soon meet them, Ma'Lock Morgan. They will look forward to conquering your dungeon and taking your station from you."

"I will prepare a welcome for them then. I wish to make a good impression on your people."

Rass paused for a little too long to be natural. "Why?"

"Because my sector will fall, and when it does, I would like your clan to take my people as mercenaries."

Rass frowned. "That would require trust that our people do not have."

"Tell your leaders that I will hold this station. They may try all they like, but it will not fall before my sector does. And if they want my help protecting their border against invasion, that is my asking price. I could easily limit my range so your enemies could skim my edge and invade you unimpeded."

Rass nodded. "I expect nothing less from an enemy, Ma'Lock Morgan."

Tumpa strode around the corner and walked past me. He wore only a ritual loin cloth without other adornments. His muscular frame dwarfed the other Kilocksin as he eyed up his opponents. "Who dares to challenge Tumpa?"

Rass and I continued to talk as his warrior fought Tumpa. The ritual fight they were doing was long and slow. It involved three rounds with a reprieve in between. There was the first to land a strike, then the first to draw blood, and finally to the death. Our conversation became less serious as we watched the ritual.

We had said our peace. This was more about building a relationship and understanding each other than trying to gain information. And I'd given far more information than Rass had, but I'd had to in order to open the door to proper communication. If I defeated their Warlords when they came to my dungeon, they might open dialogue.

A good relationship with them was necessary for Sector 13 to have any chance of surviving long-term. Tee had opened my eyes to what that would take. And the combined might of a clan and our faction in a Kilocksin sector might let them hold out for decades. And since the first decades were always the most profitable, that was important.

To my surprise, Tumpa beat both of Rass's soldiers without them landing a blow. That seemed to annoy Rass, so he challenged Tumpa himself and then lost, dying as easily as the others. It wasn't until he was dead that I asked Tee how Tumpa was winning.

Tee chuckled. "It turns out that since he's your liaison, and since their people have a lot of ritual combat, he needs to be strong enough to compete with you effectively to teach you how these rituals work, so he scales with your strength and skill. You asked the moderator to make you the best fighter in your galaxy, so Tumpa has enough skill to match you. You also currently have a genetic advancement of 18, so he's your match, which makes him significantly faster than your average Kilocksin. Tumpa was going easy on them."

I walked over to Rass's body and took the heavy shield bracer off his wrist. "Well, that will keep them on their toes, at least. Also, when you say I'm the best fighter in my galaxy, what exactly do you mean?"

"I mean, you could fight Jackie Chan, Bruce Lee, Muhammad Ali, and half the UFC all at once and still win. I mean as yourself, not as you are here."

"I didn't think I was that good."

"That's because you haven't tested yourself. The station quests and your brothers don't count. But how easily you walked through them should have given you some clue. Now give that shield bracer to Tumpa and go disconnect those shield emitters and everything else you can salvage. We need to start preparing the dungeon for the Kilocksin raiders."

15

THE 15TH CYCLE

Taking apart the wrecked corvettes to reach the functional technology within was a slow and heavy process. I only had until the end of the Cycle to finish the job. After that, everything got sent to the reprocessing facility, so I spent every waking hour pulling out as much technology as possible.

There weren't just shield emitters. There were power regulators, heat sinks, and about a thousand other pieces of technology. Each one added a new blueprint option that I could purchase. I wasn't going to use most of them, but Tee said you never knew when something might be important. You might need the technology of a dozen different species to put together a weapon that none of them could create individually. It was worth gathering as much technology as I could.

So, the rest of the Cycle was devoted to me working with my hands. It was surprisingly therapeutic. It made me feel like I'd accomplished something.

I spent my few days off on Earth looking for a new apartment and trying to help The Librarian develop a proper defence plan. The apartment search was a dead end, even though I had the money to buy entire buildings. The moment anyone found out it was me, things got complicated. Life was getting incredibly problematic. The only thing that wasn't was the Game. Everything made sense there.

So, I was happy to return to the Game and my command chair. And I was delighted that clearing the station of rats helped me level again.

Congratulations, you have reached level 39.
You have 60 Path Points to spend.
You have 755 Class Points to spend.

I dismissed the notification as I walked into the dojo, beside Diego. The tatami mats and rice paper walls made you feel like you were somewhere preindustrial, and floating paper lanterns gave a hint of mysticism. A small shrine sat against the far wall, ready to serve as a leader board.

I wanted this challenge to be ready for the Kilocksin when they arrived. I was willing to bet good money that it would be sometime today. The Cycle had just begun, but I was almost entirely certain they were coming. They liked to move quickly when they were sizing up their opponents.

I stopped in the middle of the last room, looking back through the open sliding doors to the first of the six challenge rooms. Each room was identical, but there was a real sense of progress with all the doors open like this. It sent the right impression, that getting to this point was an accomplishment.

"Tee, I can enter this unarmed combat challenge, but if I do, I can't enter the dungeon if they get past me, right?"

"Yeah, why?" His voice came from one of the bamboo and paper walls to my right.

"I want to fight their Warlords if they come. I'm thinking of making it so this room can include Tumpa and me. That way, I can talk to them before they enter the dungeon."

"You'll be weakening your dungeon."

My station leveled every time I went up ten levels, so it was now level 4. My dungeon mob limit increased by one every time this happened, so it could currently hold twenty-four dungeon mobs. I could invest class points to increase the limit, but I didn't want or need to. My immortal soldiers were extremely powerful thanks to all my D2s, so throwing more into the dungeon wouldn't help.

"Do you honestly think I'll make a difference?"

"Do you?"

"No."

"Good, you're not delusional. Why do you want to talk to them?"

"This is going to be my only chance to make a good impression. If I can make that good impression, they might be willing to work with us in the future. These people have the influence necessary to make sure that happens."

"You don't know if they'll come, yet?"

"I know. But if they do, I need to be here."

"True. It might be worth weakening your dungeon for that. You'll have to give a bigger reward for killing you, though. It would be kind of insulting if they only got a shield bracer and a laser spear."

"I'll give them 100,000 Tokens. A life for a life."

Tee whistled. "That's a reward."

"I want to make a good impression."

I turned to Diego.

A few weeks ago, I'd explained why I was building the dungeon challenge. He'd been talking with Tumpa ever since trying to decide if my plan had merit. I couldn't force him to upgrade the immortal soldiers the way I wanted. He had to decide for himself.

Diego folded his arms. "You're sure they'll arrive this Cycle?"

"Yes."

He scowled. "I'm still not certain this is the right way to go."

I could see the upgrade options for the immortal soldiers, and there was one that could help me convince him. "You need more information to make an informed decision, right? But you lack the time to gather the knowledge. I suggest you select the Kilocksin cultural package upgrade. It's cheap."

Diego looked around the dojo for a second. The tatami mats, bamboo, and rice paper walls were so different to the station that they unsettled him. This wasn't the environment he was built for. It messed with his instincts.

He sighed, as his gaze went unfocused, and then he suddenly frowned. "The cultural package unlocked other, more specific information packages but didn't provide the necessary knowledge for me to agree with your plan. However, the information provided will make my men more effective against the Kilocksin. I'm comfortable purchasing other information packages."

Tee wasn't exaggerating when he said immortal soldiers were the most versatile dungeon mob he'd ever seen. Everything in my station master knowledge package told me he was right. My station was only level 4, so the full upgrade path for them hadn't appeared yet, but the list was already twice the size of what most had access to, and that didn't include upgrades that turning an immortal soldier into a dungeon master had given them.

Diego had already purchased an upgrade that made it so the more immortal soldiers there were in the dungeon, the stronger they got. If I had six, then the sixth one would be a sergeant who was tougher.

There was a lot of talk Earthside around soldiers. Humanity seemed to have two strengths. One was our ability to build quickly. The other seemed to be extremely strong and versatile infantry. Out of all sapient species, humans seemed to be in the top .1% for reaction times, reflexes, and physical endurance.

Station masters weren't the only classes that had received AIs as traits, and the military AIs all agreed that we were capable of fielding an extremely exceptional ground force. But in order to use that infantry, we had to get them planet-side. No one was sure how to do that yet. None of our technology allowed us to get that close.

It was one of the many things we were dealing with.

Unlike living people, Diego didn't need a lot of time to gain the new information. In only a few minutes, he was done.

He grinned. It was a predatory grin. "I've purchased every information package on their faction, and I believe your assessment is correct. I've purchased the necessary unarmed combat upgrades to make this challenge into something that will entice their youth."

I returned his grin. "This should be fun."

THE KILOCKSIN HADN'T SENT their Warlords. But they did send almost a hundred waves of warriors to challenge the dungeon. I sat in the dojo chatting with another group of Kilocksin warriors while Tumpa proceeded to beat each one into a bloody pulp. Some of the warriors were respectful but standoffish. Others, like these ones, were regular chatterboxes. They were happy to sit and talk with a human Ma'Lock. They'd heard about me through Rass and were honoured to challenge my liaison for the right to fight me.

Finally, their leader broached the subject that all the talkative ones always got to. "Ma'Lock Morgan, why have you built such a strange dungeon challenge? You show respect every step of the way. But the challenges, until now, have not been insurmountable. Only three challenger teams have failed to reach the final room."

He didn't mention that none had gotten past Tumpa.

"The challenge is not for your warriors. It's for your children."

Their leader paused. "If you build your dungeon for our children, you will lose your station to our warriors."

I smiled. "The dungeon and this challenge are two entirely different difficulties. None of your challenger teams have lasted more than a few seconds in the dungeon or killed a single dungeon mob. This won't change, so I had to create this challenge to encourage your people to visit. One day, I hope to expand this challenge with another room to interest warriors like yourselves. But for now, all I can offer is a challenge for your children."

"What will be beyond this room?"

"Group combat," I said.

"I'm not sure I understand."

"I plan to have ten entrances, with ten challenges like the one you came through. They will connect after this final room, to a room where there are sixty of my warriors for your sixty to fight."

The reptilian soldier grinned, showing serrated teeth. “That sounds like clan games.”

“Yes, my clan against yours.”

“It sounds fun, but you will not last long enough for me to see it.”

Tumpa finished off the Kilocksin he was fighting and immediately challenged the next member of their group.

I smiled. “Unless your Warlords come to challenge my dungeon, you have little chance of taking it.”

“It is not us you should fear, since our Warlords are not going to challenge you. Alliances are being formed against your faction all over this branch of the galaxy. Taking your station only to then lose it to another in a few Cycles would be fruitless.”

That was considered tactical information. Kilocksin didn’t just give that away, not unless they intended to do so. The fact that this one had shared so much meant something important. He was also wearing a heavy shield bracer. “What do your leaders wish to share with me?”

“Your actions with our fleet have impressed our clan. We do not speak for our faction, only for ourselves. If you wish for us to take your offer to become mercenaries seriously, then we offer you this test. On the 20th Cycle, a conglomerate of factions will attack every station your faction has and then set out to conquer your sectors. Should your sector survive this incursion, Ma’Lock Morgan, my clan will consider your request.”

“I’ll need more than your word to take to my faction.”

“I have a data chip on my person. Defeat me in combat, and it’s yours.”

“Who are you to deliver such a message?”

“Just the son of a bored Warlord and Rass’s older brother, Tulk.”

“Beat my liaison, and you will have the honour of fighting me, Tulk. I won’t change the rules.”

Tulk hiss-chuckled. “I wouldn’t respect you if you did.”

MY VIEWSCREEN SHOWED ALMOST a thousand faces. Presidents, prime ministers, military heads, and members of parliaments and congresses were all present. There should have been more, but most didn't have access to interstellar communication yet, and Tee had only managed to hack through so many sectors. This was everyone I could connect to. I'd sent out the call, and they'd all answered.

Tee finished giving his briefing on what the data package Tulk had given us held. We didn't have the technology to make this conversation private. And I didn't want to do this on Earth. They needed to *see* what we'd been given, not just take our word on it. And our opponents weren't doing this in secret. This was public knowledge. We just hadn't known where to look for it.

"Currently, this information is unconfirmed," I said when Tee finished. "What I *can* confirm is that the Octorin and Clack who border my station are part of this conspiracy, and the scans Tee has stolen from their sectors show that they're building up for a major attack on the supplied date. I need all station masters and those with access to the mercenary guild system to make all efforts to confirm whether or not this information is true, and then all leaders to provide what support they can. Thank you for your time. If you have any further questions, please direct them to Tee."

I pressed a button on the arm of my chair, disconnecting me from the conversation, leaving someone else to sort out the chaos.

"Alex is hailing you," Tee said a moment later.

"Put her on the viewscreen."

Alex appeared. Her hair looked amazing in-Game. And she was hotter than usual. It might've had something to do with her being angry. "What was that? You can't just drop a bomb like that and walk out."

"Sure, I can. I just did."

"People need direction. They're all yelling at each other right now."

"I'm not the person to give it to them. I'm not a politician, general, or admiral. I'm a station master. I've helped where I can. Now, I need to make sure that The Crucible is ready to deal with the attack."

Alex scowled. "You're the only one who's on speaking terms with aliens. You need to ask them for help."

"I'm not going to do that. This is a test. We need to prove ourselves. You've got three factions on your border that will be part of this attack. I'm going to ask the fleets in the system near my station to move to the system bordering yours. I'm also going to ask them to sell the resources they were going to send me through your station."

"I don't need your help."

"Yes, you do. You're the only one dealing with three factions. The Librarian and Daniel only have one faction that is part of this. You're going to get rolled without help. These aliens have already divided up our territory, so only one of the factions will fully commit. The others are going to try to soften you up. You need fleet support to stop them from crippling you before the real enemy arrives."

Alex stared at me dumbfounded.

I decided I liked it when she was stumped.

"Have you been sitting on this information for days?"

"No, only an hour. If it makes you feel better, I have nineteen path points in my genetic advancement path. I'm basically functioning at my peak every second of the day."

"An hour."

"Yeah, like I told you all, it's definitely worth investing eight path points in the genetic advancement path."

"We didn't all receive ninety free path points," Alex said.

I smiled because I knew it would annoy her. "I earned those by being the perfect troll. You're just envious."

"Of course, I'm envious. You own Mars!"

This was another reason why I didn't like Alex. She wasn't happy for my success. She'd hated every time I'd beaten her at a tournament, whereas I'd been impressed whenever she beat me even when I didn't like her.

"That old thing."

"You are so annoying. I'll talk to you once I've had a chance to look through the data package."

"You might have to schedule that for when we're Earthside. I'm about to head back to the dungeon. I've still got Kilocksin trying to raid it. The opportunity to talk to them and make a good impression is not something I want to lose."

She nodded. "Do what you need to do to make sure we win."

I shook my head. "This isn't about winning. This is about surviving as long as we can."

FOR 8 MINUTES and 11 seconds, Earth stopped. Every country's leader broke the news at the same time. Humanity was going to war. And this was war. We were fighting for a chance to eliminate poverty, disease, and even death. We had a chance to turn Earth into Eden and keep it that way. But to do that, we needed to stay in the Game and win Tokens. And to stay in the Game, we needed to unite. We needed to mobilize. And most importantly, we needed to go to war.

In five Cycles, we would face a threat to the beautiful future we'd been offered. And we would beat it. That was what our leaders said. It wasn't true. We weren't going to win. But we might survive.

For that reason, I was throwing around my influence even more than I usually did. I was making a request that I normally wouldn't have made, but it was something that I felt needed to be done.

I was sitting in my hotel room when a familiar face appeared on the screen of my phone. I'd only met him once, three months ago, when I was offered the station master class, but he was the person I needed to talk to.

"General Prime, I know your time is precious, so I will make this brief. You and I both know our leaders' plan to try to hold every sector is going to fail. We only need one station to fall to lose a sector. I know you can't work against them. But in your opinion, how many sectors can we keep?"

General Prime sighed, looking exhausted and depressed. "Your separation of warriors and scholars will be your undoing. I'm happy to finally be talking with someone who understands your faction's delicate position. By my estimates, humanity could keep eleven sectors if you pooled your resources and were willing to sacrifice the other sectors. But with the current plan of action, you will likely only keep five. The leaders I've spoken with haven't accepted my guidance. They're actively ignoring it. I haven't been able to participate except in the initial class selection process. I only need one leader to work with me, and I believe I can improve humanity's chances." General Prime looked at me pointedly. "But to have such a leader, at this point, would require them to have their own country and planet and declare national and planetary independence. Otherwise, I would be forbidden from dealing with them in the way I should. If humanity had two worlds, with two governments, my time would be divided evenly between them, and I would be able to work against those holding humanity back."

I took a slow breath to calm myself. It didn't work. This was bad. *Really* bad. "They're *refusing* to work with you, as in completely refusing?" I couldn't hide my disbelief.

General Prime was our greatest asset. My station master knowledge told me that his time was the most precious in human history, which was why I had hesitated to contact him. His time was literally the most valuable asset on Earth. To misuse it was a waste. To not use it was insane.

"The majority of those best suited to holding leadership positions on Earth were culled. Those that survived are mostly minor officials who have never had this sort of responsibility. They see me as a threat, something to be distrusted. They fear I will try to take power. I don't just need a leader to rally humanity. I need someone who is willing to work with me."

I knew the legal process for what he was asking. The knowledge had been uploaded to my brain after receiving my own planet and country, and General Prime counted as a Collective official. The fact that they had side-lined him was the only reason I didn't hesitate to do what he asked. That wasn't a mistake. It was a disaster.

So, while wearing no pants and lying on a couch in a hotel penthouse suite, I changed humanity's entire governmental structure within the Collective.

"I declare myself the independent sovereign of an unnamed nation, on the planet Earth, renouncing my citizenship to the United States. I declare myself the independent sovereign of Mars, renouncing my family name and take the last name Mars in accordance with Collective law. I claim dual planetary citizenship under this unnamed nation and Mars and approve this under my own authority."

General Prime smiled. "Morgan Mars, first of his line, thank you for your help. But you could have kept your family name."

That was laughable. "I'm not going to rename Mars to keep my last name. You have no idea how pissed off people were when they said Pluto was no longer a planet. I'm not going to step into that wasp nest by renaming Mars. Now, what did you need me to renounce my citizenship for?"

"Your military's oaths do not extend to the Game. Nothing is stopping you from independently contacting the station masters and fleet admirals of the eleven sectors to try to get them to work with us. To be clear, I am not offering for you to lead these forces. You don't have the skill. I would be using you as a figurehead to form under and lead humanity's forces as I should have from the beginning."

"How do you want me to do that?"

"I will walk you through the process."

16

THE 18TH CYCLE

Life was getting crazy. Well, craz*ier.* I spent a million Tokens to rent a sky yacht the size of a cruise liner for my family to live on for the next year while I sorted everything out with General Prime. It was currently floating above the Pacific Ocean, where the country I had flippantly asked for was being formed. Hundreds of thousands of potato drones were pulling materials up from the ocean floor and bringing them down from space in a ballet of progress that would end in the creation of a new landmass.

The reason we were out here in the middle of nowhere was that I hadn't thought it was wise to remain in the United States when I was about to piss off every authority figure on the planet.

I'd been right.

They weren't happy.

General Prime had me hire a bunch of administrative AIs to organize our counter-offensive, spending all of my remaining Tokens, and causing me to have to borrow some from Tee, which he moaned about. Most of the AIs were purely for administrative work, but one of them was for writing speeches. Another one was for recording and editing images. And one exceptional AI acted as a journalist and interviewer.

The AIs walked me through one of the greatest speeches I'd ever read, having me deliver it in a way that portrayed everything they wanted perfectly. I'd spent two days filming the speech and a series of interviews, and then we'd released it on the internet and every news station that would carry it all at once, which was most of them.

I told everyone the truth.

We weren't going to win. We *couldn't* win. We didn't have the skill. Every other faction had been doing this for longer than we had. They were better at it than we were. The best we could do was smash and grab. Earn as many Tokens as possible in the shortest amount of time and then accept that we would be factionless mercenaries for the remainder of the season. To that purpose, I called them to war. I called them to become Mars incarnate. To go out and fight a battle where we didn't win, but achieved our goals.

People listened.

A *lot* of people.

No one was buying what the governments were selling. If you spent five minutes poking holes, their rhetoric fell apart. The problem was they were all sharing the same story, and no one was saying anything different. No one they could get behind, that is. But they could get behind me. I was the guy who fixed their bum hip or made grandma young again. I was the guy who was fixing the environment. And I was the guy with a plan that wasn't so idealistic but at least sounded feasible.

Tens of millions signed up in the first few hours. As each hour passed by, more people joined. The smallest countries caved first. When the number of people signed on reached a hundred million, they looked at their populations and realized they would get better terms by joining early, so they contacted me to participate on the condition that my influence did not extend outside the Game. And that was how I ended up signing my first treaty.

It had only gotten worse after that. By the time I entered the Game on the 18th Cycle, over a billion people had signed on to the plan and were actively working towards it. Resources were flowing through the stations at rock-bottom prices, and credits were being spent buying from other factions no matter the cost. Everything was being used to make the stations stronger, like they should have been doing all along. People were willing to give up their in-Game resources, so long as we didn't take their Tokens.

Tokens were all that mattered.

With them, we could change our appearance, grow younger, hire AIs to help run our businesses, and purchase thousands of other technological miracles. They offered us everything that money could buy and so much more.

I preferred to leave the Game sitting in my command chair, so it wasn't so different when I entered. And the first thing I did when I got into the Game was release an exhausted groan.

The groan went on for more time than it should have, ending with the statement every stressed-out, overworked senior statistician had said at some point. "I hate my life."

"You should try being your secretary," Tee complained. "At least, you can sleep while you're in here."

I groaned louder. "That sounds like a wonderful idea. I should just sleep for the next three days."

"Don't you dare. You have a meeting with the Japanese prime minister in a quarter of an hour."

I stood up. "I need to work out my frustration first."

"Where are you going?"

"To cause bodily harm to some station rats."

I was back and sitting in my chair within ten minutes. Wailing on a few rats had significantly improved my mood. And the next few hours passed in a blur as I went from meeting to meeting, reassuring national leaders that I wasn't trying to enact some sort of coup.

Most didn't believe me.

They thought I was some sort of puppet for General Prime. That didn't bother me. It was kind of true.

I was in the middle of talking to the prime minister of Australia, who had legitimate concerns because my new country was being formed in their backyard, when we were interrupted.

"We've got contact," Tee said, muting the prime minister. "The

Wargarg are making another move. They're about to pass through the transit ring. They have a battleship."

I unmuted the call. "I'm sorry to cut this short, Prime Minister, but something has come up." I pressed another button on my command chair, dropping the call. "How the hell did they reach the transit ring without us knowing, Tee?"

"They're a saboteur faction. Stealth is sort of their thing. Be grateful I gave you any warning."

"How large is the fleet?"

"They have 500 frigates, 500 cruisers, and the battleship."

That was a big fleet. They had to have pulled every spare vessel in their sector to the local system. The fact that they had done this without us noticing was concerning. "Focus on the battleship."

"The armour is too heavy for your D2s to damage. It looks like they've invested everything they have into it. It's built for pure defence. It might even hold up to the R9s. Do you want me to use the particle cannon?"

"No, don't use the particle cannon. No one in our faction has used it yet, so it's still our secret weapon. I don't want to use it unless I absolutely have to, and we don't have to. They're going to try to board us."

"What?"

"Think about it. They work best by attacking internal systems, but the last time they tried, it didn't work because they ran out of bombs. This time they're going to ram a battleship down my throat and flood the station with fully equipped soldiers."

"What do you want me to do?"

"You need to strip the battleship of point defence weapons and then use the Predators to take out their thrusters. They'll expect it, so I'm expecting they'll have retractable point defence. We need to destroy the first layer of point defence and fire some Hammerheads to entice out the second layer to take that out, too. If they've got more than two layers, we're going to have to repeat the process, doing this layer by layer until they have nothing left, allowing us to finally destroy their thrusters. This is going to be a pain."

"What about the rest of the fleet?"

"Destroy it. It's a smokescreen, but the combined point defence will be a problem if we leave it there. I'm willing to bet most of their fleet will remain on the other side of the ring until they've taken out the station's defences internally. They're probably here to invade Sector 13. Send the first dozen Predators towards the battleship's thrusters the moment you've stripped it of obvious point defence. I'm also going to bet they've upgraded the thrusters to get it here as soon as possible."

"Your reactor isn't powerful enough to fire all your D2s."

"Thanks for the reminder."

I'd put this off in case something different occurred, but it looked like I needed to do a little upgrading. I opened the D2 upgrade interface.

You have spent 150 Class Points to buy the D2 internal reactor upgrade from level 0-5.

Each D2 now had an internal reactor that would power them without the need for an external source.

"They've reached the transit ring and are passing through. You were right. The battleship is out front, and it's being followed by frigates."

"Only the frigates?"

"So far."

Why the hell were they sending frigates instead of cruisers?

The reason came to me a second later. "Fire on everything, right now! The frigates will launch their darts as cover fire to engage our missiles. They don't need to hit the station. They just need us to not destroy their battleship."

On the 3D map in front of me, several hundred D2s fired. The frigates were appearing at ten a second. They were immediately firing their darts.

Damn, they were predictable.

"The frigates are taking cover behind the battleship," Tee said. "It's going to make it harder to hit them. The D2 rounds need more room to manoeuvre."

The battleship was moving as quickly as I feared it would. The approach wasn't going to take hours, only minutes.

"Smart. It's not going to work, but it's smart. How many rounds do you need to fire at the battleship at once to bring it to a stop?"

"Ah, you want to stop their battleship?"

"Yeah, but only for a moment. I'm willing to bet the frigates have to move out of formation to avoid a collision, which will let the other rounds you fire take them out."

"I'll need both R9s and 1871 D2s to do that, and it will cause structural damage to the station. The inertial dampeners are still level 1, and you're basically asking me to cause the recoil equivalent of a battleship colliding with the station at full speed."

"Fire an opposing volley to compensate."

"I should have thought of that."

"Do it."

"Give me a few seconds. I need to let the railguns recharge."

I rolled my eyes. "How many frigates have come through?"

"About 250."

"Are they using stealth tech on us?"

"No. They can't both attack *and* hide their location."

"Could the battleship be doing it for them?"

"No. It's actively scanning us. I just don't know why."

I did. "It's providing point defence readings for the frigates. Have additional D2s fire at the battleship. Otherwise, this won't work."

"That's definitely going to cause structural damage."

"Do it. They've actually got a feasible plan that could take the station. We need to stop it now. How quickly will they make contact?"

"Ten minutes."

"Yeah, definitely do it then."

"Ready. Are you sure about this?"

I was.

"Fire!"

Here's the thing about inertial dampeners...when they don't work a little, you notice. When they don't work a *lot*, you die. I don't know what went wrong, but something did.

I came to inside the regeneration chamber as the lid was opening. There was a rather exciting notification waiting for me. I'd been level 43 a minute ago.

Congratulations, you have reached level 100.
You have 117 Path Points to spend.
You have 4,709 Class Points to spend.

You have completed the Station Master Tutorial.

Congratulations, you have completed the Station Master Tutorial! As the first member of your faction to achieve this result, you have been given an achievement reward:
2X Path Points up to this point and beyond.
2X Class Points up to this point and beyond.
2X Resource Points up to this point and beyond.
2X Credits up to this point and beyond.
2X Experience Points beyond this point.
Your AI Trait has been upgraded.
+100,000,000 Tokens
Tutorial Perk

Your class has changed to reflect your non-tutorial status. Your level will now equal your station's level. Your specialization paths have unlocked; Path Points beyond 100 must be spent on specialized paths within the station development path. Your secondary paths have been capped at 50 and will now scale with your level.
You will now receive 20 Path Points per level.
You now receive 20X your station level of Class Points per level.
You are level 10.
Next level: 2,321,487/10,000,000

Your Path Points have automatically been spent to raise your Station Development path to 100. ***(Maxed)***

Your Station Development Specialization Paths have been unlocked.

Your Path Points have automatically been spent to raise your Genetic Advancement path to 50. ***(Maxed)***

Your Genetic Advancement now scales with your level.

Your Path Points have automatically been spent to raise your Personal Tech path to 50. ***(Maxed)***

Your Personal Tech now scales with your level.

A cascade of notifications appeared.

You have unlocked the **Reactor Attachment**. *You receive an additional Reactor Attachment for every 100 Path Points in the station development path.*

You have unlocked the **Sensor Array Attachment**. *You receive an additional Sensor Array Attachment for every 100 Path Points in the station development path.*

You have unlocked the **Structural Fabricator Attachment**. *You receive an additional structural fabricator for every 100 Path Points in the station development path.*

You have unlocked the **Weapons Fabricator Attachment**. *You receive an additional Weapons Fabricator Attachment for every 100 Path Points in the station development path.*

You have unlocked the **Missile Fabricator Attachment**. *You receive an* *additional Missile Fabricator Attachment for every 100 Path Points in the station development path.*

You have unlocked the **Hangar Bay Attachment**. *You receive an additional Hangar Bay Attachment for every 100 Path Points in the station development path.*

The old, familiar experience of waking up to the lid of my regeneration chamber opening occurred, but this time it was different. I felt different. I felt *powerful*. I rolled off the table, walked over to the wall, and punched it.

Typically, when you punch a steel wall, your fist breaks. This time *the wall broke*.

Judging by how much the room had shrunk, I was close to eight feet tall. I'd stand eye to eye with a Kilocksin. My muscles were much denser, too. I felt like I could juggle cars. The genetic advancement was certainly living up to its description.

I grinned, but that grin faded as I stared at the notifications, feeling more than a little confused. This didn't happen the last time I got the station development path to 100. I got to the part where it said that my genetic advancement path had been pushed up to 50. I checked my path points to see if the notifications were accurate.

They were.

My genetic advancement path was at 50. That meant, I couldn't level my station rats anymore. I felt a little better when I saw I had 195 spare path points to spend in my specialty tree. But only a little. I'd just lost so much free experience.

I sighed. There was no point in dwelling on it since I had no control over it. "I take it that the attack was successful."

"And then some. Those little guys did a lot of leveling while planning their revenge. The average level of soldiers on the frigates was 30. The average level on the battleship was 35, and there were a lot of them on that battleship."

"We destroyed the battleship?"

"No, but the same thing happened to them that happened to you.

The sudden stop overwhelmed their inertial dampeners and killed the crew and raiding party."

That made more sense. "How's the station?"

"Not good. We can probably do that a second time, but a third will tear us apart. You need to invest in stronger building materials."

"I need to invest in a lot of things. Now that I've got the resources to do that, I will."

"I'm glad to see your class finally makes sense. They were setting you up with a bunch of new faction buffs. You should progress normally now. Thanks for the upgrade. I can do all sorts of fun stuff now."

"Like what?"

"Give me a minute, and I can take control of the battleship."

"Complete control?"

"I'll need two minutes for that."

I looked over my most recent rewards trying to make sense of them. I quickly realized they were a game-changer. My experience penalty had just been halved. And my other rewards made it so that the extra experience cost was fair. Growth-wise, I'd just been given back everything the moderator took from me, which made me understand why he had taken it. "I'm in the top 1%, aren't I?"

"Yes. You are probably in the top 100 at this point."

"How are *your* internal defences?"

"Better than ever, but not enough to repel their fully armed boarding. Not without you spending some of those new path points on increasing my turrets."

I ignored his last comment. "Give me a brief rundown of how my new specialization paths work."

"So, you know how you get an internal turret every time you spend a path point in station development? Well, if you spend one path point on increasing internal turret frequency, you will get two instead of one for every path point you use in station development. All the specialties are like that. Everything costs as much to upgrade as how frequently they occur. So, if you want to double the number of fighters and bombers in the hangar bay, you will have to spend twenty."

"Are there any limits?"

"There are two. You need to have space for the weapons, and you can't upgrade the frequency more times than you have station levels."

"This is big," I said, as I walked over to the locker and opened the door. A cloud rushed towards me, swarming over my body, moulding itself to my frame. "Fuck yeah, nanotech." My particle pistol came to rest on my hip without me having to do anything. I drew it.

"Be careful. That's strong enough to punch through the hull."

I smiled at my particle pistol. "Yeah, you are, you sexy beast."

I'd never gotten to 50 in personal tech before. I'd split my path points evenly, so this was the first time I'd seen it.

"You will be pleased to know that if you place it against your shoulder, it will work like the shoulder cannon Predators have."

I slapped it to my shoulder. A heads-up display appeared. It had options for me to aim or for it to work automatically. I pulled it off and looked at it.

"I'm calling you Steve."

"Lame."

I loved Steve so much that I ignored Tee.

"Ah, not to ruin your overly sexual moment with your new sidearm, but there is still a battered Wargarg battleship headed for the station. I destroyed the frigates, though, and it doesn't have any external weapons, and the R9's are now numerous enough to damage it severely. Would you like me to open fire? They don't know the station has had such a substantial upgrade. We took out their scanners, and the sensor scrambler is still working."

"No, don't fire. Are they completely blind?"

"Almost."

"Take over their systems and disable their bomb. As they get closer, start feeding them false information that the station took significant damage when we launched the first attack, and then let them board. I want to try to draw in the rest of their fleet."

We were in a completely different position than we had been a minute ago, and I needed to adapt my plan to these changes.

"I need more internal turrets."

"No, you don't. Get the squad to start clearing D2 build quests before they arrive. I can't level the station rats anymore, so we need to try to have the Wargarg do it for us."

Tee sighed. "How many do you want?"

"As many as they can activate," I said, walking into the corridor. "Remember to make our attacks on the battleship look legitimate. And I want you to fire another volley when it's three-quarters of the way here. We need to look desperate. I want their scanners to show the station taking huge damage when we make that attack."

"Why?"

"Because I'm going to let them take enough of the station that they'll tell their fleet they're making progress and that we're crippled. They know you can get into their systems, so they're going to have verbal passwords to confirm authenticity. Once they confirm that the station is damaged, you're going to take complete control of their battleship and feed them false information. Then we're going to tell the rest of their fleet that they can come."

"You're grinning again. You know I don't like it when you do that."

I laughed. "Just get me those D2s."

THERE WERE RATS EVERYWHERE. They weren't having much luck killing the fully armed and armoured boarders, so I was going around killing the boarders for them. A very beaten and battered battleship had limped to the station. We'd taken three of its four main thrusters, making its progress slower and our attempt to stop it that much more believable.

They hadn't suspected a thing.

In their defence, we were in a lot worse shape than I thought we would be after the second volley, which I survived unscathed thanks to my awesome new body and armour. There was structural damage all over the station. The shield was broken, and half the D2s couldn't reload. The fighters and bombers in the hangar bays were all damaged, and only one of the missile batteries was still operational.

I needed to upgrade the inertial dampeners.

I turned a corner and promptly shot ten twelve-foot mechs, blowing a hole in their chests where the pilots sat. Their automated weapons slammed into my personal energy shield, dropping it by 40%. It quickly began to climb back up. I'd reached the point where all of my traits came into play, and they were kicking ass.

Just because the pilots were dead didn't mean the mechs were out of action. Their weapons continued to fire at me, retaliating without guidance. I calmly picked them off one by one until I was staring at a bunch of tin cans. My shield quickly recharged, because of my reactor trait.

"They've signalled the fleet that they're making progress," Tee said, over my armour's internal coms. "I've got complete control of their systems."

"Can you deactivate their mechs, like you deactivated the ship's ability to self-destruct?"

"No. They aren't networked for remote control."

"Keep them busy."

"Why?"

I walked over to the nearby maintenance hatch. "I'm going to board them and take out a few of their regeneration chambers."

"Is that a plan? It doesn't sound like a plan."

"It's the first step of a plan," I said, climbing into the maintenance hatch. My HUD showed me that this crawl space was a straight shot to the deck above the one they were boarding us through.

"You're mad. Just give me more turrets."

I laughed.

I was having too much fun to take him seriously. "Path points are too valuable to waste on these guys. I'm only going to spend them if we really have to."

"I can deactivate the regeneration chambers remotely and feed their soldiers false information that you did everything you claimed.

"And if people on the ground see that isn't true and end up

somewhere else, they might catch on to the fact that we're not in as bad a shape as they think. Besides, I'll be fine."

It turned out I was anything but fine.

There were fifty stealth mechs that didn't appear on my scanners or the station's sensors waiting for me when I cut a hole in the floor from the deck above and dropped down to the boarding bay entrance. Every single one of them had their weapons trained on me.

The leader of the group was my old friend He Who Eats First. He was in a golden fifteen-foot mech that was kitted out better than the others. It was a rather intimidating war machine.

My HUD showed that I might be in trouble.

He chuckled when he saw me. "You thought you could sneak up on Wargarg. How foolish."

"Who's sneaking," I challenged.

I activated my particle bomb weapon. It was my once-a-Cycle weapon that my particle cannon gave me. I'd only just gotten it.

Anyone watching would think I exploded.

The surrounding corridor vanished in a flash of light, destroying everything for two hundred feet. My flight stabilizers kicked in, leaving me floating. It was the neat perk my hangar bay trait gave me. Every mech that wasn't He Who Eats First dissolved under the fury of the attack. And the hull tore open, venting atmosphere.

There was so much damage that I think I singed the paint on the battleship when I cleared the boarding bay. If this was what personal tech was capable of at level 50, then maybe the station masters who had taken it weren't going to end up entirely useless.

He Who Eats First's mech fell, landing two hundred feet below. His mech had barely survived the attack. His shield was gone, along with his external weaponry.

I slapped my pistol against my shoulder and flew down to him, grinning fiercely. My armour was linked to my thoughts, so all I had to do was think about what I wanted to do, and it happened.

I landed in front of him and had to look up. "You're taller than I remember."

The gold finish had been stripped from the front of his mech. His speakers didn't work, but my sensor could pick up his voice inside. "My people are coming. Enjoy your fleeting victory."

"I have to say, of everyone I've met in this Game, you are by far my favourite. Every time you try to destroy me, I grow exponentially. You're like a walking, talking movie montage, but you're glitching, so you keep repeating. I can't wait until you come back."

I launched myself at him, pulling back my arm. My fist collided with his armour and bounced off.

He chuckled. "You can't harm me. You don't carry a weapon large enough to penetrate my armour."

I rolled my eyes, floated higher, and patted the giant mech on the shoulder. "You can't move, can you."

"A minor inconvenience."

"We'll see." I grabbed his arm and willed myself upwards. My flight systems kicked in. To my surprise, I rose without trouble.

"What are you doing?"

"I'm taking you prisoner."

"To what end?"

"It will be funny. I think I'll add you to my dungeon as a trophy."

Your comment has been moderated.

"You won't."

My HUD showed me he'd activated some sort of self-destruct system. The energy level inside his mech was ramping up.

Fucking moderators.

I changed to internal coms. "Tee, can you shut down his self-destruct?"

"No, and it looks like you won't be able to outrun the blast. It's going to take out half the station in about nine seconds. If he had reached the centre, he could have destroyed the station. This is why you don't let the enemy board you."

I'd already changed directions and was flying the mech outside the station. My instincts made me prepare for the worst even before asking the question. Without any atmosphere, I could get some decent speed.

Not enough, of course. My HUD showed the blast radius as the seconds counted down. That asshole took out a quarter of the inner ring and a chunk of the battleship with him when he exploded.

Once again, the lid of the regeneration chamber was rising. "Send the confirmation to the fleet that the station weaponry is disabled."

I jumped off the table.

"It's a little early."

I opened the locker. The nano swarm flowed over me. "He just blew up a quarter of the station. I may have been over-eager in my assessment of what we could handle.

"You, overeager? Never! Don't be ridiculous, Morgan. Overeager would be letting an army of mechs onto your station when you didn't have to. Overeager would be taunting an entire faction. Overeager would be trying to board a battleship to Lee-Roy Jenkins it."

I opened the door, because Tee was in a mood, and I started running. "You're right. That doesn't apply to me at all."

"Where are you going?"

"To board the battleship. I still want to get my hands on one of their mechs, one without any damage." That had been my intention all along. "Did the squad survive?"

"No."

"Damn. How many mechs are on board the station currently?"

"I'm not sure. They are pushing forward and destroying my sensors. It's probably close to a hundred."

"That is a pickle."

"They are destroying the station's systems! Stop being so calm!"

"Do this math for me. Compare how fast the station repairs with how quickly they can damage it. Now factor in how fast your turrets repair with how quickly they replace their missing numbers and how much ground they will have to cover."

"They destroy all the systems on the station in eighty-six minutes."

"Now factor in what that means if we take out the second fleet?"

"How about instead of doing that, you factor in what happens if they fill the station with low-yield stealth grenades my sensor can't detect and detonate them simultaneously."

I stopped running and opened my new specialization path upgrades. My plans had changed. I was allowed to have fun. I was *not* allowed to have *so* much fun I lost my station.

The list was huge, but it seemed to have a similar layout to my class point upgrade system. I went looking for the turret multiplier. I found it in a few seconds. I spent nine path points upgrading internal turrets to its current max, giving Tee 1090 internal turrets.

"Thank you!"

"You know, you really should have told me to do that earlier. Don't drop the ball like that again."

"You're not funny."

"Of course, I'm not funny. I'm *hilarious*. Now, where are the nearest boarders?"

Directions appeared on my HUD.

I started running.

I'd definitely been overeager.

Far too overeager.

It wasn't as much fun fighting the mechs when I knew they could destroy my station. And Tee was right. They were definitely putting down grenades. They were covered in stealth tech, making it impossible for Tee's sensors to see them. I had to be right in front to see them; otherwise, they were invisible. I cleared unit after unit, trying to speed-run the engagements.

Finally, there was some good news.

"The remainder of the fleet is committed," Tee said. "It's passing through the ring as I speak. Cancel that. Part of the fleet is passing through, about 10%. I think they sense a trap."

"Fire a Hammerhead at the battleship and punch another hole in its side near something important; then, detonate the remaining missiles in the battery that fired the missile. Then inform their faction that it's a trap, that we've got more weapons active than they thought, and that they're being pushed back. Request permission to withdraw. Then have the person who requested permission to withdraw be executed by their subordinate for cowardice and have the subordinate demand a full-scale attack."

"Why are we blowing up our station?"

"It's called a bluff. The missile battery isn't going to make a difference."

"It might if they have more battleships."

"Just do it."

"Stop grinning!"

17

ROUND TWO FIGHT!

I sat in my command chair with my feet up, taking a well-deserved rest. The Wargarg had fallen for it. They were so wired for all-out combat that it didn't take much to push them into going on the offensive. Their second fleet lasted less time than the first. Tee had control of the battleship, so the moment they were through, he backed it away from the station. Any time a mech left, the R2s took it out. Without new mechs to back them up, I'd quickly cleared the station of boarders, and then I'd done my own boarding action to find a mech and one of their regeneration chambers.

After I'd found them, I'd spent half the credits I'd received from my achievement to buy an upgrade for the reprocessing facility that allowed it to dismantle the vessels and harvest their technology, then I had Tee upgrade the reprocessing facility we currently had to incorporate it. I didn't have nearly enough time to pull their technology out of their ships myself. It was a huge job.

And the station was an absolute wreck.

There was massive structural damage. Over half the weapon systems were offline. Most of the internal systems were offline. A full quarter of the inner ring was gone. My regeneration trait had a lot of work ahead of it.

"Well, that's unfortunate," Tee said.

"What's unfortunate?"

"The Horde are about to attack. They picked up the sensor scrambler information we were showing the Wargarg and think they have a chance of destroying us. We've got maybe fifteen minutes. I'm rotating the station, so the undamaged side is pointing towards their transit ring."

"How big is their fleet?"

"It's smaller in number but bigger in class. It must be several of their systems' offensive forces. They have 3 carriers, 7 battleships, 18 heavy destroyers, and 750 heavy frigates. The frigates won't be too much trouble. And the destroyers will take some time to pummel, but we still have the numbers to do it. The battleships are concerning. They aren't as heavily upgraded as the Wargarg's battleship, but there are more of them."

"What have we got to work with that can hurt them?"

"You've got 2 R9s that still function and the particle cannon. Before you ask, yes, you can spend path points to buy R9s, but the recoil of that many heavy railguns will tear the station apart. We're already going to take damage every time these ones fire."

"What's the biggest value RP-wise?"

"The carriers, but they aren't as big of a threat as the battleships."

"Target the battleship's weapons with the D2s, but point the R9s at the carriers, and take out the first one that comes through with the particle cannon a minute after they appear."

I didn't want to be the first person to use the particle cannon, but I'd left myself no other option. I needed it.

Tee sighed. "I'm not even going to bother asking why you want to do something so stupid."

"They were watching us. It means they saw exactly what happened. They think we crippled ourselves to draw in the Wargarg fleet."

"Which we did."

"Exactly, they saw us use a trap. They think the trap harmed us. They think we're vulnerable. So, they expect us to fight like someone vulnerable. But if we behave like someone who is farming them for RP, what message does that send?"

"That *we're* a trap, and we *expected* them to attack us, and we *aren't* as damaged as they think we are."

"Exactly."

"You're bluffing."

"Obviously."

"What if they call your bluff and don't retreat?"

"Then we have to figure out how to fight off 7 battleships with only enough weapons for 3. I'm assuming you can take control of one of their battleships in that equation."

"Would you stop grinning?"

I laughed. "Only when this stops being fun. Now, what would happen if I invested class points into the R9s' damage?"

"The recoil would tear the station apart, but you can't upgrade them until you've built one, remember. Your station development upgrades don't count, and you said you wanted to replace the R9s with something better when you gained access to more blueprints, which is why we didn't build them."

"I completely forgot about that. Maybe, I could upgrade the inertial dampeners to compensate for the extra R9s."

"Subsystems are a lot more expensive for you to upgrade than weapons. You'll have to pay 1,000 class points for a 10% increase in output, and you need a 50% increase for the level 1 emitter to cancel out the recoil for the R9s. Subsystems are late-game upgrades. You're still playing in the kiddie pool."

"Gotcha. You know this would probably be a good time for the Octorin to launch an early attack. We should watch out for that."

"Funny you should mention that. Their drone swarm has begun making its way to their ring. It's still several hours out."

That was annoying. Building bigger weapons was currently out. Missile batteries took 6 hours, R9s took 8, and hangar bays took 12. Even if I completed the quest, their construction time made it pointless.

Today was my crucible, it seemed.

"Contact the station masters: Priority one request for all those currently unoccupied. Send their AIs our current situation and request tactical assistance. Put them on the viewscreen."

In ten seconds, the first responder appeared.

It was Daniel. "What do you need?"

"Read the request," I said, rolling my eyes. "I'm experiencing a three-wave faction attack."

He started reading. "You have *how* many D2s! Why the hell are you worrying? Just buy the armour-piercing ammunition blueprint. Smasher and I have been getting really interested in all the different ammunitions the R2D2s can use, and those are pretty decent."

When Daniel took the AI trait, they incorporated it into his dungeon boss. They'd also made it close to Daniel's age. Smasher was better at his job than most AIs, but he was also shy. He didn't talk to anyone except Daniel.

"Keep reading."

"Holy shit! Battleships. That's awesome. Buy the corrosive nano ammunition blueprint as well. Using them won't eat through the hull, but it will take out enough of the armour around the main guns that you can use armour-piercing rounds to take their weapons out, which is the same thing as destroying the battleship."

"Tee, is the weapon fabricator functional?"

"It's not going to work at full capacity, but it could do what he suggested if you bought level 10 ammunition blueprints. They would cost you 33,500,000 credits."

"Cancel the request for assistance and buy the blueprints and start making ammunition. Thanks, Daniel."

"Can I stay and watch?"

I groaned. "Why didn't I think of that? Tee, invite the other station masters to watch my battle. We should be watching each other's fights as a way of training and developing our skills."

Daniels face lit up. "Does that mean yes?"

"Yeah, it does."

"Awesome! I'm going to get ice cream, don't blow anything up while I'm gone." He disappeared from the screen.

"Tee, send them the data from the earlier battle and make sure you mute everyone, unless they have something important to say. I don't want any backseat drivers. Leave Daniel with chat privileges. The kid saved my ass. Why didn't you suggest an ammunition change?"

"I've had to deal with this idiot at work all day, and he's left me a little too irritable to concentrate on my job."

"That sounds like a *you* problem. I just had an idea."

"The answer is no."

"Can we cheat production and make D2s that are already loaded with the required ammunition?"

"No. You could if the D2s were the same level as the ammunition, but they are currently level 2, and the ammunition is level 10. The higher-level ammunition is going to damage the weapon systems. They will fire four or five rounds off before they malfunction."

The cost for the level 3 upgrades for the D2s was in the hundreds of millions of credits, and more than I could afford, even with everything I'd received.

"We need more D2s, don't we?"

"After we send the Horde running, it would be better to be safe than sorry, but they're ten minutes away from their ring, so I wouldn't recommend it."

I nodded and then frowned, realizing I'd overlooked something, and pulled up my D2 upgrades. I'd doubled my class points. That meant my D2 class points should have doubled too.

You have 1,000 Class Points that are only available to be spent on this weapon.

D2 Upgrades			
Description	*Effect*	*Available*	*Cost*
Internal Reactor	*+5E*	*5/10*	*60*
Point Defence	*R2*	*0/1*	*500*

I had more class points than the last two upgrades cost. "Tee, the R2s are already inside the D2s like the internal reactors, right? So, when I activate the upgrade, they will pop up as a big old surprise?"

Tee chuckled. "Yep."

"I'll save that for later, then. Will it cause a problem if the reactors can produce more power than the D2s need?"

"No. But they will be able to fire faster if you upgrade the reactor. Firing faster will overload a D2's systems, but if you have to kill something fast, overloading a system is better than losing the station."

You have spent 400 Class Points to buy the D2 internal reactor upgrade from level 5-10. ***(Maxed)***

I was hoping I'd be able to connect the internal reactors to the station at some point, using them to offset the energy costs of some of the other weapon systems I wanted to build. Alternatively, I could see myself surround other weapon systems with D2s, so the D2s could be a power source.

Diego was talking with some of the other dungeon masters, and they were making progress towards synergizing their weapon systems, but nothing had clicked yet.

I closed my interface, unhappy that I'd spent so many of my class points on my D2s before I received the bonus.

About 30 station masters had joined Daniel since I'd gotten distracted, and they needed to know what was happening. "Good evening, everyone. It's come to my attention that we should be watching each other's battles for the learning experience it provides. We have so little actual combat time with our stations that this is a valuable experience. I've had Tee send you all the recordings of the first engagement I had with the Wargarg faction earlier today. I'm about to be attacked by the Horde faction and, in a few hours, will likely be attacked by the Octorin. They have seen my weakened state and are pre-emptively attacking. I expect them to fully commit to this engagement. Octorin do not like interference, and despite the fact that I'm surrounded by factions that have attacked me, they won't trust the Kilocksin not to attack them for the pure fun of it."

"Speaking of the Kilocksin," Tee said.

I rolled my eyes. "They're not."

"They are. I just received a ring proximity alert. The fact that Kilocksin managed to sneak up on me is absurd. So, I'm 100% certain the Wargarg invested in counter tech. They've probably been messing with my scanners through the transit ring for the past few Cycles. That's why we keep getting surprises."

"How big is their fleet?"

"They have 1 carrier, 2 battleships, and 84 cruisers."

I groaned.

That wasn't a battle fleet. "They're going to try to hit the Horde."

"They're not attacking you," Daniel said, surprised.

"The Horde don't build up stationary defences near their transit ring, and the Kilocksin are next door. Without the Horde's main fleet to protect them, their system is vulnerable. The Kilocksin are going to try to hit the Horde's fleet from behind and make a run on their system. They prefer to use corvettes, so this fleet is something they'll willingly sacrifice to chase credits and offer aid."

"If they're going to mess up your plans, tell them to stop."

The Horde fleet began passing through the transit ring.

"I'm not doing that. The Horde will intercept the message, and the Kilocksin just made it possible for me to destroy the Horde's fleet, instead of chasing them away. Remember, Daniel, being able to adapt to a changing battlefield is more important than having a perfect plan. Tee, hail the Horde."

Half a minute passed. "They've accepted. Would you like me to put them on the viewscreen?"

"Yes, please."

An ugly, pig-skinned minotaur appeared on the viewscreen. He looked like he hadn't eaten in months. All his bones were poking through his skin.

The name Commander Corburg appeared under the image. "You are in our territory, human. Surrender or suffer the consequences."

"Do you taste like steak or pork?"

Corburg seemed baffled by my question. "What?"

"I mean, you look like a cow, but you've kind of got pigskin, so I figure it could go either way."

"You're trying to annoy me. It will not work."

"Don't tell me you taste like chicken. Too many things taste like chicken."

Corburg ignored me.

"BBQ them, Tee."

The particle cannon fired.

Their heavy frigates were trying to use the same tactic as the Wargarg faction, so they were hiding behind their larger vessels, like the carrier that the particle cannon tore through. The particle cannon was a precise weapon, which made it easy to hit things like reactors, plasma lines, and unstable munitions. The carrier exploded. The frigates weren't destroyed by the blast, but they took damage. Well, that wasn't true; one of them vaporized. It was right behind the carrier.

The minotaur on the screen scowled. "That was foolish."

"You know someone recently said something similar to me. You're about to lose those heavy frigates, by the way. Also, that other carrier is looking a bit rough."

The D2 rounds hit a second later. The small weapons along the hulls of the battleships tried to engage the rounds, but there were so many rounds that even though they intercepted most of them, those that got through still obliterated their point defence. The same thing happened to the destroyers, and the carriers, except one of the carriers also received two rounds from the R9s since it couldn't manoeuvre without exposing the frigates. It didn't like that.

All the larger vessels, except the battleship Tee was trying to take over, had been hit with corrosive rounds and were currently losing the armour around their main weapon systems.

I gave Corburg a less-than-friendly smile. "You should check on that."

The minotaur snorted the way bulls do before they charge the matador. It was the human equivalent to an eye twitch. "You're pathetic. This is barely an annoyance."

"Don't worry, give it a minute."

"No, you've been in our territory long enough."

The battleships fired their main guns, showing their range was the entire transit junction. The attack looked sort of strange on a 3D display.

"What's that?"

"Plasma wave cannons," Tee said. "The waves move slowly, but they do substantial damage. And there are 63 of them."

"Target the waves with the D2s that aren't targeting the fleet and fire. Detonate the rounds in front of the waves."

"That won't work."

"Just do it. Fire everything."

The minotaur chuckled. "You should listen to your advisor."

"And you should take your fleet home before you don't have it anymore."

The D2 rounds began to explode in front of the waves. The waves kept coming. So did the D2 rounds. The minotaur continued to laugh, as his fleet took fire, until the moment the waves struck the main station and did significantly less damage than he thought they would. It was still a lot of damage, though. There weren't weapons attached to that side of the main station anymore, and the scanner scrambler was offline. It was a good thing most of my weapons were on the ring.

"How did that work?" Tee asked.

"The matter in the rounds absorbed enough of the heat in the plasma wave to weaken them. We threw a hundred thin walls of metal against it. The rounds didn't stop the waves, but they weakened the effect. Honestly, don't you understand basic physics?"

The fifth wave of D2 fire struck the fleet. A few of the frigates took damage this time, and the heavy destroyers discovered that their main guns were offline.

I smiled at the minotaur. "Do you feel lucky? I do. What's the cooldown on those cannons? I'm betting my ammunition eats through your armour before they're ready to fire again."

"That was clever," Corburg said. "But I can also be clever."

Their formations changed. The destroyers moved ahead of the fleet and became a wall in front of the battleships, shielding them the way they had shielded the frigates. There wasn't enough to cover all of them, so two of the battleships were left exposed.

"Okay, nice. That could be a real problem if I couldn't do this."

Ten seconds passed.

Corburg chuckled. "I'm waiting."

"Sorry about this. He has performance anxiety."

Another six seconds passed, and then the undamaged battleship turned its guns and fired at the two battleships next to it, destroying their main guns. The ship then turned and rammed another battleship before detonating its entire payload. Both ships vanished.

The minotaur scowled.

"Damn, I bet you're asking yourself, 'Will my weapons be ready before he does that again?' I bet you're also asking yourself if you've fallen for the same trap as the last guy. Whatever you do, don't let that signal telling you that the Kilocksin are making a run on your transit ring distract you. Because that would be an amateur mistake."

The Kilocksin fleet began to appear through the ring. They pivoted and then did a full burn, headed for the Horde transit ring. Their weapons weren't pointed towards the station. They were pointed at the Horde's fleet.

"This has to be the first space-based drive-by witnessed by humanity. You should feel proud of being part of that while you watch the Kilocksin ransack your territory for credits."

Corburg roared at his crew, shouting orders as the Kilocksin's weapons ripped through his fleet.

I'd taken out the majority of their mid-weight weapons and all their smaller weapons, so they couldn't counter effectively. And their new formation had left the majority of their frigates exposed, so they only got off one volley before most of them vanished, under the next wave of fire from my station.

The Kilocksin knew how to play the Game. With them skirting the back of my range and not firing on the station, I could prioritize the Horde fleet over them and let them pass unmolested. They weren't coming back. They weren't here to lose their fleet. They were lending a hand and then pillaging an undefended enemy. They were going to lose this fleet, but not before they earned a lot of credits.

The Horde battleships lost their primary weapons, leaving them little better than barges. The carriers deployed their fighters and prepared their bombers, trying to intercept the Kilocksin fleet.

That was the moment Tee made his second move. He took over the weapons systems on a handful of undamaged frigates and fired right into the carriers' open launch bays. It wasn't crippling, but the debris made launching bombers impossible. The fighters couldn't hit hard enough to cripple the Kilocksin fleet without the bombers.

Not that that would have worked. The Kilocksin were firing everything they had as they continued the drive-by.

I was grinning as I watched Corburg try to salvage his attack. "Now, since you've lost, let me clear up something you seem to be confused about. *You're* in *my* territory. And I'm not talking about this side of the transit ring. That *system*, on the other side, is *mine*. And if you don't want me to send my faction through to take it back, you're going to give my transit station 10% of everything that system produces as tribute, trading those resources and credits through my station. I don't care who you trade with or if you make or lose on the deal, but you will buy everything my faction sells you at a premium. If you don't want me taking back what's mine, you're going to do it."

I pressed the button on the arm of my command chair, dropping the conversation. The moment his face disappeared, I laughed.

"Why did you do that?" Daniel asked.

"To piss him off or scare him. If he's pissed off, he'll come back with a bigger fleet, and I'll grow my station. If he's scared, he might convince his superiors to do what I demanded. It's how his people think. Alternatively, he'll ignore me, in which case I spent five seconds of my life to take a shot I missed. You can't succeed unless you try, kid."

"Oh, I thought you were trying to get him even more tilted."

I laughed harder, happy to see Daniel understood. "Yeah, I was doing that too. Tee, when the Horde fleet turns to follow the Kilocksin, take out their thrusters."

"They're not turning. They're speeding up. They're forming a wall in front of the carriers and the last of the frigates. They look like they are going to ram us."

"Well, that's dumb of them. They just gave the Kilocksin a perfect view of their thrusters."

"The Kilocksin aren't firing on them."

"Those dickheads," I shouted, fighting the urge to laugh again. "Destroy half the Kilocksin's cruisers. If they don't fire on the Horde's thrusters within 25 seconds of that, take out the rest."

Half the station masters were suddenly yelling at me, judging by the images around the main viewscreen. It was a good thing I had muted them. It took a while for the rounds the D2s fired to reach the outer edge. But it only took a few seconds after losing half his cruisers for the Kilocksin to hail me.

A reptilian face appeared on my viewscreen. The name Commander Harosso sat under it. "What is the meaning of this, Ma'Lock Morgan?"

"I was about to ask you the same thing, Commander Harosso. And it's Ma'Lock Morgan *Mars* now. Look into the history of my new last name before we speak again. Now explain why you're treating me like an enemy?"

The Kilocksin inhaled and then started shouting. "You just destroyed half my cruisers! How dare you say that to me."

"Cruisers that had an open shot at the Horde's thrusters and didn't take it," I shouted back. "An ally would take the shot. An opportunistic enemy would have hit the Horde fleet enough to cripple them and then have left them to cause another enemy a headache. I've worked out that the cruisers I destroyed were in the latter group. I'm trying to work out whether or not the rest of your cruisers fit into the former or need to be treated similarly."

The Kilocksin suddenly hiss-roared with laughter.

I grinned back. I loved understanding how their people thought.

"You are a true Ma'Lock! My nephew was right." He turned to someone off-screen. "Order our commanders to destroy the Horde's thrusters if you want a fleet left to raid with."

The Kilocksin fleet resumed firing on the Horde, targeting their thrusters.

My grin grew. "Good hunting, and thank you for your assistance,

Commander Harosso. My dungeon is ready to entertain you, and I would like the honour of fighting you when it's convenient." I gave the ritual gesture requesting a spar with a respected ally.

The Kilocksin continued to hiss-roar with laughter. "I will come to your dungeon and take your station from you. Enjoy your hunt Ma'Lock Morgan Mars."

He ended the communication.

"Tee, threat assessment on the Horde fleet?"

"They have a 1% chance of destroying the station."

"Good, finish them off for me and start activating D2 construction quests. Send the dungeon master and Tumpa to complete them for me. I think I need to explain my actions, or some of these people are going to burst a blood vessel."

18

OH YEAH, I HAVE A DUNGEON

The Octorin swarm was a little over three hours away from reaching the transit ring, and the Horde was still headed for my station, so being grilled by General Winston, a Brit and fellow station master, wasn't exactly the best use of my time. Except, I needed the other station masters to understand what had happened, because some of their reactions were so wrong that it would cause trouble if they didn't change their thinking fast. So, I had to let him vent to calm down.

The general was glaring at me and red in the face, but every word he spoke held no trace of anger.

I needed to learn how to do that.

"You have expressed your interests in fostering a relationship with the Kilocksin clan in your neighbouring system, Mr. Mars. It is a relationship that would potentially supply Sector 13 and others with a fallback point in the future, so why did you fire on the Kilocksin fleet?"

I took a slow breath and forced away my grin.

Damn, this was fun, but I had to pretend like I was a responsible adult and not a wild lunatic getting to blow up alien spaceships while calling it a career for a few minutes.

I'm not sure anyone bought it.

"Kilocksin don't view treaties the way we do," I said carefully. "Alliances are built in the *spirit* of an alliance, *not* the *letter* of it. We don't have an alliance *yet*. We have mutual respect for each other's strength. Strength is important to them, but more important than this are personal actions and a warrior's spirit, and most important of all is being polite and respectful, even to an enemy. In their minds, we're respected enemies working towards friendship. They came to help me, which was polite and respectful and showed they were interested in working towards friendship. In return, I didn't target their ships, which was polite and respectful and showed I was serious about working towards friendship as well. Then they stopped being polite by not giving assistance and targeting the Horde's thrusters when they could have. If they were human, you could argue that they had done more than enough, but they aren't human. What they did was not polite or respectful. It was not the actions of someone working towards friendship. They treated me like an enemy, using me tactically to deal with their other enemy. By only destroying half their cruisers when they knew I could have destroyed all of them, I was being polite and respectful. I was behaving like an enemy working towards friendship. I was reminding them of my intent while showing a warrior's spirit. Try to remember their ways are not our ways."

But damn, their ways were fun.

General Winston frowned. "They were testing you?"

"Perhaps, or their commander might just be a rude prick. By my being polite, he was left with no smart option but to be polite back. He would've received a much harsher reprimand from his clan if he had lost all of his cruisers for his attitude. Unless his mission is successful, he's still going to be in a lot of trouble back home. Being rude is acceptable under certain circumstances in their society, but being so rude that it interferes with your ability to fight properly shows you aren't leadership material. But if this was a test, like you said, then I probably passed with flying colours."

Admiral Hiroshi cleared his throat before he came to my rescue. "I have a Kilocksin liaison myself. His Royal Highnesses actions were perfectly aligned with their upper warrior classes' behaviour. They're viewing him like a potential Warlord. Warlords are highly respected in Kilocksin society because they're considered forces of nature. It is said that it is better to stand behind another clan's Warlord than in front of. The implication is you work with a Warlord, or you're destroyed. If his Royal Highness achieves this status, they will be humanity's ally so long as his station remains. His title of Ma'Lock is greatly respected in their society as well. If he continues down this path and is successful, not only will this clan be his ally, but the entire Kilocksin faction. We all must adapt to this new form of diplomacy, and His Highness is doing rather well. He is also right when he says, what might be considered polite by us may be considered irrevocably taboo by another faction. And what we may view as a declaration of war may be viewed by them as polite. We should note that their commander found his actions funny, once understood."

A Ukrainian General named Fedir interrupted. "That does not mean our actions shouldn't be questioned. We no longer represent only our nation but all of humanity. We should not take it upon ourselves to independently decide humanity's relationship with an entire faction."

I shook my head in complete disagreement. "That's *exactly* the sort of power General Prime gave us, and *it's why we're here*. There are very few factions we can have an alliance with. Evolution is too diverse to allow us to co-exist with everyone. We need to do everything possible to create a good relationship with those factions we can ally with, but factions like the Horde are different. The best we can hope for is to become an enemy that they decide is not worth the trouble. With others, we can't even hope to achieve that. This is not a friendly game, and we can't treat it that way. It's a matter of survival, and we need to choose how we survive."

The station masters who had cleared their expansion quests and met the special conditions to receive station master knowledge all nodded. Those that hadn't didn't. They simply didn't understand. How could they? I hadn't understood before I received it.

Several others asked questions, but they were just rehashing what was already said. Once that had happened several times, I decided the interview was over.

"I'm sorry for cutting this short, but I can't talk any longer. I need to prepare for the next wave."

Tee muted everyone for me. "So, do you want the good news or the bad news?"

"The good news."

"Your regeneration trait will restore 2 missile batteries, the fighters, a third R9, and the station energy shield by the time the Octorin arrive. We'll also have the weapons fabricator completely back online."

"The bad news?"

"The central station will still be critically damaged. Structural damage to the entire station will be at 73%, half the D2s will still be inoperable, and a third of them won't be able to reload due to structural damage. Because of the widespread damage that is now on both sides of the main station, your armour trait is redundant. And the Octorin drone swarm is too large to calculate numbers accurately."

"Take a guess then.

"I'd guess somewhere close to two million. The only good news is the largest drones are only corvette class. The majority of the swarm are kamikaze fighter class, which are only dangerous when they're close enough to ram and detonate."

"How many D2s do we have?"

"We currently have 1,487 after using the higher-grade ammunition, but that number is constantly increasing because of build quest clearance and repairs."

"We need more or better D2s. How many credits do I have?"

"After these engagements, you have 94,285,972."

"Tee, patch me into Diego. Diego, I'm trying to improve our weapons, is there any tech I can use from the other factions' ships we've acquired for the D2 or R2?"

"You could use the Wargarg's magnetic rotator from their mechs, Sir. It's a cheap piece of tech that would double the rotating speed of the R2. The Horde's alloys are better than your faction's, but they're expensive by comparison. You need a research lab, so you can do this for free."

"When I receive a spare billion credits, I'll buy one."

I wasn't lying about that. A lab was an essential system. Free tech upgrades would save me massive amounts of credits.

"Ammunition is out," Daniel said. "The R2 rounds are too small to do anything good."

Alex's face suddenly filled my viewscreen. "You're overthinking this. Buy and build the maintenance drone facility you gained access to from the expansion quest. Then spam maintenance drones and have them finish your D2 build quests for you. You have enough RP to fill every defence slot on your station. You will have the numbers. And the maintenance drones can transport ammunition when they are done."

"Is that possible, Tee?"

"The level 1 maintenance drone facility is extremely small and limited with what it can build. The facility is expensive to upgrade, but even a basic maintenance drone would be capable of what she said. And with only one hour required to build the facility, there is more than enough time left over to fully install all the D2s. You would have close to 19,000 available when they arrive. Chance of victory in that scenario is 100%."

"That's too high. We lost the sensor scrambler to the Horde. The Octorin can see our station. If they realize they can't win, they won't attack."

The Librarian replaced Alex. "We discussed this tactic a few weeks ago. The idea of making yourself weak enough to encourage attacks but strong enough for victory. I would suggest doing as Alex said, but instead of building the D2s immediately, use the drones to transport the higher-level ammunition to depleted weapons and then have them move to where the quests need to be completed. Once the Octorin commit to the attack, begin building the D2s.

"There is a 63% chance of victory with this method," Tee said. "The maintenance drone facility cannot produce enough drones to build all the D2s between the time they begin constructing D2s and the time the first of the Octorin drone fleet reaches your defences. And the station is so heavily damaged that it won't take much to cause its destruction."

"What happens if I win this way?"

"The resource points collected from this engagement and the others will give you a grace period from follow-up attacks from any of the surrounding factions until the 65th cycle. Expansion to the second ring will be possible with complete D2 construction."

"Sounds good. Build the maintenance drone facility. Then begin constructing drones and have them transport ammunition to any D2s that can't be resupplied because of structural damage. And buy the R2 upgrade package with the Wargarg magnetic rotator Diego suggested and build one, so I can upgrade it. Destroy it once it's upgraded. I don't want its dungeon mob in my dungeon."

I climbed out of my chair.

"Where are you going?" Daniel asked.

"I'm going to clear D2 quests. I need to make it look like I'm doing everything I can to stop them."

That was a lie. If I stuck around, the other station masters would continue to complain about my behaviour. I didn't want to deal with that.

DIEGO, Tumpa, and I spent the next two hours running around and clearing D2 build quests, adding another 750 or so D2s to our arsenal. The dungeon master and Tumpa were still clearing quests, but Tee said the Octorin were approaching the ring a few minutes ago, so I hurried back to the command room.

I took a seat in my command chair. "What's the spread?"

"They've positioned their kamikaze drone fighters in the first wave. The corvettes are in the middle of the formation. They have numbers on their side, so I think they're using the fighters as a wall. With what they can currently see, your point defence probably looks like a joke. So, they likely believe it will be safe for their corvette class drones to approach by the time they pass through the ring."

“Are the functioning D2s reloaded?”

“Yes. Additional high-level ammunition has also been distributed to those that are cut off. Drone production is in full swing, and drones are ready to move to quest completion positions when the swarm reaches the halfway point.”

“Good.”

“Damn it, not again,” Tee shouted. “You really need to do something about the Wargarg messing with my sensors, Morgan. I’ve got a Clack transport passing through the ring. They have a six-man team that wants to challenge your dungeon. They’ll reach the station in five minutes.”

“Seriously, they want to try to steal the station out from under the Octorin.”

“They’re one of the factions allied against you. Why do you sound surprised?”

“I’m surprised because they normally wait longer to backstab someone.”

General Hiroshi appeared on my view screen. “They’re likely planning to offer the station to the Octorin at a steep discount, your Royal Highness. My transit station is also connected to the Clack, and I believe this is something they will do.”

That made more sense, based on what I knew about them. “Thank you for the second opinion.”

I stepped out of my command chair and made my way over to the dungeon entrance along the right wall. Five minutes wasn’t a lot of time, and it was a long walk to get to the dungeon. My command room could move like an elevator, so if anyone ever got to the last room in the dungeon, it would reposition to meet them; but since they hadn’t reached there, it was basically on the other side of the station.

The doors opened to a long corridor. I started walking, willing my armour to form around me. The nanobots covered my head, sealing me in. I did a quick diagnostics check.

He Who Eats First had shown me what a well-armed individual was capable of bringing to the table, and I’d used my one special attack for the Cycle. Since I was fielding so many immortal soldiers, I'd have five sergeants, and one lieutenant.

The weapons they had access to now were a lot stronger than in the past, but Steve was still better. He was like a micro-particle cannon in pistol form. I'd actually make a difference in the dungeon now.

A few minutes later, I stepped out of the corridor and into the control room of the transport ship-shaped dungeon. Human super-soldiers equipped with Ironman armour and heavy particle pistols stood at the control consoles around Diego.

Diego smiled at me, wearing a suit of armour identical to mine, unconcerned by the fact that he was in two places at once. He was both here and running around my station clearing build quests. "My immortal soldiers have received quite the upgrade thanks to your completed paths."

On my HUD, I watched the transport vessel land inside the hangar bay that led to the dungeon. The ship was massive, easily the size of a frigate. I thought it was overkill until the entire side of the vessel opened, showing six massive insectoid centaurs that could barely fit inside. They were the size of buildings.

They wore power armour that made them look like mobile fortresses. There were two with missile battery installations on their backs. Another had a cannon, and one had some sort of weird box that my HUD told me was a mobile shield emitter. The last two were walking anti-infantry platforms.

"What the hell is that?"

"Clack Queens," Tee said. "The dungeon has to reset to accommodate them. The good news is that if you manage to kill them, you'll kill their hives with them. They're worth a lot of experience. Clack queens grow bigger the larger their nest. These ones will each have at least 25,000 in their hive."

I ran to the dungeon exit, so it could reset, spending forty-five path points to upgrade the number of dungeon turrets so I received ten for every five path points I invested. With 154 path points invested in my station development path, that gave me a total of 300 dungeon turrets.

"Good to know. I want the Wargarg sensor scrambler from their mechs installed in immortal soldiers' armour to counter their auto-targeting systems and scanners. How much will it cost me?"

I'd seen the upgrade option pop up an hour after I stole one of their mechs, but hadn't looked into it further, because it wasn't a priority.

"It will cost you most of your credits, but only a few RP."

"Damnit!"

"I need an answer, not a tantrum."

"Pay it."

Those things were too big to mess around with.

Challenge Received
The Octorin wish to challenge your station. Vessels that enter your system cannot retreat. No other faction can enter your system while the challenge is in place. Clear the invaders from your system to remove challenger status.
Rewards:
Tokens: ???

"Um, this might create a time problem," Tee said. "You should upgrade your R2s now in case this dungeon attack takes longer than anticipated."

I pulled up the R2 upgrade path. It was more simplistic than the D2s. It would cost 605 class points to fully upgrade everything, and I needed to upgrade it all just to be safe.

D2 Enhancements			
Description	*Effect*	*Available*	*Cost*
Rate of Fire	*+10%*	*0/10*	*1*
Range	*+10%*	*0/10*	*1*
Accuracy	*+10%*	*0/10*	*1*
Targeting Speed	*+10%*	*0/10*	*1*
Rotation Speed	*+10%*	*0/10*	*1*

Piercing Rounds	*N/A*	*0/10*	*1*
Stealth Rounds	*N/A*	*0/10*	*5*

I bought everything and dismissed the notifications. Another notification immediately appeared.

Congratulations, you have completed a hidden quest by upgrading a weapon system to completion.
Reward:
+2 Path Points

The R2 will now generate twice as many station rats each Cycle.

"Fuck! No! Shit! No. You stupid fucking quest! I don't want that on my stupid R2s. Who the hell would want that?"

A whirlwind of emotion ran through me as I kept reading the notification. It was like I'd just invested in a dump stat.

"It's a trap quest," Tee explained. "It's designed to frustrate the first one to discover it and make everyone else more hesitant to complete it. The other station masters will have to make a choice between buying a full pathway early for the additional mobs or waiting until late game when it can make a significant difference. It's not quite as bad as it seems. Thankfully each of your D2s will produce another station rat because of the R2 they have for point defence. So technically, you just increased the number of station rats your D2s produce from three to five and your immortal soldiers respawns by that amount. We should tell the others, though. It isn't something that should be wasted like this."

"Fuck!"

"The dungeon has reset. It looks like Normandy beach. Don't let this tilt you."

"I'm not an amateur," I shouted. "Besides, it's a free perk. Even if I could have used it better, it's not like something bad happened. It just wasn't as good as it could have been. I just need to get my frustration out of my system."

I took a deep breath filling my mechanical lungs to capacity. "Fuuuuuuuuuuck!"

I shouted long and loud, venting my frustration at the Game that continued to screw me. As any adamant gamer will tell, the process of yelling at the game was therapeutic, and you feel better for it once it's over.

I certainly did.

"I'm good. You can go manage the Octorin attack, now."

I walked back into the dungeon.

The size had grown exponentially. It was now a quarter of a mile wide and half a mile long. Considering what I was fighting were sixty feet tall and a hundred feet long aliens, the dungeon was proportionally as large as it had been before.

I stood on a clifftop overlooking a sandy beach that went for most of the length of the room. There were only twenty yards of water on the far side, and it only went to my waist. There were trenches along the beach where the soldiers were preparing for the assault. There was no team to swarm them as they entered, because what would be the point of trying to ambush something so large in such an open landscape. All the turrets were now attached to a clifftop, which gave them a clear line of sight. But the super-soldiers no longer looked like the daunting force they had a moment ago.

I launched into the air, flying across the battlefield to perch above the entrance. I was spawn camping, which was a dick move, but fuck 'em. I wasn't in the mood to play fair. They made me waste an awesome opportunity.

My armour immediately camouflaged to match the background. My personal tech path was nuts, and it was only half of what it could have been, which was even crazier. The counter in the corner of my vision showed they would arrive in a minute.

I connected my communicator to the immortal soldiers' radio system with a thought. "I'm taking the big one."

"Sir, this is Lieutenant Dan. How will we know which is the big one?"

"I'll be attacking it."

"Yes, sir."

My dungeon mobs weren't the smartest fish in the sea. They weren't like Tee. They weren't AIs. Even Diego wasn't much brighter once you asked him something outside his skillset. There were dungeon bosses like Daniel's that were smart, but mine wasn't. That didn't stop Diego and the others from making tactically sound choices, but it did stop them from holding a conversation, so my witty back and forth was wasted on them. And I wasn't in the mood to give precise instructions.

Stupid hidden quest.

The counter lowered to zero, and the massive door under me opened. A Clack queen rushed through. It might be more accurate to say she shot through. She was moving at over 100 miles an hour. She went past me before I could decide what I wanted to do and took a face full of dungeon turret fire for her troubles.

Her head exploded, but she managed to cross 120 yards before her leg gave out. The moment she fell, an energy shield was generated from the device on her back, covering the others' approach.

I was ecstatic over the fact that the turrets could kill them, despite all the armour. I was less ecstatic to see that the shield could block the turrets' next shots. Round after round collided with the shield, making loud crashes and crackling sounds as the ammunition slammed into the barrier.

The other five approached more carefully, using the shield their teammate's death had brought them to make their way forward. When they reached the corpse, they hunkered down. The two with missile batteries moved to the sides, preparing to shoot around it.

On the beach, the immortal soldiers were firing missile launchers and aiming their particle cannons, using everything my traits had given them. Drones were flying through the air, trying to circle around the Clack's shields, so they could fire their weapons or fly into them kamikaze style.

I stopped watching both sides.

My HUD was showing me the energy cannon on the big one's back. It was charging, and the power output was enough to take out the dungeon. I immediately flew towards her, expecting to be shot out of the air, but they didn't see me. With my new sensor scrambler messing with their sensors, I was invisible to them. My HUD showed me there was a weak point on the cannon.

It was an exhaust port, about the same size as a Womp Rat. All I needed to do was fire a torpedo down it while trusting in the force, and that would destroy the Death Star. Well, sort of.

The barrel was the weak point.

The cannon was a finely tuned death machine, but that meant that its internal components were sensitive. My HUD told me that if I flew inside and halfway down the barrel, my particle pistol could fire at the device that focused the energy beam right as it was about to do its job, causing a misfire that turned it into a bomb.

It wasn't exactly how I planned to win this, but the blast radius was huge, so I flew inside. Six seconds after I entered, I respawned.

Good game.

19

MY FRIEND NICK

The lid of the regeneration chamber finished opening, and I went to the locker to get dressed for work. When my armour was on, I started flying to the command room.

"How's the dungeon raid going, Tee?"

"Your little explosion took out the one it was attached to, the two next to it, and the shield emitter. The turrets immediately took out another, and your immortal soldiers are in the process of killing the last. That's the good news. The *bad* news is that this seems like a death squad. They aren't giving as much experience as I expected. I suspect their nests are made up of level 1 Clack. You received a whole lot less experience than you should've received. It's about a tenth of a level, which is just shy of what you need to reach level 11. Diego, on the other hand, leveled a lot."

"Not bad for five minutes of work, but I'm guessing we're going to have to worry about them in the future."

"Looks like it. Clack death squads are trained to take stations. It's our bad luck that they had one in their local sector. On the bright side, their equipment was top-of-the-line. The bounty for them to get it back is 18,000,000 credits. If they don't want it, they're still worth over a million credits by themselves, and the additional blueprints will allow you to add new weapon systems to the dungeon."

The blast doors opened, and I entered the command room, landing in my chair. "What did I miss?"

The 3D map showed the front of the drone swarm was about to reach the halfway point to the station. The D2s were shooting as quickly as they could, but there were literally millions of targets. It didn't matter that every shot took out one. Their numbers made it a joke.

"The good news is they're rushing. The entire swarm will be through the ring by the time they reach the three-quarter mark."

I pulled up the specs for the R2s. I hadn't looked at them since the upgrade.

Name: R2
Level: 2
Designation: Point Defence Railgun
Damage: 20-30
Rate of fire: 240 rounds per second
Range: 10 units
Accuracy: 10 units

Ammunition:
Payload:
-Armor Piercing: Max (Light Armor)
Casing:
-Stealth: Max

"That range and accuracy is still atrocious. What's the bad news?"

"You know how I said the biggest thing you would have to face was a corvette. Well, it's not. They've built a mobile artillery platform. It's coming through last."

"What the hell is a mobile artillery platform?"

"It's exactly what the name implies. It's a big, slow mobile fortress that is barely small enough to pass through the ring. Once it gets here, it will proceed to bombard you from a distance. It's why we aren't seeing anything bigger than a corvette. They spent their credits on buying a later-stage weapon."

"Can you hack it?"

"They use drone fleets. Firewalls are kind of what their faction excels at. The best I'll be able to do is get into their system and skim information."

"Will the corrosive rounds work on it?"

"Eventually, except we probably don't have that much time."

"After today, we need to talk about your intelligence-gathering capabilities. You haven't been right *once* this Cycle. Have the maintenance drones start building the D2s. Screw fighting their whole swarm. Hopefully, they call off the rest of their attack."

"I started the moment I realized it was there. They haven't called it off despite the sudden increase."

I'd underestimated them, because of bad intel. This wasn't good.

"Launch the fighters. They're going through the middle of the swarm and we're supplying cover fire to get them through. We're going to use them as a distraction for the Predator missiles."

"You've got 450 Predators. That seems like a lot, but they don't hit that hard."

I opened my specialization path interface to see if I could increase the number of missiles, not just the missile batteries. I couldn't. The only thing I could do was increase the number of missile batteries.

"Will having more make a difference?"

"If it's as many as I think you're thinking, yes."

I bought nine upgrades, spending another ninety path points. It turned the 15 missile batteries I had into 240 and the number of Predator missiles I had into 11,520. I was going to need to upgrade my missile batteries after this.

"What sort of damage will the Predators do after the D2s hit the artillery with corrosive rounds?"

"Significantly more, but it might not be enough. The Predators don't have a high yield. You probably need a better plan."

"This is our best shot. The fact you can't see that is disturbing.

Remind me to introduce you to video games when we get back to Earth. You really need to start training."

"Would you like me to grow a neckbeard, too?"

"It will increase your click rate, so yes. Also, start targeting their corvettes. They're annoying me with the fact they aren't destroyed yet."

"I am."

"The counter says there are over 90,000 of them."

"There were more. They'll be gone by the time they reach their weapons' firing range. The fighters' sensors can't see your rounds, so they can't get in the way. But let this be a lesson. Never underestimate what a sector of a fully united faction is capable of. The more group-oriented, the more dangerous. Unless they're pacifists. Pacifists don't do too well in the Game."

"Launch all the Hammerhead missiles once you've fired the Predators. Send them after the Predators, but make it look like they're there to protect the fighters. I want to thin the ranks, so we aren't dealing with as many at once."

"The effect will be marginal."

"Marginal is better than nothing."

"If marginal is better than nothing, you could upgrade the D2s' damage output to level 3 with the credits you made from the Clack raid. It would increase their damage by 50%."

"And slow down their firing rate, without the other systems to compensate. But good idea, buy the upgrade for the new D2s and load them with the special ammunition. I want them ready the moment the platform comes through the ring. I'm assuming we have the RP and the credits?"

"We do."

"Good. I'm going to get a drink."

I walked over to the replicator. "Whiskey, full glass, brand Johnny Walker Blue Label, room temperature, with three drops of mineral water. Cigar medium, brand Cohiba."

The door opened up, with my request inside. I made my way back to my chair and lit the cigar with the tip of my armoured finger.

"You smoke cigars?"

"With my dad on his birthday, love the taste. Hate the cancer risk and the price, mostly the price."

I got the cigar going and then started on my drink. I only ever drank Blue Label after winning tournaments, and there was no way in hell I was going to lose this. It wasn't an option.

A few minutes ticked by as I tried to relax.

Our fighters were approaching the front of the swarm, flanked by a horde of missiles. The swarm looked like a massive cloud of sand flies on the 3D map, and my fleet looked like a baseball about to go through them. For the first time, the swarm drew together, bunching to engage the small fleet and disproportionately large amount of missile support. The entire swarm, from the front to the back, condensed.

"Are they close enough to hit multiple targets?"

"They are."

"Ignore the corvettes for a minute. Focus on the kamikaze fighters around our ships."

"Why?"

"I don't think they have pilots controlling the drones remotely."

"So?"

"So, they're dumb. I want to see *how* dumb."

"Why?"

"Because it will tell me how quickly their commander responds to small threats. My gut is starting to tell me there is something *off* about this attack."

The swarm continued to condense to engage my fighters. The D2s started taking out a handful with every shot, by timing the explosions of the rounds. It took 20 seconds for their commander to take notice and disperse the concentration, but that was more time than I thought it would take.

I took a sip of whiskey and frowned. "Octorin have slow reactions to change, but not that slow."

"Maybe the commander wasn't paying attention."

"It doesn't fit with what I know of their culture. All their greatest stories focus on well-thought-out plans from rich oligarchs that take time to implement and provide flawless victory. None involve improvising, except by the young and impetuous members of their species —which now makes me wonder why they're attacking. It's out of character for a seasoned leader. They should have waited until the 20th Cycle, despite my station's condition. Tee, have you tried to hack into their systems?"

"No, I didn't see the point."

"Which of these vessels would take the longest to produce in this number?"

"The corvettes."

"That platform is expensive, right? The kind of expensive that means you've got to invest heavily early on."

"Yeah."

"This fleet was probably designed to only be ready on the date that they planned to attack."

"You can't know that."

I ignored his comment. "Software and small changes in hardware are the last things Octorin will invest in, since they can be replaced at the last minute, but the platform is too valuable to cheapen out on. If I was trying to cut corners, where would I do it? Tee, try to hack into a corvette near the front of the swarm."

Tee confirmed my suspicions.

"I'm in the one I've targeted. It's only got a basic firewall system. I can take complete control."

I started to grin. They thought I was a noob, so they'd been willing to take greater risks.

Idiots.

"How many can you take control of?"

"It took me a tenth of a second to get in, so a lot. I'll get faster as I go."

That was fast. It gave me a rather nasty idea.

"Start taking control of the corvettes at the front of the swarm. Can you keep them moving forward, and make it so the Octorin don't know you have control?"

"I can keep them unaware until I make them do something their controller doesn't want them to do or stop them from doing something they want them to."

"Perfect. Take control of as many as you can! We're going to send a fleet against the Horde's system the Kilocksin just raided."

Tee laughed, evilly. "I'm on it."

I put my cigar in the corner of my mouth. "I love it when a plan comes together."

"Do you want me to try to hack the platform?"

"My guess is the young oligarch spent all their credits on rushing the platform, since it's their biggest weapon. The fighters would have been cheap to upgrade, but the corvettes would have cost them more, so that's where the money came from. I bet if you try to hack the ones furthest back, you'll find them upgraded; so, stay away from them. The ones at the front were meant to be destroyed first because they're cannon fodder, so they lack the extra investment."

The swarm continued to try to take out the fighters, but because Tee was now diverting fire away from the corvettes, they weren't having success. Our little fleet of fighters had actually managed to make some headway. The Hammerheads were doing a lot to thin the number of kamikaze fighter drones.

Another thirty seconds passed, and the oligarch panicked. The drones began to cluster again. The number heading to engage the missiles increased significantly, thinning the density of the approaching swarm, making it even easier to counter the first wave of the approach when it finally reached us.

The drones in the centre bunched. Thousands changed directions, moving in such numbers that the D2s' slow firing rate couldn't keep up. They couldn't keep up, but they destroyed so many drones in thirty seconds that it bought us another two minutes where we didn't have to worry. The front ranks were now so thin they wouldn't be any trouble.

The fighters and missiles went down in a hail of drone laser bursts. The Predator missiles remained unnoticed, passing through the swarm unchallenged.

"I'm making a path for the Predators through the corvettes," Tee said. "I've worked out which have the upgrades, and which don't. I can leave a gap in their sensors that will look natural."

"Good work."

"We've got three minutes before the platform arrives and the last of the swarm is through."

I took the cigar out of my mouth, blew a smoke ring, and enjoyed my drink. Johnny Walker Blue Label was like drinking a cloud. The flavour made you float. Drinking it with a cigar was kind of a sacrilege, because the cigar overpowered the flavour, but since I didn't have to pay for it, I didn't care that the flavour wasn't as clean as it could be.

The swarm continued to approach the three-quarter mark. The number of corvettes Tee had taken over appeared above the map, increasing at breakneck speeds. By the time they reached the three-quarter line, it was over 20,000.

We weren't done.

The Predators were happily making their way through the back of the swarm as the artillery platform finished passing through the transit ring.

It was huge. It dwarfed everything I'd seen on the battlefield. It was larger than the station was when I first received it. It was going to be worth a lot of RP.

"I've upgraded the damage output on the new D2s, and the first wave of corrosive rounds is on its way to the platform. We can fire four, maybe five rounds before it deploys."

"Let's hope that's enough. Try to get into their system."

"Doing that will stop me from being able to take over corvettes. You're grinning again."

"You said you can see what they see, but you won't be able to affect anything, right?"

"Yes."

"Well, it seems to me like if we knew what they were shooting at, we could put something in the way. Something like a corvette, perhaps."

Tee chuckled. "I'll see what I can do."

The swarm continued to gain ground. They were about four minutes from reaching the R2s' range. The artillery platform began to turn. Armoured plates retracted, exposing a massive array of heavy weapons.

"What am I looking at, Tee?"

"I'm still not in their systems, but if I had to guess, ion cannons. 210 of them. They will turn this station into Swiss cheese."

A wave of D2 corrosive rounds slammed into the artillery platform and began eating through the armour surrounding the ion cannons.

The Predator missiles were still 30 seconds out, and the next two waves of D2 rounds would hit it before they did. Hopefully, that would be enough to thin the number of cannons pointed towards the station.

"I'm in." Tee chuckled. "Yeah, they've lost. It's just a matter of time. I'm going to take control of more corvettes."

The second and third waves of rounds quickly slammed into the ion cannons, followed by a hail of Predator missiles that damaged three-quarters of the weapons so heavily that they couldn't function. The Octorin must have thought they had me then, but the moment their ion cannons fired, their corvettes moved in to take the hits for me.

"Wololo, bitches!" I shouted gleefully.

More rounds bombarded their artillery platform, taking out a few more cannons and bringing the rest closer to being inoperable. The oligarch tried to find out which corvettes we controlled by moving them. Tee let them. They must have asked someone for advice, because a half a minute later, the corvettes tried to leave the formation entirely. *That* we couldn't accept. The jig was up, but by then, Tee had control of a third of the corvettes.

War broke out. The fighters had to join because Tee started targeting the corvettes he couldn't take over with the spare D2s. Every second brought more of their corvettes onto our side. And the second wave of fire was only as effective as the first.

It was chaos and violence on an unimaginable scale. Millions of spaceships, against thousands of weapons, causing unholy hell levels of destruction and carnage.

It was glorious.

I was grinning like a madman.

This was my purpose.

This was where I wanted to spend the rest of my life.

The front of the swarm eventually reached the station, expecting to finally have their revenge. I opened my D2 upgrade path fifteen seconds before they reached range. Thousands of R2s appeared out of the tops of D2s, where seconds ago, there had only been 260.

"Surprise, motherfuckers!"

The R2D2s were finally complete.

Another barrage of D2 fire slammed into the artillery platform, taking out more cannons and doing serious damage this time. At this point, some of the D2s were shutting down due to internal damage from the higher-level rounds, but they had done their job, and there were hundreds of them and more joining every second as the maintenance drones completed quests.

The battlefield quickly changed. If the Octorin could have left, it would have been a full rout; but they had committed to this, so it was an all-or-nothing scenario. And they got nothing.

The R2s shredded the weakened front line. The D2s shredded everything else. Corvettes fell by the hundreds, as the artillery platform succumbed to the corrosive and armour-piercing rounds.

I'd done it.

"Tee, give additional cover fire to the corvettes. I need them functioning so I can attack the Horde."

"That's not going to be a problem. At this point, I'm gaining corvettes faster than I'm losing them."

Within a few minutes, Tee had control of the remainder of the Octorin corvettes. There were 42,874 in total. They were the only large vessels on the board. They moved through the swarm, taking out vast swaths of fighters for fifteen minutes before only the dregs of the once-massive swarm remained.

"Tee, it's time to go demand tribute."

A moderator has been contacted. ***An AI investigation has been***

***launched.** Please standby for disconnect from the scenario while the investigation is underway.*

"What the hell?! Not again? I'm playing by the fucking rules."

Tee chuckled. "No good deed goes unpunished."

"No. Not this time. I followed the rules. They're not an AI faction. They're players. They did this themselves. You can't take this from me. Tee, attack the fucking Horde!"

The station faded as I was shouting instructions, and I found myself sitting in the same office as the first time I'd been moderated. The same tired-looking old man sat behind his desk in a cardigan. And the same ceiling fan was spinning a little too slowly to do its job. Somehow the smell of scotch had grown stronger.

"Case number 002 for human faction," he said, using the same stupid slow droll, with the accent I couldn't place. "Investigation of station master acquisition of substantial corvette drone fleet with intent to destroy crippled Horde faction's systems. Station master will kill 145 billion Horde players due to crippled defences from Kilocksin's invasion in the first system alone, resulting in extreme credit and experience acquisition. Individual created possibility by befriending Kilocksin faction and surviving three substantial faction assaults back-to-back. Rules were adhered to. Certain actions were against an AI faction whose reaction was proportionate to sapient races, but the AI's actions caused a ripple effect resulting in the end scenario. Scenario was legitimate. Chance of occurrence 1.626%. Investigator suggests partial course correction. Station current trajectory flagged as indestructible."

"Request denied," said the same nasally female voice from above. "Faction is new faction. Partial course correction is unacceptable. Achievement must be exchanged."

The moderator looked like he wanted to swear at the other speaker but sucked it up and scowled instead. "Individual has already received an exchange."

"Calculate chances of faction receiving additional exchange?"

"Fine, I'll make a deal…again." He glared at me. "What do you want this time?"

I glared back at him. "What am I losing?"

"You are about to attack a defenceless system with a fleet of more than 40,000 corvettes. You have the firepower to kill everything in that system and move on to the next, where you can repeat your performance several times before the Horde pulls together a large enough force to counter you. The kill count will be in the trillions. The credit count will be quadrillions. You will receive multiple first achievements. This can't be allowed to happen unmoderated. A compromise must be reached."

Because of Dad's advice, I'd put a great deal of effort into studying the moderators since the last time I'd been here. I'd discovered how badly I'd been screwed. I had a lot more leeway than I was led to believe.

It was time to get some payback.

"Here is what you are going to give me in-Game. In exchange for the loss of experience from killing all those players, all my station and R2D2 rats now start max level, and if my R2D2 rats should evolve into something else and become new mobs, they start at the max too, so long as my station defences are adequate to take care of them. If they aren't, then they start at a level where my defences can handle them and automatically level when my station becomes stronger. I assume removing the increased experience cost of leveling is off the table?

"It is."

"Then that's all I'm going to ask for there. Now, as compensation for the loss of credits, I want every upgrade for the human faction up to level 10 along with the alien technology I've acquired. On top of this, I want you to give my station a fully upgraded lab that will level and receive all upgrades each time my station levels for the rest of the season."

He frowned. "That is a little more than I was thinking."

"I'm not finished. You screwed me last time. It's not happening again. I get to keep the achievements. In exchange for any experience modifiers you don't want me to have, I receive double the class points and path points, but I get to have the experience modifiers back when I reach level 100."

"There are other modifiers you can't have."

"Then double my class points and path points every time you take something."

He scowled. "This is barely acceptable."

"Good. That's in-Game. Now we're going to talk about out-of-the-Game. You're going to pay me one Token for every credit I would have earned in-Game from this raid and ten Tokens for each level of every kill I make. And for taking my experience, you're going to replace it with knowledge. I want everything you can give me on the Kilocksin, their way of life, their goals, and everything else. And I want to know how to run a successful planet. I want to know everything a great ruler should know, from how to negotiate a treaty to how to build a functioning economy in the Collective and how to treat those who don't want to participate in the Game."

"I can't give you the last request. If you had that knowledge, you would be significantly more effective in the Game. It would unbalance everything else. However, outside of the Game, I can give you an administrator with all these skills and undyingly loyal to you and your values. They will be given an organic body, so they're not omnipresent. You're welcome to learn from this administrator, but you cannot receive that much knowledge freely. This sort of entity is different from others, so it will be a few Cycles before you receive it."

"That's an acceptable compromise, so long as you give me everything else I asked for."

"I would think so. It is at the very limit of what I can give you."

"Good."

"Request approved. Negotiations successful. Case closed. Now, this time, please don't come back."

"Hell no. I'm coming back as often as I can, Nick."

He scowled at me. "My name isn't Nick."

"Are you sure? Because I'm pretty sure you're Santa Claus since every time I see you, it's Christmas."

"Goodbye, Morgan."

"See you around, Nick."

The office began to fade, and I was back in my command chair. The last of the Octorin drones had been destroyed, and the fleet of corvettes were on their way to the Horde transit ring.

Challenge Complete

You have destroyed the invaders.

Rewards:

Tokens: 2,500,000
Drone Fleet

A fiery grin spread across my face. "Buckle up, Tee. We have systems to conquer. Contact the Kilocksin. They're welcome to the scraps we leave behind, but it's going to cost them their cooperation in my new dungeon."

"Negotiations went well, I see."

"Less talking. More conquering!"

20

THE WAY THE DOMINOS FALL

I'd spent the last two and a half Cycles raiding the Horde's sector, screaming at them for entering my territory and then not paying the tribute I demanded, despite my crusade starting only a couple of hours after they attacked me. The fact the Kilocksin attack had made it impossible for them to meet my demands was something I was wilfully ignoring. I'd even raised the amount of tribute they had to send through my station from 10% to 25% when they eventually restored their systems.

I'd utterly destroyed their first system, bombarding it back into the Stone Age, finishing off the Kilocksin's work, before moving on to the following systems. The Kilocksin had accepted my offer and conditions, and a convoy of corvettes and freighters had passed through the transit ring within a few hours of starting the invasion. They arrived well before my station could repair the damage which I intentionally caused to let them pass through safely.

The Kilocksin had to spend a ridiculous amount of resources to get through in time, but the payoff was worth it.

My station accidentally destroyed some of the fleet when it repaired a few weapons and auto-targeted them, but the ones who made it through reached the Horde's planet and set up regeneration chambers and industrial fabricators, bringing in waves of their people, to strip the systems of every credit they could.

They'd shipped entire cities of scrap, turning them into massive balls of slag, strapping a small engine to them to push them to my station for sale. The Uon and Octorin started a bidding war, buying them as quickly as they appeared. So, the Kilocksin were making bank, even if they couldn't take any of the resources for themselves. I'd tried to get humanity to participate, but they weren't organized. It was a massive, missed opportunity.

But my position was secure.

The trade going through my station meant the credits were rolling in, and the RP was stacking up. My holographic display showed a new ball of metal appearing through the transit ring every few minutes. Trading vessels were coming from the Uon and Octorin at nearly the same rate. This level of trade was even better than what a good station was supposed to see.

The corvette drone fleet I controlled still had two-thirds of its ships, and it looked like I'd finish my attack on the eleventh system by the time they got a large-enough force together to wipe it out sometime later tomorrow.

I wasn't too worried. My attack was already more successful than I imagined. If only the rest of humanity's situation was as good as my station's, then I wouldn't have this cold feeling in my gut.

The 20th cycle was turning out to be everything we feared it would be.

"We just lost another station. This one led to Sector 17," Tee said quietly.

The map of the area around my station shifted. In its place was a local galaxy map of the human sectors. With the new station upgrades, Tee had managed to piece together what our local branch of the galaxy looked like. None of humanity's sectors bordered one another, everything was at least two sectors away, and everyone else was in the same position. All the factions attacking us were trying to push closer towards their faction's other territory. Five of our sectors now glowed red, meaning they had lost at least one station. Two shone green, because all their stations had won their battles, and the rest were a neutral yellow, including Sector 13.

"That makes it the fifth sector we've lost today," I said unhappily. "But the first of the ones we thought we could keep."

There were three maps on the viewscreen. Alex's, Daniel's, and The Librarian's stations were all under attack. The factions attacking Daniel and The Librarian were alone, so they opted to challenge their stations, hitting them as hard as possible. A win-or-lose scenario. I'd had a strong feeling that was exactly what they were going to do, and their local fleets were ready to support them, having to experience their first major engagement. The fleets weren't doing well, but every little bit of support helped.

There was no way anyone was getting past my station anymore. Not when everything was level 10. My D2s could hit with more force than the R9s could at level 1, and their range was far beyond the current battlefield size. I needed to figure out what other weapons systems I was going to install, since we were directly connected to the other stations and dungeon masters, but that could wait a few Cycles. Now that I had all these options, Diego and I needed to get more creative.

I was glad my station was so powerful, because it meant I could safely send the entire local fleet to reinforce Alex. She was having a rough time. Three faction attacks were not an easy thing to take care of, even with the help of a fleet made from half the systems in Sector 13, but if she survived, she'd have the second strongest station in our sector. And that's all I cared about. I couldn't help the other sectors, but I could help ours.

Well, that wasn't technically true.

At the end of the tutorial, I'd gained access to the challenger's hall and challenger transit ring systems. They were currently under construction, but the build time for the level 10 systems was seven Cycles, and they wouldn't be ready until the start of the 25th Cycle. So, I could help soon, but not yet. That didn't change my views, though. Humanity needed to fight. We needed to get stronger.

For that reason, I hadn't told anyone how many Tokens I now had.

Not even Tee. I hadn't told them that I could personally keep humanity alive and solve our problems until the start of the next season. People needed to do this for themselves. It was the only way we were going to be ready next time. If they coasted along because of what I'd done, then nothing would change. And we needed to change.

There was a big, old universe, and most of it was against us.

"The station and inner ring have finished reconstruction," Tee said. "I don't know why you wanted them so big."

The central station was now eight miles wide, which was about where the edge of the first ring had previously sat. I'd also changed the shape of the station from a sphere to a tiered, double-sided ziggurat, to make it look more in line with the inner ring, which was now gargantuan after growing to keep the same proportions.

"It's to deal with the Clack Queens. They're so damn big they turned my dungeon into a single room. Now I can make them fight their way through a dozen rooms."

"That's smart. The corvette fleet is about to hit the tenth system. Do you want me to change the display?"

"I'm good. Now that the expansion is finished, I can finally get to work setting everything up."

I pulled up the station's current information.

Station Name: The Crucible
Level: 11
Armor: 600
Energy Shield: 1,000,000/1,000,000
Damaged Systems: 0%
Resource Points: 183,234,657
Credits: 12,588,974,235

Station Systems:
-L10 Phoenix Reactor: 64,000E
—Secondary Phoenix Reactor: 64,000E
-L10 Sensor Array:
-L10 Sensor Scrambler Array:

-L10 Communication Array:
-L10 Reprocessing Facility:
-L10 Weapons Fabricator:
-L10 Structural Fabricator:
-L10 Missile Fabricator:
-L10 Hangar Bay:
-L10 Laboratory:
-L10 Maintenance Drone Fabricator:
-L10 Challenger Hall:
-L10 Challenger Transit Ring:

Station Defence Slot: 1,000/100,000 (Current Structure Max)
-L10 R2D2: 500

Inner Ring Defence Slots: 50,000/500,000
-L10 R2D2: 25,000

Station Development Path: 249
External Weapons:
-L10 R2: 249
-L10 R2D2: 83
-L10 Missile Battery: 249
—L10 Hammerhead: 249
—L10 Predator: 49
-L10 R9: 16
-L10 Hangar Bay: 12
—L10 Fighters: 249
—L10 Bombers: 124 Internal
Weapons:
-Turrets: 2,490
Dungeon Weapons:
-Turrets: 490

My station was undoubtedly better than when I received it. I was significantly ahead of the curve, but my progress was going to stall. I was gaining 2.5 million experience points each Cycle from my station rats, but even with that, it would still take me an average of six Cycles to level without any attacks. When I reached level 20, the cost of leveling would increase again, making it even harder. The RP I had coming in from the station rats was a joke at this point. So, it was time to move on to stage two for my plan for galactic domination.

I pulled up my recent achievements.

The moderator had taken all my experience, resource, and credit modifiers, and in return, Nick had doubled my path and class point rewards. For some achievement rewards, he'd taken more, but he'd also doubled the bonuses again when he had, and I had no clue what he'd taken, only that he'd taken something.

The EXP, RP, and credits that were part of the rewards had been traded for more Tokens, which were nice, even though it wasn't that helpful. But at least I'd gotten to keep some of my perks' effects. And they were good, which made me wonder what the hell I'd lost.

Congratulations, you have successfully invaded a system! As the first member of your faction to achieve this result, you have been given an achievement reward:

+80 Path Points.

+800 Class Points.

+10,000,000 Tokens.

Invader Perk.

+10,000 Tokens a cycle.

+100% Attack and Defence when you are invading a system.

Congratulations, you have successfully declared war on another faction! As the first member of your faction to achieve this result, you have been given an achievement reward:

+80 Path Points.

+800 Class Points.

+10,000,000 Tokens.

Warlord Perk.

+10,000 Tokens a cycle.

+100% Attack and Defence against factions you're at war with.

Congratulations, you have conquered a planet! As the first member of your faction to achieve this result, you have been given an achievement reward:
+160 Path Points.
+1600 Class Points.
+100,000,000 Tokens.
Planet Conqueror Perk.
+100,000 Tokens a cycle.
+100% Attack and Defence when attacking a planet.

Congratulations, you have killed the entire population of a planet! As the first member of your faction to achieve this result, you have been given an achievement reward:
+160 Path Points.
+1600 Class Points.
+100,000,000 Tokens.
Planetary Genocide Perk.
+100,000 Tokens a cycle.
+100% Attack and Defence when attacking the Horde.

Congratulations, you have conquered a system! As the first member of your faction to achieve this result, you have been given an achievement reward:
+320 Path Points.
+3200 Class Points.
+1,000,000,000 Tokens.
System Conqueror Perk.
+1,000,000 Tokens a cycle.
+100% Attack and Defence when you control a system.

Congratulations, you have killed every inhabitant of a system! As the first member of your faction to achieve this result, you have been given an achievement reward:

+320 Path Points.
+3200 Class Points.
+1,000,000,000 Tokens.
System Genocide Perk.
+1,000,000 Tokens a cycle.
+100% Attack and Defence when attacking the Horde.

Congratulations, you have invaded a second system and started a crusade! As the first member of your faction to achieve this result, you have been given an achievement reward:
+320 Path Points.
+3200 Class Points.
+100,000,000 Tokens.
Crusader Perk.
+100,000 Tokens a cycle.

+1% Attack and Defence when you fight any faction. The longer you fight, the more this bonus increases.

These achievements were insane compared to my earlier ones, but they were also harder to gain, and something a station master rarely earned. The damage modifiers were why I was able to steamroll the Horde. After the first system, it had gotten easier. As the king of Mars, I was able to declare war on them, which because of the first warforger perk and the new one I received modified my damage further.

It pissed off a few governments back home because we could only declare war on one faction at a time, but I didn't care. My station was humanity's best chance of not being kicked from the Game. It was a territory. As long as I held on to it, no one could make us an independent faction.

The new path points called to me, asking me to spend them, but I held back. I wanted to be ready to deal with what came next, but I didn't know what that would be, and they provided an immediate change. The ability to add new weapons or systems to my station mid-battle was not something to be squandered. I was going to hold off on spending them for now.

I felt the same way about my class points. They could just sit there until I had a plan and better weapons.

"You should look into hiring researchers when you are back on Earth," Tee said. "You're going to want to research as quickly as you can now that you're level 11. I know it seems okay to let the lab just tick over and automatically research the tech you've got right now, but a lab is only so fast by itself, and when you let it do research automatically, you strip your researchers of the opportunity to level."

"I'll add it to the to-do list, but it's not like there is anyone on Earth who knows what they're doing in that department. This tech is completely beyond our understanding."

Tee groaned. "They don't do actual research. They play puzzle games. Each time they clear a puzzle, they gain experience and progress the research."

I hadn't looked into how other people played the Game. I'd been too busy, but his answer surprised me. "Seriously, they play puzzle games."

"Not everything in the Game is about combat. There are just as many support roles. There are entire factions who abhor violence, and the Peacekeepers give them a way to participate. What do you think the children from your world have been doing all this time?"

"I honestly hadn't thought about it."

"Well, they aren't blowing things up, that's for sure."

"Good to know."

"Unless their parents are nuts, so there are probably a few million who are blowing things up. Maybe a few tens of millions. A couple of hundred million tops. Though you do let children play violent video games, so maybe it's like 50%. It can't be more than 70%. I'm sure there are some decent parents out there. Did you play violent video games as a child? Of course, you did, but you turned out mostly alright, so the 90% of kids out there participating in the war effort should be fine."

I tuned Tee out as he continued to babble but listened when he turned serious again.

"An information package on dungeons and dungeon mobs just became available for purchase. This is a special one-off item. It will give every station master, station AI, and dungeon boss an information package on dungeons and dungeon mobs."

That was intriguing. "How much does it cost?"

"Twelve and a half billion credits."

That was stupidly expensive. "And the rest of our faction will learn from it?"

"Yes."

"Why didn't you suggest it earlier?"

"The bidding war on the second system's slag only finished recently, and I didn't know you could purchase it until you had the credits to purchase it. It's a hidden item. They appear from time to time. And before you think of saving up to find more, hidden items only appear one at a time. You need to buy this one to gain access to another."

"Buy it and tell everyone it's coming."

"Done. Also, Daniel just won his battle. And he's accepted his first prestige."

I looked up. The battle was still raging on the viewscreen, but the battleships attacking his station were all destroyed. Now, all he had to do was mop up the weaker targets, and he was done.

"Why'd he prestige?"

"One of the factions that neighbours the one attacking him is massing at their ring. They're going to make a move on the faction that just attacked him while they don't have their fleet."

I chuckled. "Makes sense. There are way more credits in invading a system than in attacking a station. He should gain a fair bit of experience taking them out in transit."

I spent the next eight hours going over the new information package that was being added to my head, working out how everything fit together, as I let the knowledge add to my existing understanding while

I worked. There was a lot to process. The station master knowledge from the special clearance rewards for the expansion quest had let me understand my role as a station master. This one let me understand how weapons systems created dungeon mobs and how dungeons worked.

It let me go through the R2D2 weapons system and understand how each component added up to creating the immortal soldiers. I wouldn't be able to recreate it from scratch with this knowledge, but I would be able to make half-decent dungeon mobs. It also let me go through the other station masters' unique weapon systems and understand how good they were.

Alex's reactor was top-of-the-line, while the weapon Daniel had designed was only average. The Librarian's station armour was even better than Alex's reactor. I could now see other station masters had also created several promising unique systems and weapons.

"The Librarian just won his engagement, and the final faction has begun their assault on Alex's system. You finished looking at everyone's toys?"

"Nope. I've got days of work ahead of me."

The immortal soldiers had been ineffective against the Clack. The knowledge in my head said that was because they weren't designed to fight something that big. If I designed a second dungeon mob that could assist them, they could participate in that sort of fight. Hell, they could take down the Clack without the turrets if what the information package was telling me was true.

Tee asked me what I was doing, and I told him.

"I've got you covered," he said.

A heavy railgun weapon system appeared in front of me. The name of the creator, Sabastian, sat above it. It was the general from Germany.

"This baby will make short work of the Clack if they invade again," he said.

The dungeon mob it produced was a massive, four-legged combat drone that functioned like a tank, but the weapon itself was terrible.

"This weapon sucks, Tee."

"It does?"

Tee sounded upset. He'd been actively trying to learn more about strategy, but there were only so many hours in the day, and he had to manage a trillion-dollar company as well. It would take him time to catch up.

"Yeah, this is the sort of weapon you build early in a game because it gives you an advantage, but the advantage quickly disappears as the game progresses."

"But the dungeon mob is good, right?"

"The dungeon mob is good. The guy who made these has probably spammed the weapon system. In the future, he'll only have one of these in his dungeon, because they'll become redundant, too."

"They're redundant?" Tee sounded despondent. He was really trying to be better.

"Just because something becomes redundant eventually, doesn't mean it doesn't have a place."

"Oh, so he thinks about this weapon the way women think about your penis."

I smirked, knowing he was making a joke because he was insecure. "No, I doubt he thinks it's saintly."

"How the hell do you quip that fast?"

I laughed. "Two older brothers."

"I've met your brothers, and neither of them is that fast with comebacks."

"You misunderstand, Tee. When you're the smallest in the family of boys, the only way to win a fight is with words. You either learn how to use them, or you lose every fight."

"You got your butt kicked a lot, didn't you?"

"*So* much."

Tee laughed. "Would you like me to bring up our invasion while we wait to see how Alex does? My risk assessment programs show me she has an 87% chance of success, so we don't have to worry anymore."

"Yeah, I might as well relax and try to ignore how badly everyone else is losing. It's going to be political hell when we go back to Earth. Those who sided with us are going to be hailed as kings and queens for seeing what was coming, and those who didn't are going to be trying to blame us and say we should have done more."

"That's the joy of being in charge."

"I'm a figurehead. The moment I get the administrator, they're taking over. Then when they finish making my country, I'm going to build myself a beachside bungalow, where I can spend my days fishing and swimming and generally relaxing, so I can focus on what's important."

"And what's more important than holding General Prime's alliance together?"

"Making a station that can survive *independent* of the human race when our last sector crumbles."

"To what purpose?"

"*Sanity.* There is no way in hell I'm going to survive not playing the Game as a station master for the next 300 years if I lose my station."

Tee sighed. "You're grinning again."

The End

ALSO BY BENJAMIN KEREI

UNORTHODOX FARMING

Oh, Great! I Was Reincarnated as a Farmer

Oh, Great! I Discovered How to Cultivate a Farmer in 52 Easy Steps

THE VAMPIRE VINCENT

Death Loot & Vampires

FIRST LINE OF DEFENCE

First Line of Defence

www.ingramcontent.com/pod-product-compliance
Lightning Source LLC
Chambersburg PA
CBHW030826310726
48980CB00006B/649/J

* 9 7 8 0 4 7 3 6 9 1 7 9 0 *